RUN 2

The Crossing

Rich Restucci

SEVERED PRESS
HOBART TASMANIA

RUN

ISBN: 978-1-925342-91-8

This book is for all the hardworking folks that pushed me to work harder. Except for Mrs. Miller, my first grade teacher. She was mean.

Foreword by Eve Bellator

Zombie enthusiasts are a motley group. This niche community is comprised of a seemingly limitless array of people, and those drawn to its ranks represent every walk of life. We are survivalists, preppers, horror fans, gore whores, authors, producers, directors, bloggers, artists, singers, photographers, geeks, nerds, military, schizos, sociopaths, gangbangers, rednecks, yuppies; we are mothers, fathers, sisters, brothers, husbands, wives, and children. We come in every color and size, race, creed, and socioeconomic class. Yet, zombie enthusiasts all identify with one common denominator: Humanity. Unequivocally, this can be attributed to the fact that zombies do not discriminate.

Zombies level the playing field in a way that no other catastrophe could. This playing field is set against a gruesome backdrop of complete annihilation- not merely the collapse of society, but life as we intrinsically understand it. The zombie apocalypse reduces the equation of life to its most basic formula: Us versus them. In the face of such a decimating adversary, humans have no other option but to set aside their differences and kiss their prejudices goodbye. Those of us who consider ourselves zombie fiends join forces under one stalwart banner that flies for the human nation.

Throughout my years as an administrator of social zombie websites, I have had the honor to virtually shake hands with the most eclectic mix of people. Rich Restucci is one such individual, and his novels are an excellent example of the way humanity will rally on a playing field scorched by the zombie apocalypse. His characters are not cookie-cutter, white bread individuals, but rather they are a mad mix of survivors, a hodge-podge sample of humans. Rich's storyline aptly demonstrates his indiscriminate perspective and his own passion for the genre. You will find that his words weave a mesmerizing tale that is at once both horrifying and fun. Therefore, without further ado, I take great pleasure in introducing Run 2, The Crossing.

Eve Bellator
5/27/2015
Zombiefiend.com

1

The streets and buildings of the San Francisco Bay area were quiet, the formerly bustling structures now dark sentinels under the luminescent glow of the early evening moon. Some of the concrete and steel towers still smoldered, but most were lifeless, in one way or another. The streets were no longer alive with movement, as they had always been in the evening, but empty, with trash strewn about, and the occasional corpse left to putrefy in the July heat. There was stirring in some places, the furtive movements of a survivor taking his chances on a supply run, or the lurching stagger of people who didn't survive, but continued to exist.

The suburbs weren't spared the terrible fate of the city either, as the plague which had ravaged the metropolis was rampant throughout the country, throughout the world. Infection was everywhere, and indiscriminate in whom it chose to taint. The power of this new disease was such that death itself no longer held its sway, and shortly after an infected human perished, something else, something evil returned. This evil inhabited the body of the person who once was.

The infected had had names, but their names no longer mattered, and had died with them. The presence of this new sub-species mattered to the uninfected, who were now hopelessly outnumbered and fighting for the very survival of civilization. Humans in every hastily fortified attic, broken-down vehicle, and converted building died every day for a can of Spam or a bottle of water. Each death was a brace against humanity, the numbers of the enemy swelling when a person's expiration date was reached.

More terrifying than the fact that the dead now walked and sought the flesh of the living, was the truth of who these creatures had been. Your grandmother, the pizza delivery guy, the little boy next door, your girlfriend's Rabbi; all slavering things, now looking to end your life with tooth and claw. Looking to eat you. Those unfortunates not entirely consumed by mobs of creatures but merely bitten or scratched, joined the ranks of the undead and hunted for anything with a heartbeat.

On a trash-strewn beach on the outskirts of San Francisco, one such thing stood staring, its head hung slightly to the side. A cold hand, just beginning the preliminary stages of decomposition, rose from its resting position and felt the tough rubber hull of a rigid inflatable boat. Footprints in the sand of the small beach led from the boat toward a continent full of insatiable cannibals. Not having the intelligence to realize what the footprints meant, the dead thing didn't follow them, but continued to stare at the craft, wondering dully if this had been the source of the sound which had drawn it stumbling to this area.

Dressed in the tattered rags of what was once a police uniform, the thing removed its appendage from the boat, and the hand brushed an empty weapon holster. Slowed synapses fired in the dead policeman's brain, and if understanding was possible for it, it understood that there was no food here. It moved to leave, but stepped on an oversize stone and fell. It didn't put out its hands to attempt to break the fall, it simply crashed face first into the rocky beach. The fall damaged the creature's nose, but the trip had broken its ankle with an audible snap. Feeling neither of these injuries, it rose with painless determination, intent on travelling down the beach. It now had a noticeable limp, the left foot at a ninety degree angle from where it should be. Bones grinding, it didn't have the mental capacity to read the warning sign placed next to a small, convex piece of green plastic slightly raised on two sets of scissor legs. The claymore mine detonated when the policeman walked through the tripwire, the thin layer of C4 explosive propelling dozens of tiny steel balls outward at approximately twelve hundred meters per second.

The creature fell forward as its legs were peppered with the steel projectiles, bone and muscle shredded into non-functional meat. Undeterred, it tried to stand but was unable as its legs were mostly gone. The hand that had recently rested on the boat was also now missing, but the former policeman reached both its arms out, sinking the fingers of its good hand in the sand attempting to pull itself forward. It failed as it didn't have the strength in one good arm to do so. It settled for a tripod approach of using its two arms and what was left of its midsection to move at a pathetic pace in the direction it had been blown. Although it did not comprehend this, it was now following the footsteps that would eventually lead it to those that had made them. It would seem even Lady Luck had abandoned humanity.

2

A large Texan smiled and elbowed another former policeman, this one very much alive, in the ribs. "Boom. He he. Tole ya them claymores was a good idea," he whispered.

"There's only a few of them in the road," Chris whispered to Boone. "We could run right past them, or even club them to stay quiet."

Lt Commander Boone was lying prone on the warm roof of a single car garage with SEAL members Cole and Seyfert, and civilians Chris Rawding and Martinez. Boone didn't know Martinez's first name, but he knew the guy had been an SFPD SWAT sniper. He looked across the small street at the Wavy Road Surf Shop, then raised his night vision binoculars and looked up and down the length of the road. There were eight dirt bikes chained together under a carport to the left of the shop. "Yeah, but there's about a hundred and fifty right up the road that way," he pointed left, "and another fifty that way," he pointed right, "not to mention there's movement inside the shop. Half the city could be in there for all we know."

Chris looked crestfallen. "This is actually a suburb, and the population is only about thirty thousand. We need those bikes!"

Boone considered the idea for a moment. "Too many variables. If we get in the shop, and it's full of Limas, we're in trouble. If we get the keys but the bikes are out of gas, we're in trouble. If one of the Limas in the road sees or hears us and starts to moan, we're in trouble. Lastly, if nothing goes wrong, and we get the bikes unlocked, and they're full of gas, then what? The second we start them up, those things will hear it and come after us. There're too many in both directions to effectively negotiate them without becoming a hot lunch. The worst bitch of it is that there're only eight bikes, but twelve of us. Those bikes won't really run with two. Sorry Chris, but the bikes are a no-go." Boone saw the look of dejection on Chris's face and put his hand on his shoulder. "It was a good idea though."

3

Boone's group of twelve was going to have to hoof it through the suburb to the first waypoint of their journey. The goal was getting to a civilian maintenance depot where three military Light Armored Vehicles were in for repair, and subsequently using those vehicles to gain access to a weapons cache at an as-yet undisclosed location. Boone did not like to hoof.

A loud moan came from below them to the left, and Boone threw his closed fist up in the air signaling for quiet. His radio came to life with a whisper. "Sir, target spotted, twenty meters, two Limas closing slow. Claymore might have tipped them off. They're looking for something."

Yeah, us. Boone thought. "Androwski, can you evade?" Androwski was on the ground in the smashed and ransacked store attached to the garage with Benotti and Stark, two more of the SEALs. Covering the rear of the structure, in an alley, were civilians Rick Barnes, Anna Hargis, and Dallas (Boone didn't know if this moniker was his first, last, or middle name, or just plain made up) along with SEAL team member Usher.

"Negative, they'll be on us in twenty seconds and there's no place to hide in here."

"Go quiet."

Boone's earpiece received two squelches in rapid succession, indicating Androwski would comply with the "go quiet" order. He would dispatch the targets with as little sound as possible.

Boone turned around and looked at the other members of his team, holding up two fingers. Everyone on the roof nodded in affirmation. They all had radios as well and had heard Androwski, but Boone wanted to make sure they had all heard correctly.

The veteran SEAL peered once again through his field glasses to the larger, closer group of undead up the street, and kept his eyes on them. He was interested to know if they would have to bug out alone, or with a shitload of company.

The ratcheting mechanism from Androwski's suppressed MP5SD3 sounded like a cannon shot to Boone, but the Limas at the end of the road seemed not to notice. As he was panning right to check the smaller horde, he noticed that three of the ones nearer to them had turned to investigate.

"Danger close! Twenty meters, straight!" Boone whispered to the radio.

Three more undead dropped in their tracks as the SEALs in the store took them out. Unfortunately, the huge plate glass display window of the Wavy Road Surf Shop imploded, showering surfboards and wetsuits with beads of shiny safety glass. That got the attention of some of the larger group, and they began to stumble and jerk their way toward the commotion. Soon the whole pack was on its way. "Contact in the zone!

Right, left, and forward! Fall back to the rear and secure the alley!" As silently as possible, the six on the roof made their way down the back of the garage and met up with the other six. The alley was closed five feet behind them with a dumpster against the wall. Ahead of them it was about twenty meters long, with buildings to their left and a chain-link fence on top of a low concrete wall on their right, ending in a paved street. Usher and Stark were at the far end of the four meter wide passage, both on one knee, each with their weapon's advanced combat optic gun sight (ACOG) to an eye peering in different directions.

"We need to bug out!" Boone whispered into the radio. He noticed that there was trash throughout the narrow path. "Keep it quiet and watch your footing. Ush, Stark, point. Andy, Benny, rear. Cole, Sey, with me and the civvies. Barnes, have your people keep their safeties on. No chatter!" The dozen people slunk down the alley, looking behind dumpsters and boxes as they moved. Halfway down, Usher lifted his hand and made a fist. Everyone froze, and Boone had time to think that maybe the civvies would be okay on this mission, when a lone creature banged against the chain-link fence and growled loudly, its shabby fingers reaching for them through the obstacle. Boone raised his suppressed MK23 handgun and ended the thing's misery. Other undead could be seen in the near distance stumbling toward the link fence and their re-killed brother, and possibly dinner. The mission team heard moans and mewling off to their right, and knew that their position had been compromised.

"Sir!" Boone heard Usher whisper. "Whole fucking town is on the way, left! Sixty meters!" Crashing could be heard as the things thundered through the store the survivors had just exited.

Boone started down the alley. "Let's move! Now!" The group reached Usher and Stark, and waited for Boone's orders. Across the street was another alley, but it was shrouded in darkness and could be a dead end. Boone pulled a small mirror on a collapsible stick out of his tactical webbing, and stuck it out past the building. His whisper of *Oh shit…*was enough to send tendrils of fear spiraling down Rick Barnes' back, and his testicles tightened accordingly. Thumping came from behind them. The things had found the back door to the store and wanted out.

Quickly, Boone did mental calculations. Left was not an option, as a tide of undead was slowly plodding toward them. Back was a death-trap, and forward was too risky, as nobody could see the end of the alley opposite the one they were in.

"Keep to your assignments, we're going right. As soon as we can find a place to lose them, we take it, keep moving." As Usher and Stark moved to the right, Boone added, "And look for a vehicle we can use, something big!"

The group moved to the right, and suppressed weapon fire from the two SEALs in the front cleared the way. They were being quiet, but not silent. Corpses littered the road ahead of them, all with head trauma, as they fled north through the suburban sprawl. They slowed when they reached a hill overlooking a housing district, and everyone paused to catch their breath.

Boone pulled out his night vision binoculars again and looked the development over. "Sporadic movement, but no hordes that I can see."

Dallas pointed. "There's a Fed Ex truck at the corner. Could we use that?" Boone panned to the intersection Dallas had indicated.

Martinez looked through the scope of his rifle. "Seems to be clear too."

"Yeah. We've got maybe ten minutes to get a couple of vehicles before the group we just left catches up to us."

"Dirt bikes would be nice," Chris said sadly.

Boone smiled, a rare occurrence. "Yeah, they would. Alright people, we need to keep moving. Martinez, cover from this hill, Benny, cover Martinez. Andy, Sey, point. We're fifty behind you."

The two SEALs rushed off quietly, checking low areas and behind obstacles as they moved. They reached the truck and Androwski checked underneath while Seyfert hopped up on the runner and looked in the cab. Simultaneous whispers of "Clear!" came through everyone's radio earpiece. What little undead presence there was in the immediate area was stumbling in the other direction. Seyfert turned to his buddy. "Andy, check the back, I'll cover."

"Fuck that. Rock, paper, scissors."

Androwski lost the kid's game, and proceeded to open the rear door of the parcel truck while a smug Seyfert covered him. As they opened it and peered inside with their night vision goggles, the rest of the group minus the two on the hill arrived. "Back's clear of hostiles too, but it's gonna be tight with all these packages."

"Pile in everybody," Boone ordered. "Sniper team to our location ASAP."

Dallas looked back to the hill and saw the two men running toward him. "They're comin'."

He walked toward the driver's side and swung into the cab. "Keys are in it!"

Boone was peering through his night vision binoculars down the street. "Wait until the sniper team gets here and then start her up." Seven people squeezed in, and it was indeed, tight. There were two shelving systems, one on each side of a small corridor that ran all the way up to the cab. Some packages on the floor made for even less room, and Anna started a bucket chain, the group removing twenty-six packages before Martinez and Benotti showed up breathless. "Sir. Limas," Benotti relayed to Boone, "too many to count. Five minutes to the rear."

"Catch your breath, Benny, you might need it. Dallas, can you drive this thing?"

Dallas chuckled and turned the engine over. It started on the first try. "I'm a truck driver, Boone." Dallas turned on the headlights, and saw a mauled woman in a gore-covered Federal Express uniform lurching toward them. "We got Dead-Ex bearin' down, can we go?"

"We're all aboard, head northwest."

The parcel truck was parked such that Dallas had to back up to move. He sped backwards about twenty feet or so, then threw the truck into first gear. The noise from the vehicle was loud, and slow, lumbering shadows approached from all sides.

Boone looked out the back window with his NVGs. "That's a lot of fucking green! Go Dallas!" Not needing further incentive, Dallas pulled away from the curb and hung a left, continuing down a residential street. The dead encroached from all sides, but in minimal numbers. The main horde was behind them somewhere. After only about a minute, the headlights illuminated a thick cluster of staggering forms in front of them. Dallas slowed some, not sure how to proceed other than to run them down, but at the same time he didn't want to damage the vehicle as he plowed the cannibals under. Androwski had taken the passenger's jump seat and pointed toward a small group of creatures coming toward them down the middle of the street.

The first thump took the riders in the cargo hold by surprise. "What was that?" demanded Anna.

"Road kill, ten points!" Dallas shouted over his shoulder. *Thump!* "It's gettin' thick up here, Boone." *Thump! Thump!* He was forced to slow the truck some. "Hey, roll up your window, will ya pard?"

Androwski realized he had his elbow resting on the open truck window and he jerked it in, feeling foolish. He locked the door and rolled the window up. It was sweltering in the truck, and Dallas, reaching right, flicked on a small fan.

Boone struggled through his group to get to the cab. "Time to check in. Andy, switch with me so I can make a call." Androwski got up and moved past Boone without a word. Boone sat in the passenger's seat, put on his seatbelt, and pulled the comm-unit out of his ear letting it rest on his shoulder. He then reached for a second radio, switched it on, and began to transmit, "Rock, this is Wanderer, come in, over."

Almost instantly there was a reply, *"Wanderer, this is Rock, we read you five. SITREP, over."*

"Transport acquired, proceeding northwest to acquire superior transport. Moderate Lima presence, over."

"Final coordinates to follow on next transmission. Be advised, new intel on Limas: Unconfirmed reports suggest some Limas are much faster than previously determined."

Boone was confused. "Say again?"

"Repeat, some Limas reported running. Repeat, running."

Dallas looked over at Boone. "Is that boy serious?"

Boone pointed in front of them. "Watch the road."

Thump!

Dallas looked forward and steered slightly to the right.

Boone keyed the microphone again. "Unconfirmed?"

"Affirmative. Intel comes from the last group to arrive at base. Intel not confirmed by base personnel; however, many newcomers concur on Lima speed. Caution advised. SITREP required when first mission objective met, Rock out."

Dallas smirked. "Caution advised? Does he think we're out for a Sunday drive?"

"It *is* Sunday." Boone pointed again. "The road."

He keyed the mic again. *"Copy that base, Wanderer out."*

Boone spun in his seat and looked over his shoulder. "Listen up people: Apparently the Limas have decided to put on some track shoes. Alcatraz has reports of some of them running now. I would say we need to be extra cautious, but that would be ridiculous under the circumstances. From this point forward, consider all Limas as fast as you are. Do not underestimate their speed, because we have no idea of their new capabilities."

Nothing but stunned silence came from the cargo area of the truck, as the occupants exchanged worried glances that carried a new level of fear.

3

Eighteen corpses littered the area just outside a locked chain-link fence in front of a vehicle service depot. All of the corpses had severe head trauma. Three large garages and a hangar-like structure sat next to a large canopy, under which resided a row of gasoline and diesel pumps. All were inside the fence. Martinez was on his stomach on the roof of the appropriated parcel truck, scanning the area past the mil-dots of his weapon optics. There was no movement inside the fence, but he took out one more zombie that came into view across the street with a perfect head shot. He had dispatched the contingent of mobile deceased in under two minutes, and now his people were sneaking down a hill and making for the locked gates.

The SEAL Benotti had remained with him to provide tactical close-combat cover for Martinez as he removed threats. Benotti was on the roof of the vehicle with the sniper, and Anna and Chris were still inside its relative safety. He looked at his watch, 19:40. "Clear," Martinez whispered into his comm-unit.

At once, the forward team started moving by twos to the gate. Even the civilians remained exceptionally quiet as they quickly removed a pair of bolt cutters from a pack and cut the heavy chain from the fence. Sliding the left side gate open slightly, they moved inside. Behind them, Stark wrapped the chain back around the two gate posts and zip tied the links together, securing the gate. It wouldn't stop a human for long, nor a horde of creatures, but it would slow down any singular unwanted undead visitors as they lacked the capacity to reason out the chain.

Dallas and Rick moved forward together into the depot, taking positions behind a parked Ford F150. Their job was to cover the gate while the rest of Hammer Platoon Detachment Bravo searched for fuel for the vehicles they were there to appropriate.

The SEALs had spread out by twos and were attempting various tasks. Usher and Seyfert were checking out the two LAVs that were outside the hangar, Boone and Stark were quietly breaking in to the office in the first garage, Androwski and Cole were placing fuel cans next to fifty-five gallon drums marked with a diamond-shaped placard reading simply, UN1202.

Twenty minutes into the operation, Boone and Stark appeared from the second garage holding folders with yellow tags on them. Boone pinched his throat mic. "Recon is complete. To Dallas and Rick in thirty." All six men showed up at the Ford in a few seconds. "Okay," Boone began, "good news and bad news. Good news is that the service reports for the C-2 and the M indicate that the onboard electronics upgrades and drive train service was complete. Bad news is that the R," Boone pointed toward the third garage, "had the boom removed and they were working on the front axles before the shit hit. We could fix it, but Actual tells us there is a significant Lima force nearby."

Dallas raised his hand, and Boone raised his eyebrows. "Yes?"

"What's a C-2, and R, and M, and who the hell is *Actual*?"

Stark stepped forward and whispered to Dallas and Rick, "The letters are different types of LAV, and Actual is Commander McInerney. That will change when we get out of radio range, and then Boone will be Actual."

"Oh. So how does Kevin know there are pus bags near us?"

Boone looked uncomfortable with the name *Kevin* being used in reference to his commanding officer. "Satellite feeds must still be up. Either someone is still manning them, or the orbits haven't degraded enough to screw with the signal. How he knows isn't really important. What he tells us is." In the waning light of the day, he spread a map across the hood of the pickup and traced his finger across it diagonally. "This is our route, and we will get further instructions when we reach this control point." Boone stabbed his finger at a nondescript point on the map. Looking at Usher and Seyfert, he pointed his chin at the military vehicles. "We have any issues with our rides?"

"Sir," Seyfert began, "LAVs One and Two are fueled and ready. We have another sixty gallons of diesel for each rig, but we haven't powered up yet. The ramps were down for the electronics upgrades, and we cleared both vehicles just to be safe, no evidence of hostiles."

"Dammit, I wanted that boom. Okay, two LAVs will have to do. Rick and Dallas with—"

The SEALs each pressed fingers to their left ear as all the tactical radios came alive with Benotti's voice. "Contact right fifty meters, closing on your position!"

Boone pressed his throat mic again. "How many?"

"Too many to count through the NVGs, dozens, maybe a hundred or more."

"Well folks, it looks like our secret's out, let's load up and hope these things work. High squad, fall in on the gates ASAP, we're bugging out."

The parcel truck started three seconds later, the headlights piercing the dusk shadows. It sped to the rendezvous point, and Boone quit whispering, "Dallas and Rick in LAV One with Andy, Cole, and Ush. Chris can jump in with you when he gets here. Everybody else in LAV 2. Start 'em up!"

The LAV One crew ran to their large, green vehicle and gained access via a ramp that was also the rear hatch. The inside of the vehicle was tight, although not tall enough to stand up in. It was still more spacious than the civilians would have believed. There were two padded benches opposite each other, with webbing behind each for storage. Underneath each white bench was a large storage locker, and up front were two bucket seats. Two hatches, for use with an M252 mortar system on the ceiling, now allowed for egress from the transport compartment, and a single hatch up front allowed the driver to maneuver the rig with his head sticking out should he want. Panoramic windows, approximately ten inches high and tinted red, were the windscreen, but there was also a video monitor near the driver, one near the front passenger, and two more in the rear. A big smile came across Dallas's face. "I'll drive!" he blurted. "Like Hell," Cole yelled as he made his way to the driver's seat. "This is a military op, Texas, not a mud-fest, I'm the wheel man here."

Dallas looked stunned, but acquiesced in silence and sat on one of the benches opposite Rick. "Oh shit that's cold," Usher chuckled, shaking his head as he passed the two civilians on the way to the passenger bucket seat. As Usher sat and buckled his seatbelt, Cole pushed a lever forward and turned a dial. A hum filled the steel monstrosity, and lights turned on throughout. Cole looked at Usher with a sideways half-smile, pressed a flashing yellow button and the beast came to life instantly with a throaty diesel roar. Cole yelled back to the civilians, "Cover the hatch until the high team gets here!"

Androwski showed up a few seconds later. He had cut the zip tie, removed the chain, and slid the front gates wide open. "It started! Damn, I was worried for a minute."

"We are five by five baby!" Cole yelled from the front. "Waitin' on the sniper crew and we is out!"

Outside LAV One, Boone and Stark had gained access to the second vehicle. It also powered up quickly. The parcel truck arrived, smashing down a few of the undead vanguard, and the four sniper crew abandoned the truck, running for the armored transports. The dead had also arrived in full force and were beginning to stagger through the open gate, arms outstretched.

Chris bolted for the back of the LAV and sprinted up the hatch door. "I'm in, close it!" he yelled, and Cole flicked a switch. The rear hatch began a slow ascent from the ground. The few seconds it took to close seemed like a lifetime, but the dead weren't close enough to pose a threat.

Anna, Martinez, and Benotti reached LAV Two quickly gaining access, and Benotti smashed his hand on the yellow hatch button near the rear of the vehicle. The hatch didn't budge. He hit it again with the same result, the dead were forty feet away and stumbling toward the open door, slow but steady. Benotti hammered the hatch button repeatedly, but it wouldn't close.

"Close it for Christ's sake!" screamed Anna.

"I'm trying! It won't go! Sir, the fucking hatch won't close!"

Boone got up and made his way to the open door, Benotti was now hammering on the button.

Boone pressed his throat mic. "Cole, our door won't close!"

"Red and white striped handle above the yellow button, push it up then press the button!"

Benotti grabbed the handle and pushed up, then pressed the yellow button. Boone opened fire on the encroaching dead, carefully picking headshots using his night vision. The door began to close, but the dead had reached the ramp and were coming up. Boone switched to full auto and fired into the small crowd as the door pushed upward painfully slowly. Three zombies fell off the back but a fourth gained access and went straight at Boone, propelled forward by the rising door. The overweight, middle-aged dead thing struck him hard and they both went down in a heap, Boone's MP5SD3 pinned against his chest. Benotti let go of the button to pull out his sidearm, but Anna got there first with her combat knife, thrusting it into the fat dead guy's eye. The creature didn't want to miss a late dinner because of a blade in its face, so it kept pressing the attack while Boone held it off. Anna wiggled the knife and thrust it deeper, and the thing collapsed on top of the SEAL, who frantically pushed it off. "Go, Stark!" he yelled.

LAV Two started to move forward, and Benotti returned to wildly pressing the yellow button on the bulkhead. Several undead arms that had been reaching in through the mostly closed rear door were amputated and fell to the deck of the LAV.

Boone sat up and nodded at Anna, who nodded back. "Cole, SITREP," he said without taking his eyes off of her.

"Locked tight, sir. We have one from high team and five from depot team, and we're ready to move."

"Roger that. Follow us, out."

"Copy, out."

The two LAVs rumbled forward, crushing some undead in their path. Stark maneuvered LAV One through the gate and past the still running Fed-Ex truck, but Cole ran his side of the gate over, and it folded like cardboard under the weight of the heavy armored vehicle.

The dead gave chase, but were no match for the speed of the LAVs, and soon the depot and the small horde were lost to the darkness. The team travelled in silence for fifteen minutes or so, and they were well out of the town and into the surrounding hills when the commander called a halt.

Boone pointed at the blood smears from the severed arms and dead man, "It's been all over the news that fluids from a Lima are infectious, so stay away from that crap as much as you can. Stark, Cole, can we stop? Do you see a significant Lima presence here? I want to get this poor dead bastard out of the LAV."

"We're good up here," Stark yelled back, and Cole's voice came over the radio: "LAV Two is secure behind. Recommend you power up your vid screens and check all four sides."

"I dunno how to do that, Cole, instructions please?"

"Small panel to the right side of the driver should read *Vid 1*, hit the soft key. Passenger should have a four-way split screen for all cameras, same deal with the soft key. The two screens in back turn on just like a TV. Starboard views starboard, and port port."

Boone sat on the bench, checking himself over while Anna and Martinez turned on the video monitors. A moment later, both sides of the vehicle were shown bathed in green on the screens.

"Port is clear," Martinez told everyone.

Anna followed suit. "Yeah, there's nobody on this side either."

Stark peered into his driver's monitor. "Clear to open, sir."

Benotti pulled the lever down and pressed the button. Boone stood, as much as was possible in the confined space. "Try not to touch any of the fluids. Andy, grab him by the shirt, I'll grab his pants." The two SEALS lifted the re-killed man and brought him out into the deserted street. Anna noticed that they didn't dump the unfortunate victim, but placed him gently to the side of the road. She and Martinez used their boots to kick the five severed arms out of the LAV. There was still quite a bit of thick, black blood on the door and floor of the vehicle, but they had no means to clean it.

Anna waved to the other LAV, but couldn't see if they waved back as the headlights were in her face. She stood at the top of the ramp, just outside the cargo area, her MP5SD3 pointed at the ground when a piercing shriek almost made her piss herself. "Get back in!" she yelled to the two pall bearers.

Not needing any further encouragement, the two SEALs ran for the ramp at full sprint. Boone came in first, but Benotti stopped at the base of the incline, looking to his left into a dark field. He flipped his NVGs down over his eyes, and Boone was starting to tell him to get inside when Benotti was tackled from the rear, and thrown tumbling forward out of sight.

Guttural grunts and growls could be heard mixed with Benotti's swearing as Boone and Martinez bounded from the LAV to see what was happening.

Boone couldn't believe his eyes. There was a teenage girl beating the shit out of a US Navy SEAL. She was all fury, claws and teeth. She was whacking at him with one hand while he fought to keep her head and other arm restrained. She fought like a cornered tigress, all the while screaming and screaming. Martinez stepped forward, grabbed her by her backpack, and threw her to the side. She landed hard, but was up immediately. She scanned the three men in front of her, threw her head back and screamed long and loud. She decided Benotti was her enemy and she sprinted toward her original target, who was beginning to stand. He stood fully and met her as she came at him, grabbing her outstretched arm and flipping her over with a grace that belied how big he was. She ended up on her belly, with him atop her back, her left arm pinned behind her. She screamed again, but the SEAL put his knee on the back of her neck, effectively pinning her.

"How do ya like that, ya little bitch?"

"Stow that shit, sailor," Boone said as he reached for a zip tie. Pulling a wide, white tie from his belt, he grabbed the flailing arm of the helpless girl and fastened it to her other arm. Then he did her legs at the ankles, and Benotti warily let go of her and stood.

She looked up at her captors and growled, struggling so hard against her bonds that small trickles of blood dripped down her arms. She couldn't have been any older than seventeen or eighteen, but the rage she was displaying made the men back up a step. She was actually trying to get to them while she was cuffed, inching pathetically toward them while scraping her skin on the asphalt. Her eyes were blood red, and there was a very small semi-circular mark on her left arm.

Chris, Dallas, Androwski, and Rick showed up from LAV Two. Anna and Seyfert from Boone's LAV. They all stood clustered around the prone girl, watching her.

"So now what?" demanded Dallas.

Benotti harrumphed, "Fuckin' shoot her that's what."

Anna looked horrified. "But she's not, dead. She's not one of them!"

"How do you know she's not dead? Bitch tried to kill me!"

"Look at her neck, see the vein," Anna countered, "it's throbbing, she has a pulse."

Benotti drew his sidearm and began screwing on a suppressor. Boone looked at him hard. "You secure that weapon."

"Sir, that thing is not human. I'm sorry she's just a kid, but look at her. She'd kill any one of us given the opportunity."

"He's right," agreed Rick.

"Rick, you can't mean—"

"I can, Anna. We can't take her with us, she's too dangerous." The bound girl affirmed this by snapping her teeth together loudly and hissing. "What's the alternative? Do we leave her here tied up so that she dies slowly, or cut her loose so she can attack the nearest person, probably infecting them?"

Dallas put his big hand on Anna's shoulder. "Rick's right, kiddo. We ain't got a cure, and killin' her'd be a piece of mercy. What if it was you? Would you wanna attack an old lady, or some kids?"

"No. No, I wouldn't." She raised her pistol, but Dallas put his hand on hers.

"Gotta save our ammo, hon," he told her, and pulled out a two-foot piece of rebar from his belt.

"Hey, let's get back in the tank-thing," Chris said to her. "It's no good being out here."

Wordlessly, she went with him.

Benotti sat on the bench across from Anna after he shut the door to the LAV. "Sorry it had to go down like that."

"I know. This plague thing sucks."

He put his elbows on his knees and leaned forward. "Are you going to be able to pull the trigger if need be?"

She matched his pose and looked him in the eye. "Yes."

He smiled and leaned back, resting against the seat-back. A stinging sensation in his neck caused him to put his hand under his tactical vest and shirt. His middle and ring finger tips came away with the slightest bit of blood on them.

4

Using the LAVs to skirt most of the larger towns, the team of twelve made good time on the empty highways and back roads. Most of the roads had been jammed full of deserted cars at the early part of the trip, but it was easy for the monstrous tires of the armored vehicles to tread outside the tarmac where the average car couldn't go. They used the westbound lane to travel east where they could as well. Just east of Sacramento, a huge tow truck had smashed into the Jersey barriers, effectively blocking all eastbound traffic on I80. The doomed travelers in their vehicles had been swamped by the dead flooding from the city. Many car doors were open and even more windows were broken. Hundreds of corpses had been straining to escape the confines of their metal and plastic tombs only to be confounded by a simple seatbelt.

After the unintentional roadblock, it was easy to get back on the interstate and head east toward their destination. Boone would not relay their objective's location until they were almost on it.

The LAVs crested a hill and looked down on the town of Brent in the early morning the day after the events of the depot. The small town sat in a valley in western central California, with scrub land on three sides, and high hills leading into mountains on the near side. The mountains would have been able to be viewed off to the west if the light was good.

Brent was dead, just like every other town they had gone through. At least it looked dead, with trash strewn about, three burned-out hulks of vehicles, and a few corpses littering the one wide, main street. Spread out over a few square miles, Brent's draw certainly couldn't have been tourism, as there was nothing to see here. Perhaps it had no draw at all.

Somewhere on the far side of the tiny municipality, and as yet unseen through the waning darkness, was their goal: a compound of three brick buildings surrounded by yet another chain-link fence a few miles outside the town proper.

Unlike the previous towns they had been through, this one was pitch black, no sodium-arc street lamps nor light of any kind perforated the darkness save for the headlights on the LAVs. The electricity was truly out here. It would probably stop working throughout the entire country soon enough, as unmanned power stations and relays began to fail.

Other than Cole and Stark, who were at the controls of the LAVs, the entire team gathered outside looking to their commander for guidance. Boone folded his map up and stowed his radio. "Okay people, the population of this piss-ant burg was nine thousand before the shit hit. That's nine thousand potential enemies and nine thousand infection risks. We're going to drive down that road," he pointed at the main road, "and get to the facility ASAP. Once there, we'll do what we did at the depot, with one exception. No sniper team. Get inside the gates and lock them behind us, then we'll get the guns and canvas the buildings in three teams of three, with two remaining in LAV Two and Stark in LAV One. Do not take chances. Check everywhere. Even if you don't think a human could fit in a tight place, check it. Nobody goes anywhere alone, and use your suppressors. We'll give ourselves away when we drive through town, but still, be as quiet as possible when we reach the buildings. Dallas, you and Stark drive the LAVs in, and button up when we get out." Dallas smirked and winked at the red tinted glass where he knew Cole was listening. "Anna, you hop in LAV One with Dallas and monitor the perimeter with the LAV cameras. Chris, stick with me. Everyone maintain constant contact, but zero chatter. The LAV weaponry is located in the storage shed to the left of the main building, so all three squads will hit that first, and if we have time, the other buildings. Load up the guns in the back of the LAVs, and we'll sort it out when we have thirty miles of desert on all sides. Benny, you okay?"

Everyone turned to look at Benotti who had his eyes closed and was pinching the bridge of his nose. He looked up startled. "Yeah. I just got this really fucked headache is all. Ain't slept in a couple days."

"Okay. Well make sure you get some fluids in you before we get out of the LAVs, and more when we get back in."

"Copy, sir."

"Any questions? Then let's go."

They entered their respective vehicles and hunkered down for the fifteen minute drive through Brent. Dallas switched seats with a dejected Cole and gave him a friendly punch on the shoulder as he passed him. "That's the button to open the back, you have to push the switch up and hold the button down," Cole said pointing. "This is the monitor switch, and this is comms. Don't break my truck, you redneck prick."

Dallas looked at him smiling. "Your truck just got a driver upgrade, ya Jarhead wannabe."

"Fucking bumpkins," Cole said as he shook his head and sat down.

LAV One rolled forward and the second vehicle followed immediately behind at a slow speed of twenty KPH. Not long into the town it was evident that the plague had not spared many here. Smashed in storefronts and hastily built barricades were everywhere. Many of the buildings and homes had broken front doors with spatter marks on the jambs and exterior walls, indicating the holdfasts were overrun from the exterior. Cole was using the spotlight on LAV One to illuminate alleys and shine in upstairs windows, but no humans were evident. Numerous corpses could be seen however, and not all of them were still. From alleys and doors, from open cars and windows the dead came out to see what was for dinner. Some of the bodies lying in the street sat up and attempted to grab the vehicles as they rolled through the town. Anything foolish enough to get in front of the big wheels was crushed beneath.

"Aww shit, look at this," Seyfert said pointing at his monitor. Three figures were running from the south, directly at the slow-moving hulks. "Fuckers are damn fast."

"Seyfert, confirm they're infected."

"Sir, they're pushing shufflers out of the way to get to us, and the pus bags aren't grabbing for them."

"Shit, step on it then. Stark, maximum safe speed, and watch for road hazards, Dallas keep sixty feet off of us minimum."

"Copy, sir." Stark looked at Seyfert, covered his tactical mic, and said, "Whole damn place is a road hazard."

Both vehicles picked up speed and soon the sprinters were left behind with the rest of the town. The LAVs thundered out of Brent and continued down the road for a few more minutes before they came to a turn off. The sign read I-80 East to the right, but no sign indicated anything to the left. Stark stopped, waiting for instruction.

"This is us," Boone told Stark, pointing left. "Follow it for about three miles, and we're there." He looked out the window of the LAV. "It'll be light soon. I haven't decided if that's good or bad."

"At least we'll be able to see better," Seyfert surmised.

"So will they." The lieutenant commander pointed out the thin window to a lone undead, ambling toward them in the pre-dawn light with its arms outstretched.

Stark took a left and brought the vehicle to speed. "Seyfert, think that dead guy was from the town?"

"Dunno, but I'm glad we're out of there, I didn't like it at all on that street with all them fuckers drooling over us."

"Agreed."

The minutes passed slowly until they reached the facility.

"Oh shit," Seyfert blurted.

Boone looked up from his map. "What is it?"

"Somebody beat us here."

Boone moved forward, hunched over in the LAV, to look at the forward monitor. Between two natural rock formations, a yellow, tube-steel gate was across the road barring entrance to the parking lot. Seyfert shined his searchlight on the area. The tollbooth-style guardhouse was almost completely destroyed, the glass broken and blood everywhere. Four dead men lay on their backs in front of the little shack, and two more blocked in the broken doorway.

"That gate is some serious business; we need to get it open."

Seyfert started to get up. "Roger that, sir."

"I got it," mumbled Benotti from the rear. He flipped the handle down and pressed the yellow button. Grabbing a huge pair of bolt cutters clamped to the bulkhead of the LAV, he jogged down the ramp not waiting for it to finish opening. Benotti casually strode to the gate and applied the cutters to the lock, which fell away in two pieces when he was done. He pushed the gate wide and motioned the vehicles forward. When they were both past the gate, he closed it behind them and hopped in the back of the open LAV, closing the door behind him. He sat down on the bench across from Martinez, who looked at him strangely.

"You're soaked."

Benotti drew his sleeve across his forehead. "It's fuckin' hot, and that thing was heavy."

Martinez nodded and the two vehicles drove forward. A kilometer up the access road, they arrived at the outskirts of the small facility. The fence was knocked down and there were bodies everywhere. Dozens of them. The buildings themselves looked secure, but there had definitely been a stand here.

There were lights on in the building indicating that either this facility had its own generators, or it operated on a different functional grid than that of the town of Brent. The vehicles pulled up to within thirty feet of the front door, and after a cautious three minutes, both rear hatches opened, unloading nine of the twelve passengers. They came out in spread formation, checking in all directions with weapons leveled.

"Clear!"

"Clear!"

"Okay, we do this quick. Rick, you're with Martinez and Ush, Chris, with Andy and me, Benny, you're—"

The window one story up opened and an older man stuck his head out, "Can I help you folks?"

"Yes, sir, you can tell me who you are and then open this door."

"Well, as to the who, name's McNalley. The other part is a no-can-do."

"Why are you in a military facility, Mr. McNalley, and why won't you let us in?" Boone demanded

"I work here. Worked I guess. You ain't gettin' in because I got my grandkids and my daughter-in-law in here and I don't know you."

"Sir, we are elements of the United States Navy, and we need—"

"Don't give a rat's ass about the Navy, and don't rightly care what you need either. You can mosey on out of here or I can kill all of you."

Boone smiled. "Mr. McNalley, we have armored vehicles, but I promise you we aren't here to hurt you or to take—"

"You ain't gettin' me, son. I told you to move on. Why don't you look in them bushes next to the door, or under that ashtray-thingie there." He pointed to a tall chimney-type ashtray behind them. "Might wanna be careful though."

Usher strode forward, got to one knee, and moved the brush aside. "Claymores."

"Christ, there's a brick of shape-charged SEMTEX in here with a cell phone detonator." Androwski put the top of the ashtray back on carefully.

Boone shook his head and looked up, "Well done, sir. All we want are the armaments for these LAVs and we'll go."

"There's three Bushmasters in that building there," he indicated the building to his left, "but there's a dead guy locked in there with em'. Got about a ten thousand rounds in twenty cases too. There's two five fifty six SAWs for the pivot turrets too, the fifty cal HWMGs that are standard for them LAVs," he pointed at LAV One, "ain't here. 'Bout eighty thousand five fifty six rounds, and then there's the grenade launcher, but she's a heavy sumbitch, and I only got smoke for her."

"Benny, Andy, Rick, check for the Bushmasters. Watch out for the infected."

"Hang on a sec there, Admiral," McNalley said and ducked his head back inside. He came back out in a few seconds jingling a key ring. "These'll open the door for you, I disabled the key card system when I got here a week ago. I got APMs and IEDs all over, so if you try gettin' in or shootin' at me, well, it's gonna get messy."

"You have my word, we aren't here for anything but the arms for these vehicles."

"S'what the last group of National Guard fellas said. They killed my son." He tossed the keys to Boone.

"That's reprehensible. What happened?"

"Don't matter. They killed him, I killed them. They're over there under that tarp if you wanna see. Gonna burn em when I get a chance."

"I'm sorry for your loss, sir." Boone tossed the keys to Androwski. "Get the guns."

The three men hustled to the other building, Androwski fitting the key in the lock. "Get ready."

Benotti got down on one knee ten feet from the door, and Rick moved to Androwski's side, raising his weapon and sighting down the barrel.

"Do it," Benotti said with a nod.

Androwski banged on the steel door three times. After a few seconds, clawing and scratching, and the distinctive mournful moan of the living dead could be heard from the other side.

"On one. Three, two, one!"

He yanked the door open, and a man in woodland camouflage fatigues came stumbling out straight at Benotti, whose body picked that moment to betray him, and he vomited on his shoes. A round from Rick's M4 passed through the side of the dead soldier's cranium, re-killing him before he could reach the puking SEAL.

Rick turned on his tactical light and shined it in the open doorway. Benotti looked up wiping his mouth with his sleeve. "Thanks."

"Don't mention it. You okay?"

"No. I'm FUBAR." He stood up and nodded his chin at the open door. "Let's go check shit out."

Rick looked at Androwski who shrugged, and they both peered into the darkness. Rick went first with his light panning side to side. There was a push-button type light switch, and Rick turned on the overhead florescent lights. They were in a large storage area with a loft above them. The LAV armaments were exactly where McNalley said they were. In addition, there were crates and crates of ammunition and racks of weapons in chained cases on the wall. One area had a dozen or so Pelican cases stacked against the wall, each with a large hammer insignia and THOR in capital letters in a semicircle above the hammer.

Androwski gave a low whistle. "Mother-fucking-lode."

Rick looked at Androwski and half-smiled. "Let's get the LAVs over here and get the guns mounted."

The three men bounded back to the rest of their party. Boone paused in his conversation with McNalley, "Report."

"Tons of goodies, sir, we should load up."

"Yeah, you should," shouted down McNalley, "then beat it."

"Are you sure you don't want to come with us? We could find a safer place for you."

A comical look came over McNalley's face, "Safer'n here? This building has two-foot-thick reinforced concrete walls with a two-inch steel plate in the middle. I'm surrounded by natural rock formations to the east, canyons to the north and south, and the gate to the west. I'm gonna blow the rocks near the gate to block that route, I just ain't got around to it yet. No windows on the lower level, and the door is four-inch steel with a compression wheel-lock. I got MRE's to last half a hundred years, and chlorinated water for twenty. I was attacked by twenty sumbitches with automatic rifles and I kicked their ass. A safer place don't exist."

"Again, we're not here to tell you what to do. I have nothing to give you except a radio. You can contact our group on Alcatraz if you wish."

"Alcatraz? You the guys sending messages? I might just give them…" He pulled his head inside and was gone for a solid thirty seconds. He reappeared looking concerned. "Damn son, you done brought Hell with you."

"I'm sorry?"

"There's a sizable force of dead folks making their way up the road by the gate. Be here in an hour, and before you ask, I got video surveillance for two miles in three directions. Saw you comin' too."

"Alright, load up! Get the guns in the back of the LAVs, and—"

"Won't take but ten minutes to fix them Bushmasters on the LAVs," McNalley told Boone. "The coax is harder, but the pivot will go on in a jiffy."

"I can do it, sir, it's easy," Stark said over the radio.

"Okay, get the LAVs into the garage and hurry. If this takes longer than twenty mikes, we quit and stuff 'em in the back. Get moving! Stark, you got point on this one!" The LAVs moved across the parking lot of the facility and into the garage and the team got busy. Boone had Martinez and Androwski climb a small ridge and scan for signs of the approaching menace.

McNalley was indeed correct when he said that it wouldn't take long to install the weaponry. They had the pivoting light machine guns attached to pin-swivels in ten minutes, and were working on the Bushmaster belt system for LAV Two when Androwski called Boone on the tactical radio. "Sir, we have far range contact, a mile, maybe mile and a quarter."

"How many?"

"How many people in that town we went through?"

"Nine thousand."

"Then I'm going with nine thousand."

"Shit. When the vanguard is half a mile out, hump back to us, we're almost done."

"Copy, sir."

Boone surveyed his team. Things were under control. Chris and Anna had loaded three cans of twenty-five millimeter ammo into both vehicles, and all of the 5.56 crates. It was significantly tighter in the crew compartments now, but that was a small price to pay for the goodies they just received. Seyfert was attaching a wiring harness to the chain feeder of

LAV Two while Usher examined the Pelican cases. Boone jogged back to the window to engage McNalley one more time.

"Mr. McNalley, thank you for your help. I have some C4, and will lay a couple of strings to block that narrow gateway if you would like. How can I get you the radio, I would rather not throw it."

"You got C4? Coulda blown your way in here after a while I guess, but it would have taken half a day. I appreciate you not trying. Blowin' the gate would save me a dangerous trip down there, so yeah I would appreciate it. Here." He dropped a length of clothesline out the window, and Boone attached the radio to it. McNalley hauled it up with appreciation. "You're gonna lose comms when you get over them mountains to the east. Best take care of yourselves out there, Admiral," and with that he shut the window without another word.

A single shot rang out and echoed throughout the facility.

"Who's firing? Does anybody have eyes on?"

"It was me, sir," said Martinez. "There was a speedy one coming faster than the others up the road. He's history. Also, it's time for us to bug, they're about a half mile out."

"Roger that, Martinez, you guys get back here ASAP."

When the two scouts returned, LAV Two was buttoned up, but Seyfert was manning a light machine gun in the two-man turret. LAV One was waiting for them with its ramp down. They rushed in and Usher shut the door behind them. Chris passed them both a pair of wireless headphones like you would see in a helicopter. "Stark says that when the Bushmasters start to fire, you'll need those to save your hearing and listen to commands. It's gonna get loud."

Both LAVs roared toward the gate area. Boone's voice was already coming through the headphones when Martinez put his on, "...to blow the gate area. This op needs to be most ricky-tick, but only if there's time to get our folks back in the LAVs. McNalley has some defenses of his own, but I want to give him as much protection as possible."

The vehicles stopped between the sixty-foot-tall natural rocks that flanked the gate. The LAVs opened up their rear hatches and Benotti, Usher, Martinez, and Androwski started placing the explosives at the base of the small cliffs. They rolled the plastique out in small bundles, each attached to the others by detonation cord.

"Okay, we see the horde, back inside pronto!"

Boone's command didn't go lightly, and three men ran back and up the ramps to the safety of the interior of the armored vehicles. Benotti remained outside. Usher gaped at him. "Benny, get the fuck in here, quit screwing around!"

"Not coming. I'm infected. That little chick with the backpack must have gotten me." He pulled his shirt collar down and exposed a small scratch that looked like it had been festering for a week. The occupants of LAV Two knew instantly that Benotti was doomed. His lower neck and shoulder were inflamed and red, the area around the scratch was black, and the wound itself was oozing a thick, dark fluid.

Boone came over the radio from LAV One. "Benotti, what's happening? We don't have time to fuck about, they're three hundred feet away." Apparently he hadn't heard Benotti's confession.

"I'm humped, sir. The speedy little girl that jumped me scratched me on the neck. I'm dead already. Gimme the detonator and go."

"Benny, you can't be sure, get in the damn boat and we'll check it…"

"Due respect sir, negative. I'm done, I can feel it inside me."

Usher nodded and handed him a double-click detonator. He nodded at Benotti, turned the striped door handle and pressed the yellow button. The ramp started to rise and Usher reached into one of the pockets of his tactical vest. He got a small package out and tossed it to his friend just as the ramp closed. Turning towards the other riders in the LAV, he noticed they were all looking at their shoes.

"Godspeed, Benny," Boone said through his throat mic, and the vehicles started to move forward.

Benotti looked at the package that Usher had tossed him and smiled. He opened it, popped three huge pieces of grape bubble gum into his mouth, and leaned against the yellow gate near the guard house, watching his friends depart.

"Don't plow into them yet," Boone told Stark, "let's open up on them first to keep them off us for a while. I don't want to gum up the wheels."

Usher climbed into the two man turret of LAV One and turned on the M242 Bushmaster chain gun system. It came on with a hum, and a small heads-up display came up over a green monochrome view screen. The things were sixty feet away when he asked permission to fire.

Boone was also looking through a view screen. "Light 'em up. Concentrate fire in the center and we'll go through the three hole."

Even with the headphones on, the cannon was incredibly loud. The twenty-five millimeter high explosive, incendiary rounds turned the vanguard of the living dead horde into a flaming mushy pulp in five-round bursts. After the second burst, half a thousand of the densely packed creatures were destroyed, or so damaged that they were useless, and there were small fires where the things' clothing had begun to burn from the incendiaries. Everywhere the tracer rounds were sent, a column of dead exploded thirty deep in a straight line, the ones in the back falling like dominoes, and the first few unfortunates simply liquefying in a spray of gore and bone from the chest up.

LAV Two had moved up on the port side of LAV One, and Seyfert also fired into the crowd. Short bursts with his light machine gun from the open turret blew off limbs and destroyed craniums. Many of the undead tried to rise after being knocked over only to be trampled down by their hungry brethren trying to reach the canned food in front of them. Seyfert wasted no time and kept firing at chests and heads.

The vehicles gave deep diesel grunts and moved forward, the twenty-five millimeter firing to the front. LAV Two fell back in behind LAV One and they drove in a single column. Seyfert spun left and right in his turret and tried to take out anything that got too close, but there were so many creatures that the pocket created by the Bushmaster began to collapse, and some reached the sides of the LAVs. The uncoordinated and lumbering dead were immediately knocked away by the speed of the moving vehicles, and in a moment they were through the horde, one fast creature running after them. Seyfert sighted her and gave her a short burst of 5.56 rounds. She collapsed, and he got back inside and shut the turret hatch.

There weren't nine thousand undead as first surmised, but Seyfert did mental calculations to come up with about three thousand. More than half wouldn't be getting up, but some on the ground still moved, and others were untouched. The mobile ones stumbled after the LAVs, or made their way in the other direction toward a sure meal; the sailor waiting patiently.

Benotti watched them come, leaning against his gate and blowing bubbles between coughs. He harrumphed and shook his head, "Well this sucks."

They didn't take long to reach him, maybe three minutes, and when he could make out individual men, women, and children he swore out loud and taunted them. "C'mon fuckers, come get some! You bitches like Italian food? I had a shitburger this morning, hope you like the taste of it!" As the first of the significantly smaller swarm, an older man with horrible wounds on his face and neck, reached for him, Benotti spit his gum out, flipped him off, and double clicked the detonator paddles.

More than a mile and a half away, Usher witnessed the spectacular explosion on his rearward monitor. His disciplined manner allowed him two words of farewell. "Bye Benny."

5

Salt Lake City was burning. The highways and bridges outside the city had been bombed with high yield ordnance, probably to stop people from spreading the infection west. The city itself was covered by a dark smog, the smoke from the fires unable to escape outside the ring of mountains. It was impossible to tell if the military had destroyed the city or if it had been the dead, but the city was in ruins.

Several of the taller buildings (there weren't that many) were obscured by the smoke, and the streets were awash with corpses, walking and not. At the western end of I-80, just north of the city, was a huge plywood sign with scrawled block print telling folks to turn back, or subject themselves to medical inspection. It was evident that a military outpost had been hastily set up here as two medical trailers and an olive drab canvas tent sat vacant. Two Humvees were present, one with its hood up. Concrete barriers stood resolute across the highway. A white tent sheltered the remains of an aid station. Cots, some with still squirming victims strapped down, became visible when the wind blew the bloody flaps of the tent open.

Dozens of black and twisted hulks of burned vehicles were blocked in by two immobile M1 Abrams tanks, the barrels of the huge guns pointing toward the city. The hatch on one of the behemoths was wide open, and there was blood all over it and the exterior of the machine. The other was crawling with fifty or so living dead beating bloody fists on the Chobham armor. Most were ordinary people clothed in Western garb with cowboy boots, but many others wore military camouflage fatigues or doctor's scrubs. This outpost had been overrun.

Boone passed his binoculars to Rick, and Rick to Dallas. Three others pairs of binocs also surveyed the scene, less than five hundred meters away. Some of the dead had already begun to shamble toward the LAVs, but most remained with their eyes on the prize, and continued in their futile attempts to gain access to the tank.

"What's the plan, sir?" Rick asked Boone.

"Well, there's nothing in the city we need, but those Limas pounding on that Abrams tell me that there's someone alive inside. We're not leaving him to die in that tin can."

Martinez unslung his SR25 sniper rifle from his shoulder. "I'll take the twenty on the right."

Rick opened one of the Pelican cases that they had affixed to the outside of the vehicle. He pulled out one of the new weapons they had acquired at the weapons depot back in California: a Thor Weapons Systems XM408E sniper rifle, of which there were two. Cole grabbed its twin before Dallas could appropriate it for himself.

"Drive your tractor, hillbilly, this is mine today. I already stripped and zeroed this bitch. That's what I was doin' when I dry firin' her in the boat, and was shootin' them cans yesterday."

All three men took their time setting up on the road. Cole coughed, the dust and smoke in the air momentarily too much for his lungs. "Jesus they look like ants from here." The new rifles had attached bipod stands, but Martinez's SR25 had to be rested on an empty diesel can with a fatigue jacket on the top. The twelve-times magnification ballistic scopes cut the distance down considerably, but the area of effect inside the scopes was small. "What's this wire?"

"Gotta admit," Rick contemplated, "I have no idea. It looks like an ear bud for a Walkman."

"Huh."

"Okay, the thirteen I can see coming up the road are your target practice," Martinez told the other two shooters. "Right now they're a little under a quarter of a mile away, so you won't need to account for too much bullet deviation. Wait until they're three hundred meters out and aim about an inch above the bridges of their pus bag noses. Don't fire until I tell you, but I'm going to take a few shots now."

Rick looked quizzical. "You're not going to use the suppressor?"

"No need. They know we're here, I don't want to burn out the suppressor through overuse, and the cold-loaded rounds and barrel length actually hurt the shot."

Martinez took a deep breath, let half of it out, and squeezed the trigger. The top half of the head of a zombie that looked like a macabre Elvis Presley popped up in the air and the thing dropped to the ground. The sniper did this six more times before he told the other two men to follow his lead, "Remember, don't yank on the trigger, squeeze it. Squeeze it like a tit, like you were caressing a nipple. Slowly curl your finger back until it fires. There are seven left, Rick start on the far left and work your way in, Cole, start from the right."

Rick squeezed his trigger and the leftmost zombie keeled over. He sighted the next one and missed. Then missed again. "Damn."

"Feel the shot, don't let anything bug you."

Cole fired and missed, but scored a hit on the next try. Unfortunately the creature got right back up. "What the hell?"

"You must have grazed her, try to—"

"*The TA-52 Target Assist System is an electronic range and deviation calculator that is calibrated for each weapon during the initial test firing phase prior to shipment from the Thor manufacturing facility.*" All three men turned to look at Anna, who was reading from a small pamphlet. "*Simply plug the tactical earpiece pin into the electronic receiver input at the base of the ballistic scope and turn the pin clockwise to activate the…*" She noticed that they were all looking at her. "What? You said you didn't know what the wire was so I looked in the case." She shook the little booklet. "Big instruction manual, duh… *Turn the pin clockwise to activate the holographic targeting reticule, then sight the target center mass. The smaller green dot in the reticule will move to auto compensate for deviation, elevation, target speed, and certain atmospheric conditions. Adjust the weapon such that the green dot covers the red. A sonic indicator will sound single tones as the firing solution is calculated. Three rapid tones will sound when a firing solution has been acquired. The weapon is now ready to fire. Depress the firing mechanism within one point five seconds or the algorithm will recalculate.* Uh… those are the quick instructions, but there's a bunch of stuff in here on calculations and recharging the system batteries and recalibrating and stuff."

Cole was still staring at her, but Rick already had the ear piece in and was aiming. He fired and dropped his target. He adjusted the barrel of the rifle slightly, and fired again, and again, and again. Each time the weapon fired one of the undead dropped.

Boone was looking through his binoculars again. "Holy shit."

"*Bullshit* is what it is," complained Martinez. "Now an eight year old can be a professional sniper with zero training or discipline."

Rick looked at him and stuck his tongue out.

Cole attached his earpiece, and soon all the approaching zombies were down. "Way better practice than soda cans. Zombie noggins are the best way to practice. Not that I need it with this thing."

Rick stood and brushed grit from his shirt and pants. "Shall we see who's in the tank?"

Boone nodded thoughtfully and pulled out his radio. Switching frequencies, he spoke to the tank, "This is Lieutenant Commander Boone of the US Navy calling to the Abrams on I-80 outside of Salt Lake City. Is there anyone alive in the tank? Please respond." Repeated attempts went unanswered.

"What's the plan then?" demanded Dallas.

"Shit. Kill the Limas and get the person out of the tank."

"Thought you was gonna say that." Dallas pulled his rebar from his belt. "You boys is pretty good with them rifles, cover me."

Boone raised his eyebrows. "Where the hell do you think you're going?"

"I'll go down there and make some noise. Pus bags see a free lunch and come run... ah walking. You guys shoot em."

Usher stepped up. "I'll go with him for close cover, sir."

"Alright. Sniper team take out any approaching Limas. Runners would have been on us already. Seyfert you're on the LMG for support if necessary. Everybody else in LAV One, with Stark. Andy, you man the Bushmaster, but stay off unless ordered. I'll provide close cover for the sniper team. Forward team, stay in the center of the road, and drop if we radio you to do so."

Everyone hustled to follow orders, and in short order Dallas and Usher cautiously advanced toward the dead city. The first of the dead turned toward them about two hundred feet short of the tank barrier.

Dallas cupped his hands in front of his face and shouted, "C'mon pus bags, we're over here!"

The result of his shout was instantaneous. Dozens of blood red eyes turned toward them, and the things climbed down from the tank. The undead formed a procession following their attentive friend.

"Ya know, Ush ole buddy, this seemed like a great plan when we was way back there, but I ain't too fond of it no more."

"Agreed, let's get scarce."

Both men started backing up, and they had moved maybe sixty feet back toward the LAVs, keeping pace ahead of the zombies, when they noticed a disturbance in the center of the oncoming horde. Several of the dead were pushed aside and some fell. Two in the front fell forward as a large shape in fatigues came hurtling through them, barreling them over.

Usher dropped to one knee raising his MP5SD3. The former soldier came swiftly, and Usher fired when it was fifty feet away. He hit it in the chest and stumbled back but didn't fall. It let out a scream and kept coming. Usher fired again, hitting it center mass with the same result. "What the fuck!" He raised his weapon higher and sighted on the thing's cranium as it continued to scream and run at them. He fired but missed his headshot. "Fucking suppressor!" Firing three quick shots, he saw the infected spin and fell down. It was up quickly and running again, screaming. Dallas started backing up, but Usher remained on one knee and switched to automatic fire. He gave the infected a short burst, the creature's head jerking back, and the thing fell down and stayed down. It was ten feet away and Usher got up and walked toward it. He kicked it in the ribs and nodded. "Body armor," he said and looked up. The approaching crowd was closing. He trotted back to where Dallas was and both of them made a slow return to their friends.

The rifle fire started a moment later, and the dead were re-killed quickly. Soon it was only the team that was moving. Boone kept his sidearm in the ready position as he advanced on the tank. "Let's check that tin can. LAV One, you follow at twenty meters, LAV Two remain behind and stay buttoned."

Several *rogers* and *affirmatives* rang out, and the party moved forward as a cohesive unit. Rick and Boone cut a wide path right, Dallas and Usher left, Cole and Martinez down the center. They made it to the tank and checked under and around it.

The carnage in front of the armored behemoths was becoming commonplace. Hundreds of bodies and smoldering vehicles dotted the road behind several concrete barriers. The windows on the vehicles were broken, and where not charred, bloody. It looked like the doomed civilians had tried to make a hasty escape from the infected city only to be met by a blocked road and two Abrams tanks. The dead had followed, and the folks had either been trapped in their vehicles, or made a break for it into the flat lands of Utah. At some point, the tanks must have opened fire with their one-hundred-five millimeter cannons because there were huge swaths of destroyed vehicles and shell-torn asphalt a few hundred meters forward of them. Several overturned or completely destroyed vehicles were off to the sides of the road, appearing to have tried to run the blockade and failed. Several of the vehicles and two large, green street signs had been peppered with what looked like buckshot from an enormous shotgun.

"Jesus, they used M1028's on these poor bastards."

The big Texan looked at Boone. "Wassat? A M28?"

"M1028. It's a canister round fired from the tank. Anti-infantry. It couldn't have been pretty."

"Why would the army not let them out?" demanded Anna over the radio. She must have been watching through the monitors of LAV One.

"Standard containment protocol," answered Boone. "The army was trying to contain the infection." He climbed on the Abrams and rapped his fist on the hatch. "Anybody home? This is Lieutenant Commander Boone of the US Navy. We can help you."

There was a screeching noise, and the hatch opened. A young man crossed his eyes as he looked into the business end of Boone's sidearm. "You gonna shoot me?"

"Of course not." Boone stuck his hand down to help the man out of the belly of the M1.

"I'm good," the guy said and climbed out of the tank. There were mewling sounds behind him, inside the vehicle. The man had a white T shirt on, and it was covered in sweat and gore. "Thanks. I thought I was going to die in there. Jesus it was hot."

"What's your name?"

"Ben Griffith. I'm afraid you saved me only so I can die out here in the fresh air though." He pulled his shirt up and there was a clear semi-circular tooth pattern on his side. The skin had been broken and he was bleeding from it. The wound wasn't rank or oozing yet, indicating the man had been assaulted recently.

They climbed down from the beige beast and Ben began talking.

Ben's story was the same as countless others. He didn't flee the city when everyone else did, but got caught in his apartment too afraid to leave. He ran out of food and water and was attacked while scavenging. "Had to run, and this was the only way there weren't any of the dead people. 'Course that changed when I got to the cars here. Then there were plenty. The hatch on this tank was open, so we jumped in it and shut the lid just as those dead bastards were on our heels."

Rick looked at the man, "We?"

"Yeah, I had Joe with me but he kept giving me away when I was trying to sneak around. He's too little to understand when I tell him to be quiet." He wiped his hand across his brow blinking in the sun, "I didn't see the infected soldier inside the tank until he grabbed me and bit me. I got his knife from him and stuck it up under his chin, but by the time I was done, the other walkers were trying to get in there after me. There's a pole inside the tank, I don't know what it's for, but it was great for pushing those dead ones off the lid. That was this morning. The only damn thing that works in this thing," he jerked his thumb at the Abrams, "is the clock. And the radio, but I couldn't figure out how to send, I could only hear."

"Where's the boy?" demanded Dallas.

Ben looked confused. "What boy?"

"Your kid, Joe."

The man smiled, then gave a whistle. A small bark came from inside the tank. "Joe's my puppy. I only got him two months ago, then the world ended."

"I'm sorry, son, but ya know you're infected right?"

"Yeah. I saw it all over the news for a week, then I saw it first-hand. Nobody gets better." As if to punctuate his statement, he started a hacking cough, and spit up bloody sputum when he was finished. "Yup, fucked. I sure could use a gun for a minute if you don't mind. At least one bullet anyway."

"Kid's got balls, Boone. What we gon' do with 'im?"

Boone looked angry and sad at the same time. "Are you sure you want to do this, Ben?"

"Better than being one of them," he said and pointed at a dead doctor stumbling toward them from the medical tent.

Boone raised his sidearm and ended the thing's misery with one shot. Then he looked at his crew, "Ush, Cole, cover him." Both men raised their weapons. Boone ejected the magazine from his sidearm, flicking single rounds into his palm, leaving one shot in the weapon, and then passed it to the unfortunate man, who began to cry softly.

"This wasn't supposed to happen. I never even asked her out," he raised the weapon to his temple. "Take care of my dog, will you?"

Usher and Androwski tensed as the man lowered the pistol slightly. "Oh, one of the things I heard on the radio before you got here was to *join the three*. There's a guy broadcasting that over and over again with instructions on how to get there, and that they offer safety, food, and shelter."

Boone was stunned. "When was the last transmission?"

"A few hours ago. The group is supposed to be someplace south of I-80 in Nebraska. The guy said he was US military, and they have thousands of people there." He raised the gun to his head again but didn't pull the trigger. "I...I can't," he said and began to sob, lowering the weapon. He put the pistol on the road and looked back at the city.

"Best if you do it now, son," Dallas told him.

"I never heard from my parents. They live just inside the city. I'm going to go look for them."

"Fair enough," Boone handed him another bottle of water. "Stay quiet. I might recommend telling your parents that you've been bitten too."

"If I find them."

"If you find them."

Ben turned and started walking back toward Salt Lake City.

When he was out of earshot, Dallas asked Usher, "How long you think he'll last?"

"An hour if he's lucky." He waved his hands at the bodies around him. "These are just the ones who made it out of town. There's got to be thousands back there. I would have taken the bullet."

"Alright, saddle up," Boone shouted as he picked up his handgun. "There's nothing here we need, and there's a rest stop sixty miles east of here. We'll get some fuel there." He keyed his radio. "Stark, monitor all frequencies for chatter. There may be a large group of survivors broadcasting from someplace in Nebraska."

"Do we make contact, sir?"

"Negative, Cole, no contact yet. Our mission is the priority, and we don't know if they're friendly."

6

Most of the screen was light gray, but it was dotted with some occasional white moving shapes as well. Anna furrowed her brows. "Shouldn't they give off no heat if they're dead?" A beagle puppy was asleep in her lap.

"They must possess some residual warmth," Chris said pointing at the screen. "I mean, I'm no scientist, but they are moving under their own power. They must be generating some type of heat."

The thermal optics in the LAVs were registering movement six hundred meters away at the McDonalds restaurant on I-80 in southern Wyoming. They had seen nothing between Salt Lake City and here. Not a car, or a shambler, or a jackrabbit. Two other rest stops had been razed to the ground, and they had skirted all the towns along the way, preferring to stick to the scrub land and drive around. There was one can of diesel left between the two vehicles, and LAV One was on fumes.

Dallas moved his finger across the screen, tapping the white moving shapes. "There's only eight of 'em. Let's kill em and get the gas."

"Diesel," corrected Boone, "and there are only eight that we can see. That place is huge, and there could be dozens that we don't see."

"There might be, but there's only two big rigs, and seven cars, how many could there really be? If we wait until sunrise, they can see us."

"Yes, and we can see them. We button up and wait for morning. Cole, you and Stark have first watch. Wake up Andy and Ush at zero-two-hundred, the rest of us will get up at oh-six. Let's get some chow and some rack before we hit that station tomorrow."

Rick blinked sleep from his eyes as Usher gently prodded him with his boot. He cracked his back as he stretched, the LAVs had reclining seats for sleeping, but they were extremely uncomfortable. Rick wanted a quality night's sleep in a king-size bed, with a continental breakfast the next morning. Fat chance. He settled for weak coffee and a pimento loaf MRE.

After breakfast in bed, he made his way forward. He was startled to see a dead man in coveralls looking directly into the starboard camera. "That's Victor," Usher told him. "He's been here since before Cole woke me."

"Is he the only one?"

"You mean is he the only former-American that I've seen since taking over watch? No. I saw a few walk past us and go for the truck stop, but I also saw some walk off into the wild black yonder never to return."

"Why did you name him Victor?"

"I didn't. I would imagine his parents did. His name is on his coveralls."

"Oh. Nobody else came for a look?"

"Some. They all moved on except for Victor. There's been little activity at the truck stop, but my attention has been on my buddy Vic here."

"Why?"

"Because he's extremely focused. Whenever one of the other Limas would come toward his side of the LAV, he would get riled and push them away. One of the speedy ones fought back for a second, knocking poor Vic down, but then it just ran away, and Vic stood back up and stared into the camera. Watch this." Usher moved a small metal joystick below his monitor. The effect on Victor was immediate, his red eyes grew big, and he followed the camera with his entire head. He became agitated and put his dead hands on the hull of the LAV.

"Maybe he was a mechanic, and he remembers something about vehicles," Rick opined.

"Either way he poses a threat." Boone was also staring into the monitor now. "He's infected, and his interest in us is irrelevant. They aren't pets, Usher, they're dangerous."

"Understood, sir. It's just that this one seems different somehow."

"That's even more reason to shoot him here rather than have him follow us." Boone picked up his radio. "I hope everyone had a good breakfast. The plan is the same as before. We'll drive LAV Two up to the truck stop and make some noise. The Limas will come and follow us back this way as we back up. We'll dismount snipers at one hundred yards and take them out on the road. Seyfert, you're on the LMG, and Andy, you're on the Bushmaster for backup in LAV One, which remains on station at this location to conserve fuel. If we get in hot water, bring up the second LAV, and save our asses. Any intelligent questions?"

"Yes," answered Rick. "Usher told me that other walkers came and went in the dark. Where did they come from and where did they go?"

"Good question, but I don't know the answer. We'll stay on our toes."

Victor got even more agitated as LAV Two fired up its engine and rumbled slowly toward the truck stop. The dead man followed them at a quick shamble. He loped along, swaying his arms instead of putting them out in front of him zombie-style. This creature was slightly faster than the other undead they had come across, but he wasn't sprinting, and was clearly dead. There were bloody bullet holes stitched across the back of his coveralls, indicating he had been shot while his blood was pumping. He wandered after the LAV, and was soon very small in the distance. Cole radioed to Boone to let him know that Victor was coming behind them.

True to the plan, LAV Two rolled up to the outskirts of the gigantic truck stop, and a baker's dozen dead things took notice. As before, the LAV reversed and the snipers got out and took positions on the hot road. The thirteen undead were re-killed in less than a minute. Easy peasy. After a good five minute wait, no more undead came to greet them.

LAV One thundered forward and met up with LAV Two, then both of them made for the diesel pumps. The passengers dismounted, and the LAVs locked all access points. Stark and Cole remained in the LAVs, and Seyfert was on the light machine gun for support, but the rest of the team made for the gas pumps.

"No power. How we gonna pump the fuel?" demanded Dallas.

Chris started looking at the ground near the pumps. "There have to be vents. There will be pumping equipment with long hoses someplace too."

"Chris, what do the vents look like?" asked Boone.

Chris pointed at the ground. "Like that." He indicated a small metal circle in the ground, slung his rifle, and went to one knee. He pulled ring tab, but the circle wouldn't budge. "Locked. There should be keys in the office, and maybe the siphoning gear, which we should probably take with us."

"Yeah, and they'll have food in there too," Dallas said, throwing his chin toward the diner which was the main attraction of the rest area.

"Can we pry the vents with the wrecker bars from the LAVs?"

"Yes, Commander," Chris answered, "but we can't get the fuel without those vent pumps. They'll have long hoses with a hand-crank mechanism for siphoning."

"I don't like the idea of going in those buildings, son, are you sure we can't get the fuel any other way?"

"I can't think of any, no."

Boone considered, pacing for a few seconds. "Dammit, alright. Cole, Stark, we're going off mission to find some pumps, and maybe some keys for the vents here. Stay frosty. Cole, keep on the thermals and apprise if necessary."

"Roger that sir."

"Chris, you, Rick, Andy and me are going in the office building to look for keys and the pumps. Ush, you take Dallas, Martinez and Anna and check out the diner. I'm fucking sick of MREs too. Stay low and quiet. Maintain constant comms, but zero chatter, and use hand signals."

The team split and went to work. Androwski led his group into the office, which wasn't locked. He shined his tactical light in a wide arc across the workspace. The place was big, but empty. It looked as if nobody had been here for quite a while, with no evidence of firefights and no blood or walking dead in the area. A corridor ran toward the back with doors on either side. The diner was attached to this building via that corridor. This section held travel accoutrements and a large counter area. Candy, bags of chips, road atlases, novelties, and magazine racks were prevalent, and Chris reached for a bag of Cheetos. Boone put his hand on Chris's, and Chris was startled. Boone mouthed *Not yet*, to Chris, who nodded that he understood.

Androwski panned his light back and forth, checking corners and behind the counter, but there was nothing. He pointed to Rick and indicated that he should follow, and they moved down the hall to the first door. Andy looked at Rick signaling with raised his eyebrows. Rick nodded and placed his hand on the door. Andy held up three fingers and Rick nodded again. The SEAL silently counted down from three, and when he reached one, Rick yanked the door open. The first room was storage, and there were cups and plates and napkins and the like, with a small sink and janitor's equipment. Rick closed the door, and they repeated the process on door number two.

This room held an occupant. He was sitting in a chair with his head thrown back and his brains on the wall behind him. A small automatic was on the floor next to him, and there was one line scribbled on a yellow notepad on the desk: *Too many, I'm so sorry, Barbara.*

Androwski picked up the weapon and flicked the safety on. He stuck it in his thigh pocket and they started to leave when Rick noticed a key ring on the dead man's belt. They grabbed it and proceeded to the last door, which when opened held an assortment of crap, including two of the long hand pumps that Chris was so adamant about. Rick grabbed the pumps, and they retreated back to the desk area. The group moved silently outside, and Boone was all business.

"Chris, Andy, get those cans filled ASAP." He glanced around. "I don't like this place."

Chris used the keys Rick had found to open one of the circular vent caps, and stuck a long hose down into the underground diesel storage tank. He put the other end of the hose into the five gallon can that

Androwski had hurriedly brought up from LAV Two, and the SEAL started cranking the handle on the pump. The sound of liquid sloshing into the cans followed a few seconds later. Chris handed Androwski his pump and moved to a second vent cap to repeat the procedure and double their efforts.

After the third can was full, Boone keyed his throat mic. "Usher, SITREP, what's your twenty, over? Usher come in." No response.

Rick looked at Boone. "I don't like that so much."

Chris paused in his cranking. "What's up?"

"Keep working, but stay on your toes. The diner team isn't checking in. Seyfert, maintain cover on the LMG. Stark, sit tight. Rick and I are going to check on the diner team."

Rick looked uneasy as he and Boone moved toward the open diner doors. "Why wouldn't they check in unless—?"

"Either they can't hear me or they can't send." Boone tried to contact them again to no avail.

"Maybe we should—" Gunfire from the diner area cut him off.

7

Dallas and Anna were packing chips and packaged cookies, along with giant, industrial-size tins of soup into three huge, green duffel-bags. They already had canned corn, beans, maraschino cherries and a large can of peppers. They also got a case of Mountain Dew cans, and a thirty pack of Bud Light. Usher was checking doors, while Martinez covered the scavengers with a suppressed MP5SD3.

Usher nudged open a pair of café-style swinging doors that opened into a corridor which overlooked a huge parking lot on the far side of the diner, and down an embankment. He swung his tactical light in both directions, one a dead end, the other ending in another set of swinging doors thirty feet away. Both directions held no undead, but then he looked into the parking lot. There were hundreds of cars and trucks parked down the hill out of sight of the front of the diner. Some undead were stumbling around, but the number of vehicles was just too much for the amount of zombies.

"Oh shit."

The door to his left swung open, and a swarm of dead faces looked at him with hunger in their blood-red eyes. They came through the doors, moaning and grasping at him.

Rather than open fire, he hurried back through the door yelling, "Out! Out! Back to the LAVs!"

Martinez raised his weapon, "What's—"

"What the fuck do you think? Move!"

Dallas shouldered one of the packs, but Anna couldn't lift hers. Dallas was reaching for the second one when Usher screamed at him, "Are you out of your fucking mind? They're right on us, leave it!"

Dallas dropped his bag and pulled his shotgun from his back. Anna, Usher, and Martinez were already across the large kitchen, and Dallas was making for the exit when the back doors swung open and the dead poured in. There were too many to count.

Usher held the door for Dallas and the Texan sprinted across the tiles, dead in tow. Usher switched to single shot and fired into the crowd, felling the front three creatures. Their dead friends piled over them, but some tripped, slowing the others but only slightly. Dallas fired the shotgun into the throng, and the boom was earsplitting even in the large room. He hurried through the door and Usher followed him out. They ran through the diner, only to find Martinez and Anna firing into another horde. More dead were coming from in front of them.

Usher frantically looked for an exit, as Boone's voice came over the radio, but the SEAL had no time to answer. "In here!" he shouted, and ran behind the diner bar to another door. It was the only direction that no dead came from. They all followed him into the manager's office, Dallas, Martinez and Anna pushing the heavy metal desk in front of the door. The room was approximately ten by ten and the only way in or out was the door they came through.

"Fuck!" shouted Usher, who then pressed his throat mic "Sir, shitloads of Limas! There's hundreds of cars out back! We're trapped in a small room off the south side of the diner."

Thuds from many fists came from the other side of the door.

"Now what?" demanded Anna.

"I...I don't..." Usher looked around quickly, but there was no secret passage to safety. He switched his weapon to full auto and fired into the ceiling. Dust and insulation rained down on them, and Anna put an arm in front of her face.

Usher jumped up on the desk, reaching for the ceiling joists. He pulled himself up enough to look into the unfinished attic of the diner. Dropping down satisfied, he used the butt of his rifle to break out remaining pieces of sheetrock, and then he and Martinez pulled enough down for them to get through. Usher looked to Anna. "You first, then Martinez, then Dallas, come on!"

Anna slung her weapon over her shoulder and used Usher as a ladder while Martinez pushed her by the legs through the joists into the area above. Anna could hear gunfire from outside over the wails of the dead below her.

The door had broken in, and filthy hands were reaching through the shattered jamb. The desk was keeping the door mostly closed, but even with the combined weight of Martinez and Usher, it was slowly sliding away from the door. Dallas put his foot on the end of the desk and heaved forward, it didn't move back toward the door, but it stopped moving away. Martinez jumped up with Usher pushing him from below and Anna pulling from above. He made it up and noticed that there was no floor up there, just joists with sheetrock screwed to them and pink insulation stapled to the tops of the cross members. He kicked a bigger hole as Dallas made his way up.

Usher pushed Dallas's giant ass, and as he did so, the desk jolted forward two feet spilling him on his side, his head toward the door. A hand raked down on his face, digging furrows into his cheek and forehead and scratching his eye. Blood welled up and he pulled away from the thing that almost had him, rolling to the end of the desk. Dallas still had his legs dangling, and two of the dead had grabbed his pant leg. He kicked for all he was worth and one let go, but the other had latched onto his leg with both hands, its torso half in the room. It was trying to pull a size twelve boot to its mouth.

Blood dripping from his shredded face, Usher fired a burst into the creatures, and the one yanking on the Texan was destroyed, letting go. The desk had begun a steady slide into the room as Dallas was pulled to safety, and a deceased grandfather crawled over the desk coming for Usher. The boom of the shotgun from above made Usher's ears ring, but he was thankful nonetheless. All three of his friends in the attic were firing into the crowd, the dead half plugging the door with their numbers.

Usher fired another burst into the horde, and in one motion jumped on the desk and leapt for the opening. Dallas and Anna caught him and started hauling him up as Martinez fired into the sea of lifeless faces. Usher's ascent stopped abruptly. His weapon had snagged on the ceiling between the joists, and the sling was around his shoulders. Try as they might, they couldn't pull him up. He looked at Dallas pleadingly as the things filed into the room and grabbed his legs. He kicked and flailed, but there were fifteen of the dead in the room now and they all grabbed him, biting and pulling. He fell into the crowd as Dallas screamed, "No!"

Martinez tried to shoot him, but he disappeared screaming under a mass of the things. His friends could only see the backs of the creatures as they knelt and reached over each other to get to the man. The screaming didn't last long. The creatures piled into the room until they were packed tightly. Those who couldn't get to Usher's more tasty bits reached toward the hole in the ceiling and the three terrified humans.

Anna fired a few rounds until Dallas put his hand on her arm. "Won't do no good kid, there's too many."

"Bullshit! I've got fifty rounds, and so do you and him," she thumbed at Martinez. "We can blast them as they come in the room, one at a damn time 'til there are none left! If there are more than that then we'll use your rebar if we have to." Her words were underscored by muffled gunfire from outside.

"We won't have to do either," Martinez interjected. "We have two armored vehicles outside remember? Boone, come in, this is Martinez."

"Wait one, Martinez, we've got issues."

"So do we," he replied, but not into the radio.

The gunfire slowed to sporadic shots, and Boone came back on the comms two minutes later, "Usher, SITREP!"

"He's gone, sir. We were surprised and got swarmed. Anna, Dallas, and me are in the attic above the diner. We can't get out, but they can't reach us."

"Dammit, how many? Are you sure Usher's dead?"

"Yes, sir, and there are dozens, maybe a hundred or more, I can't tell from this vantage point."

"Okay, sit tight, we'll figure something out. For what it's worth, there were quite a few out here as well, they came from your area."

"Roger that sir, we'll wait." Martinez looked around and saw a trapdoor to the floor below about twenty feet away. Stepping on the joists so as not to put his foot through the sheetrock, he arrived at the folded ladder and noticed the knotted end of a string that was used to pull the unit down. He pulled it up and cut it off with his knife. "Dallas, can I borrow your club?"

The big man pulled out his rebar and held it out to the sniper as the man gingerly stepped his way back. "Anna, could you hold this please?" He handed his SR25 to her and let his MP5SD3 dangle on its single point sling. He walked to the inside of the peaked roof, and using the end of the rebar, he began to chisel away at the plywood in the roof. He started at a roof rafter and began to break his way through the plywood joint. It was slow going, but he eventually moved the plywood away from the rafter enough that he could see the underside of roofing shingles. Prying the plywood up, he used his knife to poke through the tar shingles and could see sky.

"This is our way out if they can't get to us," he spoke into his tactical radio. "Boone, can you get to us if we can get to the roof?"

"Affirmative. Can you make the roof?"

"I think so, we have to do some cutting and breaking, but we can get out."

"Be careful. If you can't access to the roof, I'm going to use the bushmaster to blow a hole in the fucking wall, and I'm going to drive an LAV up their asses."

Anna smiled and looked at Dallas. "Hardcore SOB huh?"

"Can you two help me push this plywood?"

Dallas and Anna joist-stepped to where he was prying the roof. "I'll use this, you two push." Martinez used the rebar against the rafter to pry the plywood. It was extremely difficult as the roofing shingles were nailed to each other, and acted as a spring, pushing the wood back as they pushed it forward. In addition, the roofing nails were poking through the wood, the pointy ends toward them, so they had to find a safe place to carefully position their hands to avoid being stabbed.

They heaved hard, and the wood moved outward perhaps eight inches. Martinez pushed as well, and as all three pushed with all their might, Dallas slipped and fell backward on the joists. The plywood slid in Anna's hands, and she was raked across the palms by the roofing nails. She howled and pulled her hands back, and the plywood snapped backwards pinning Martinez's arm between the plywood and the rafter. He yelled as well, long and loud.

Dallas and Anna got back to pushing, and Martinez got his arm out. He cradled his left wrist with his right hand. It was already beginning to swell.

"Broke it," he yelled. "Fuckin' broke my wrist! Shit! Fuck!" He gritted his teeth, and continued swearing and cursing. Blood dripped from his arm in fat droplets that splattered on the insulation paper.

"Screw this," Dallas hollered aiming his shotgun at the roof. *BOOM! BOOM, BOOM!* Eight inches of clear, blue sky could now be seen through the semi-darkness of the attic. Dallas grabbed his rebar from amidst the insulation, and began to hack at the hole to make it larger.

As Anna inspected an injured wrist, Dallas broke a hole large enough for him to fit through. He pulled himself up and began throwing torn roofing shingles off the roof so no one would slip on them.

There were dozens of bodies newly strewn about the truck stop parking lot. Seyfert was firing sporadically with the light machine gun two lots over, but nobody else living could be seen. Anna and Dallas helped the injured sniper on to the roof, and the three of them surveyed the carnage below. Several undead were making their way toward the LAV, and more seemed to be coming from the diner. Dallas pinched his throat mic. "We made it t' the roof, an' we can see Seyfert blastin' the dead-uns, but where's everybody else?"

"We're in the LAVs. I can see you on the roof through the monitor. There's a wall of windows under the overhang in front of you. Move to your left about fifty feet, and there's solid wall, no surprises when you jump down. Wait until we get over there, and you can all land on the LAV and climb in through the turret hatch."

"Got it. We're gonna need some meds, Martinez is hurt."

Boone's voice was hard. "Bitten?"

"Nope. Smashed his hand. Might be busted, but he ain't bit."

"Alright, we're coming now, move left until you're in front of our nose. We'll come in sideways and you jump down. Martinez first, then Anna."

The three on the roof moved to the designated spot, the armored vehicle rumbled toward them. The LAV spun sideways and ran up on the curb, knocking over a Pedestrians Crossing sign and reducing a wooden bench to splinters. The top hatch next to Seyfert flew open, and Boone popped his head out, searching in all directions before lowering his weapon back into the vehicle and motioning for the three to come. Dallas helped Martinez down, and Anna was next. Gunfire erupted again as Dallas made his way from the roof to the hull of the LAV. He snapped his head up to see a small army of the living dead headed toward them from across the tarmac.

"Sir, there's lots. Request permission to cease fire, I'm wasting ammo."

"Good call, Seyfert, quit firing. We'll button up and bug out."

When the team was safely inside, the LAV departed, leaving the undead mob behind. They reached LAV One and opened the back hatch to add some diesel to the tank. Three cans later, they transferred some personnel, and shut all the hatches. Fifty or so dead were shuffling up the road toward them from the rest area. The LAVs headed east. As they passed the far side of the diner, the rest of the team noticed a hundred or so vehicles out back in a huge parking lot.

"Piss poor recon," Boone said angrily. "I killed him. I killed him for pork rinds and Cheez-Its that we didn't even get. He was our God damned corpsman." He sat down on the bench hard.

"They killed him," Anna said pointing at the monitor, "not you."

"Thanks, but no. He was my responsibility, acting on orders from me. The blame is mine."

8

Salt Lake City may have been on fire, but Cheyenne, Wyoming was gone. Simply gone.

There were craters and lots of rubble, but not much more, and no free-standing buildings in the city proper. Whatever had hit this city had completely destroyed it.

"Dammit, we need to find something," Rick said angrily. "He's bad off."

Androwski and Seyfert had both been cross-trained as corpsman, the Navy's medics, but neither was as experienced as Usher. The SEALs had given Martinez what medical assistance they could. Androwski had shaken his head at one point and spoken low to Seyfert. *Shattered* was the word Martinez had heard.

Seyfert had used a syrette of morphine on Martinez's shoulder to counter-act the intense pain. They had also tried to give the injured man a broad-spectrum antibiotic from Usher's back-up medical pack in the LAV, but when it came to injecting him, Martinez had stopped Androwski. "Allergic to cillins and mycins. Need a flaxin."

An IV hung from the bulkhead of the LAV, the line ending under some tape in Martinez's un-injured arm. Seyfert had given him Narcan, a drug to counter the morphine's respiratory-depressing effects, and Phenergan, an anti-nausea med that would also increase the pain-reducing effects of the morphine.

Martinez raised his pasty face to look at Rick with some flare in his eyes. "I'm fine."

The man's face belied his words. He was the color of rancid cream, and he was shivering. His forearm and wrist were swollen to three times their normal size. Both were so purple they were almost black, with yellow bruises blotching the area. His condition had deteriorated significantly during the four hundred fifty mile trip from outside of Salt Lake City to Cheyenne.

The trip, which would have taken less than seven hours when the world was still alive, had taken the better part of three days. The US military had been diligent in destroying roads and other infrastructure during the plague. The idea was probably to contain the contagion by not allowing travel, but as far as the group in the LAVs knew, the plan had failed, as they hadn't come across a single living person in any of the small towns they had been through since leaving Ben to his fate in Salt Lake. They had seen plenty of dead folks though, both ambulatory and not. They had gotten more diesel in a town along the interstate, and this time Boone had circled the gas station twice before using the pumps Chris had appropriated from the truck stop. The diesel tanks on the LAVs were full, and the cans were almost there as well before the dead showed up in force. They had bugged out without incident.

Then they came across the destroyed roads. The tarmac simply ended, and for quite a while there was no interstate, just broken shards of asphalt and twisted guard rails. The carnage didn't end at the interstate either; the secondary roads were also destroyed, and there were huge craters making passage slow overland. They had skirted the highway as much as possible, but in some places it was extremely difficult to get by without using I-80.

Now Martinez had a fever, and Cole, who also had some corpsman experience but claimed he was not a medic, surmised that the broken bones in Martinez's wrist or forearm had cut into some blood vessels. He was bleeding internally. His fingers looked like fat, black sausages, and the pain must have been extreme, but Martinez didn't give a shit about it because the morphine had kicked in. Cole told Boone and Rick that the fever meant probable infection, and if they didn't fix the issue, Martinez could lose his hand, or worse. Androwski and Seyfert both nodded in agreement. The bandages that had been on his wrist and arm had to be changed twice, the tightness and swelling restricting the blood flow in his arm.

The occupants of the LAVs popped the rear hatches and Boone unfolded a map as they assembled around him in a semi-circle. He held the map on the hull of the LAV.

"There's an airport there," Androwski pointed to the map, "on the other side of the city. Can't see it from here. They must have some kind of medical facility at an airport, no? Like a med-flight helicopter, or at the airport fire department?"

"Yes, but the thing they definitely have at airports is lots of people." Boone shook his head and sighed, resigned. "We've got a man down, and we need to get him on his feet, but I want full recon of the entire facility before we go in."

"This is Wyomin'," Dallas drawled, "and I'm thinkin' that there wouldn't be too many folks at the airport, plus I bet that anybody living would have gotten out if they could."

Boone shifted his weight. "It's the ones that didn't get out that concern me. Alright, around the city to the south, then north to the airport." He traced the route with his finger. "Full circle with LAV One, LAV Two stays in reserve a mile out."

Joe started whining, and let loose with two puppy barks. He had taken a liking to Anna, and was in her arms or near her most of the time. He started struggling and barked again.

"Never liked beagles much," Dallas said as Anna put the dog down. "Yippy lil' sumbitches."

Anna put her hands on her hips, and glared at him, "Let me guess, you're more of a bloodhound guy right? You like your dogs big and dumb, and capable of all kinds of howling?"

"Well yeah, actually, I kinda do. The only thing a pissant dog like that is good for is addin' extra meat t' my stew."

As they emerged, Joe ran to the opposite side of the road and barked at a gigantic green road sign. The sign had been toppled into the weeds in a gulley next to the broken highway. He whined and looked over his shoulder at Dallas and Anna, then continued to bark.

Dallas strode over and stood next to the dog. "Well I'll be god dammed. Friggin' mutt might prove useful after all." Anna joined them, followed by the rest of the group. Joe was barking at a pair of legs that were sticking out from under the sign. The legs were moving.

"Guess yer sniffer ain't busted there, kiddo." He reached down and scooped up the puppy, and gave him to Anna.

"Back in the LAVs," ordered Boone. "Last time we thought a place was clear, there turned out to be a hundred Limas playing died and seek."

The reactions were all the same: Shock. Boone did have a sense of humor.

"Everybody in LAV One. Cole, you stay in Two with Martinez until we get back. Stay here unless we call you for exfil."

"Copy, sir."

Rick entered LAV Two to check on his friend. Martinez was stretched out on one of the benches, his broken arm re-bandaged and in a sling on his chest. His chest was rising and falling, but Rick checked his pulse anyway. It was weak, but present.

"I'll watch him," Cole said from up front.

"Thanks." Rick left the LAV and Cole closed the rear hatch from the driver's seat.

9

After circling the small airport for a half hour, the team of eight pulled up on runway six next to the charred remains of an airliner. It was unlikely that anything stumbled from this wreckage, but Boone was not taking any chances. He ordered everyone to stay in the LAV until they could see a medical facility. There was a Mountain Airways 747 airliner pulled up close to a jet-way that jutted out from a terminal. A ten foot gap or so separated the jet-way from the open door of the plane. Several non-mobile corpses were broken on the tarmac below the jet. The evidence suggested that they had fallen from either the plane or the access tunnel leading to it and smashed their heads on the airstrip.

"I'm not seeing any medical signs," observed Anna.

Chris pointed at the terminal. "There's bound to be some meds and stuff in there someplace."

"Out of the question," said Boone. "That place is a death-trap. We can't properly recon it from out here, and look," he pointed toward the large glass windows on the first floor, "there's plenty of Limas. We'll have to find another way." Many mobile deceased were staggering around on the lower level, some smacking the glass in an attempt to get to the LAV that had driven onto the runway.

The med-flight helicopter was nowhere to be found, and the fire station looked like it had been a failed last stand. Doors and windows were boarded, but the barricades hadn't held. Part of the station had burned as well. The garage doors were open, and the terrified occupants of the fire station had tried to escape in two fire trucks and an ambulance. The trucks were twisted together just outside the station itself. The ambulance was on its side a bit farther down, a black hulk that had charred to next to nothing. Perhaps some scared folks panicked and smashed the vehicles together, or there had been too many dead to plow the trucks through, and someone had gotten overzealous with their driving. Dozens of shuffling forms, some crispy, were meandering around the scorched station and vehicles.

Rick put his hand to his temple and rubbed. "Boone, I'm not trying to buck the chain of command here, but Martinez is in deep shit. I'll go alone if I have to, but we need those meds."

"Rick, we'll find meds if they're here, but you're not going in there, it's—"

"He's going to die if we don't. He needs help now."

Boone frowned. "I understand that, but we—"

Anna interrupted, "What about the plane?"

Both Rick and Boone looked at her and chorused: "What?"

Anna pointed toward the plane in front of them. "There has to be medical stuff on the plane right? I mean what if there's an in-flight emergency?" She started shaking her head. "Gotta be. Gotta."

"There is," Dallas blurted. "There's two med stations, one aft of the cockpit in the attendant's quarters on the second floor, and one to the rear of the cabin by the bathrooms on the first floor."

Chris looked at him, "How do you know that?"

"Used to work for Shiner Air as a cabin inspector."

"What kind of supplies are in those stations?"

Dallas began ticking items off using his fingers. "Band-Aids, aspirin, gauze, tape, scissors, bandages, splints, insulin, maybe some single-use morphine injectors, and a defibrillator."

Seyfert looked disgusted. "All that shit would have been in the LAVs if they were combat ready."

"Yes, and Usher had most of it too, but he's gone."

Cole piped in over the radio. "At the very least, he could use the morphine and a better splint. He still needs an X-ray, and someone who can pin his wrist together though. A real doctor."

"We don't have one," Boone said and looked at Rick, "but we'll get what meds we can." Boone glanced to his left into the port monitor and saw three forms staggering toward them. "We already have company. We tow the plane to that hangar," Boone pointed toward a huge hangar to the side of the runway, "we use those stairs, and get on the plane!"

They sped to the plane inside the safety of the armored vehicle. Androwski produced a fifteen foot length of yellow carrying strap from the bowels of the LAV, and he, Dallas, and Rick affixed the strap between the tow-package of their vehicle, and the pin on the front of the aircraft landing gear. Seyfert plugged a few dead that were getting close with the SAW.

As they were moving back to get into the armor, undead started dropping out of the jet-way and onto the tarmac below. The ones on the bottom broke the falls of the ones to come out after, and the secondaries decided to get up and come for lunch. They were between the LAV and the plane, so Androwski, Dallas, and Rick had to go in the other direction.

"Sir, it's fuckin' rainin' pus bags here! Take off and tow this big bitch, we'll catch up."

"Roger that, Andy. Watch your asses."

The six-wheeled behemoth began to angle away from the concourse, easily pulling the big aircraft with it. The three people on foot ran at a slant to the vehicles, with ideas on a rendezvous a few hundred meters down the runway. Zombies began to pop up from different areas in ones and twos and they all staggered toward the men on foot. One of the glass windows on the lower level of the terminal gave way as well, and the dead emptied out and began the slow chase.

Seyfert opened up on the few creatures in front of the LAV, but couldn't get a shot at anything behind him as the plane was in the way. The three men on foot slowed to a trot as the immediate danger was behind them. They caught up with their friends as Boone, Anna, and Chris unhooked the tow strap from the plane. "Now what?" demanded a huffing Dallas as they all surveyed their surroundings.

"Now we go to that hangar and pull that mobile stairway over here," said Boone pointing.

A hundred feet away was the hangar with the doors wide open. Just outside was the stairway on wheels, used to enter and exit aircraft not at a terminal. "We would have pulled the plane all the way, but the front strut got caught when we went over that embankment." Here Boone pointed again, this time to the strut that held the two front tires of the plane. It was stuck on a foot-high curb. "This is as far as she will go. Anna, you and Chris back in the LAV with Stark, the rest are with me. Stark, get the LAV to the staircase and we'll hook it up so you can pull it to the plane."

Everyone did as they were told, but Rick grabbed Boone by the shoulder when they reached the stairs. "Been doing the math here, Boone. We can't possibly hook up the stairs and get the meds before they get here." He pointed to the growing horde two hundred meters away and closing.

"Agreed. We'll need bait." He looked right at Rick and Dallas. "Androwski and I will herd them off, you two get on the plane and get the materials we need."

Rick was dubious. "Can't we just all leave and come back when they've dispersed?"

"You willing to bet Martinez's life that we can get back quickly, or that the Limas will just move on?"

"Dammit!" Rick yelled, but their vehicle arrived and he got to work without further objection. He and Dallas hooked up the set of steps while Boone and Androwski started toward the horde. With help from the LAV, Rick and Dallas maneuvered the mobile stairway so that it was in front of the open door of the airliner. Dallas was armed with a SPAS12 combat shotgun that he had appropriated from Rick, and Rick had his M4. "After you, Hoss," Dallas told him, and they hurried up the steps.

Rick switched on his tactical flashlight as he took a tentative step toward the dark opening in the side of the plane. He pinched his throat mic. "Stark, do you read?"

"Loud and clear."

"Pull the stairs five feet back from the plane."

"We just put the damn thing next to it! What the hell do—?"

"Because if this thing is full of dead folks, or if they come in behind us, I don't want them to be able get on or off the plane! I don't think they can jump the gap!"

"Actually, that's fucking brilliant. Hang on."

Dallas and Rick grabbed the railing as the stairs jerked slightly then moved a few feet back.

Chris and Anna jumped from the back of the LAV to unhook it from the stairs.

"Stark, pull off about two hundred feet, I don't want a crowd out here if we need to get out in a hurry."

Dallas looked at the gap. "More like seven feet."

"What? You can't make it, fatty?"

"Rick, I gots me a shotgun, and I'm sensitive about m' figure."

Rick smiled then focused on the door. He shook his head. "Jesus..." He jumped the gap with ease, spinning first right, then left, then right again, and motioning to Dallas, who quickly followed. The tac-lights on their weapons illuminated a torn curtain to the right, and a stairway leading up to the left, with another curtain pulled all the way open past the stairs.

There was blood everywhere.

"Thank you for taking me along, sir, this is the best outing I've had since training."

"Secure that shit, sailor," Boone said with a grimace, "this is about to get real."

"So what's the plan?"

Boone stopped walking and Androwski followed suit. "We wait. Check our six."

Androwski turned around to check behind them. "There are some coming from the sides, but none close. Maybe three hundred meters." He ran his thumb over the selector switch to double check that his suppressed MP5 was in the single fire position. "I'd feel better if Martinez was covering us with his cannon."

"Agreed. We back up when the ones in front get to one hundred meters. Keep an eye on the ones behind us."

"Copy that."

It didn't take long. When Boone was able to make out individuals in the undead horde, he told the other SEAL it was time to move back. They moved at a quick trot another hundred meters back and stopped. The horde was closing.

"Sir, firing one." Androwski shot one creature that had stumbled to close to their nine o'clock. "Danger at sixty meters left, firing one!" He shot at another but missed. "Two!" The second shot dropped the thing.

It had been approximately twenty minutes since the team had separated, and Boone wanted to get back into the safety of his light-armored vehicle, as the two hundred or so zombies were closing faster than he liked. "Okay Andy, this party's over. They must have found the meds by now. We're bugging out. Boone to Rick, SITREP! Rick, SITREP!"

"Sir? Let's go yeah?" Androwski sounded nervous.

"Stark, do you read?"

"Yes, sir, loud and clear."

"Do you have Barnes and Dallas?"

"Negative, they're still on the plane."

"Shit! Androwski, get back to the plane and help them."

"But sir, we—"

"That's an order, squid! Move!"

"Copy that, sir." Androwski sprinted back toward the jet as fast as he could. Boone ran laterally against the crowd, all of whom turned to follow him. He made as much noise as he could, yelling insults at them to egg them on. They were fifty feet away.

10

The plane smelled like rot.

Rick and Dallas walked left and found the lower-level first class cabin to be devoid of anything living or dead. All the seat backs and tray tables were in their upright positions. They turned and walked back toward the coach cabin. There was a white box with a red cross on the side, indicating a first aid station on the wall just inside the door, but it was open and drenched with blood. The door of the small box was still dripping, and gore soaked bandages were on the floor of the cabin.

"Watch the stairs," Rick whispered to Dallas, who nodded and stepped onto the first stair with his right boot.

"There're more aid stations on both sides," Dallas whispered back, "in the third part of the plane."

It was Rick's turn to nod. A bloody blue curtain was hanging from four of its twelve chrome rings, partially obscuring the view of the coach cabin. Rick used the barrel of his battle rifle to nudge the remains of the drape out of his way. He could see carnage throughout the cabin. There was blood on the forward seats, and a body in the aisle in front of him. The front of the cabin was partially illuminated as most of the window shades were up for the first fifteen rows or so, but the rear of the aircraft was shrouded in darkness.

Rick shone his light right and left across the aisles to clear the area as he moved toward the rear of the plane. He was in the right side aisle with three seats to his right, four to his left, another aisle, and then three more seats.

Six rows back there was a dead person in the widow seat to his left. The man, if it had been a man, had been devoured. Its right arm was gone, as was all the flesh of his right side. The abdominal cavity was just that, an empty cavity, and the face was torn away. Rick shone his light on the thing, and the person still had their seatbelt on. The top if the victim's head was missing, and the brain was gone as well. The stench of blood was so strong Rick gagged.

There was a body in the aisle in front of him, the back of its head missing. There were two more farther on, and some slumped over the seats. Several bullet holes in the fuselage let small beams of light in through the side of the cabin bulkhead.

Rick checked each body and they all had holes in their heads. He was almost to the second junction, and the curtain on this one was missing, when he heard movement on his right, but the beam of his light couldn't detect anything. Rick was sweating profusely. When he got to the flight attendant's station, there was a thump in the bathroom next to him. He brought the tac-light up and noticed a barf bag with something scrawled on it in large black letters had been duct taped to the bathroom door.

It read: *I'm dead, and I'm in here.*

The latch had been turned from the inside, and the red *Occupied* indicator told Rick that there was indeed someone in the bathroom. While he didn't relish the thought of a zombie between the exit and himself, Rick decided that opening the door to exterminate this poor victim was too risky, and he moved on.

Reaching the back of the first cabin compartment, yet another blue drape was between him and the rear cabin. Fortunately, there was another flight attendant's station, this one with a closed white box complete with red cross on the wall. He let his rifle hang from the single point sling and quietly opened the box. Although the box was only half full, there were many supplies in it. He didn't think perusing them at the current moment was the best plan. He pushed up on the box while holding two pressure release locks on the side, and the box slid free of the wall. Taking it under his arm, he decided to go one cabin farther to get another box if there was one.

He nudged the curtain open again as he had done before. This time his tac-light illuminated dozens of people sitting in the cabin seats, all of whom looked at the light, and all of whom were dead. They started standing as he heard Dallas start yelling.

"Rick! They're comin' from upstairs!" The boom of the shotgun spurred Rick into action, and he turned and sprinted back down the aisle. Dallas was running at him, and both were blinded by each other's tactical lights. Rick threw his arm in front of his face as he ran back at Dallas. Just before he ran back through the attendant's station, the small bathroom door burst open, and Rick ran into the one arm of the occupant, who immediately bent in to attempt to snatch a morsel from Rick's shoulder as they crashed to the carpeted aisle.

Waiting for the inevitable pain took two seconds before he realized it wasn't coming. The thing had two arms, but one was duct-taped to its side, the fingers on the other were taped together, and it had half a roll of tape around its mouth. Rick easily pushed away from the dead man and stood, his boot on the guy's chest. One round spread the back of the man's head on the carpet.

Dallas arrived a second later. "We gotta go back! They're comin!" He looked past Rick and noticed the passengers coming for them. "Christ!"

Dallas turned and ran back the way he came. "C'mon!" The shotgun boomed again. Rick followed him. He fired toward the front of the plane again. "Cover, Hoss!" He slung his shotgun and turned a handle on the wall, opening a door which let in the bright sunlight. Dallas squinted before reaching up and smashing his hand against the wall. He did it a second time, then yelled, "Shit! It ain't workin'!"

He pushed the door all the way open so that it banged against the fuselage of the aircraft, then smacked his hand on the wall again, "Goddammit!" Rick began firing toward the rear of the plane.

"Rick, we gotta jump!" Rick backed up, and between shots, looked down to the tarmac.

"Fuck that."

"You got a better plan?"

"Yeah, anything that doesn't include jumping twenty feet to an asphalt runway! Where's the damn emergency slide thingie?" Rick fired as he spoke: *Pap! Pap pap pap!*

The dead were starting to get close, twenty feet from Rick's side, and ten from Dallas'. The stink off the things was incredible, and Dallas began to gag.

"It won't deploy, I dunno why!"

Rick fired twice more and looked at the bulkhead of the plane, running his finger across the pictograph of how to deploy the slide as he read it.

Dallas fired two booming shots into the small crowd in front of him, destroying a granny zombie and a dead hippie. He then fired the shotgun at the door, and there was a whoosh as the escape slide speedily filled with compressed air. The slide was fully extended in less than five seconds, but that was long enough for the dead to reach Dallas. His weapon clicked empty, and he pulled his rebar club to go hand to hand with two creatures. A sideways whack to the head of a blue-faced pastor sent the creature sprawling, but the two things behind the priest reached past him and grabbed Dallas by the shirt. Dallas was shrieking four letter curses when he was grabbed by the waist from behind and thrown unceremoniously from the plane.

Rick, Dallas, and two monsters tumbled down the inflated silver escape ramp all the way to the tarmac. Rick was able to extricate himself immediately, but Dallas had two zombies on him. The big man was using his rebar to keep them at bay. Rick raised his rifle, but a shot rang out before he was able, and dropped one of the dead men. Dallas jammed the pointed end of his rebar up under the second thing's chin and kept going until the metal would go no farther.

Androwski was at the top of the mobile stairs, aiming at the escape hatch. "Get to the LAV!" Less than two seconds later, dead began to spill down the ramp. Rick and Dallas sprinted toward the vehicle and Androwski ran down the steps. "Stark! Stark, exfil!"

The turret on the LAV spun toward the plane, and machine gun fire belched from the gunner's position as Seyfert let loose on the growing group from the aircraft.

All three men made it to the LAV quickly and gained entry. "Why the fuck didn't you answer your radios?" Androwski demanded as the hatch closed.

Rick checked his radio and noticed that the ear bud cord had been ripped from the receiver. He held it up for Androwski to see. Dallas checked his radio and it seemed to be fine. "Didn't hear ya."

"LAV One to Lone Wolf, come in," Androwski shouted into the com unit, "Lone Wolf, come in! Do you copy? Over."

Cole's deep voice came over the radio, "One this is Two, SITREP?"

"Objective secured, but Actual is unaccounted for. How's our boy?"

"Bad. Still unconscious, breathing ragged. You're gonna need to hurry back."

Androwski clicked the mic off. "Shit!" His eyes glazed over while he thought.

Seyfert poked his head down from the gunner's emplacement. "Limas are almost on us."

Androwski looked up. "Boone can take care of himself. We need to get the meds back to Martinez before he kicks it." He looked at Rick as he spoke into the radio, "Lone Wolf, this is LAV One, if able to receive but not transmit: One is bugging out to accomplish primary objective. One will return in two hours to retrieve Lone Wolf. Sit tight, out."

Seyfert looked at Stark with raised eyes while Androwski pinched his nose with his thumb and forefinger. "Go, Stark."

The thumps of dead fists rang through the armored vehicle as Stark shifted into gear.

11

"Cole, do you copy? Cole, we're almost there, how's our man? Fucking radios are for shit." Androwski raged as he slammed the radio into his hip. "First order of business when the world gets back together is to find the dickweed responsible for these radios and string him up!"

The return trip to the other LAV only took half an hour. There were three zombies stumbling around outside when they arrived. Seyfert took them out with single shots from his suppressed sidearm. "Clear!"

The back of LAV One opened and the team got out. Androwski was fuming. "Cole! Cole, open up, we've got some meds for Martinez! Stark, try the comms in the LAV."

"Nothing, sir," replied Stark after a few seconds. "He's not responding."

Androwski rapped his fist on the hull. "Cole! If you're sleeping in there I will kick your ass, I shit you not!" The SEAL walked around to the front of the vehicle, swearing. The blast shields were open over the windows, and he climbed on the nose of the LAV. Putting his hand up to the red window to shield his eyes from the sun, he peered in but couldn't see anything. He rapped on the window and still there was nothing.

"I need to get in there, Stark." The man's voice was past angry, there was now a tinge of worry. "How do we open her up?"

"Can't. The vehicle is specifically designed to repel invaders. Without somebody inside, or an access code that's on the manual, which is also inside, we aren't getting in."

"Fuck! Are you telling me that if the driver goes outside to take a piss and shuts the hatch behind him, he can't get in without the code?"

"Roger."

"So how…" Androwski thought he saw a shadow move behind the armored red glass. Again he put his hand above his eyes and pressed his face to the window. Cole's face slammed against the other side. Thick fluid splashed the pane from the inside as Cole attempted to bite through it. Androwski pulled his face away fast, but not before he saw the malice in his teammate's dead eyes.

He hopped off the vehicle and walked directly to Rick. "They're dead," was the only thing he could think to say. Rick ran around the front of the LAV, and following Androwski's example, peered in the window.

Sighing, he got down from the LAV and walked back to the group. Androwski was on the radio asking Stark how they could blow their way in to retrieve the ammo for the other LAV.

"Not advisable. We don't have any cutting tools, and if we did it would take a while. We could try the Bushmaster, but it would probably put holes in the armor before it blew the door off. One stray round could cook off the ammo and then twenty millimeter rounds would be firing in all directions."

"What about the C-4?"

"It's in LAV Two, and I don't know what would happen if a Bushmaster round hit that."

"I have a brick," Seyfert interjected. When he noticed everyone looking at him, he went on the defensive. "What? One brick of C-4 and some det-cord is worth having on you on missions like this. I got it from Benotti before he…"

"Alright. Seyfert, shape-charge the bottom hydraulics and the top lock. Let's pop this bitch open. Stark, man the LMG and check our six while we're busy. Everyone else keep watching for stray Limas, we'll let you know when we're gonna blow this."

It only took three minutes or so for Seyfert to wire up the explosives. He molded some into the small crevice between the hatch and the hull on the back of the vehicle, and some on the hydraulic pin catch on the bottom of the door. One more larger amount on the locking mechanism at the top, and he thumbs-up signaled to Androwski he was ready. Two suppressed shots hissed out on the left side of the street they were on.

"Contact left," Chris told them. "They're down… I mean, clear."

Androwski pinched his throat mic. "Everybody on me." When the rest of the team minus Stark, who was manning the LMG, showed up, Androwski told them to get in the LAV. "We'll blow it from fifty meters back." The team complied and soon they were backing up.

Seyfert pulled what looked like a small hand-held radio from his tactical vest. He looked at Androwski. "Boom?"

"Boom."

Seyfert flicked a red safety switch up and moved a silver toggle switch down. A loud popping sound came from outside, and Androwski called to Stark to open the door of LAV One. The team got out and examined LAV Two. The rear hatch was bent and burned and hanging from one hydraulic piston, but what really drew their attention was the occupants that slowly stumbled from the rear of the vehicle.

Martinez came out first. The front of his T-shirt was stained crimson, as was his bandaged arm. His face and neck were a dingy gray, and his eyes were blood red. Cole followed and he looked worse. There were huge chunks missing from the meat of his neck, and the right side of his face had been savaged. Everyone raised their weapons, but Androwski and Rick stepped forward. The live men looked at each other, nodded and then raised their rifles. Two quick reports followed, and the dead men collapsed.

The rest of the team walked up to their dead friends. "Martinez must have died on the bench and then attacked Cole," Seyfert said. "See? He's not bitten but Cole is. We didn't know how bad off he really was, but who dies from a damn broken arm?"

Rick got down on one knee. "Sorry Pabs. Nobody deserves this." Rick closed his friend's eyes with a gloved hand. He stood again. "We need to bury them."

Androwski looked at his shoes, "Rick, Boone might not have that kind of time. We need to hump the ammo from Two to One, and get back there for him. We can move them," he indicated the dead men, "to the side of the road and cover them, then we can come back."

"We did that damn plane fer nothin', Boone is by hisself too," Dallas said under his breath.

Rick nodded in the negative. "We did it for our friend, and I wouldn't do it any different for any of us. Boone wouldn't have it any other way either."

"Yer right on that, Hoss. Let's go git 'that tough bastid."

"Lieutenant," a deep voice came over the radio, "I've got movement in the woods on the thermals. My door is open and I'm lonely."

"Roger that, Stark. Everybody saddle up."

Rick, Dallas, Androwski and Seyfert dragged their fallen comrades to the side of the road, and then helped the others wordlessly carry the extra ammo back to the undamaged LAV. Rick made sure to take Martinez's SR25 and all its ammo as well. "What about the other guns on LAV Two?" asked Chris. "Shouldn't we take them?"

The Bushmaster is too big," Androwski told him. "We could strap the barrel to the outside of this rig though, and we'll definitely come back for the LMG. Let's roll, Stark."

"Solid copy, Lieutenant."

The light-armored vehicle rumbled back toward the airport.

12

"Jesus, look at them all." Anna was looking at monitor that was displaying thermal optics. "There must be two thousand, where did they all come from?"

"How do we find him in alla that?" Dallas demanded waving his hand at the screen.

Androwski was leaning over and looking into the monitor as well. "Lone Wolf, do you copy? Lone Wolf, this is Wanderer, are you receiving? Lone Wolf, if unable to speak, squelch twice, over."

There was no response, just dead air. The population of undead at the airport had grown substantially. The team couldn't figure out why though, as there were no living people in the area that they could see, and the dead weren't attacking any fortifications of any kind, they were just milling about. Androwski began to check his weapons.

Rick put his hand on the lieutenant's shoulder. "Andy, we have no illusions about who's in charge, but you cannot go out there. You can't."

"Boone wouldn't leave anyone behind, and I mean to find him."

"We can look, but not outside this vehicle. Do you think Boone would want you to die looking for him?"

"Rick, I'm a SEAL. We don't leave people behind."

"I understand, but don't you think that the mission is more important? A possible cure for this plague? If you get killed, that's one more trained person that can't help us get where we need to be."

"Rick's right, Andy," added Seyfert. "You go out there and you're just gonna get dead. And Boone will have your ass if you go looking for him with no recon."

Androwski glared at Seyfert. "So we leave him? We just leave Boone? Is that it?"

"No, we recon and give him some time to get to us."

Stark interrupted from up front, "Well whatever we're gonna do, we gotta do it now."

All eyes went to the monitors. The horde had noticed them and was on slow approach. Two were sprinting toward their position, only a few hundred meters away.

"Stark, zoom in, how many are coming after us?"

"Looks like all of 'em, Chief, they look damn hungry too."

"Fine then," began Androwski. "We let them come. We'll back away when they get to a hundred meters out. When they close the gap again, we back away again until we're a mile off, then we boogie around or through them back to the airport and look for Boone from the LAV." He looked at Seyfert. "Sey, take out the runners with the short gun."

"Roger that, sir, good call."

"Lone Wolf, this is Wanderer, if you can receive but not transmit, we're backing up to draw the Limas out. Stay put and we'll be back for you in thirty mikes."

The undead presence at this particular airport, with the only nearby city a smoldering ruin, was extremely large. The runways were also intact, and considering the military had destroyed most of the highways and byways in this area, this was an anomaly. Androwski surmised that the runways were not destroyed in case the US armed forces needed a place to land and refuel in this part of the country. This might also account for the large numbers of zombies in the area. The uninfected were trapped with no way to escape when the undead hordes reached their doors. The only thing left for the creatures to do was to search for food in the immediate area, or move on. Apparently they hadn't reached the moving on stage yet.

Doing some quick math in his head, Stark calculated that there were approximately three thousand undead marching in their direction.

"Can't we just run 'em over?" Dallas asked.

"I don't know," Stark told him. "Enough of them might get stuck in the wheels and gum up the works. Then we would stop moving. I don't want to stop moving."

Dallas harrumphed, "Me neither. You keep drivin', Stark ole buddy. I'ma shut up now."

It took longer than thirty minutes to lure the undead from the tarmac and into a nearby field. Almost an hour after the LAV had begun tactically withdrawing, Stark threw the vehicle into high gear and skirted the swarm heading east back to airport. Not wanting to miss a canned dinner, the mass of bodies began following immediately. The team would have less than an hour to collect Boone before the undead arrived on their heels.

The vast majority of the former humans had followed the vehicle, but some strays remained at the airport. Rick, Seyfert, and Androwski used the sniper rifles to cull the herd, and then the search began in earnest.

"We can't go in the larger buildings," advised Androwski, "but we can run around and look in the windows, and look in those hangars." He thumbed at two large hangars on the east side of the facility. "God help me, but we need to split up. We'll cover twice as much ground twice as fast. Dallas and Anna, you go with Seyfert and check out those outbuildings. Don't go inside! Rick and Chris, you're with me."

"Where are we going?" asked Chris nervously.

"To check out those hangars on the east side. That's the direction Boone was heading when we separated. Stick together, nobody leaves a twenty-foot circle from the others in your squad, and don't engage unless absolutely necessary, just run. I want everybody back here in thirty mikes regardless. Constant contact, zero chatter. Stark remain on station unless we call. Any questions?"

There were none.

"Thirty mikes, no more, or I assume you're in some shit and we come looking for you. Radio check."

Everyone said *Check* into their throat microphones. Androwski nodded and began jogging away, Chris and Rick following. They skirted a hissing thing on the ground with broken legs in a runway worker's uniform and made it to the first hangar. The massive aluminum doors were spread open, and the sun was glinting off of the tinted glass windscreen of a private jet.

There was a small parts loft above a work area in the back of the hangar. Metal stairs on the left side ran up to the loft, and the four large windows were all broken out of the workshop. Androwski was moving forward slowly, taking in everything as he progressed. Rick had their rear, with Chris in the center.

"Androwski, can you fly—"

The SEAL's left fist flew into the air, and Chris silenced himself instantly, falling to a crouched position. Something was moving in the workshop. Androwski signaled the men to follow him towards the back of the hangar and they did so with great stealth. Rick caught up to the other two and put his hand on the SEAL's shoulder. Rick indicated the oval windows on the port side of the plane. One of them was covered in streaks of gore from the inside. Androwski pointed two fingers at his eyes, then Rick, then at the plane. Rick nodded understanding and slung his M4. He drew his suppressed sidearm, sighting at the door to the aircraft.

Chris was sweating profusely as they made their way toward the workshop. It was pitch black inside, the bright sun outside not being able to penetrate this far back. All three men switched on their tactical lights and scanned the area, Rick looking back toward the plane at all times. Gore spatter was evident on some jagged triangles of glass still in the workshop window frames, and several bodies were strewn about with holes in their heads.

Something was slapping on the concrete floor inside the dark room. Androwski lifted his weapon up so that the tac-light could pierce the gloom through the smashed windows. Two huddled forms were pulling choice morsels from a third prone shape. When illuminated, they turned almost casually, faces dripping. One stood up, immediately and began to stagger toward the light, the other continued his meal uninterrupted. The bolt ratcheted on the lieutenant's MP5SD3 as he sent a suppressed round through the walking creature's cranium. Adjusting his aim, he destroyed the second thing as well.

Peering into the room, they were able to discern that the unfortunate victim had been a man in a business suit, and not Boone. Androwski put a round through the victim's head before turning away.

As they moved from the area, Androwski pointed his light up into the loft area. He couldn't see over the lip of the loft. Putting a booted foot on the first aluminum step, he looked back at his friends. There was no place left to hide in this hangar, and they had checked it thoroughly except for the loft. The SEAL called out softly, "Boone. Sir, are you up there?"

There was no response.

"Shit. Stay here."

He took the stairs slowly, slashing his light through the darkness above. He peered over the edge of the loft but was unable to visually clear the room because of the racks of airline worker clothing and lockers. "Sir, are you up here? Sir?"

He couldn't detect any movement through the racks and banks of lockers, but there were blood drops on the plywood floor leading toward the back of the loft. He started to move further up the stairs when he heard Rick through his earpiece.

"Contact! Fifty meters and closing."

Androwski rushed back down the stairs and met Rick and Chris, who were aiming at a small group of dead people plodding toward their position. Rick holstered his Beretta and unslung his M4. "You guys fire with the suppressors, and I'll hang back unless they get close."

Androwski wiped his forehead. "Keep our six clear, and don't fire unless you have to." He sighted a small boy and fired, but missed. "Fuck." He ran forward and Chris followed, raising his pistol. Rick followed as well, glancing back to keep from being surprised from the rear. Chris fired and the boy fell. He fired again and woman in a security uniform fell beside the boy. Androwski looked at him with his brows raised, and Chris shrugged and fired again.

The SEAL followed suit, and soon nine more undead had been destroyed. Both men reloaded, and Rick caught up with them.

"Where'd you learn to shoot like that?" the SEAL demanded.

Chris had already slapped a fresh magazine in his Glock and was filling the empty magazine with loose rounds. "I never fired a weapon in my life until you guys trained us in San Francisco. I used to kill the hell out of people in the Battlefield games though. My KDR was almost nine to one."

"What's KDR?"

"Kill-to-death ratio. It's how many times you kill others versus how many times you get killed."

"Fascinating." Androwski shook his head. "So you learned to shoot by playing video games. Why am I not surprised?" He smiled and looked at Chris. "You keep your head. If I knew nothing else about you, I would accept you on my team. I'm glad you came."

"Yeah, well, zombie plagues notwithstanding, I'd rather be shooting people that *aren't real* while sitting in front of my computer."

The SEAL smirked at Chris. "Nerd. Oh, and my KDR is like, two hundred to one. And those fucks were firing real bullets at me. Let's find the chief."

Chris jacked the slide on his weapon. "Sure. Noob."

"We've got twelve minutes left, let's hit this next hangar."

13

Dallas couldn't help but look at Anna as they jogged toward a small, windowless, white building constructed from cinderblocks. She reminded him of someone from long ago. Not just the fact that she was extremely fit, or the color of her auburn hair, but her attitude. She was tough as nails, and brave. Hell, anyone who would agree to cross a zombie-infested United States to secure a possible cure for humanity was damn brave. Dallas smiled. He snapped back to reality when a dead woman came around the corner of the tiny structure and started ambling toward them.

Seyfert stopped and drew his combat knife from a shoulder sling. "Hold fire!"

Incredulous, Dallas stopped him with a hand on his shoulder. "You touched, boy? You got an eight-inch reach with that pig-sticker." He pulled his shaft of re-bar from his belt. "Time ta' cowboy the fuck, up...er...sorry Anna."

"I'm twenty six, I've heard the F word a couple times."

Red-faced, Dallas nodded and strode forward.

Anna looked indecisive. "Wait! Androwski told us not to engage!"

The rebar looked wicked as he pointed it toward the dead thing. "Anna, that thing is in the way. We can't git to that building without her comin' up behind us." He squared off ten feet in front of the creature and let her close the distance. He used a backhand swing and she dropped, but started to get back up. Two more overhand whacks and she stopped moving.

Dallas was wiping his forehead with his sleeve when he noticed Seyfert standing next to him looking between him and the twice-killed thing. "Damn."

The three of them spread out and approached the structure. When they reached it, they came together and looked at the door. It was heavy steel and locked. Seyfert knocked on the door, but Boone didn't answer. They moved on to the next structure, which was significantly larger. As they came upon it, they realized that the half that they couldn't see had burned, and the far side of the roof had collapsed. Two motionless corpses guarded the building, both shot in the head.

The third and fourth buildings didn't have much in the way of anything, but as they approached the fifth, a large crowd of undead coalesced. "We'll never make it to that building," Seyfert told them as he looked at his watch, "and we've only got eight minutes left to get back."

"What if he's in there?"

"Then he's fucked. We can't get to him like this. Maybe we can use the LAV to get closer, but I'm making the decision to bug right now." The cries of the oncoming pack of monsters were getting louder.

Seyfert pinched his throat mic. "Chief, do you copy?"

"Roger that, Two, you got anything?"

"Big pack of dead fuckers coming, but no Actual."

"Is it the group we tricked with the LAV?"

"Negative, this is a new group, smaller than the other, but there are still plenty. I'm calling this end of the mission and we're gonna RTB."

"Solid copy, we're doing the same."

"Copy that, Chief. See you in eight mikes, out."

"Okay civvies, move out. We're gonna hoof it back to the LAV, and meet up with squad one. We can discuss the plan of bringing up the armor to check that last building with the chief when we're snug."

The three of them jogged back to the LAV. Squad one was waiting with the rear ramp down, and Androwski was inside speaking to Stark.

Rick turned when he heard them coming. "Nothing at all?" Seyfert ran past him up the ramp.

Anna shook her head as she caught her breath. "Doughnut. There was one more outbuilding we couldn't get to because of a group of dead, but he wasn't in any of the places we checked."

Rick looked past her. "Yeah, I see them. We should get inside."

Chris hit the button to close the rear ramp, and noticed everyone listening to Stark and Androwski speaking. Stark in the driver's chair, and the lieutenant in the front passenger's seat.

"It was the same message, but it wasn't on a loop. There two were replies, and at each reply, directions were given to a secure location to be picked up. The city itself is crawling with the dead, it had a population of just over a quarter million before."

"And you're sure the message was live?" demanded Androwski.

"Yes, sir, they were quite specific. They said to…" Stark put his hand to the left side of his headphones and looked down, his eyes focused. "They're on now." He flipped a switch, and a tinny voice filled the LAV.

"…can make it to any of the coordinates stated, we will come for you and bring you to safety. There are over eight hundred members of the United States armed forces guarding us. We have armored vehicles and aircraft. Food, shelter, and huge walls. Do not give up hope. Come to The

Triumvirate, and the Three will provide. Repeat, you are not alone. There are nine thousand of us, and we will help you. Get to the following coordinates in rural Nebraska, Iowa, Missouri, or Kansas. The Crossroads Mall, forty one degrees fifty eight minutes point four one seconds north by..."

The voice listed more locations with coordinates, then repeated itself one more time, adding that it would be back on at the top of the hour, and every half hour after that.

"Sir, do we respond?"

"Negative. Our mission is the priority. McInerney told us to help anyone we could as long as that help didn't compromise the mission or time to complete. Besides, I'm not sure I trust a voice on the radio." The sounds of the approaching dead could be heard through the hull of the LAV, and the lieutenant shifted his attention to the monitor. "Damn, here they come."

The dead were almost on them when Stark fired up the diesel engine, and with a belch of black exhaust from the snorkel pipes, the behemoth began to move.

"Actual, this is Wanderer, we need to..." Androwski sighed, "Wanderer is moving out. Suggest you RTB at Rock by any means necessary. Good luck."

The eight-wheeled vehicle turned in a wide arc and fled back toward the other LAV. Leaving one friend behind, they would bury the friends they had lost as the sun set.

A solitary figure stood alone in the control tower, watching the LAV drive off through his binoculars. As they faded from sight, he tossed his broken and useless radio on a lightless air traffic console and sat in a wheeled chair. Putting his feet up next to the discarded radio and leaning his head back, he thought about his parents. They couldn't possibly be alive, they were in San Antonio Texas. He hissed his breath in as pain lanced through his left forearm. He looked at the semi-circular wound and pulled his MK23 HANDGUN, unscrewing the suppressor and placing the weapon in his lap. *There's always a zombie in the bathroom*, he thought to himself.

14

It was early afternoon, ten miles south of I-80 in central Nebraska when an A10 Thunderbolt screamed over the heads of the mission team. Joe the puppy had started whining, and Anna had needed to pee, so now Rick and Androwski had their backs to her while she took care of business behind a small trading post in the middle of what seemed like a million miles of corn fields. Joe was running around happily near them. Androwski had forbidden anyone to go into the restrooms, as there was a bloody hand print on the men's room door.

Rick was staring up at the noise, but the SEAL had dived on to the ground and covered his head. He looked up into Anna's eyes. She was squatting with her pants around her ankles. "Like the view?"

Androwski looked in all directions. "Fuckin' Warthog!"

Anna stood and pulled her pants up. "I didn't think I was that ugly."

"What? No! No, no, no, the plane! The plane is called a Warthog."

She stuck her bottom lip out in mock despair. "I never did go to prom…"

Androwski stood and brushed himself off. "Dammit, he must have seen us. Stark! Anything on comms?"

"Negative sir, no chatter."

"Keep monitoring, and let me know if anybody else is out there."

"Copy."

Two helicopters, a blue and white Channel 8 traffic copter and a military Blackhawk followed shortly after the jet. The traffic chopper slowed and looked down at them for the briefest of moments, but then continued after the other aircraft to the south.

Dallas, Seyfert, and Chris came out of the trading post, arms laden with appropriated foodstuffs, and staring into the sky. Dallas had a full Native American headdress on, the faux white feathers blowing in the warm Nebraska wind. Seyfert was chewing on a Slim Jim. "Place is a gold mine, Chief, tons of packaged goodies. Maybe—"

A huge explosion shut Seyfert up mid-sentence. The blast was far off to the south, but that was the direction they had intended to head. A massive mushroom cloud of fire erupted a hundred or so feet into the air, and the team felt the wind and heat from the blast a few moments later. Even from the two or three mile distance away that they were, they could tell that the cornfields were ablaze.

Androwski and Seyfert looked at each other wide-eyed. "Jesus, they dropped a Hades."

"Is that a nuke?" Chris demanded in a panicked voice.

"No, but almost," Seyfert answered while still looking at the conflagration. "It's a bad-ass MOAB full of napalm-like stuff that they can ignite by remote control. Everything within half a mile of that detonation just reached about a thousand degrees. It will burn for days. Weeks if all the corn goes."

Dallas took the headdress off. "Well, I'm pretty damn happy that we wasn't a mile further south."

"Agreed. I wonder if they knew we were here and dropped anyway."

"We're alive, so I don't give a shit about any of that," Androwski said. "What worries me is why they would drop ordnance like that here. The only thing I can think of is that there were a shitload of Limas over there, and we're only a couple of miles away. Button up, we're out. And Dallas, that ridiculous thing is not coming in my LAV."

Chris came down the LAV ramp empty-handed. "One more trip into the store?"

Androwski nodded, "Yeah, I'll come with."

When they had loaded their booty of canned goods and bottled liquids, they pushed on. The lieutenant decided that they would go north. Directly east was out of the question as Androwski didn't want to meet up with this other group of survivors near Lincoln. He thought they might get conscripted into whatever rag-tag military operation was in this part of the country, and his commanding officer had given him specific orders to do no such thing.

Four hours north, and they shifted east again, on Route 20. This route would keep them a hundred twenty miles north of the Lincoln area, and hopefully out of sight of prying eyes.

No contact had been attempted from the group with the air support, but the message from the Triumvirate was broadcast on all frequencies every half hour. The signal was significantly stronger than it had been in Wyoming.

After two hours of flatlands and small farming towns heading north, it was back into the corn again. Both sides of the road had three meter stalks as far as the eye could see, which was about twenty feet into the yellow vegetation. An hour east, and they came upon a crossroads in the waning daylight. Half a mile north of them was a farmhouse.

Chris looked longingly at the large house. "I could sure use some sleep in a bed, a real bed."

"We all could," agreed Androwski. "Stark, let's recon that homestead."

The LAV turned northward and they circled the farmhouse and huge barn before parking in the dirt driveway. The recon went smoothly. Chris, Seyfert, and Rick checked out the house, while Dallas, Anna, and Androwski looked into the barn. The house was locked up tight, with boarded windows on the lower floor. Repeated knocks on the door yielded nothing from the inside. The barn wasn't an animal barn, but housed a huge green combine harvester and big dump truck. Various other farming equipment adorned the walls and hung from hooks all over the place. Two fifty-five gallon drums of diesel fuel were found as well. The loft was empty except for a desk with a small computer and a dead man. He had taken his life with a shotgun, and there wasn't much left to see. There was a photograph with a pretty woman in a floral print dress and two little blonde girls clutched in his decaying hand. Androwski said not to touch anything, and they left the man in peace.

Seyfert reported the locked house to Androwski. "Three doors, front, back, and bulkhead to the basement. Bulkhead is the strongest, it's made out of steel. Back door is the weakest, flimsy wooden thing, but it's braced from the inside. Front door is solid oak, also braced. That window," he pointed to an open window on the second floor, "looks to be our best way in without destroying the barricades."

"Okay then, you and I are on point. Chris, Anna, back in the LAV. Rick, Dallas, cover our six while we get in. We'll recon and let you know if it's safe. Stark, button up. If a hundred Limas come out of the corn, I want you to lead them away then get back here to pick us up."

"Copy."

Ten minutes later, a different window opened up on the second floor and a roll-out fire ladder tumbled down, and the lieutenant stuck his head out. "It's clear. The barricades are so well built that I think we should come and go through the upper floor. Bring the sniper rifles."

The civilians climbed the ladder and entered the house with Seyfert's help, passing their weaponry in first. They looked around at a child's bedroom, immaculate, with a Littlest Pets bed spread, and picture books on shelves on the wall. AMY'S ROOM was on the front of the open door, neatly printed in block letters on yellow construction paper. Pictures of SpongeBob torn from magazines, and some other cartoon characters nobody knew adorned the door as well.

Androwski was sitting on the bed, rubbing his face in his hands, "Rick, you and the civvies will stay in the house with Seyfert. Stark and I will bunk in the LAV. Try to keep the noise down, and no lights on without the windows covered."

"Ain't you gonna sleep in a bed for once?" Dallas demanded.

"Somebody has to stay in the LAV, and I don't want anybody alone while we sleep."

"Fair enough. I'll bunk with Stark when we get to the next Motel 6."

"Thanks, Dallas. There's a full cupboard downstairs, and the gas is still working in the stove, so a hot meal is in order. I want a guard at all times just in case, two hours each ought to do it. We'll leave by zero nine hundred, after a good breakfast. Oh, and the basement door is locked, and we couldn't find a key, so we pushed a table and the fridge up against it. Nothing will get in without making a shit-ton of noise, and the back bulkhead is secure. Feel free to explore, but nobody goes anywhere alone except the armed guard, not even to the bathroom. Take whoever is on guard with you if you gotta pee. Now let's get cooking, I want to get some food to Stark, and get him a shower if the water's working. Poor bastard hasn't been out of that LAV except to piss in two weeks."

"I heard that!" came a tinny voice from the radio.

"Dibs on the shower," Anna said with a yawn.

Shouldering his shotgun, the big southerner volunteered his services. "I'll cook us up some vittles then."

Rick looked at him in mock surprise. "Hillbillies can cook?"

"Yeah, ribs n' brisket are my specialties, but yer probly gettin' soup tonight Hoss."

"Everybody should get some quality rack," Androwski said. "Remember the lights and noise. There isn't a town for fifteen miles, but who knows what's around."

15

Androwski woke with a start as Stark shook him gently. He woke confused, which was unlike him. Normally he would spring up like a cat and be instantly awake, as his SEAL training kicked in, but two weeks on the road had taken their toll.

After the civvies had eaten, he had brought out some soup and boiled corn on the cob for him and Stark. They had eaten and then stretched out on the benches in the LAV for a night's rest. Now Stark had his hand on his superior's mouth and was *shhhh*-ing him. Androwski nodded and sat up rubbing his right eye with his palm. Stark pointed at the thermals on one of the monitors.

Dozens of undead were streaming out of the corn.

"Fuck me." The chief looked at his watch and calculated who would be on guard at the current time, four forty one AM. "Dallas, don't answer me, just listen. There are Limas on station. They're pouring out of the fields. We can't tell how many, but it looks like a hundred or more. Wake everybody up, but don't make a sound. I don't want you to look out the windows either. Click your radio twice if you copy."

The radio squelched twice.

"Wake Seyfert first, then everybody else. Don't let them speak. If we keep quiet, the Limas might pass us by."

In the house, Dallas stood from his armchair at the top of the stairs on the second floor. His size thirteens didn't make a sound as he trod lightly to the first bedroom. The door was wide open, and Chris and Anna were asleep in a queen size bed. He moved past them and went to the second room, where Seyfert was sleeping in a kid's bed. The SEAL was fully dressed, with his boots on. As Dallas made his way into the dark room, he heard the all too familiar sound of the hammer clicking back on a pistol. "Speak or I shoot you in the face," came an unmistakable New Jersey accent.

"It's me, Dallas, an' keep your voice down. Ya boss just tole me there's pus bags outside, tons of em. He said ta keep quiet, an' they might move on, but he wants ever-body up in case they don't."

Seyfert sat up quickly, his voice an almost imperceptible whisper, "I'll wake Chris and Anna, you go get Rick."

Dallas nodded and moved out of the room. Soon all five survivors were huddled in the master bedroom, speaking in hushed voices and armed to the teeth.

"So we just sit here and hope?" demanded Anna.

Seyfert turned his palms up. "What do you wanna do? Make a break for it? What if there's a thousand of them out there, we can't see through drapes!"

Rick put his hand on Anna's shoulder. "Relax, both of you." He looked at Seyfert. "We sit tight and hold out. First thing is we stop talking unless absolutely necessary, and remember, whispers carry farther than low voices." Rick pointed toward Dallas's radio and motioned for it with his fingers. Dallas handed it over.

"Androwski, you copy? How many?"

"At least a hundred. I can't figure out where they came from. I can see them on the thermals. One came close, and he looked burned. Maybe there was a…hold on…" Stark pointed toward one of the dead people on the monitor. While the others around it kept moving past the house and the LAV and down the road, this one had stopped and was looking at the house, his mouth impossibly wide open. He walked to the house and put his hand on it. His other hand followed suit, and it looked as if he were pushing. He looked left, right, and up, then he reared his right hand back and slapped the siding. He did it again and again, then started using two hands. Other undead had stopped to see what the ruckus was all about.

"Androwski, what the hell is that?"

"You have an admirer, now keep quiet."

The dead man continued to smack the house, and an obese woman in a flowered mu mu decided to join him. They stood next to each other playing patty-cake with the clapboards. A young woman also came to the party and soon there were six, with more coming. In the LAV, Stark pointed to the starboard side monitor, and Androwski saw that some of the dead that had walked past them were starting to return.

"This got fucked up fast. Rick, put Seyfert on."

"Sir?"

"Looks like these sons of bitches either know you're in there, or they just got lucky. The whole troupe is coming back, and there's still more coming out of the fields."

Seyfert's steadfast voice came back. "Orders?"

"Shit. Sit tight, we'll try to draw them away like we did at the airport. Barricade the stairway, and if they get in retreat to the roof.

"Solid copy, sir, good luck. Did everybody get that?" Nods all around. "As quietly as possible, bring some stuff out here to block the stairs with."

"Damn son, I dunno if that'll even slow 'em down."

"I'm out of options here, Dallas, what are you thinking?"

"There's a chainsaw downstairs, fulla gas. Guy musta used it to cut the boards for the windows."

"You want to go out there with a chainsaw and eviscerate them like Freddy Kruger?"

"I dunno who that is, but no. I was think'n more like we cut them stairs out so they can't get up."

"That...that's a good idea. Of course the second they hear that thing fire up, they'll know for certain we're in here."

"Don't' think that matters none. They's poundin' now, sounds like a Baptist Revival out there. They's gonna get in"

A deep diesel growl outside indicated the LAV had come to life, and then the moaning and hissing began. The pounding stopped almost immediately, as focus was directed toward the machine. The living dead did not operate machinery, and even though they had only the basest of brain functions, they knew that when a vehicle started, a meal was close. They didn't reason this, hypothesize, or calculate it, they just knew.

Androwski's voice came over the comms. "We're moving out. Be ready, we'll come back as soon as we can."

As the engine noise faded in the distance, the group in the farmhouse took stock of their situation. "Suddenly I'm feelin' a mite anxious, with no tank around me."

"I hear that, hillbilly, douse the lights, I want to recon the exterior." They all turned off their tac-lights, and Chris turned off the electric lantern that they were using. Seyfert made his way to the window in the master bedroom, and pulled the corner of the comforter they had strung up to keep the light in. He released the curtain, backed up and looked at his shoes.

Dallas strode forward and moved the drape slightly himself. He turned and looked at the rest of the group, "Jumpin' Jesus but there's a lotta dead folks out there."

Anna looked anxious as well. "How many?"

"More'n fifty probly. I seen this movie, it don't go too good for them folks in the farmhouse."

"I saw it too," Seyfert said. "*They* didn't have any of these." He produced his suppressed MP5SD3. "Stay away from the windows." He immediately removed the tac-light from his weapon and put it in his mouth. He put the rifle on the bed, where he began to field strip it. He produced a small leather case from his web gear.

"What the hell're you doin'?"

"Cleaning my baby. You might want to do the same."

"Cleanin' it now?"

"Better *before* they get in than after. Getting that chainsaw now might save our lives. I would be quiet about it too." As if they read his mind, the things outside began to slap on the side of the house again.

"How do they know we're in here?" Rick whispered.

"Maybe they don't," Seyfert said as he pulled a long spring from the slide and slid a round bristle brush into it. "Maybe they just want a bed to sleep in, or to admire the furnishings," he mused, blowing down the length of the spring. "It doesn't matter, they want in and they're extremely unfriendly, so we prepare as much as we can. Dallas, the chainsaw?"

Dallas hurried off, and Chris went with him. Rick watched them go and then turned to Seyfert. "So the plan is we saw out the stairs and wait for the LAV to get back?"

"I am certainly open to intelligent suggestions should you have any."

"Well I was thinking…"

Seyfert clicked something together, pulled the slide back and sighted on a picture of an apple on the wall. "Yeah?"

"What if they don't come back?"

"Then we escape, and meet them at the next rendezvous point in Iowa. And if they don't show in twelve hours, we consider and move on to the next rendezvous point, and so on. We'll leave coded messages at each point, or receive them should the LAV get there first. I'm hoping they come back, because I like the safety of that tin can."

Seyfert looked to his right and noticed Dallas and Chris approaching with their newly appropriated Stihl Farm Boss chainsaw. "I'm a fan," Dallas whispered with a smirk.

"The second you pull on that cord, they're going to go apeshit out there."

"They're already somethin' apey. Now I'm a big fella. Y'all gonna be able to haul me up when there ain't no more stairs? I ain't gon' get et!"

"Big is one word for it, hillbilly. Chris, you ever use a chainsaw before?"

"Nope, but I'm ready."

Dallas instructed Chris on the use of the machine. They all looked at each other, and Chris set the choke. He pulled on the cord rapidly four times, and the engine sputtered. He set the choke again, then tugged once and the thing came to life. It was loud. He ran down the stairs and started cutting through the wooden railing. In thirty seconds, he hit the far wall, and sheetrock dust filled the air. "You gotta get the stringers underneath!" Dallas yelled to him. Chris looked confused. "Dammit!" the big southerner yelled and stomped down the stairs. He bent down and literally ripped up two of the sawn-through stair treads with his bare hands. "That Z lookin' thing there!" Chris nodded and sawed through the two-by-twelve quickly. He was moving on to the second one when Dallas noticed a zombie round the corner from the kitchen. The thing couldn't be seen from upstairs, and Chris was still sawing, so he couldn't hear Dallas's warning shouts immediately. Feeling the fool for leaving his shotgun upstairs, Dallas tapped Chris on the shoulder and pointed behind him. The stairs started to shudder.

Chris turned around and saw the threat. He released the trigger on the saw and started up the stairs. He dropped the saw when the lower stairs collapsed, but Dallas grabbed him by the shirt and pulled the pin-wheeling kid up. They paused, exchanging relieved glances when the upper part of the stairway collapsed with a crash, sending them both sprawling back into the foyer in a cloud of dust.

The dead woman that approached them was by no means alone, and Chris looked at a dozen dead faces as he lay on his back. He pulled his sidearm and fired as he stood, his ears still ringing from the chainsaw and the crash. A strange calm came over him as he fired again and again. He glanced at Dallas, but the big man wasn't moving. Chris kicked him as he continued to fire. Seyfert, Rick, and Anna were screaming something at him, but he was in the zone, scoring headshots. He kicked Dallas a few times and the man stirred.

Seyfert was reaching for him, yelling for him to leave Dallas and climb up.

Chris didn't look at him, but reloaded and continued to fire. The things were closing, and as they came into view, Rick and Anna began shooting into the crowd from above. Dallas came to, but was groggy. There was a lull in dead people coming from the kitchen area, and Chris did something insane. He left Dallas and ran into the kitchen. A single shot echoed through the house, and Chris returned to see Dallas getting up. "Give me your hand!" Seyfert was screaming to Dallas, but Chris had company. "No time!" He grabbed Dallas and the both of them disappeared into the front room. The zombies followed. A few moaning-filled minutes passed, Rick and Anna terrified for their friends, then Chris was on the radio.

"We broke the lock off of the basement door and came down. The door is barred from this side, but it won't hold for long. I can hear them pounding."

Seyfert pounded the bed with his fist. "Shit! Shit! Shit!" He sat on the bed and put his head in his hands, trying to think over the incessant hissing and growling. He raised his head and looked at his two compatriots, "Okay, this is what's going to happen, and I don't want to hear shit out of anybody about it, especially the words *suicide*, or *in vain*. Anna, you drop the ladder out the back window again when I tell you, and cover it. I don't think these things can climb, but if they do, get them off of the ladder. Use your knife if they get close to you, and shoot them only as a last resort. Rick, you and I are going to the front windows, we're going to provide a diversion."

"What diversion?"

"I'll take care of it. You're going to cover me. Use one of the rifles if you need to. Chris, Dallas, do you copy?"

"We're here."

"Anna is going to call you when the back yard clears, I'm going to divert the Limas such that this can happen. When she calls you, you open that bulkhead and run for the ladder, it's only fifteen feet or so from the bulkhead. When you get out of the basement, hang a right and get up that ladder like a pack of hungry zombies were chasing you."

"Dallas says he's dizzy."

"Dallas deals with his dizziness or you both die. Any questions?"

"No, sir."

"Anna, call them when the things leave the area, don't wait until they're all gone, just until Chris and Dallas can successfully negotiate any Limas in the way without getting snagged. Snipe what you can from here to cover them, but don't waste ammo. Rick, follow me."

The two men moved to the front of the house, into another bedroom. This room looked out over the cornfields twenty meters away. It also just happened to be above a quaint farmer's porch.

"I'm going to jump down there, and when the pus bags follow me, you shoot any that get too close."

"There are a lot."

"Yeah, I know. I've got to do this sooner rather than later, or that basement door will cave in and our buddies are chow." Seyfert swung his legs out the window, sitting on the sill. "You ready?"

"Yeah, good luck."

"Damn, Rick, you're not even going to try to talk me out of it?"

"You'd only get pissed and do it anyway."

Seyfert walked to the edge of the farmer's porch and looked down, then looked back at Rick, "Don't miss. Tell Anna to drop the ladder now!"

Rick nodded and yelled to her, and Seyfert started yelling for all he was worth. It didn't take long for many undead to come looking, and soon there were a baker's dozen right under him, with loads more on the way. He adjusted his weapon strap on his shoulder, took two steps back, then ran forward and leapt out into space. He flew over the creatures below him gracefully, and rolled when he landed, coming up in a crouch and aiming his weapon's tac-light. Comically, the creatures stared at him momentarily as if to ask: *Are you fucking nuts?* A moment was all he got though, and then they started to amble toward him.

A wall of shadows was coming out of the pre-dawn darkness from both the left and right sides of the house too, but Seyfert didn't move. "I forgot the hot sauce, you dead fucks!" he screamed, and then spit at them. A *pap!* came from Rick's M4, and the dead kid that was behind Seyfert dropped. The SEAL had just enough time for one half of his brain to think that this was a terrible idea before the other half kicked in and told him to run. Unfortunately, he was a peninsula in a sea of rot. They were coming for him from three sides. With no choice, he turned and darted into the corn, yelling.

True to their nature, the creatures followed, and Rick watched the tac-light bob through the corn twenty meters in front of them. He watched the steady stream of undead pour back into the rows, then ran back to Anna.

There were nine creatures remaining in the back yard, two near the ladder, but the others spread out pretty thin.

"I'm going to call them!"

"Okay, tell Chris to come up the ladder first."

"Why?"

"Because Dallas might have a concussion, and if he falls off the ladder with Chris under him, they'll both get killed." He aimed his suppressed handgun and destroyed the two creatures near the ladder.

"Chris, you come up the ladder first, are you ready?"

"Hell no, but we'll do it!"

"Now!"

The latch bolt on the steel bulkhead sliding back made a loud noise, but it was nothing compared to the horrendous creaking screech that sounded when Chris threw open the old doors. All seven creatures in the back yard turned to gaze at a potential meal, their red eyes shrouded by the shadows.

Rick fired five suppressed rounds and scored two head shots as the men outside made their escape. Other dead had noticed the commotion, so more visitors were on the way.

Chris was up the ladder in less than three seconds, Rick and Anna pulling him in the bedroom window, but Dallas was struggling. From where Rick stood, half out of the window, Dallas looked unsteady as he very slowly climbed the chain rungs. Half way up, and just out of reach of the growing crowd below, he hooked his arm through a rung and stopped moving, swaying slightly.

"Rick, the ladder might not hold him!"

"Come on buddy, you're almost there," Rick called down. "Don't stop now."

The big man blinked a few times, looking up at Rick. "Hurt my noggin, pard. Feel like I gotta puke."

"Puke when you get in the damn house, now climb, you dumb redneck."

Dallas smiled through his misery and did continue his climb. When his three friends finally pulled him through the window, and he was lying on the floor on his back, he tried to sit up. "Damn," was all he managed before he passed out.

Anna pulled her wrist across her forehead. "Jesus, the guy weighs a freakin' ton!"

"I know, right?" agreed Chris. "You'd think now that he's been off the pasta for a month, he'd lose weight."

Anna tried to pull the ladder back in, but an enterprising young dead man had the bottom of it clenched in both fists.

"Good idea," Rick said. "Pull that up, you never know."

"It's July, ain't it?" asked a groggy southern voice. "There ain't no snow. And I know one of y'all said somethin' 'bout spaghetti." He promptly passed out again.

Anna fired two shots outside and quickly retrieved their means of egress, then all three conscious survivors moved their large friend to the bed with difficulty.

Anna looked at Rick. "So now what?"

"We wait for our ride."

16

Every time the breeze blew through the stalks, it sounded like one of those things was right next to him, hissing. Seyfert had jogged through the yellow rows yelling with the things in tow for what seemed like an eternity before he decided to go into stealth mode. He stopped yelling and picked up his pace. The problem was he had no idea which direction he was travelling in, and it was still mostly dark. It was also extremely difficult to be quiet as he ran past the corn, and it had cut his face and arms. The lacerations were small, but one was in the scalp over his left eye, and it gave a steady trickle, partially blinding him. He didn't know if the dead could smell his blood, and he was leaving a trail of it on the husks.

He had only come across one dead person in front on him in the corn so far, and had dispatched it quickly, moving on. He knew they were around him, and he was pretty sure they knew he was there too. Suddenly, an elephant loomed in front of him, scaring him witless. He raised his rifle, to shoot this living dead Goliath, but realized it wasn't moving. It was a tractor abandoned in the field. He lowered his rifle, breathing heavily and thinking himself a fool when hands grabbed him from behind, and something bit into his shoulder. The SEAL did a forward roll, and the thing released him as it flew forward. He shot it in the face as it tried to stand and continued on his way. He now knew, beyond a shadow of a doubt, that he would not live through this night, and made an extremely quick peace with himself. He was a SEAL, the baddest of the bad, and his job was to die if necessary. Bitching about it wasn't going to change the job.

He wouldn't go out puking and crying just to turn into one of the Limas though. Uh uh. He'd shoot himself as soon as it got bad. Until then, he'd continue fighting, destroying as many of the pus bags as possible. He could hear them following, crashing through the stalks behind and to the sides of him. One stumbled in front, reaching, and he juked to the side, spinning and running. Was he going in circles? Was there a town load of zombies in the fields? Two more emerged, arms outstretched, and he shot one, and ran from the other. Now they were in front of him too, or maybe they always had been. He wiped his hand across his eye and it came away bloody. His shoulder ached where the thing had clamped down on him.

His warrior's mind was racing. Would it be better to be caught and torn to pieces or to die slowly, enduring hours of terrible sickness only to swallow a bullet before expiring? Being eaten alive would hurt, but it would be over in less than five minutes, probably in less than two. The corn was starting to play on Seyfert's mind, every noise amplified, and coming from every direction. It was almost sunup, but even when the sun rose, he wouldn't be able to see anything past the tall stalks. He had gotten lost in a corn maze when he was eight, and had to sit between the rows crying until his father had come for him.

A growl from his left made him jump right, and the lunging dead farmer in denim overalls missed him. He ran. They were everywhere. He hoped that his friends would make it, and that they would find the cure. He hoped his mom and dad were okay, and his sister studying abroad in Australia had escaped the plague. He was hoping that his parents' Dalmatian Sparky was still alive when he burst through the corn and stumbled into a shallow roadside ditch.

Dawn's first light peeked over the stalks as he looked up into the barrels and blades of several different weapons. "Lookey what we got here boys," a gruff voice said. "A bona fide soldier." Seyfert looked at the speaker, a barrel-chested man dressed in jeans with a black leather vest, forearms covered in tattoos. The waxing sun glinted off of the chrome from a line of silent motorcycles stretching down the road in both directions.

Oh shit… thought the SEAL as visions of murderous post-apocalyptic biker gangs flew through his head. He would endure a thousand tortures before he revealed the location of his buddies to this trash. Saying a silent prayer, and a sorry to his parents, he started to bring his weapon up to fire when a little boy showed up behind the big biker's tree-trunk legs.

"Who's that, daddy?"

"Why don't you ask him, Danny?"

The boy looked up at his father and shook his head. *Uh-uh.*

"Forgive my son, soldier-boy, he's shy. Before you join my group, I gotta ask, are you bit?"

A shot rang out and someone yelled, "Rotters!" and then all hell broke loose.

"Get up here, boy!" the man yelled to Seyfert, who didn't need to be told twice. What unfolded next stunned the SEAL. Men on both sides of the road aimed into the corn with rifles and shotguns, while the women and kids unfolded poles and snapped them together. Each was two meters long, with a crossbar on the end so that the thing looked like a T. The firing began, but soon the odd items were passed to several of the men, who in turn passed their rifles to the women and kids. Several more shots rang out before the poles could be put into use, but they were still brought to bear quickly.

"Stand back, son, and save your ammo until you need it," the big guy told Seyfert. As the dead poured out of the corn, the men stopped them in their tracks with the T-poles. Others used harpoon-like spears to pierce the skulls of the impeded zombies. One or two more shots echoed across the fields before Seyfert looked upon the carcasses of more than forty re-killed bodies. The operation had been executed with military precision.

"How many were chasing you?"

"More than this, I think."

"Eyes open! There are more out there. Calvin, are you finished with the tire?"

Seyfert noticed a man fixing a flat on one of the motorcycles. He also noticed that no self-respecting homicidal scumbag would ride some of the bikes in the procession. There were big touring bikes, rice rockets and even a Ducati racing motorcycle with the Harleys. There were women and kids, and even a bird in a cage. These were families.

The guy fixing the tire wiped his hand across his forehead. "Three minutes! If you leave me the hell alone."

The big man laughed, "That there's Calvin. My name is Teems, Mark Teems, and this is my family." He spread his hands in both directions.

Seyfert stuck his hand forward. "John Seyfert, US Navy."

"Navy? You're in Nebraska, sailor, you lost?"

"No. You've got a pretty extended family."

The man chuckled. "Yeah, most of them are strays we picked up along the way. Started off with me, Danny, and nine of my biker buddies. We picked up a guy and his kids outside of Sturgis, and we've picked up everybody else since. Couldn't leave them behind."

"Thanks for saving my ass, Mark."

"Teems. Nobody calls me Mark.

"Teems! We got Rotters in the corn on the same side as before."

The biker looked at Seyfert with a wry smile. "See?"

The group took care of the emerging dead as efficiently as before. None of the creatures ever reached the road. The mechanic said he was done with the tire, and Teems decided it was time to go. "I don't like being inside this damn corn." Everybody packed up quickly, and Teems with two of his friends continued to speak with Seyfert.

"You're welcome to come with us, sailor. Oh yeah, back to my original question, are you bit?"

"Yeah, yeah I am."

Instantly three weapons were pointed at him. Half the column of people were looking on now.

"Sorry, sailor, but you know how this works. Pass me your weapon slow-like."

Seyfert nodded and did as he was told. "Where did they get you?" He pulled his tac-webbing to the side and his shirt down so they could view the bite. One of the three with a gun on Seyfert stepped forward. A skinny man in glasses, he leaned in and inspected the wound. Moving his fingers across the SEAL's shoulder, he pushed the shirt this way and that.

"How long does he have, Doc?"

The doctor shook his head. "Fifty, maybe sixty years unless he really gets bitten. They didn't break the skin, son, but you're going to need new gear." The man showed Seyfert teeth marks and a tear in the padded part of his tac-webbing. "You're a lucky man."

Teems passed the MP5SD3 back to Seyfert. "Guess you can come with us. We could use a man with military training. What did you do in the Navy?"

Seyfert smiled. "I was in the Teams."

That earned him a guffaw and a hearty slap on the back. "So what do you say? We've got room, and your fortunes would improve some if you were mobile."

"I'm sorry, Mr. Teems, but I've got some friends trapped in a farmhouse, and some more that are missing. I've got to figure out how to help them."

Teems looked at the doctor, who nodded. "We'll help you, kid, that's kind of what we do."

"I couldn't ask—"

"You didn't, as I recall," the biker yelled over the sounds of the bikes starting up. "Calvin! Calvin, where's this depot you've been promising me?"

"Eight miles east on twenty, and a mile south on RR nine."

"You take everybody there and hole up. I'll take the Steadys with me and help this young man's friends. Calvin knows where there's a big garage-type place with its own well," he told Seyfert. "He says it's built like a fortress, so we're going to catch our breath for a couple days and then move on."

Seyfert was puzzled. "What are Steadys?"

"That's the name of my bike club, the Rock Steadys."

Nodding, Seyfert reached for his radio, only to find it missing, "Damn." He noticed Teems looking at him queerly and relayed the information about the missing radio. "Must have happened when the one almost got me at the tractor. I've waded through rivers and swum oceans, crossed mountains, traded fire with insurgents, and spent a week in a sandstorm as a SEAL, but I have never had so much radio trouble as I've had in the past two weeks."

A suppressed gunshot sounded, and everyone looked to see another dead woman fall just inside the corn. Seyfert had his weapon trained on the corn looking for more targets.

"So where are your friends?"

17

A few dozen undead milled around a solitary farmhouse in the center of miles of corn. Some walked into the back of the house through a broken rear kitchen door, and others came up or went down through a bulkhead into the basement. Access to the first floor of the dwelling was no longer limited. More undead had shown up since Seyfert's brazen act of heroics.

The noon day sun was high overhead and it was hot. The stench from the dead wasn't overwhelming, but it wasn't by any means easy to take.

"Do you think he made it?" Chris whispered to Rick.

The live humans were hidden on the second floor in the master bedroom, with the door closed. With no stairs, the things below couldn't figure out how to gain access to the second floor.

"I hope so." He looked at his big friend, unconscious on the bed next to him. "I hope we all do."

"What do you think happened to the tank?"

"I can't figure that out. If they broke down, they would have radioed us. I'm worried about them too."

"So do we just wait here?" Anna inquired. "What if more of them come?"

"Anna, we don't have enough ammo for the ones that are here now, and even if we got to the yard then what? We don't have a ride. We can't outrun them on foot forever. Besides, Dallas isn't running anywhere. We'll wait for the LAV, and if they don't show up by tonight, then we'll I'll make a break for it and find a vehicle. We need to plan first."

"You can't go out there alone, Rick..."

"Well, somebody has to. We stay here and we starve, but we should wait for a while before making any rash decisions. We could..." Rick noticed that Chris had his head cocked and was listening to something intently. "Chris? Chris, what—?"

"Ssshhh! Do you hear that?"

"All I hear is them. What do—?"

"Music!" He smiled. "I hear heavy metal dammit!" Apparently, so did the things in the back yard, because they all started moving back into the corn. Rick peeked through the curtains, and noticed that they were all leaving, heading toward the sound, which was now clearly audible. He could see them filing out of the back door and the bulkhead as well.

"What the hell is this?"

Anna put her hands to her face. "It must be Seyfert or the LAV! They've come back!"

Teems gave a cockeyed smile. "So once the ruckus starts, they all hit the road to see what it is, and we swoop in and save the day. We've done it a bunch of times."

Seyfert nodded his head understanding. "A sound diversion. That's how I brought them into the corn and away from the house in the first place."

The two and four others had left the main group two hours previous, and were now within sight of the besieged farmhouse. They had ditched their bikes in lieu of a red Dodge Ram 2500. All their eggs were in one basket, but Calvin had modified the vehicle to be extremely quiet while driving.

"Well, they aren't that bright," Teems said, "but they're no fun in numbers.

Where—?"

An argument had broken out behind Teems and the SEAL, and they both turned around to see what was happening.

"...a total whack job, Ed," said the doctor to one of the bikers. "You can't start with *Stupify*, you have to start with *Down with the Sickness.* The irony is too significant to go unnoticed, even by the living dead"

"Ridiculous, Doc, you start with *Stupify* and it leads into *Down with the Sickness. Both* are significant. Have you seen a zombie yet that isn't both stupefied and down with the sickness? Duh."

Teems stepped in. "You're both crazy. Drop some plates on their ass. That's what you do."

Ed and the doctor looked at each other. "That's why he's the boss," Ed said. "Genius."

"He really is," agreed the doc.

"What the hell are you talking about?" demanded Seyfert.

"Disturbed," all three men chorused back to him at once.

"Who's disturbed? What do you mean?"

"Jesus Christ, who is this person?" asked Ed.

All the bikers were chuckling. "Disturbed is the name of an extremely powerful rock band. They're loud. Very loud."

Seyfert stared blankly.

Teems shook his head. "We're going to play some loud music as the diversion remember? Disturbed is apparently today's diversion."

"I was always more of an Elton John fan myself…"

Jaws dropped all around. "I thought we were mighty kind not shooting you when you might have been infected," the doctor said, "but this is not as easily forgiven. Elton frigging John indeed."

Teems laughed and looked at Ed. "How many discs do we have left?"

"Nine. Of the Disturbed disc anyway. Hang on." Ed strode forward, hefting his baseball bat. A lone zombie had discovered them and was stumbling out of the field. Ed pointed, calling his shot and thumped the creature in the temple. He returned as if he had just gotten the morning paper. "Discs are okay, but we're running out of radios and batteries." He cleaned off his bat with a rag.

Teems harrumphed, "The only thing on the damn box in two weeks has been those nut-jobs out of Lincoln."

The SEAL looked at Teems. "The Three?"

"Yeah, you heard them too?"

"Yeah, and we're pretty sure they have functioning aircraft, which means that their claims of having a shit-load of people must be true. We saw an A-10 drop some serious ordnance a few miles from our position yesterday, and it was followed by two helicopters, one of which looked to be an appropriated news chopper."

"This is not good news," said the doctor. "We found a man and his teenage son the other day. They had been in with the group from Lincoln, and they said it didn't go to well for them. Apparently one of the leaders of the group liked one of the women that was in the guy's group. The family was invited to dinner with the top brass of the organization, then they disappeared. The guy tried getting the rest his group to leave, but they wouldn't go. He cut out with his kid when they were on a scavenging detail."

"I would like to talk to this man."

"He wouldn't come with us," Teems said. "We gave him some food and water, but we couldn't spare any weapons. He thanked us and we went our separate ways."

"Okay, we can talk about that later, but first let's save my friends."

A map was spread across the hot hood of the red pickup. "There's a small access road here," one of the men pointed to a winding red line on the map. "It's only three hundred feet away from the house, but you can't see it through the corn. That means they won't see us coming and we can get out quick."

Teems and Seyfert nodded. They all jumped in the truck and drove toward the access road. Ed was unwrapping a new CD to put in a new boom-box they had appropriated. He noticed Seyfert looking at him. "Eight D cell batteries would have been a small price to pay a year ago, but they're almost priceless now. Can't just walk down to the convenience store and grab them anymore." He fumbled with the boom box for a second more and then the most horrible sound (other than a zombie) that Seyfert had ever heard belted from the machine.

"That's the music you guys were talking about?" he shouted over the cacophony. "It sounds like chainsaws cutting through steel!"

"That's why they call it heavy metal boy!" Teems shouted from the driver's seat, which was immediately next to him. All the others were now singing: *It seems what's left of my human side is slowly changing in me. Will you give in to me?*

Several minutes later Ed was putting the now silent boom-box in the middle of the road. The truck was pointed away from it, and they were ready. Teems gave a double thumbs up and Ed pressed the play button and cycled through the song numbers until he found the one he wanted. A rumble came from the box before the lead singer screamed. Then Ed increased the volume and ran for the truck.

"Damn that's loud," Seyfert said.

"I turned that shit up to eleven!"

Teems' grin went from ear to ear. "Every rotter in a mile radius will be listening to the musical stylings of Disturbed up close within the hour."

"Don't they attack the radio?"

"Nope. Sometimes they'll touch it, but they never hit it or pick it up. They just kind of wander around looking for who's singing."

Plates on your ass bitch! Plates on your ass!

Teems put the truck in gear and they drove back toward the crossroads. Seyfert looked in the mirror and noticed an undead farmer in blue overalls mosey out of the stalks and stare at the boom-box. He couldn't tell if it was the same one who he had seen in the corn earlier.

18

Dallas was awake but woozy when Rick dared a peek into the first floor of the now stairless farmhouse. No zombies were immediately visible, but there was some shuffling going on down there, so he knew where they stood on that score. He looked through the back window in Amy's room, and through the front window over the farmer's porch, and couldn't see any of the dead around.

He was thinking that this would be a perfect time to make a break for it when a red pickup came skidding to a halt outside in the dirt driveway. Several armed men dressed in biker's gear were in the back, and Rick had time to think *Oh shit!* before a familiar face jumped out of the passenger's side of the vehicle.

"Do you need a God damned engraved invitation? Come on!" Seyfert yelled at the house.

"Rotters," one of the men in the back of the truck yelled, and two shots rang out. "Clear the house," yelled someone else. Three men and Seyfert entered the house and one more shot was heard. "Rick! Come on you guys, we don't have time to screw around!"

Chris and Anna poked their heads over the second floor railing. "Nice to see you, Jarhead!"

"Dammit woman," Seyfert said with a smile, "how many times I gotta tell you, I'm a SEAL! Get your asses down here, this is a rescue!"

Rick showed up with Dallas, and they passed the three sniper rifles down. Low whistles came from two of the men dressed in leather when the saw the guns. Anna dropped down and Seyfert caught her, Chris followed, and then Rick helped Dallas. Soon all four were clasping hands with their friend, and they were rushing for the door, Dallas on unsteady feet.

"There's food in the pantry," came a shout from the kitchen. Two of the bikers ran into the kitchen and another shot was heard. Then another. They came running back out in less than a minute with their friend, and all jumped in the back of the truck. "The basement's full of rotters," one of the leather clad guys said, "we couldn't get all the food."

"Forget it," said the burly driver. "Is everybody in?"

"Yeah, Teems, hit it!"

"I see dead people," a middle-aged man with glasses said from the back seat and pointed back toward the homestead. He was the only one save the friends from Alcatraz not dressed in biker garb. Exhibiting extreme patience, the driver put the vehicle in gear, did a three point turn, and drove back toward Route 20. Several undead had lurched into view near the house and seemed confused as to which way to head, after the truck or the music. They kept turning their heads, some eventually going in each direction.

Dallas, Chris, and Anna had gotten in the back of the truck with the other men, but Seyfert had Rick get in the cab. "Rick, this is Ed and Doc, and the guy driving is Teems."

"Thanks for the rescue, Mr. Teems."

"Just Teems, and you're welcome." He extended his hand toward Rick, who accepted it. Teems didn't take his eyes from the road when he asked: "Didn't you say there were two more Navy guys?"

"Yes, they're in a vehicle. They drove off to try making the dead follow them. We haven't heard from them since."

"Well I'm not going to lie, that don't sound too good. We're going to have to find them too I guess, huh?"

"You've done enough for us, Teems," Rick said. "We couldn't ask you to do any more."

"Been over this with your soldier friend, Rick, you don't have to ask. The way I look at it, humans have become an endangered species. As long as we don't throw away our lives needlessly, we should save as many as we can." He looked in the mirror. "Your friend back there, the big fella, he ain't bit is he?"

"No, he took a blow to the head, he should be fine in a day or two."

"I'll take a look at him when we get where we're going," the doctor piped up. "A concussion could be serious with no treatment."

The doctor did just that a half hour after they arrived at their destination. A large concrete service building poked out of the fertile Nebraska soil. It was a depot for combines, tractors, and other large farm equipment. There were no fences or gates, but Calvin had been correct, the building itself was indeed a fortress. Two huge steel garage doors and one smaller door opened on the front of the building, and a service window was already being boarded up. There were men on the roof with binoculars and hunting rifles. The exterior of the place had the look and feel of an armed encampment. A diesel and gasoline pumping station adorned the left side of the depot, with one pump each.

The interior was enormous; a hangar-like structure with multiple levels, a kitchen, an extremely large work area, and two full-size bathrooms complete with multiple stalls, showers and lockers.

The newcomers were welcomed with open arms. Anna was playing with some kids, and Chris was helping to get a wind-driven generator working with a few of the bikers. Dallas was laying down on a steel medical table and the doctor diagnosed him as having a mild concussion. Rick and Seyfert were yet again in front of a map, but this one was framed, and attached to the wall in one of the upstairs offices. The map was a series of aerial photos strung together to make a large chart of the area. They were pointing at different locations with their index fingers and talking about each one.

Seyfert looked at his surroundings again. "What is it?" Rick demanded.

"This place. I understand the need for the vehicle lifts, and all the tools, and even a bathroom, but what the hell are medical facilities doing here? What kind of tractor repair depot has medical diagnostic equipment, and a wind-farm for power?"

"Wind-farm?"

"Yeah, look," Seyfert pointed again at the chart. He traced his finger from the depot along a blue line to a series of poles half a mile away. "Those are windmills. They must power this whole facility." The structures Seyfert pointed at were difficult to recognize as windmills until Rick looked at the shadows on the ground. He could see the shadows of three huge blades in varying positions at the top of each pole and he understood.

"It does seem a little odd," Rick agreed with furrowed brows. "The walls are double thick concrete, and the garage doors are like nothing I've seen."

Seyfert nodded. The seaman looked over the catwalk and spotted Teems moving a box of stuff. "Teems! Where's Calvin?"

Teems looked around and nodded his chin to his left. "I'm here," the mechanic shouted. "What do you need?"

"You, could you come up here for a sec?"

Calvin showed up in short order and looked confused. "What's busted? I should tell you that I don't know shit about computers."

"That's okay. How did you know about this place?"

"I used to drive by here on my way to Sturgis and back on my bike. I live... lived in Ohio." He looked away for a moment. "Ohio is bad now."

"Did you ever see anything...weird here?"

It was Calvin's turn for furrowed brows. "Weird? What do you mean?"

"I don't know, any strange vehicles, or did the road close down near here?"

"Nope, nothin' like that. I drove by all the time, and thought that the place looked a little like a castle. When all this," he waved his hand around, "happened, Teems came and got me, and we high-tailed it out of Ohio using back roads. We got to Sturgis, but it was overrun, and the Army was shooting people up there, so we left before they could decide all bikers were degenerates and tried to shoot us. I thought of this place when we hit Nebraska, and we came almost straight here."

"Not all bikers are degenerates, but you sure as shit are." Teems had come upstairs and was leaning against the door frame. "What's going on?"

"They were just grillin' me about this place."

Yet another furrowed brow. "What about it?"

"The place is an actual fortress," Rick said. "Look at how it's built, and it has its own power source, and I'm guessing water too."

"And medical stuff way beyond what a tractor shop should have," Seyfert added, "and lockers for fifty, and I swear," here he pointed to a shelf attached to a wall, "that is a rifle rack."

Teems stuck his lower lip out. "Don't look like one."

"Because you're thinking of horizontal display racks for rifles, that one is vertical, to store more in less space."

Teems tilted his head. "Yeah, it could be. But so what? Maybe they were hunters."

"What would they hunt? Are there bears in the corn? Deer?"

"What difference does any of this make?" demanded the big biker. "We're here, and we're safe for now. Also, don't we have to find your friends?

"We do."

"Then let's talk about that."

They moved on to a conversation about what could have happened to the LAV. That particular vehicle would be hard to stop, and only a huge ditch or a break down or heavy ordnance could stop it. They hadn't heard any explosions and the LAV had just been serviced the month before. Insofar as ditches or cliffs, they were in Nebraska, and it didn't get any flatter than this. A big hole in the ground maybe, but who would have a big hole in the middle of their cornfield? Besides, they had last seen the LAV driving down the middle of the road. The conversation lasted a half hour before they decided what to do. The entire time Seyfert couldn't shake his feelings of unease about the building they were holed up in.

19

"We've had bad luck with airports," Rick told Calvin. "We lost a man, technically three, at an airport."

The doctor rubbed the back of his neck. "I understand your apprehension, but this is just a dirt runway with a small building and a fuel truck. No hangars, no tower, and no zombies. I would call it an air *field*. It's your best bet."

Rick looked again at the digital photograph stored on a small point and shoot camera, and passed it to Seyfert. The viewable image was of three small single engine planes, a biplane, and a small helicopter off to the side of a very small outbuilding. Calvin, Ed, and Seyfert had reconnoitered the airfield when Calvin had remembered it was *down the road a piece*, as he had put it. It was entirely zombie free, and only two miles away. Several undead had been shot from the roof of the tractor depot as they made their way toward it, however.

"And you can fly that bird? You're sure?" Seyfert demanded of Calvin.

"I was a helo mechanic in the army. I thought it was a good idea to learn how to fly, so yeah. I can use a cyclic and a collective."

"Fair enough. That bird will only hold two, so it's you and me. Teems, may we borrow your truck for one more jaunt? We'll need a driver and a man to ride shotgun too."

"Of course. I'll drive."

"And I'm yer shotgunner," drawled a voice from behind them.

"Dallas," Rick said with a smile, "nice to see your lazy hillbilly ass is finally up."

The big man pointed to a bandage on his head. "I busted my noggin, Hoss. Shut it."

"Which is exactly why you should be laying down," the doctor interjected. "I can't properly diagnose your condition with this equipment, but I can tell you for certain, you took a nasty whack and probably have a concussion."

"A whack says the quack. Damn, doc, I coulda toldja that. I'm fine."

Seyfert shook his head. "He's right, Dallas, you shouldn't even be up let alone going on a foray."

"I'm goin'."

"What if you pass out when you're needed?"

"Then I'm et. I'm goin. Take three in the truck, but I'm goin."

Teems was grinning. "Now I'm a big man, but this fella here is downright *large*. I for one ain't telling him he can't come."

Forty five minutes later, Dallas and Teems were talking about college football while they fueled a Robinson R22 helicopter outfitted for crop dusting. Ed and Rick watched the area with a hunting rifle and an M4 as the big men worked, using an almost full fuel truck to accomplish the task. Calvin had already removed the wires holding the rotors to the ground, and was using a clipboard he found in the cockpit to fill out an included pre-flight checklist. It only took minutes to fill the chopper with fuel, and Calvin gave a thumbs up when he was ready. He hopped out of the vehicle with a small yellow tube and added a little fuel to it.

"Checking the fuel is all," he said to no one in particular. "We're ready," he announced in short order. They had done a radio check, and the helicopter could be heard on all the radios, but the throat microphones could not be heard by the chopper. "Security reasons," was all Seyfert would say. The good news is that there was a full radio room in the depot and the bird could receive loud and clear using that equipment.

"You ready, Navy?" Calvin shouted to Seyfert, who was speaking to Rick.

Seyfert came trotting back to the Robinson. "Will the roof at the depot hold this helicopter?"

"That roof would hold a 747. Didn't you *see* that building?"

"Okay, when our recon is done, we fly back and land on the roof. Rick will take the fuel truck back, and then you guys will have a helicopter at your disposal too."

"Good plan. Let's fly."

Goodbyes were said, and then the helicopter lifted off. The trucks wasted no time in leaving either, and they drove back toward the depot. No signs of undead had been seen at the airfield. For the few minutes of time they spent there, it was like the plague had missed that small patch of land. Until they got in the air.

Looking down into the vast sea of yellow stalks, Calvin could see dozens of shapes crashing through the corn toward where they just were. In minutes, fifty or so undead would be on the runway.

Seyfert must have seen them too. "Jesus, they really are everywhere."

"Yup," Calvin said into the headset. "You should see where we came from. Ohio was thick with them. Thousands upon thousands."

"I came from San Francisco, but I never really went into the city, we went around it."

"Roger that, Navy, where do you want to look for your buddies?"

"They were travelling east the last time we saw them." Seyfert held on as the chopper banked to the left and climbed. Seyfert was scanning out the right side window of the helo with his binoculars not three minutes later when he heard Calvin's voice over his headset. "There's your huckleberry."

The biker was pointing down the highway toward a crossroads a mile or so away. The LAV was indeed there. It was pulled off to the side of the road with the rear hatch open, and three large fires were burning next to it. Even from a mile out and three hundred feet in the air, Seyfert knew that the greasy columns of smoke could only be one thing. Bodies. What really got him thinking was the military checkpoint complete with Abrams tank and Bradley fighting vehicle that had most assuredly held up the LAV. There was no sign of Androwski or Stark.

There were two school buses parked to the side of the road, and they appeared to be full of people. A large tent was in front of the buses, with several personnel in black fatigues strutting about near it.

"Let's get the hell out of here," Seyfert said into his headset.

"Ain't those your friends?"

"That's the LAV yeah, but I don't see Stark or Andy."

"So shouldn't we go down there and see where they are?"

"Negative. They would have come back to us if they could have, so somebody stopped them. One of the things that could stop an LAV is a tank, and they just happen to have one," he pointed to the checkpoint. "We return to the depot and come back with guns."

Calvin spun the helicopter southwest. "What are guns going to do to that tank?"

"Not a damn thing. We still need to get my friends though, so I'll think of something."

20

The rotors hadn't stopped spinning when Seyfert jumped from the helicopter and made his way to the roof stairs. He gathered his people and some of the inhabitants of the depot and told them what had happened.

"But they're the damned army," Dallas drawled. "Ain't they on our side?"

"I don't know. There's no law anymore, so who knows what their intentions are. We saw heavy armor and men in black camo. They could be anybody."

Chris looked at Seyfert. "We can't just leave them. They'd come for us."

Anna nodded in agreement, and ejected the magazine from her pistol, checking her ammo. She slammed the magazine home and made sure the safety was on before she holstered it. "Let's get them."

"We can get them as long as it doesn't compromise the mission. If nobody is left alive to get to our destination, then the mission fails. That can't happen."

Teems raised a bushy eyebrow. "What mission?"

"Top secret, ya dumb hick," Dallas said and punched Teems in the arm. They had become fast friends. "Which is why you can't come with us, Hoss."

"What? What are you talking about?" demanded Rick.

Seyfert looked at Rick sympathetically, "He's right, Rick, you can't go. You have vital information that can't be lost or the mission could fail." Everyone was looking at Rick now. "Commander McInerney would have my balls, but Boone might actually kill me if anything happened to you."

The bikers weren't brought in on the details of the Boston mission, but there was a discussion about the detained LAV in which Rick got a little heated. In the end, he acquiesced to the fact that he knew exactly which buildings in Boston they would need to visit, and in the case of MIT, the layout of those buildings. He had been a police officer in the New England city, and as such had been to the university on numerous occasions for various reasons. An explosion in one of the labs, two murders, and frequent parties that needed to be rousted when he was a younger patrolman. In addition, his ex-wife had worked in the specific laboratory facility that they would need to gain access to, and he knew how to do it. That building was a fortress in itself, and the lower administration levels were a maze of cubicles and offices that nobody would want to negotiate without a plague of living dead let alone with one.

Seyfert, Dallas, Ed, and three of the other bikers would attempt to gain some intelligence on what had happened to their friends in the LAV. Teems had demanded to go, citing he wanted to help, but his son had come down with something, and had asked his father to stay with him.

Ed, and two bikers named Crackers and Smitty, now looked down from a giant white water tower, positioned under giant red letters reading GARSVILLE. They watched as Dallas and Seyfert drove a beat up blue Chevy Cavalier toward the checkpoint. Two sniper rifles and a scoped hunting rifle were following the Chevy.

"Check, check," came Seyfert's voice through the radio.

"We've got you," Ed replied. "We'll stick to the plan."

Seyfert stopped fifty feet shy of the checkpoint, and four men in black camouflage approached. There was an emblem on each of their left breast pockets: a simple III embroidered in gold. It was unfamiliar to Seyfert. The turret on the tank swiveled toward the car. "Sirs, would you exit the vehicle please?" asked a young man. He was very polite. Seyfert had doffed his tactical gear for farmer's clothing, and was in jeans and a white tee shirt with boots traded from one of the bikers. No tactical clothing had fit Dallas at the outset, so he was garbed as always, but had left his webbing with Rick.

This part of the road didn't have any cornstalks for a few hundred yards, just a crossroads with the tank, tent, buses, and a hastily built wooden guard tower. Men in the tower scanned in all directions with scoped rifles. As Seyfert and Dallas opened their doors, they noticed that the buses were full of people. They were also somewhat armored, with bars on the windows and steel plate covering the back escape door. The SEAL was certain the forward door was also armored, although he couldn't see it. The bars made the buses look more like prison transports than armored personnel carriers.

Chain-link fence laced with concertina wire had been strung up to surround the area off to the side of the road. The tower overlooked the area, and the tank was manned. There was an anti-vehicle spike mat across the road.

The young man who had spoken before piped up again. "I'm sorry, but we will have to confiscate your weapons."

"You ain't takin' my gun, boy."

The men raised their rifles slightly but still didn't point them at the two friends.

"Sir, please, I would rather not have to shoot you. It's been a good day and I haven't killed anyone living today. If you resist, you'll be shot. It is against the law in Nebraska for anyone to carry firearms without the express written permission of the governing body."

That line sounded rehearsed and was probably used quite frequently. "What body?" asked the SEAL.

"Until such time as the United States is re-formed, all executive and judicial decisions will be carried out by the Triumvirate or a designee of their choosing."

More rehearsed bullshit, thought Seyfert. Three more men began to walk forward from the camp. The soldiers in black were getting antsy, and the speaker had started getting loud, when the three other men showed up. "Sir, I will not ask again, please—"

"That's okay, Corporal, I'll take it from here." The younger man seemed startled, and immediately answered with a *Yes, sir.*

"Gentlemen, I am Captain Brady of the Triumvirate," said the newcomer. "This is a military checkpoint, and you must surrender your weapons, for the time being, and be subjected to a search." A rifle shot sounded and Dallas raised his shotgun slightly. "Please do not be alarmed, the tower will be firing on the Fallen throughout the day. Now will you surrender your weapons or do we need to take this to the next level?"

"The next level?" demanded the big man.

"Yes, that's the point in time where we shoot you in the head and burn your bodies with the Fallen."

"Dallas, give up your gun. They'll give it back to us."

The Texan put his weapon on the hood of the car and put his hands on his hips. Seyfert followed suit with his pistol. He had left his MP5SD3 with Rick at the depot.

"Search them," the Captain said.

A quick search yielded Dallas's rebar and two combat knives on Seyfert. The weapons and Dallas's belt were put in long plastic bins and labeled. The young corporal approached with two white zip ties.

"I'm sorry, sir, standard procedure until you're cleared."

"I got a bum shoulder boy, could you tie me up in the front?"

The corporal looked at the captain, who nodded that it was okay. It was then that the corporal noticed the small bulge in Seyfert's tee shirt. He reached in and pulled out the small throat mic, which came away with the earpiece that had been draped down his back. He held it up for the captain to see.

The captain's eyes narrowed. "What's this?"

"It's so's we can talk to each other if we get separated."

"I was speaking to him," the captain nodded at Seyfert.

"It's so we can talk to each other if we get separated. Sir."

"Sir?"

"My father always told me to respect the military."

"Did he? Corporal, bring them to the tent please." The officer spun on his heel and the other two followed him.

"Yes, sir!" Dallas and the SEAL were hurried forward and moved into the tent. It was an army medical tent with gurneys and stretchers. Some medical supplies, food, and water were readily available as well. It was good to get out of the heat of the Nebraska sun, and Seyfert thought that the men in the black camo must be dying out there.

They were seated in metal folding chairs and offered bottled water. Seyfert declined, but Dallas accepted, and a man put a straw in a bottle for him.

The captain leaned against a gurney and folded his arms. "Normally I would sit across from you at a desk for this procedure, but desks are hard to come by nowadays. I have only one question for you." He leaned forward slightly. "What is your mission?"

For the second time in two days, Seyfert absolutely knew he was fucked.

21

Danny was watching a DVD of Shrek 2 with Joe the puppy and the little kids. They were only five and five and five and four. He was eight, and way bigger, but he wasn't bossy or mean. They were scared all the time, but he only got scared when the rotters came.

They were ugly, the rotters. They walked funny, and they didn't talk, they *growled*. The worst part of the rotters wasn't their looks or the way they walked or even that they growled. It was that they ate people. They didn't use stoves or even a campfire to cook people either, they just ate them. Ate them *alive*. Danny had seen it happen a few times and it was horrible and gross. There was screaming and lots of blood. Those things didn't even need to kill you for you to die either. All they had to do was get in a bite, or even a scratch and you would die. He had seen that even more.

What with travelling and the rotters, there wasn't much time for Danny to play with his dad anymore. Dad was always busy. Always helping people, or fighting the rotters, or planning. So when Dad came to see him and said that there was a game of catch going on down in the service bay, Danny jumped at the chance. He told the kids that they should all play, but little Stevie wanted to watch Shrek. Stevie didn't have anybody, his mom and dad got eaten, and he was shy.

Danny, Robbie, Rosie, and little Savanna wanted to play though, so they all followed Dad and one of the new people down the stairs and into the garage. The garage was big! It had three things that could lift up a whole truck, and right now Calvin was under one of the trucks and black stuff was coming out of the bottom into a bucket. Danny thought it was oil, but he wasn't sure.

Rosie had told Danny that the new guy was a policeman. Rosie said she knew a bunch of cops, but Danny didn't know any. The policeman threw the ball to Danny (underhanded) and Danny whipped it at his dad, who caught it and threw it to Robbie, (underhanded, lame). Robbie dropped it and it went rolling so he ran after it. He picked it up and threw it to Rosie, and they went around in a circle for a while, throwing it back and forth. Robbie only caught one ball. Danny thought it was funny to see

Robbie laugh when he chased the ball after he dropped it. If it was Danny who kept dropping it, he would have gotten mad, but Robbie laughed and so did everyone else.

Danny threw the ball extra hard to Robbie so he would drop it again, but this time he caught it and threw it back to Danny, who wasn't expecting it. The ball sailed over his head and went rolling against the wall. Thinking that maybe it was kind of fun to chase the ball, Danny ran for it. It rolled under a metal shelf-thing with all sorts of car parts on it. "I'll get it," he yelled and crawled under the table next to the shelves. He couldn't reach it, so he had to crawl behind the storage system. He got the ball, but when he stood up he bumped his head on something. It was a doorknob. He came out from behind the shelf and under the table rubbing his head. The bump had hurt but it wasn't terrible, and he was done crying. Danny would never cry again.

"You okay, kiddo?" his dad asked.

"Yeah, I bumped my head on the doorknob."

"Doorknob? There's a door back there?"

"Yeah, it's metal."

Teems looked at Rick with raised eyebrows.

"Can we play now?" asked Danny.

"In a minute. Rick, gimme a hand?"

Rick and Teems strode to the shelving system and pulled on it. It wouldn't budge. Rick put his hand through the shelves and felt smooth concrete on the back. The table was bolted down so Rick got on one knee and was about to crawl under when he noticed a slight semi-circular wear-mark on the floor. "Look at this. This shelf must swing out, look at that mark."

"I told you, nobody calls me Mark."

"No, the dig in the floor!"

"Oh, yeah."

It took a few minutes, but Teems found a small catch on the inside of one of the shelf brackets, and pushed it. The unit unlocked from the wall behind it, and they swung it out. There was indeed a door behind it. There wasn't a knob, but a metal handle. It was locked. "Calvin! Calvin come here!"

Calvin showed up quickly, "Why is it every time I'm working you gotta bug me?" He saw the door and pointed at it. "What's that?"

"A locked door, can you open it?"

"Uh...what if there are three hundred rotters on the other side?"

"Dammit, Calvin, the wall is only six feet thick, there can't be. All the same, let's get the kids upstairs and bust out the poles and guns."

When the children were safely staring at the group through a window on the second floor, and there were eight rifles six pistols and nine T-poles pointed at the door, Calvin looked at the lock. He scratched his head.

"Can you open it?" demanded Teems.

"Yup, gimme a sec." He ran off and came back with a giant sledge hammer. Before anybody could say anything, he swung the hammer and smashed the handle off the door in one blow. The handle went flying and the door stood ajar about two inches.

"Jesus, did you have to break it?"

"Do you have a key?"

Weapons were raised as Rick cautiously moved to the door and pulled it wide. A six-by-six-foot room was behind the door, empty save for an open hatch in the floor. Standing at the edge of the hole, he peered down with his tac-light. A ladder that descended fifteen or so feet down into another room.

He circled around to the back of the hatch cover and shone the light at it. There was nothing printed to indicate what was down the ladder.

After some discussion, Teems decided he needed to know what was down there, especially since they had broken the lock off of the door. He took a flashlight and a pistol and climbed halfway down the ladder. There was a larger room below with a military style heavy door on massive hinges. The door was slightly ajar and had a box of something in front of it. Teems climbed the rest of the way down and found an old push-button light switch which he pressed. With the room bathed in light, they couldn't discern anything spectacular about it. The box contained old magazines as far as he could tell. He called for Rick and Calvin to come down, and soon there were six people in the small room.

Rick wiped dirt off of the heavy door, and there was printing under a dusty aluminum American flag.

It read simply, LF 66.

22

"What mission? What are you talking about?"

"Your friends in the LAV were tight-lipped about the mission as well," replied the Captain. "All I could get out of them was that there *is* a mission."

Dallas also knew that there was trouble here. "What in the hell is an LAV?"

"It takes a soldier to know a soldier, sir, and you aren't one. I was speaking to him," he looked at Seyfert. "The United States is in peril, son, and I have been given leave by the current government to save it by any means necessary." The captain stood and walked to a privacy curtain. He whipped it back so Seyfert and Dallas could see what was on the other side. At first Seyfert couldn't recognize the man in the chair, but as he studied him further, he could tell it was Stark. Zip tied to a metal chair, he had been beaten to a bloody pulp, and was unconscious, his swollen face lolling backward slightly.

Dallas looked at their captor. "You son of a bitch."

"Sergeant, if this man opens his mouth again, close it for him," He looked back at the SEAL and pointed to Stark. "This man and his lieutenant came through here yesterday in the armored vehicle you see out front. The proximity of time in which you came here today is indicative to me that you are together. In addition, your sniper team on the water tower was another dead giveaway. They are in custody now and will be questioned later." The man walked up to Seyfert and pulled the SEAL's left T-shirt sleeve up. The tattoo that was there gave him away completely. "Navy. Figures. Now are you going to tell me what I want to know, or do you want to join him?" Again, he pointed to Stark. "He has proven himself an enemy of the Triumvirate, and of the United States."

"I noticed you put the Triumvirate first. *Sir.*"

"We are in charge. This is going nowhere. Sergeant, bind *him*," he pointed at Dallas, "to one of the chairs. We'll see how long it takes the SEAL to give in while his friend is questioned." The sergeant stepped forward, and snipped Dallas's zip tie with a cutter and moved him to another seat with arms. He was in the process of trussing the burly southerner up when another man came in and whispered something in the Captain's ear.

The captain looked unperturbed. "ETA?"

"Three minutes."

"Very well, prepare to receive him. Dismissed."

The man hurried out after issuing a *Yes, sir*, and the captain began a new tactic, "You are very lucky. One of the elite will be here shortly. One of The Three. He's coming to question you personally, but I wouldn't want to give him the impression we weren't trying." He slipped a black glove on and moved to Dallas. Looking over his shoulder, he asked with an air of finality, "Last chance, SEAL."

Seyfert looked helplessly at Dallas, who smiled and spat on the captain's boot. "You could use a shine there, Private Gump."

The man back-handed Dallas, punched him in the stomach, and then in the face. Dallas spat blood. "You hit like an ole' woman. Speakin' of ole' wimmin, your mom says hi. She was hangin' out with me—" The man punched him twice more.

"Captain, you could kill him, he has a concussion."

"Then you should probably tell me what I want to know soon." He punched again. And again.

"So this is your new world order, killing civilians?"

"To save my country?" the man asked incredulously. "I would kill as many as I needed. So should you." Dallas was unconscious, so the Captain slapped him, disgusted. "Typical."

Seyfert could hear the engine and rotors of a large helicopter. His captor perked up when he heard them as well. "I tried to be nice," was all he said, and he began removing his gloves. He strode from the tent, and Seyfert was left alone with two unconscious men, two guards and his thoughts. The captain had never even asked him his name.

After repeated futile attempts to rouse Dallas by calling to him, Seyfert pleaded to one of his guards to check for a pulse. The guard acquiesced, and told the SEAL that his friend was still alive. Then he and the other guard apologized for the terrible treatment they had received. One man slung his weapon and brought forth a wet cloth to wipe the Texan's face. Dallas's eyes fluttered, but he didn't wake.

The noise from the helicopter had grown extreme, and then diminished as the machine powered down. The captain returned ten minutes or so later with another group in tow. In addition to the returning soldier, there was a shorter man, older than the captain also in black camouflage, with the embroidered golden III on his breast. This man had a black beret, which he promptly removed when he entered the tent. He was armed with a pistol. Flanking him were two more men, each with a P90 submachine gun, and behind them was a giant, six foot ten easy. He had to duck when he came into the tent. He stood to the rear, holding on to a bloody and disheveled, albeit conscious and walking Androwski. His mouth was taped with duct tape.

Seyfert breathed a sigh of relief. At least they hadn't killed anyone yet.

The shorter man stepped forward. "You've been busy, Captain."

"Yes, sir, I have been trying to get them to reveal the mission specifics about their operation, but they have been…resolute."

"As well they should be." He looked at Seyfert. "This is the other SEAL?"

"Yes, sir, we haven't questioned him yet."

"Don't bother, it would be a waste of time." He glanced at Dallas and said matter-of-factly, "This man isn't military."

"No sir, he came in with this one just an hour ago."

"You worked him over pretty hard, Brooks would be impressed."

The captain half-smiled. "Thank you, sir."

"But I'm not." The new man pulled his pistol and shot the captain in the face. Two more suppressed *Pap!* noises came from behind him, and the two men with the submachine guns dropped to the floor. The leader aimed his weapon at the two guards. "Where did you serve before the plague?" The huge man had picked up the P90s from his fallen companions, and had one in each massive hand.

The guards looked nervous. "Uh…seventh infantry under Doherty. Sir."

He holstered his suppressed weapon. "Regular Army. Good, you can come with us. If you had been National Guard, I would have shot you both. Release this man, we need to get out of here. There's a sizable force of undead on the way, half an hour out. Five or six hundred at least, and they will follow the noise of the helo." As if to punctuate his statement, several rifle shots were heard from outside.

One of the guards stepped up and cut Seyfert's bonds. Rubbing his wrists, he stood and looked at the newcomer. He was confused. "What just happened?"

"I shot a brutal bastard, and Barry shot two more." He nodded toward the giant. "Look, son, I don't have time for bullshit, if we're still here in a half hour, we're all dead. There isn't enough ammo for the pack I saw on the way. I hear tell that LAV is yours?"

"Yes, sir."

"Take it and your injured friends and get out of here. I will ride in the Abrams with what soldiers are loyal to me that can fit, and Barry will drive one of the buses with the civilians and the rest. The other bus will have to stay here. We'll follow you, and assist you on your way to Boston, depositing the civvies in a safe place."

Seyfert was flabbergasted. "Sir, I...how did...when...?"

"You weren't the only group that was contacted by MIT. In fact, you are the back-up plan. We can discuss this along the way."

Seyfert folded his arms across his chest and scowled. "Sir, I don't trust you."

"Good," the man said without hesitation and drew his weapon, "My name is Colonel John Lester Bourne, and we are coming with you, or more to the point, you with us." He turned the weapon around and handed the butt end to Seyfert. "Change of plans, Barry you drive the tank, I will go with them." He then took Stark and threw him over his shoulder in a fireman's carry, Stark easily outweighing him by sixty pounds. "I will ride with you in the LAV and tell you what's going on, I can be your hostage if you want to call it that. Once I've given you the details of your mission, you will understand we are on the same side." Seyfert didn't move. "He's heavy, son," was all the colonel said, and he strode from the tent.

The giant soldier named Barry cut the zip tie on Androwski's wrists and passed him a P90. "You two," he said to the guards in a baritone voice, "with me."

The three left the tent with Androwski and Seyfert staring at each other, speechless.

23

Rick and Teems were staring at dusty old computer monitors in a computer room in the secret facility they had located. It looked as if the computers hadn't been touched in years. There was a huge screen over the monitors and smaller ones throughout the room. Chris Rawding, the resident computer geek, had been summoned and was on his way.

The underground installation they had found was fairly sizable, perhaps three times the size of the depot above. There were numerous doors and several tunnels that led to who knows where. Some of the doors were locked, but most were open, and even ajar. The Rock Steady's were exploring, and exclamations could be heard here and there. In one of the huge rooms were racks and racks of military MREs, meals ready to eat, and on others were older K-rations. Dozens of fifty-five gallon drums filled the rest of the room, and when one was opened, Teems said it smelled like a swimming pool. "Preserved water," Rick told him. "Probably good forever, although I bet it tastes like you're drinking out of a Jacuzzi."

There was a sleeping area with twenty bunk beds, the smelly mattresses rolled up and tied together with wire. A bathroom with community showers done in yellow tile was found near the sleeping area, and a workout room next to that with an ancient but functional Universal machine and some free weights. The other rooms were as yet to be explored or locked.

Chris showed up, awe on his face when he saw the banks of computers. "Those are old Micral P6's!" he shouted. "Nobody's seen one of those in forty years!" He looked around some more at the large screen and the radio equipment in the corner. Slowly he turned to Rick and Teems, "Do you know where we are right now?"

"No, that's why we called you. We figured you're our nerd and would tell us what all this is."

Chris swallowed hard. "This is your basic nuclear missile silo. It looks abandoned, and I doubt these rigs," he pointed at the computers, "will even fire up, but this is a missile silo!"

His obvious excitement was making Rick smile. "We got you kid, it's a silo. Why is that so wonderful?"

Chris looked at him like he had three heads. "Rick, if there was say, oh I don't know, a horrible plague of some kind, the safest place on the planet would probably be NORAD. After that, it would be a missile silo. This place probably has food and water for up to twenty people for thirty years if they didn't remove it! Not to mention escape tunnels, and a nuclear missile!"

"This place looks kind of...unused...don't you think they would have removed all the weapons and the missile?"

"Yeah! The military would have removed the warheads, and weapons, but left everything else. They probably plowed over the launch tube, and there are cornstalks over it now. There are probably two or three other silos attached to this one, each capable of sustaining two dozen or so people for years. This place is perfect for your group, Teems! Once we figure out the locks on the doors, a million of those things couldn't break in. They could wander all they want up in the depot, but they could never get down here."

"Well, that's good news. The thing is, we tend to move around a lot. Nomad-like, you know what I'm saying?"

"Teems! Do you know what *I'm* saying? This place is impregnable, probably stocked, and safe. You're on motorcycles. I've never heard of an armored Harley, so the first time you come over a hill or around a corner into a swarm of those things, you're history. You've got kids, stay here."

Rick was still smiling. "Kid's got a point, Teems. You might want to hole up here at least for the time being.

Danny showed up and called to his father. "Dad, can we play now?"

"You shouldn't be down here yet, buddy, we haven't cleared it."

"But Mr. Calvin said it was okay. He said that there was nobody but us down here."

Teems and his son continued to talk while Chris looked under the tables and benches and pored over the computers. Here and there the computer whiz would give short exclamations, and he was deep into his search of the area when Anna came in looking for Rick.

She pulled him aside and spoke in low tones while the others were busy. "Rick, we've got trouble."

"What kind of trouble?"

"The kind that rolls in with two tanks and a very familiar armored vehicle. There's a school bus and some other vehicles as well."

Rick put his fingers through his hair. "Jesus, a tank?"

"Looks just like the one we saw outside of Salt Lake, and it's coming up the road now. There's another tank thing with it too."

There were shouts inside the complex now, and Teems told his son to stay with Chris. By the time Rick and Teems got to the roof, the school bus, a blue Chevy Cavalier, two Humvees, and the LAV were already parked in the depot parking lot. The tank was rolling in. Men in black camo were exiting the Humvees with their hands on their heads. The back of the LAV opened, and Seyfert, Androwski, and a man Rick didn't know got out. Ed and the other bikers got out of the Humvees.

"Rick," Seyfert shouted, "we need Doc. Dallas and Stark are busted up! Hurry!" Two men Rick didn't know moved Dallas from the LAV to the ground in front of the depot door. Rick hurried downstairs and grabbed the doctor on the way. He told Teems to shut and lock the door, and not to let anyone in without his okay.

The doctor looked at Stark first, and concluded that the SEAL suffered from multiple contusions and abrasions, possibly a concussion and maybe a broken jaw. "Basically he had the shit beaten out of him," were his words.

Dallas was in worse shape.

"I told this man not to take any whacks to the head. What happened? He looks like he was on the losing side of a bar fight."

"He was interrogated by one of my underlings," the shorter man said. "That particular problem has been rectified, but others have arisen, I'm afraid."

Rick narrowed his eyes. "Who are you exactly?"

"We can discuss those formalities soon, but we should get inside. A sizable force of undead were almost upon us at the checkpoint, and they most certainly will follow our engine noises, not to mention any undead presence in the general vicinity of this facility. I believe your friends have vetted me already."

"He's on our side, Rick," Androwski agreed. "Or if he isn't then we're all screwed anyway."

24

The depot had ample room for all the vehicles as it had been devoid of any farm equipment. Once they were parked inside, and twenty six new family members from the school bus were introduced, the new man told an interesting story.

The Triumvirate was nothing more than three men with power. Bourne, Brooks, and Recht. Bourne had the military personnel and most of the equipment, as he was a colonel in the US Army. Initially, his mission was to contain the spread of the plague by destroying highways and off ramps using explosives and heavy machinery. That had failed. Command had then decided on a new tactic, and the mission parameters changed to the fortification and holding of Lincoln, Nebraska against the undead menace at all costs. There had been significant success at first, then contact with command was lost, as were supply routes and reinforcements. Short on fighters, equipment, and food, Bourne had resorted to asking the locals for help.

He came across a group of about two thousand people holed up in Cornhusker Stadium following a televangelist by the name of Zachary Recht. Recht had an unbelievable hold on the people of the mid-west before the plague, but now his grip had been solidified. People thought he was the second coming. Literally. Bourne soon found out that whatever Recht asked of his people, they did it. They did it without question, and Bourne realized that he could get things done with this man in charge of the civilians. A week after Bourne met him, Recht had his own security squad armed with submachine guns, and he had converted a luxury box in the stadium to his own private penthouse, complete with kept women. Apparently his sexual proclivities leant toward the weird, and he had more than enough women willing to further said depravities. He and all his followers believed that the undead were sinners who hadn't or wouldn't repent, and he referred to them as *The Fallen*. His daily sermons had an odd effect on many folks, and even the most devout atheists were soon in his camp. He also walked almost daily through the tent-city that was the inside of the stadium, personally ministering to the sick or injured, or giving spiritual guidance to the faithful and unfaithful alike. The people loved him.

One final supply chopper had landed in the stadium, and that chopper had contained a bona fide Superman. Brooks. This man was a CIA asset of the most unpredictable kind, and came with all kinds of wonderful toys. Satellite links, locations of weapon caches in rural Nebraska towns as well as in Lincoln and nearby other cities, and security codes to almost every covert installation in the mid-west. The man was a genius with everything from fixing the plumbing at the stadium, to hacking the security system on an A10 Thunderbolt attack jet, to killing undead with his bare hands without so much as a scratch. He was the kind of guy that knew everything about everything, and was *always* the guy who could kill everyone in the room. He even had a military airfield at his disposal. The only problem was he was an evil, sadistic bastard. He had no compunctions about killing anyone who he thought posed a problem of any kind, and people who so much as disagreed with him tended to go missing, or were found stumbling around with their throat cut or even worse, with no visible wounds at all, looking for someone to eat. He was a master at interrogation, and could get information from most people without torture, but he enjoyed the torture so much that he would often "interrogate" someone for days without asking any questions.

After they had fortified the stadium, the three men got to talking, and they formed an alliance.

Bourne controlled the fighters and military equipment, Recht the people, and Brooks knew everything. There was no more government as they knew it, and supplies were not coming in anymore, so something needed to be done. Forays were organized into the city proper to gather equipment, supplies, and more people, which they had found in droves at first, and then they started to dwindle. As the survivors waned, the undead waxed, and soon there were fifty thousand undead beating against the walls and fortifications of Cornhusker Stadium. Weapons and ammo were running short, so a plan was made. Bourne would train soldiers, Recht would provide morale, and Brooks would procure everything they needed and provide "security." In two weeks, the undead population outside the gates had grown to almost eighty thousand, and in four weeks the soldiers, equipment and training had reduced that number to stragglers that came out of the city or the surrounding countryside. The gates to the stadium were opened, but remained well-manned, and teams had begun to scour the city in earnest.

One day, Brooks and his team had come back driving an eighteen-wheel semi-truck full of goodies, not the least of which were black BDUs. Hundreds of them. Recht thought that the community should have a name, and he went religious, but Brooks was a huge fan of Roman history, so he came up with The Triumvirate. Recht loved it. It didn't focus on a place, or even on a government, but on a ruling class of people.

It was then that things started to go awry. An officer close to Bourne, Major Cushing, discovered that there were people going to see Recht that didn't come back. Mostly men, whose female partners Recht had taken a fancy to. The evening after Cushing had told Bourne about his discovery, Cushing had gone missing. After a search conducted personally by Brooks turned up no trace of the major, one of Cushing's men had come to Bourne with a cell phone. Cell phones hadn't worked in about a week. This call came from the wife of Major Cushing, who worked at the Massachusetts Institute of Technology. Dr. Cushing told Bourne exactly what Rick's ex-wife had told Rick's group, down to the last detail. Bourne said he would get there as soon as possible, and Dr. Cushing told him that a colleague would try to phone her husband in California to try to get him to rescue them as well. Apparently, the man was capable. A second phone call confirmed the contact between MIT and a military group containing SEALs, who had fortified Alcatraz. The group would come for the scientists, but they were a long way off. Bourne had to move fast.

The problem was that Recht now had a huge security staff, all were undyingly loyal, and all had P90 submachine guns supplied by Brooks. Recht strutted around like the President at a high-school commencement with personal security and snipers in the stands. He had become untouchable, and started to flaunt his religious superiority.

The radio broadcasts had started soon after, and people came in droves. In another two weeks, the population of the enclave had grown to nine thousand. Then the checkpoints started. At key locations on both interstates and rural roads, soldiers waited for travelers, and stuck them on buses all headed to Lincoln, whether they wanted to go or not. Refusal meant serious consequences.

Anyone bitten was executed on the spot, children included, and those who refused to be inspected were beaten into submission and inspected anyway. More often than not, these people, or anyone else who didn't conform, had "bites" in undisclosed locations, and were put down immediately.

When Bourne had gone to Brooks and Recht to speak to them about the executions, they told him that while he was in charge of the military, Brooks was in charge of security, and he could conscript whomever he chose, including Bourne's men. It was then that Bourne realized these men didn't need him anymore, and the gold stitching on the BDUs might just have two IIs instead of three in the near future.

That night when he picked up his volume of *The Art of War*, (which he read passages from every night), a transmitter had fallen out of the worn spine. A bug. The colonel found two more in his room, one in a light switch, and one under the desk, both in his luxury box. There were probably ten more he couldn't find.

The next day, Brooks was waiting for him when he woke up at 0430 hrs. Brooks was sitting across from his makeshift bed reclining in a chair reading Bourne's copy of *The Art of War*. He called out, and two of Recht's men came in shortly after, both with submachine guns. They were to be the colonel's security detail, and he wasn't to go anywhere without them anymore. Bourne had just received his first order from someone other than a general.

When the call came in from Captain Brady, who had been under Bourne's command, that they had detained elements of the military complete with armored transport, Bourne knew he could use this opportunity to bug out. He brought his most trusted man, Gunny Barry Steele, and seven others -including his security detail- with him on a Blackhawk helicopter to intercept and question the detainees.

Brady had always been a little over the top, but Bourne thought he was loyal, until Brady had started working with Brooks over the last two weeks. Bourne was certain he was in on the disappearance of Cushing, as Cushing stood in his way on the military hierarchy. So did Bourne.

Bourne was not a murderer, but there was no way Brady could be allowed to report back to Brooks. He had to go.

He planned to rendezvous with the military elements that had been detained, and conscript them if necessary. When Bourne found out that Seyfert was a SEAL, he took a chance, dropped non-integral information and was instantly rewarded. He now had mission capable soldiers at his disposal, or so he hoped. They were even on the same mission.

Immediately prior to leaving for the depot, the colonel had the Blackhawk destroyed, hopefully with any of Brooks' transmitters aboard. Every one of the men at the checkpoint had agreed that they didn't want to go back to the stadium, back to Brooks and Recht, so they all came with the colonel.

"So here we are. The real question is, do you trust me enough to combine forces and go get those scientists, or do we split up? Either way, I'll see you in Boston if any of us survive."

Barry Steele was an intimidating man. At six foot nine and almost four hundred pounds of muscle and sinew, he scared the average MMA fighter with his size alone. Most doorways barely fit him, and three of the extra-large black BDUs that Brooks brought in had been needed to tailor the big man's Triumvirate uniform. When he got out of the tank after parking it in the depot, everyone stared. He was used to it, and shrugged it off. When the tiny boy named Stevie came up and asked if he was a giant, he got down on his haunches, looked in Stevie's tiny face, and said yes.

"I've never met a giant before. Can I ride on your shoulders?"

Barry stood. "Nobody's ever asked me that before."

"So, can I?"

Scooping up the boy, Barry lifted him until his small legs were on either side of the soldier's massive cranium, and then he proceeded to walk around. In ten seconds, every kid in the depot was begging for a turn, and when they had all received a ride, Barry showed them the inside of the Abrams and the Bradley.

While the big gunnery sergeant kept the kids busy, the colonel and most of his soldiers, the SEALs, Rick's group, and Teems were planning the rest of their trip to Boston. Dallas was awake and the doctor was ministering to him, but Stark still hadn't regained consciousness. Calvin and one of the army engineers had gone up to the roof and were installing a fifty caliber heavy machine gun, and the other new-comers were making themselves at home, and figuring out a work schedule. Many of the civilians on the bus hadn't wanted to go to Lincoln in the first place, and the ones who had come looking for it all decided that the place they were in now was probably safer.

Bourne was impressed with the installation, but soon had an epiphany. He looked at Teems and said, "It's a fair bet that Brooks knows about this place."

"How could he know about this?" the biker said, spreading his arms. "We just stumbled onto it today."

"The man just knows. He knows everything, that was his job, and apparently he's the best at it. I'm torn between thinking you won't find a safer place than this, and that it might just be your tomb."

"We can fight."

"He won't come knocking at the door. He'll send scouts, and when they report back to him, he'll send a small army. Or a large one."

"We can hold this place forever."

The colonel was skeptical. "I hope so."

Bourne was marking a road atlas of the US with red marker. The marks were where roads and throughways had been destroyed at the outset of the plague to curb the spread of infection. The colonel looked alarmed when there were shots from outside, but Teems told him that it was probably a few rotters that had gotten too close to the depot, and the snipers were taking care of them. They continued to talk and the shots went from sporadic to continuous. Then the fifty cal opened up and Bourne's engineer called on the radio.

The colonel looked at the people with him in turn. "We may have a problem."

Everyone looked nervous. "What it is?" demanded Teems.

"Let's get to the roof to confirm."

The fifty cal was very loud as they climbed the stairs to the second floor catwalks. Looking out one of the office windows, Rick could see that they might just be in serious trouble. It would seem their secret was out, as hundreds of zombies were again pouring out of the corn heading for the depot. The main body of the horde was just starting to reach the killing field of the fifty caliber machine gun and dozens were on the ground either not moving or missing body parts and crawling toward the sanctuary.

Bourne went into high gear as he made it to the roof. "WILCOX! Lay off the fifty until they're bunched! Anyone with a rifle get to the roof and defend! Pick your targets, head shots only! Barry! Where's Barry?" The colonel spun around and the giant man was behind him. "Barry! Get in the Abrams with Richards and Monahan and get it out of the depot. Use the treads, but don't fire the main gun. You'll have to hurry so we can get the door closed before they reach the other side of the building." The man kept firing off orders to others he had just met, or barely knew, and they jumped to follow him. Rick thought of his friend submarine commander McInerney back on Alcatraz. Both men commanded authority, and Rick was amazed that Bourne was able to remember the names of the colonel's new recruits.

Rick pulled Teems aside. "Get the kids and anybody else who wants to go into the silo, make sure Chris and Anna are down there, and then lock yourselves in. Shut the top hatch but leave the bottom door open so you can hear us call for you. Don't let anybody in if you can't figure out who they are."

"Rick, I'm staying up here to fight the rotters off, I can..."

"You can help Dallas, and keep your son safe. There's no time to discuss this, and don't let Dallas give you any shit, either, get him down there."

The Abrams tank fired up its diesel engine with a growl. Sixteen people stood on either side of the tank ready for whatever came through when it opened, and the Bradley and the LAV had the back hatches open to receive these folks should something go awry. Three of Teems' T-poles were in use on each side of the tank, with three gunners and two men wielding harpoons per side as well. The rest of the depot community was either on the roof or in the silo.

It had taken almost ten minutes to maneuver the vehicles out of the way so the Abrams could move into position in front of the garage door, and Bourne inwardly cursed himself for being so stupid as to not foresee of the problem beforehand. In the time that it took to move the other vehicles, the mass of dead had reached the depot and were smashing their fists on the concrete walls. A minimal force had traversed to the far side of the building, and the snipers above culled as many as possible before someone figured that more dead were coming to that side because of the shots.

"Open it!" someone yelled, and the door began to rise. Several undead knees were revealed as the door slowly ascended, and several of the more impatient zombies dropped down to crawl under and into the facility.

The men with the poles went to work and held as many creatures as they could at bay while the ones behind hurried to spear them. The door moved painfully slowly as the men and women fought off the onslaught. Calvin was one of the spearmen, and six inches of his pointed pole was protruding from the back of the skull of an undead housewife wearing a brown-stained apron with *Kiss the Cook* on it, when two zombies broke the front line and one grabbed him. A shot rang out as he frantically pulled on his harpoon, the dead weight of the re-killed woman dragging it away from him. One of the breachers dropped, but the one who had grabbed his shirt sleeve lunged and snapped at his arm. He let go of the spear and used his hands to fight the thing off. He punched it in the face as the tank rumbled forward, the door already closing.

The commotion at the door had attracted many more undead, the snipers on the roof trying to deal with as many as they could. The fifty caliber was firing steady too now that the horde was closer and bunched together. The massive shells blew the encroaching host limb from limb, scattering bits and pieces of undead flesh, bone, and organs on the dirt.

As soon as the tank was out the door, the gap was filled by more zombies, but the giant metal door was mostly down. A surge pushed the defenders back as the roll-down gate reached head height, and the young woman manning the push-button door control screamed for the defenders to drive the creatures back or the door wouldn't close all the way. The door would get stuck on the bodies.

The door continued to close, cutting the enemy down to sixteen inside and dozens outside. The snipers could see that several of the exterior creatures had turned to chase the rumbling Abrams. The undead who had breached the depot began to spread out, and the defenders fought for their lives. Two creatures grabbed a young man from the bus and fell on him, biting and clawing. He became hysterical as he fought them off, and received help when a harpoon pierced the skull of the skinny girl who was trying to bite his stomach. The other thing, a dead orderly by the looks of his stained blue scrubs, was held at bay by the young man as he pulled the thing's hair with one hand and held its face away with the other. Someone shot it and it went limp, the man pitching it off to the side.

With the T-poles, the harpoons, and the guns, the battle lasted less than a minute. There were twenty nine re-killed creatures, and the defenders looked around and started cheering, but trailed off as the young woman with the door control started yelling that the door wasn't all the way down. There was a ten-inch gap where the metal frame couldn't reach the ground. Several undead lay in its path blocking the closure. Three had been destroyed, but two were still moving, one with its legs moving feebly on the inside of the door, the other trapped at the waist and pushing up with its hands, hopelessly trying to free itself.

Calvin grabbed a harpoon off the floor and strode to the pinned zombie, who immediately smashed its face on the ground when it reached both arms at Calvin and snarled. "Stupid fucker," he said and stabbed the weapon into its head. The defenders used the T-poles to shove the rest of the things that were caught under the door back outside as best they could. Apparently, the word was out though, and many of the creatures had dropped to their hands and knees and were trying to get through the gap.

As a creature would get its head under the door, the defenders would stick it with a spear, and someone else would shove it back out. Soon there was a small wall of lifeless people on the outside of the door, and it was able to be closed all the way. A second cheer went up.

Doc was looking at the man from the bus, who had deep red furrows on his right forearm and cheek from the things that had pinned him. It didn't look too bad, but the doctor wanted him isolated and watched just the same. The doc stood up and looked around, wiping his brow, and noticed Calvin. Calvin was staring at his hand as everyone else was congratulating each other on the victory, with hearty claps on the back and high fives.

Calvin looked up as the doctor approached, his eyes glazed. "It must have happened when I punched the one that grabbed me." Doc took his friend's hand and examined it. There was a small gash on the knuckle above the ring finger. Calvin looked at the doctor knowingly. "Shit. After all this, I kill myself."

Doc swallowed. "Now, we don't even know how you got this for sure. We'll clean it out and watch you, but don't assume that it's fatal just yet."

The biker nodded, but the look on his friend's face spoke volumes.

The tank used its treads to do the job outside, and it ground the wretched former humans into pulp as it ran them over. The problem was that there were so many of them that it was difficult to get them all, and the procedure took the better part of the day. The snipers had stopped firing to conserve ammunition, as had the large machine gun. Bourne was in constant contact with Barry in the tank giving him orders and locations of pockets of stragglers via the radio and his rooftop vantage point. When all was said and done, better than eight hundred undead had been pulverized, shot, bludgeoned, or harpooned.

Bourne came down off the roof five hours after the first dead person showed up, to see three people on stretchers. He knew the names of two of them, Private Hobbs and a biker named Calvin, but the third man was unknown to him. All three looked to be in bad shape. Hobbs was vomiting, and the unknown man was unconscious, and in the process of being secured to his gurney with restraints by the resident doctor. A single blood-red tear ran from the man's eye. Calvin was coherent, with a damp cloth on his forehead. Several people, including the big man Teems, Seyfert, and Rick were talking with Calvin.

"Bullshit," joked Teems, "you'll be fine, ya dumb hick. It isn't a bite."

"I punched him in the face and his tooth cut my hand. What's the difference, a bite or a cut by a tooth? I'm screwed, and it would probably be easier on me if you all just quit bullshitting me about it."

Bourne furrowed his brow as he approached the group. "What happened?"

Private Hobbs wiped his mouth with a rag and tried to sit up. "Sir, when—"

"Lay back down, soldier, you can tell me from there."

"Thank you, sir. When we opened the garage door to let the Abrams out, there were more than we anticipated outside. Several got in, and we had no choice but to go hand to hand. Sir, the folks here are good people and damn good fighters."

"Agreed, son. Why are you sick, were you bitten?"

"Negative, sir. That guy," he indicated the unconscious man, "had two of the Fallen on him, and I dragged one off and shot it. There was some spray and it hit me in the face." He looked away. "I must have become infected because of the shit that got on me."

"We don't know you're infected, it could be anything."

"Due respect, sir, but *I* know. I can feel it."

"Me too," Calvin said from the other gurney. "I can't tell if it's something extra or if I'm missing something, but I can feel it just the same."

The doctor gave a sharp intake of breath and backed quickly away from the man who had been unconscious. The man was feebly struggling to sit up, and was emitting a low, guttural growl.

Doc wiped his brow with his sleeve and shook his head. "He was alive five minutes ago."

The private vomited again and closed his eyes muttering. He was obviously scared. Calvin was angry. "Dammit. I didn't want to go like this. Not like this. Puking and feeling like shit until I try to get up and eat my friends." The private began to sob quietly on the bed next to him.

"Calvin, you are too damn pretty to die. You'll be fine."

The biker mechanic sat up so fast the cool cloth on his forehead went flying. "Knock it off, asshole! I'm fucking dead already!" he spat venomously. "If you keep..." Calvin caught himself and immediately looked horrified. "Sorry Teems, I'm... I'm just mad. It's so... so *unfair*," he lay back down. "Doc, best tie me down too. I honestly wanted to jump off the table and kill my best friend for a second there, and that ain't me, I don't get mad."

"Do it, Doc," Teems said in a heartrending voice. "Calvin is right, he never gets pissed."

Rick spoke up. "What do we do with him?" He pointed at the young zombie strapped to the stretcher.

Doc reached down to a gleaming stainless steel table and picked up a small instrument. He put on a face shield, grabbed the dead man's hair and yanked his head to the side. The surgical drill entered through the ear and the dead man's struggles ceased. "We bury him."

25

Private Hobbs died at 20:44 hours on as near as anyone could tell, a Sunday night. The colonel sat with him next to his gurney until he lost consciousness, then he called the doctor. By the time the doc got there two minutes later, Hobbs was snapping through his restraints at his commanding officer. The doctor's drill did its job again.

Calvin's left eye had started turning crimson at 18:00 hrs according to Boone's watch, almost three hours before Hobbs died. The biker began to babble about his mother and a dog named Lug Nuts soon after that. He lost consciousness at 18:40. He never puked once.

He didn't die either. At 20:51, as they were unstrapping Hobbs from his steel slab, Calvin started screaming. He thrashed against his bonds, and Teems came running.

"Calvin, are you..." Teems backed up slowly.

The mechanic did everything he could to break the leather straps holding him in place. He thrashed so violently he tore the skin on his arms under the straps. He slammed the back of his head against a now blood-stained pillow repeatedly in frustration. It was clear he wanted to kill something, and his friend was the closest to him. One of his teeth cracked and fell out as he snapped his jaws closed.

"I'm sorry, Teems," the colonel said. "He was a good man. Irreplaceable as well."

"You don't know the half of it. This is gonna be real hard on Danny, and the rest of the Steadys."

The doctor came over with his drill yet again, but stopped short, "This man isn't dead. Look at his chest, he's still breathing."

"He's a runner then," Rick said. "We've seen some before. They're feral, and will attack anyone they get close to. They're infected, but not dead."

"We've seen them before," Teems said.

The colonel nodded. "As have we. The good side is that they can be killed like any normal human, then they get up again. The bad is that they are very fast and resistant to pain."

Teems brightened. "But if he ain't dead, doesn't that mean he can take this cure and be okay?"

Rick shook his head. "I don't know. My ex-wife told me that anyone that was already infected was incurable, but that was before we knew about the runners. The cure, if it works, can only prevent people from getting back up. You'll still die if bitten, but once you die you stay dead."

"I'll take that, it's better than the alternative," said Bourne.

"Yeah but what if it does work? I can't just kill Calvin knowing that he could have been saved."

"I'm sorry, Teems, but we don't even know if the cure works at all, let alone on a runner. Besides, we're fifteen hundred miles away. How would you contain him for as long as it will take to get the cure back here, assuming we survive the trip and get it in the first place? The country is crawling with zombies."

"Don't forget the Triumvirate," the colonel added, "Although now they're probably calling themselves something else. They're going to be searching for me, and no doubt Brooks knows about a secret mission from San Francisco to Boston by now, so he'll be searching for you as well."

"Gentlemen, this doesn't solve our immediate problem," said the doctor. "What do we do with Calvin?"

"Can you sedate him?"

Doc rummaged through what looked like a tackle box and came out with a syringe and a small bottle of clear liquid. He injected the now shrieking Calvin in the forearm with the stuff, and the infected man calmed down almost immediately, although he still lazily snapped at the doctor while he was close.

Ed was standing behind the group. "What did you give him?"

"Valium," answered the doc. "Actually, it's a concoction of valium and morphine I mixed together. I could have used Thorazine, although I don't know why they would have that at this facility. The Thorazine would drop an elephant. Normally, I wouldn't mix an opiate with—"

Teems pointed. "Jesus, look at him, he looks almost normal."

Calvin had indeed calmed down, and his blood red gaze was locked on to Teems, who took a tentative step toward his friend. He stooped to pick up Calvin's tooth and the doctor yelled at him, "Don't touch it! It has infected fluids all over it." Doc used a surgical glove to pick up the tooth and he discarded it in a plastic bag. "Therein lies the problem, my friend. If we keep him here, eventually he will infect someone else, regardless of how he's isolated or how careful we are around him. Not to mention he might not eat. I've seen the runners attack people and tear into them, but they don't eat the people like the rotters do. Besides, if he does eat, who would feed him? You can't get close enough without him trying to kill you."

Calvin's hands were clenching and unclenching into fists, and his eyes began to leak what appeared to be blood. His breathing started to speed up, and he turned his gaze from Teems to the others nearby.

"How much of that shit did you pump into him, Doc?" demanded Ed.

"Enough that he should barely be conscious, and extremely happy besides."

The restrained biker started moving more quickly on his stainless steel bench, and he began to emit a low growl as he looked back into Teems' eyes. His lip curled into a snarl and he clenched his teeth.

Doc looked at his syringe, and then at the small vial he had used. "That should have put him in a near coma. I... I don't understand."

"The dead are walking, Doc," Rick said. "The rules have changed."

"Now what do we do?" Teems asked, his eyes locked with Calvin's.

Bourne stepped up. "Considering this infection is strong enough to oust whatever medication you gave him in less than five minutes, I think the answer is clear."

"What answer? What's clear?"

"I'm sorry, Teems, but you need to put him down?"

"You mean kill him? Put him down like a...a sick dog?"

"If you need to think of it that way, please do." Teems started to argue, but the colonel raised his hand. "Consider the alternative, he bites or scratches someone, and then your enclave here is infected from within. Let me ask you this: Would he want that? If it were you, would you?"

Teems looked down, defeated. "No. No I wouldn't."

26

The Rock Steadys took the news hard, but Calvin wasn't the first person they had lost, nor would he probably be the last. The doctor had given him an overdose of his concoction, enough morphine alone to kill three men, he had said, and when their friend had stopped breathing, Doc used his drill again.

Teems, six foot three and two hundred seventy pounds of Harley Davidson-riding Biker, cried like a baby. They buried Calvin, Private Hobbs, and Mitch, the young man who had been scratched that evening, under the cover of snipers and the Bradley. The zombies left them alone while the humans completed their cheerless task.

When they were finished, Bourne called the SEALs, Rick, and Teems to a meeting in one of the second floor offices.

"The folks in Boston are running out of time. They have maybe two weeks of supplies left, and then they start getting hungry, and that will make them sloppy. We should be able to make decent time in your LAV but it will be extremely crowded. We will have to appropriate transportation for the extra muscle I'm bringing along the way."

Androwski looked confused. "Muscle?"

"Yes, in addition to your SEAL team, I will be taking ten of my men with me. The rest will stay here and defend this place against the undead and, once they figure out where you are, the Triumvirate too. We blew the Blackhawk when we left the checkpoint, as I have no doubt that Brooks put some type of locator on it, but that was only a few miles from here. Eventually they'll see this facility and come knocking."

"How are these people supposed to fight off those soldiers?" Rick asked. "They're all civilians!"

"As I said, I'm only bringing ten of my boys with me. Barry will stay behind as he's the only one qualified to drive the Abrams. He and some of the other members of my team will train your civilians in the proper use of firearms and munitions, tactics, and stealth. The civvies will also be trained on how to use the armor, both the tank and the Bradley. Trust me, loading a Bradley is not a five minute operation." Bourne looked at the biker. "Teems, you always have the silo to fall back into should things get out of control up here. Barry can more than fortify what you have below such that a nuclear warhead would be needed to gain access."

"The kids do think that place is cool."

"So do I. The fact that it's a nuclear launch facility notwithstanding, you have an underground fortress with multiple egress points, food and water for years, and probably weapons once you get all those doors open. That boy Chris might just be able to get sat signals with those archaic computers as well, assuming the satellite orbit hasn't degraded too much."

"Chris is going to want to come with us," Rick said.

"Absolutely out of the question. Your civilian team, with the exception of yourself, will need to remain onsite here while we carry out the mission."

"Due respect, Colonel," began Androwski, "we were given orders by my CO to both keep Rick and his team safe. All the way to Boston and back. Following your orders would compromise my CO's, and I'm not willing to do that. Not to mention, telling Dallas he can't come could get...unpleasant."

In the end, the colonel acquiesced to bringing Dallas and Anna along with Rick, but Chris elected to stay behind. Androwski and his SEALS couldn't make Chris come with them, so they were relieved of responsibility as far as he was concerned. The kid hadn't come up from the silo since he first went down there, and he had already figured out how to power down some of the electronic door locks.

There were six of Rick's original team, plus four others including the colonel, in the LAV. Eight others would also be coming, four each in a black Dodge Ram pickup and a Humvee. The second Humvee would remain behind as additional light-armored transport.

Dallas was on his feet and demanding to go in his most belligerent tone before anyone told him he was already slotted to go. "Concussion my ass, I'm fit as a goddam fiddle." He looked at the doctor and smiled. "Damn quacks dunno what they're talkin' 'bout anyway."

Good-byes were said, and Anna actually kissed Chris on the cheek when he came up from the silo. Stunned, he put his hand to his cheek and remained silent. "Well don't get all emotional on me, you big sissy," she said, "and don't go getting eaten."

"I would like to see you again," he answered and smiled a wan smile, "so if you could please not die, I might let you kiss me again."

She raised her eyebrows, "Let me? Huh. We'll see when I get back."

She left him blinking, and moved off with the soldiers. Rick and Dallas came up next, and Rick grabbed his hand, as Dallas put his hand on the young man's shoulder, "Been through a lot with you boy, gonna miss your sorry ass."

"What our red-necked hillbilly is trying to say is that he's going to worry about you."

"About him? Ha! He should be worryin' bout us! Take care of yourself, kid."

"You too, big guy." Chris leaned forward and embraced the Texan. Surprised, the man hugged back and then pushed hastily away. He thumbed at Anna. "Thought you liked *girls*."

Rick shook Chris's hand again. "I must admit, I'm glad one of you has the sense to remain in a safe spot."

"Sense?" Dallas asked in mock rage. "Sense! If *you* had any sense you'd stay here with the kid. Can't shoot worth a damn anyway, prolly shoot me for we git out that damn LAV," he muttered as he strode off.

Chris got serious. "Rick, don't take any dumb chances, you've got Sam to think about."

"Dumb? Me?"

"Yeah, you. Remember to save your own ass when you're saving everybody else's."

"Will do. You and I have been together since the beginning, stay safe."

Chris hugged Rick as well. "Always." He looked over Rick's shoulder. "And if you wouldn't mind bringing her back, I would be happy with that."

"She's feisty, I'll do what I can. Take care of these folks, they're good people."

Rick looked around the depot once more then joined his team inside the LAV. Teems poked his head inside when he was done shaking hands with Dallas and Seyfert. "Watch them rotters," he said to the crew, "they bite! See ya, hillbilly!"

"You sure will, psycho! Back before you can say Harley Davidson!"

The cheerful expression on Teems' face dropped away as the hatch closed on the LAV. "Harley Davidson," he said to himself and moved to the side.

27

A small fire crackled in the waning light of the Iowa sun. A group of nine sat around the fire on the road, or broken debris from it as they spoke back and forth. Several others kept watch from atop the LAV or in the bed of a Dodge pickup. The back hatch of the armored vehicle was open, and Anna strode out of it, using a fingernail to pick her teeth. "Nobody thought to bring any floss?"

The fire they were sitting around was a cook fire. An empty cardboard case of MREs sat nearby, it served as a trash can for the discarded plastic packages associated with the military rations. Each Meal Ready to Eat had its own flameless ration heater, essentially a water activated, environmentally safe, plastic bag. Heating the beef stew and chunk-chicken dinners was always better over a fire though, and the team was in the middle of nowhere on a barren, partially destroyed road, so the colonel called a halt to heat the food and stretch everyone's legs.

"Seriously, nobody? This damn chicken is stuck in my teeth."

"Use your toothbrush," the colonel said and went back to his map.

"Tried that," Anna replied to herself and made sucking noises as she continued the attempt to remove the lodged poultry.

Bourne rubbed his jaw as he traced his finger on a Rand McNally road atlas. "Better than six hours and no Triumvirate. I thought for sure they would have this road watched."

Androwski pointed at the atlas too. "We're more than a hundred miles north of I-80, did they have patrols out this far?"

"Patrols? Probably not anymore, the Warthogs and birds were fuel eaters, and both fuel and maintenance techs are hard to come by, not to mention pilots and the constant threat of undead roamers at the airfield. Checkpoints though, those I can envision this far north."

"Do ya think they'll look for ya?" asked Dallas.

"I'm sure of it. The average guy would see the downed helicopter back at that checkpoint and assume we crashed. There were hundreds of undead a few miles from that position too, so hopefully they came to investigate and at least wandered through. Best case scenario, the dead decided to hang around, and the Triumvirate stooges sent to check will assume the area was overrun. Brooks isn't the average guy, though. He will want to see the destruction for himself, regardless of undead infestation, and when he does, he will understand immediately that it was a tank shell that took out the copter." Bourne smiled. "Then he's going to get pissed and shoot somebody. Hopefully it's one of his guys. Make no mistake though, he'll come looking."

"With any luck, they'll miss the depot and not come this far north or east," Rick thought out loud.

"Sir," one of the lookouts said from the back of the Dodge. "Sir, there's a vehicle inbound from the west. Make that two."

Bourne was all business after that. "Rick, Dallas, and Anna back in the LAV, Stark, you're driving, button up. I want snipers on the LAV, and get the truck on the other side of the armor. Weapons hot, people, safeties off! Androwski and Seyfert, remove your suppressors. If they fire on us, return fire immediately, focus on the vehicle drivers and any heavy weapons first. If they are Triumvirate, I would rather they not know I'm here, but you guys will stick out like sore thumbs. I will man the Bushmaster. Fire at will if they get hostile!"

"Radio check!" yelled Androwski. Several *check-checks* and *five by fives* came over everyone's radio, as folks scrambled to follow orders. The Dodge was moved in front of a now sideways LAV, and the Humvee was pulled off to the side of the broken road.

The vehicles had been coming at high speed, but they seemed to slow, then stopped about a quarter of a mile away. The soldier who had spied the vehicles coming shouted through the radio, "Sir! Two just jumped and headed into the brush. I have scope glare! Snipers, repeat snipers!" Everybody got down behind something, and the turret on the now closed up LAV swiveled toward the road.

"Biggs, Keleher, do you have the snipers?"

"Roger that, sir, these rifles are unbelievable! Kelly, I got left."

The soldier standing to the right of the LAV with one of the THOR sniper rifles swiveled his bipod and braced against the hull of the vehicle, adjusting his aim. "Copy. Right is mine. Five by five."

"Take them on Androwski's signal or if any hostile opens fire, then pick targets at will."

"Signal is *copasetic,*" Androwski said. "Repeat, fire on copasetic."

"Roger that."

Two more military Humvees came speeding up the road and stopped thirty meters short of the small convoy. "Shit," somebody said over the radio as men in black BDUs got out of the lead truck.

Androwski and Seyfert moved forward as two of the newcomers walked toward them. The SEALs pulled their black face covers down as they approached. Both of the men in black were armed, and although their rifles were pointed toward the ground, they looked anxious.

"That's far enough," Androwski said when five meters of pockmarked and burned asphalt separated the two groups. "What do you want?"

The man that had gotten out of the passenger's seat was unshaven and unkempt, and he spoke first. "Interesting way to meet new people. What's with all the hostility? We're here to help."

"How exactly do you intend to help us?"

The man smiled, showing a gap where his left front tooth used to be, "Relocation!" he said as if it were a saving grace. "We're here to help you to Lincoln, Nebraska, where there's food, shelter, and a military presence to guard the people against the Fallen."

"Not interested. And if you're military, I'm Bugs Bunny."

Unfazed, the Triumvirate man tried anew, "As I said, we have a strong military presence with armor and aircraft support. If you would please follow us, we can take you straight there. Of course, you will have to surrender your weapons and that tank to us immediately. Security, you understand."

Seyfert snorted. "I believe the man said we were fine. We're headed north, and don't need your protection. Thanks all the same."

The man's smile disappeared. "I'm sorry, I really am, but you are travelling in US military vehicles, and those have all been recalled to Lincoln, as have all military personnel and any civilians in the area. You and your companions will need to come with us."

Two more men got out of the first desert camo Humvee, and another popped through the hatch at the fifty caliber M2 machine gun on the second, although he didn't cock it. All the newcomers now had their fingers on the triggers of their assorted weapons, even though they were still pointed at the ground.

"My friend told you we're heading north, not south west. Thanks for the offer, but we're on our way to a military base in northern Iowa."

"Iowa?" the driver said and cocked his head. "What's in Iowa?"

"That's classified."

"Is it now? I believe you have mistaken our intentions. It wasn't an offer, but a demand that you come with us. This is your last chance to comply."

Seyfert shook his head and smiled. "Look, Chief, we're not coming, and quite frankly you're out gunned and out trained. We don't want to shoot you or get shot at, so this is *your* last chance. Fuck. Off."

The driver narrowed his eyes. "We have an attack chopper two miles out, if we—" He was interrupted by one of Bourne's men who walked around the LAV holding a green tube with what looked like a blast shield on the side of it. "What's that?"

"If you were actually military," Androwski said, "you would know that is a Stinger missile. Anti-air. We have six more, and if you look at the LAV behind me you will see tubes on the side. Those are also anti-air missiles. You're full of shit on the helicopter anyway, but tell your bird if he comes within *three* miles of us in the air, we'll shoot him down. Also, if you don't leave in the next thirty seconds, we'll fucking kill you all." At this, both he and Seyfert raised their MP5SD3s and pointed them at the driver and passenger.

The Triumvirate men began to raise their weapons, but Seyfert screamed, "Don't!" and they stopped. The driver's eyes were wide, but there was a smirk on the passenger's face.

"Something funny?" demanded Seyfert.

"Yeah, you're being covered by—"

"Two snipers three hundred meters back?" finished Androwski. "I guess we're not *copasetic*."

Two pops sounded, and then more weapons were pointed at the Triumvirate men.

"Your snipers are down. Twenty seconds, nineteen, eighteen..."

The passenger nodded, obviously angry. "Good luck on your trip up north." He turned. "Saddle up, let them go!" His men got back in the Humvees and they turned their vehicles around. Dust and broken asphalt spewed from their tires as they began speeding back the way they had come.

Seyfert looked back at the LAV then at Androwski. "You told him the snorkels were missiles?"

"Yeah, I didn't think he would know the difference."

"Pity we don't have any Stingers," Bourne said thoughtfully as the LAV thundered down the road. He smiled and looked at Androwski. "Great bluff by the way, but they have probably already radioed our position to Lincoln, and I'm sure they're dispatching help as we speak."

"Then we best haul ass, sir," Stark yelled over his shoulder from up front. The convoy of three vehicles picked up speed and they ate up the miles as they travelled due east through the Iowa flatlands.

"The Stinger we have is functional, sir," Seyfert replied, "but we only have one shot, and flares or ECM from the bird may counter it. Then they can stay a half mile up and take us apart with their guns or rockets."

"With any luck they'll be chasing us north. Where are we anyway?"

Anna looked at one of the screens in the LAV, then back at a map. "This is Route 18, we just passed the turnoff for Route 69 south, which puts us about...ten miles west of a town called Clear Lake."

The colonel was smiling at her. "Maybe it's a good thing we did take you along. Who taught you how to read a map?"

"Taught me? You just look at it."

His smile widened. "I guess you do at that. It's getting late, and we should pick up fuel at a truck stop, or one of these smaller towns." He picked up his radio. "All units, we need fuel, so keep your eyes open for stations, or farms with pumps."

Twenty minutes later, the LAV pulled up to a white sign on the side of the road, the Humvee and truck behind. The sign had originally read Welcome to Clear Lake, Population 786. The 786 was crossed off with a red slash, and the number 522 was below it, also crossed off in red. Several other numbers were below or to the right and left of the original, all crossed off. The numbers dwindled down to 51, and then ALL DEAD was scrawled in the right corner. A truly dead man with a pistol in his lifeless hand was crumpled under the sign.

There was no gas station in sight, not that anyone could see farther than was illuminated by the headlights of the LAV. The town was dark, and as the sign indicated, dead.

"Our pickup is vulnerable," began Bourne, "so you boys need to stay on your toes. We'll proceed through town in the LAV, and check for a pump station and assess the hostiles. Don't get complacent, and keep checking your six. Maintain radio contact at all times, and engage undead only if they pose a direct threat. Deal with human threats appropriately, but don't get trigger happy, anybody left alive in this town is probably starving and scared." They transferred twelve fuel cans from the back of the truck to the armored vehicle.

As the LAV moved away, a soldier got out of the Hummer with a high-powered light and flashed it in all directions. A lone undead was slowly making its way toward them from the south. The man got back in the vehicle and pointed right. "We got one coming from over there, keep an eye on it, and we'll take it out with a suppressed weapon or an entrenching tool when it gets close."

The light was extremely bright and, according to the manual, illuminated up to a hundred yards, so the soldier had been able to see the zombie, and the zombie had seen the light. Some of the other hundred or so zombies that were approximately one hundred and thirty yards away had also seen the light and heard the vehicle engines. Like a flock of birds, their direction changed from south to north, and now they plodded toward the unaware men.

Clear Lake may have been picturesque once, with its pretty store fronts all facing the main road and its single traffic light suspended over the thoroughfare. Now there was trash in the streets, burned stores and crashed vehicles. Festering corpses with holes in their heads, unattended and left to rot, lay here and there as well. Newspapers blew across the headlight beams like tumbleweeds through the darkness.

A military presence had been in this small town as well. An abandoned deuce and a half transport truck, the torn canvas top blowing in the wind, had come to rest halfway through the front window of a barbershop. The driver's door on the truck was still open.

It didn't take long for the townsfolk to come out to greet the newcomers. Several shapes materialized out of the shadows, and made for the LAV on dead legs.

"How many?" Bourne asked Anna.

She was looking at the thermals on the screen in front of her, white shapes stumbling in the gloom. "Nine, but there are a lot of places they could be hiding."

"Strictly speaking, they don't hide. They do just pop out though, don't they?"

"I know, right? They...hold on..." She peered into the starboard monitor. "Stark! Stark that road we just passed has a gas station, I saw it!"

The LAV braked, Stark managing to turn the behemoth in the middle of Main Street. He backed into a red Toyota Tundra, leaving a huge dent in the driver's door of the truck. "Shit."

"You want me to drive, Navy?" Dallas shouted from the bench in the back.

"I want you to shut it, redneck!"

Androwski looked sheepishly at Bourne, "Sorry, sir."

Seyfert stood and climbed into the turret hatch, as John's Gas and Go came into view through the front windows. He donned his night vision glasses and popped the hatch open, cocking the light machine gun on the hull.

"Thirty seconds people," Bourne said almost casually, "smooth and by the numbers. Seyfert, are we clear?"

"Negative sir, we have hostiles. Six at least, and the window front of the station is gone. Take them?"

"Negative, we'll go hand to hand until it gets bad. Henson, Wilcox, provide close cover, the rest of us will fill the tanks. Rick, you stay in the LAV with Stark and cover the back hatch. If this gets out of hand, fall back to the LAV. It takes one minute to fill a five gallon jug, we have four gasoline and fourteen diesel to fill. I want to be out of here in twenty minutes."

The soldiers Henson and Wilcox snapped together two harpoons that they had made using a crude drawing provided by Teems. They were the first out of the hatch, and within seconds had dispatched their first undead. Several more were staggering toward the station, but rather than meet them, they covered the others as they used Chris's pump to put fuel in the tanks.

It went smoothly. The two soldiers speared any approaching zombies, and Seyfert shot several more from his perch atop the LAV with his suppressed MP5SD3. Dallas and Bourne humped the cans back to the LAV as Anna filled them with the pump. They had three diesel cans left to fill when Seyfert opened up with the LMG. "Contact right! Fall back, there are too many!"

Not needing to be told twice, the fuel crew pulled the pump and ran for the safety of the armor, three cans left behind on the concrete. The undead appeared from nowhere, and there were dozens. Two different howling screams came from behind, and Henson spun to face them, fumbling for his sidearm. Sprinting up the road from the east, two fast movers came directly at the young man. "Screamers!"

Forty feet from the hatch, he realized he wouldn't make it even though the others were yelling for him. Henson turned, took aim, and fired at the first one, scoring a hit at chest level. The thing flopped down and scraped across the road, leaving skin. His infected cohort kept running, and Henson fired again, missing. Adjusting his aim, the soldier fired two quick shots, both hitting the other blood-soaked thing in the abdomen. It staggered and fell, putting one hand to the ground and one on its bleeding mid-section. Looking at the man the creature closed its eyes hard in pain, and tried to scream at him. Only choked gasps came out, and it fell forward on its chest trying to crawl.

Henson realized that he had just shot a teenage boy and was saddened to his core. He immediately thought of his little brother, but that thought was shaken by the hollering behind him. He turned toward the LAV and saw the hatch closing as Wilcox, Bourne, and Dallas fought off a small horde of undead clawing at the rear of the vehicle. More were coming from his right and behind him. Seyfert gave one more burst to the front of the LAV, and spun his weapon at Henson. "Run! That way!" He pointed south. "We'll pick you up!" He opened up on another group coming from the east, behind where the sprinters had come from. Seyfert fired over Henson's head into the smallest group coming from the south, the clearest direction for Henson.

"RUN DAMMIT!" Seyfert screamed at him and he finally got going. The LAV was backing up to meet him, crushing some undead in its path, when another runner appeared and jumped up on the side of the vehicle.

Henson reached the small crowd blocking his path and fired at their heads. He holstered his weapon and deployed his harpoon, destroying another creature, but as it fell, it dragged the harpoon with it, spinning the living man sideways. Getting a good look at the LAV as he twisted, Henson saw the runner climbing up after an oblivious Seyfert, who was carefully firing into the crowd. As he lay on his back, he pulled his sidearm and drew a bead on the sneaky creature to Seyfert's side. Henson took a deep breath as three creatures fell to their knees around him coming to his level to feast. He let half the breath out and squeezed his trigger.

Seyfert couldn't understand why Henson didn't get up, they were right on him! The SEAL's eyes went wide as he saw the fallen soldier aiming at him. His ears were screaming from the machine gun fire, so he was unable to hear the shot from Henson's pistol, but he saw the muzzle flash. He felt rather than heard something slump next to him on the hull of the LAV, and he spun to see a farmer with a hole in his head rolling off the hull to the street.

Henson tried to roll to his left, but he ran into the bare and bloody feet of a dead woman in a blue bathrobe and she fell on top of him. Frantically, he pushed at her, but the others had reached him and halted his escape, and she had fastened her hands around his tactical webbing. Her head snapped back when he shot her in the face, and she released him. He felt a searing pain in his left hip and ear at the same time, and he continued firing until he was empty. The creatures were pulling on him, his weapon arm snapping to the right. He felt more pain in his forearm as he thrashed and kicked. Then they were biting him all over. The soldier saw an old woman chew his ring and pinky fingers off with a jerk of her head. He heard machine gun fire, and had a moment to think that this was a terrible time for a headache, before he mercifully died.

The barrel of the light machine gun was still smoking as Seyfert closed the turret hatch. "He…"

Bourne put a hand on his shoulder. "We saw, son. You did the right thing." The colonel shouted up front, "Stark, get us back to the rendezvous point ASAP."

Seyfert sat down hard on the padded bench. "Guy scored a headshot from a hundred feet with a pistol on a moving target. He saved my life and I shot him."

"An' wherever he is, he's thankin' ya for it," said Dallas. "I promise."

28

"Shit!" Murray yelled and threw the mic at his feet in the Humvee. It dangled by the cord and he watched it swing. He and the other three men in the vehicle heard what had happened to Henson from Stark via the radio.

The dead thing they were keeping an eye on was forty feet away now, and moving steadily toward the parked vehicles. "Fuckin' things! They're everywhere," Murray said, grabbing an entrenching tool from the clip on the passenger door. He opened the door and got out, starting toward the thing coming at him. "This is not your country!" He unfolded the spade and snapped it in place. Murray yelled a battle cry and swung the shovel with all his might in a sideways arc. He took off damn near half its head, and the dead man in an orange jumpsuit crumpled to the ground. The back of the jumpsuit had letters on it, and as he had left the powerful flashlight in the Hummer, Murray pulled his pistol and used his tac-light to read I.S.P. in black bold print. He was using the jumpsuit to clean the entrenching tool of blood and brain, when he heard a noise in the scrub behind him. He spun, but couldn't see anything as he squinted into the gloom. Raising his tac-light, he panned right to left, "Holy fuck..." he whispered and ran back to the vehicles.

"Look at Murray running," laughed Biggs as he pointed out the right side of the Humvee. "Looks like a little school girl getting chased by a bee." Keleher and Stenner chuckled as well. They were still laughing when he scrambled into the vehicle, slamming the door and picking up the mic. Keleher leaned forward from the back seat. "What're you runnin' from, chicken shit?"

Murray used the interior handle to swivel the exterior spot light on the passenger's side and clicked it on. "Them," he shouted, as the light illuminated dozens of undead staggering toward the vehicle.

"Holy fuck," Keleher, Stenner, and Biggs said in unison. The red Dodge pickup beeped its horn and Webb, the driver, screamed over the radio: *"Fucking move, Biggs! Go!"*

Biggs threw the Humvee in gear and floored it, the Dodge pickup following close behind. Murray keyed the mic, speaking concisely, "Wanderer, this is Roadtrip One, do you copy over?"

"Roadtrip, this is Wanderer Actual, we have hostiles, bugging back to your position as initially communicated."

"Negative, Wanderer, we have hostiles as well. Dozens, maybe hundreds just outside of town. Roadtrips One and Two en-route to your position."

Undead were staggering out of the gloom on both sides of the road now, the headlights of the Hummer illuminating them more and more as they got closer to the pavement, "Request alternate evac route, things are getting bogged here." Men, women, and children were materializing out of the darkness now all with the same intent.

"Standby Roadtrip, we're looking."

Up ahead the things had already stumbled onto the road and were coming straight at the oncoming headlights, looking for a quick dinner. The Humvee had some light armor, while the pickup was unshielded although faster than the military vehicle. The undead were beginning to pinch the vehicles from three sides, and it wasn't long before evading them wasn't possible. The first thump on the driver's side of the Hummer sent chills down Murray's spine. The creature went spinning away, but two more took its place and followed behind the vehicles. "Roadtrip Two, tighten up, we can plow for you."

"Copy One!"

The pickup sped up slightly, and soon the vehicles were only ten feet apart as they sped down the rural road at forty miles per hour. The thumps were more common now, and one went under the Humvee with a satisfying crunch. The truck behind braked and swerved a little as the crushed zombie was spit out from under the tires of Murray's vehicle. Several more creatures in the road, heedless of the danger, moved straight at the front of the oncoming trucks, and were plowed under or pushed to the side. Inevitably, one rolled up the hood and over the roof of the Hummer, getting caught in blast shield in front of the machine gun turret.

"That thing is still fucking kicking," shouted Keleher. "I can hear it!" The zombie was indeed making some noises from above, as it scratched and scrabbled on the roof of the vehicle.

"Roadtrip One, Wanderer, what's your twenty, over?"

"Wanderer, we're a klick out and coming at mid speed. The road is getting thick, any alternate routes would be appreciated!"

"The only alternate route is overland Roadtrip, recommend you remain on the road until it becomes impassible. Rendezvous two klicks east of town, unless you require assistance, out."

"Roger that, Wanderer, stay tuned. Did you get that, Two?"

"Copy that, five by five. And you have a hitch-hiker on your fucking roof."

Murray looked out the back window. "Tighten up, Two, you're back too far." He let go of the mic and looked out the front. "We have to get off this fucking road. Where are they all coming from?"

"Dunno," said Biggs. "But there are a shit-load of them."

The speed of the vehicles had decreased to twenty miles per hour as the road became bogged with dead people. The Hummer plowed them down, but the truck was having difficulties, and began to shimmy on the driver's side. Murray looked at all the dead faces out the window as they drove, "Shit, we're not gonna make it..."

Stenner looked back over his shoulder out the window. "Well, *we* will..."

"We're not leaving them, Stenner, if you—"

Stenner interrupted him. "Due respect, Murray, but that's shit and you know it. It's one thing saving a buddy behind enemy lines, with motherfuckers shooting at us, but there's *always* a chance. If that truck stops on this road, there's no chance to get to them. None. We would have to stop and get out in the middle of *that*," Stenner pointed to the throng of dead things encroaching from all sides. "There's no coming back from that for any of us. Four dead is better than eight dead, and we need the soldiers."

Murray keyed his microphone. "Wanderer, we're going to need an extraction. Roadtrip Two is in trouble."

"Roger that, One, we're coming."

"Webb, did you copy—?"

Roadtrip Two didn't get a chance to answer The left front tire blew, sparks flying from the wheel rim as it made contact with the asphalt. Three undead were run down, but two more went over the hood, one spider-webbing the safety glass windshield before rolling away into the night. The vehicle carried on for another fifty feet then jerked violently to the left, going down a slight embankment. The driver's side headlight impacted a mound of earth, and the rear of the truck jumped into the air, tires still spinning. Dazed, the men in the truck tried to gather their bearings. "Jesus..." Webb said when the first ghostly palm smacked the passenger window. The driver, Slone, wiped his hand across his brow and looked at it. It was bloody. Past his hand, out through the front windshield, a woman was pinned between the truck and the dirt pile. She was scratching the hood of the truck trying to gain purchase in her single-minded pursuit of what was inside the vehicle.

There was frantic pounding all over the pickup. Webb pulled a grenade from his tac-webbing and looked at Slone. He nodded, also pulling a grenade.

"Fuck that," came a voice from the back seat.

"You'll never make it, Carr," Webb said, shaking his head. Without answering, Carr threw open the rear window slider and threw his M4 into the truck bed. He shimmied through the window, picked up his weapon, and began firing behind the truck. He threw a grenade behind the vehicle and ducked down into the bed. The muffled explosion threw limbs and gore in all directions, and Carr jumped into the crowd and ran, shooting.

A hand reached through a hole in the front window glass, the skin flaying away on the green safety glass to show purple muscle. Both the driver and passenger windows were beginning to crack, and an undead had made it into the truck bed. Kimball, the other rear seat passenger, shot it with a suppressed round. "Do it," he said.

"Wanderer, Roadtrip One, this is Two."

"Go ahead, Two."

Webb looked at Slone and spoke back into the mic, "Good luck."

Both Webb and Slone pulled the pins from the grenades. Slone smiled. "Spoons off in three?" Another suppressed round came from the back seat, and blood sprayed the inside of the cab and back window. "Sounds good."

Sloan's window let go and hands grabbed him, "Three!" He screamed and shoved his grenade into the mouth of the dead mailman trying to pull him out the window. More hands were reaching in, and they pulled at him while he fought them off. At the same time, Webb let go of the grenade's primer handle and put the weapon on the seat between them.

Murray put his head down as the Hummer cleared the swarm. A small explosion lit up the night behind them, just as headlights appeared from the right side. "Wanderer, Roadtrip Two is down."

"Copy that, One. We see you, can you exfil to us?"

"Roger that, Wanderer."

29

"So that's the Mighty Mississippi then?"

Anna looked up at Seyfert from her map. "Yeah, it forms the border between Iowa and Illinois."

A Texas drawl added to the conversation. "She don't look so mighty from here. Kinda like a junk yard."

They were viewing the river from the embankment under the Black Hawk Bridge in northern Iowa. The bridge had been destroyed, the girders twisted and the concrete broken. Cars, also broken, could be seen piled up and partially submerged under what used to be a road over the crossing. There was movement in the crushed mountain of cars, and a sizeable force of creatures on the far side of the river milling about.

"They blew the bridge with people on it?" fumed an irate Dallas.

"I would imagine," began Bourne, "that in an attempt to control the spread of infection, many bridges were destroyed. The loss of human life here is reprehensible, but to keep the plague on the east side of the Mississippi, I would have ordered the same destruction."

"Yeah, but wouldn't ya have cleared them folks off first?"

"They probably wouldn't leave. They were so desperate and scared they disregarded orders to get off the bridge, or were stuck in gridlock when the planes came. Or maybe they didn't believe the army would actually destroy it in the first place."

"How do you know it was planes an' not explosives?"

"The blast pattern and the way the bridge looks now. See how the bridge is mostly twisted and bent, and there are huge pieces of it missing? That is indicative of aerial bombardment. Explosives would have taken out an entire section, north to south, neatly and cleanly."

Anna traced her finger down a blue line on the map. "The only other crossing on the map is the one on I-80 to the south of us."

"That will undoubtedly be gone as well. We'll cross here."

"Uh…the jeep ain't gonna make it over that wreck of a bridge, and it ain't gonna swim neither."

"We'll have to take on the four men in the Hummer and find more transport on the other side." The colonel strode from the back of the LAV and into the red light of the early morning sun. Rick was talking to Biggs and Murray, while Androwski urinated behind the Hummer. Stenner was in the Hummer's turret scanning with binoculars, with Keleher walking a close perimeter.

Six eyes surveyed Bourne as he walked up to Rick's small group. Androwski finished his task and was coming around the corner of the vehicle when he heard the colonel's voice. "There's no way to get the Humvee across the river. You boys will have to pile in with us, this mission is about to go amphibious."

Androwski keyed his mic. "Stark, how many people can the LAV hold?"

"Comfortably? Seven, three crew and four passengers, but we've been running between six and ten since we got her."

"Can it carry twelve of us?"

"I don't know if twelve will fit. But we'll have no room and we'll piss through fuel if we try. I wouldn't recommend it for the entire trip anyway."

"Can it carry all of us across the river?"

"Negative. I don't know what the extra weight would do. But we could pull a boat or raft."

Bourne pointed at the other side of the river, where the undead mass had seen the survivors and were starting to get frisky. "Not into that. Alright people, options. We didn't come all this way to be stymied by a busted bridge."

"Contact, sir, four hundred meters." Stenner was pointing to the north past the bridge. "Six hostiles, speed is slow, ETA twenty."

"We're out in five people, lock and load and button up." The colonel looked around, paying attention to the far side of the river. "I'm not getting any warm and fuzzies coming off this location."

Androwski ejected his magazine and checked his rounds. "Sir?"

"Why are all of the dead on the other side of the river? Where are the ones from this side?"

"Maybe they's all gone," drawled Dallas. "Maybe they got lucky and escaped the bombin'."

"We're behind enemy lines, Dallas, we don't have time for maybes when it concerns the enemy."

They piled into their respective vehicles and drove south down the river. There were several bait and tackle shops, convenience stores, a gas station, a movie theater, bar, and some homes. Everything looked pretty well looted, and most of the shops had broken front windows or kicked in doors. Evidence of panic was everywhere as well, burned buildings and vehicles were prevalent, and corpses on the road. Many corpses. Dallas looked wistfully at the bar through the video screen as they drove past.

Larson and Sons Marina sat a mile south of the Black Hawk Bridge in a small cove almost invisible from the street. The road had pulled away from the river, and the only indication that there was a marina was a small sign at the head of a dirt access road. The LAV and the Hummer turned down the dirt road and followed to its end. The street opened up into a rather large area with two dozen or so boats on stands or blocks. Some were shrink wrapped in plastic, but others showed signs of activity. Half a paint job on a hull, shrink wrap partially removed. Tool boxes and an arc welder next to one boat, buckets and scrapers next to another. These were signs that people had been starting to get their boats ready for another summer when the plague had cut their plans short.

A small structure with a corrugated metal roof and a sign that read "Get your bait here!" was located near the two docks and boat ramp. The windows were intact, but the door had been left open, and there was gore spatter on it.

"Androwski, take Seyfert and Wilcox and check out that store. Murray, have your group run a perimeter sweep. Check between the boats for unwanted visitors and deal with them quietly, from inside the Humvee if possible, and nobody gets out alone. Remain in contact."

The Hummer pulled away with an *Acknowledged,* from Murray. Androwski, Seyfert, and the jumpy kid Wilcox moved off to check the store while Rick, Dallas, and Bourne examined some of the boats.

"This one here's a real beaut."

"I agree hillbilly, but it's up on blocks."

"Damn shame. I coulda used a cruise right about now."

Bourne held a fist up. "Quiet!"

Rick tilted his M4 to the side, double checking the safety and selector switch, and Dallas flicked the safety off on his shotgun.

The safety was off Bourne's M9, and he held the weapon with both hands, pointing it at the ground. He went into a semi-crouch and looked under the boat Dallas had thought was pretty. He saw two sodden work boots and a pair of jeans from the shin down. The colonel nodded his head toward the boat and raised one hand with one finger extended. Rick and Dallas nodded, and Dallas put his hand on Bourne's wrist. Dallas slung his shotgun and pulled his rebar, and it was Bourne's turn to nod. A pungent odor wafted through the air.

The feet moved, crunching across the gravel beside the boat. Dallas strode around the front of the vessel, rebar held high, Rick and Bourne followed with weapons ready. The thing on the other side of the craft was disgusting. Worms dropped from it as it walked, and maggots infested its empty eye sockets. Hairless, sightless, and shirtless, the repulsive creature stumbled, its one arm hanging limp, the abdominal cavity completely devoid of anything resembling organs. Shreds of flesh and whatever was left in its chest dangled down into the empty stomach area.

The smell was unimaginable, and as Dallas approached it, an eel slid from its middle and plopped on the ground with a wet slap. Dallas put his forearm to his mouth and gagged loudly. That was all the impetus the creature needed, and it moved toward the Texan with astonishing speed for a dead thing, the one arm reaching blindly, mouth open wide. It was on him quickly, and he swung the rebar in an upwards arc, catching it under the chin. The mandible broke with a loud snap, and something black and slimy fell out of its mouth and landed on the gravel. The creature fell backward but immediately started getting up again. Dallas finished it with a coup de grace swing to the top of its skull.

"Jesus. Thing stinks." Dallas retched again. "Is that black thing its damn tongue?"

Bourne got down near it and looked it over. "Why's it so rotten? This is the worst one I've seen. It's even worse than the burned ones."

"Well," Rick began. "The plague hit the east coast first, then made its way west and then jumped across the ocean. Maybe we're looking at one of the first victims."

"Maybe. But if that's the case, why aren't the others around here like this one?"

Dallas spit. "Yeah, well, it's dead, let's leave it be b'fore I lose m'lunch."

"*Sir, the bait shop is clear,*" came Androwski's voice over the radio. "*There aren't any keys for the boats in here, though.*"

"Roger that, Androwski. We just took care of a dead one, so stay frosty. Continue recon and meet back at the LAV in five."

"*Copy.*"

The three men walked through the boat maze carefully, listening to the sound of the Hummer driving around the yard. They made it to the docks and everything looked clear. They weren't actually on the Mississippi River anymore, but on a canal that must lead to it. Small trenches were cut into the surrounding marshland, probably for drainage. The boats undoubtedly put in at the ramp and took a quick jaunt to the river. There was little current and the reeds blew noisily in the breeze.

Rick pointed at a small barge tied to the end of one of the docks. "Can we put the Hummer on that and drag it across?"

"You think it'll fit?"

"Let's take a look." Rick began walking down the small pier to the end, Dallas and Bourne following. They reached the barge and climbed aboard. There were tools and hardhats, welding equipment and two gas cylinders on a dolly. There was no wheelhouse, and no motor. "This here's a work float," Dallas told them. "I worked on a couple o' these in Corpus Christi. Damn solid."

"Will it hold the Hummer?"

"It'll hold that damn tank of ours, but we gots ta tie her down some or she'll fall off with the first stiff breeze. These things won't sink, but if they tip a little, anythin' with wheels'll get ta movin' then the barge gets all a kilter and before ya know it, ya lost yer cargo. That's what them rings is for." He pointed to a series of rings that were welded to the barge in various locations. "And them chains too." Rusty chains with hooks at both ends were piled in boxes in the center of the barge.

"I'm tellin' ya, this baby would float a team o' elephants across this river. Solid," he said again, and stomped his boot on the barge three times.

The bass boom from his stomping echoed across the small marsh, and Bourne scowled at him.

"Oops," said the big man looking back at Bourne sheepishly. "Sorry, I..." he broke off and craned his neck slightly to the right so he could see past his friends to the dock behind them. "Shitfire." Creatures were rising from the water on both sides of the dock. Two had already begun to climb up, as the water was only waist deep halfway back to the land. There were ripples in the water all around them, as more dead things ambled back toward land.

Bourne was already on the radio when Dallas and Rick unslung their weapons. "Stark, Murray, we're in deep shit at the dock, we're going to need an extraction!"

Stark's voice sounded tinny as he answered the call. "Roger that, sir, we're on the way!"

Rick noticed small swirls and eddies in the water. They were swirling toward the dock and the barge. Apprehensively, he peered over the side of the vessel. "Look at that, look there." He pointed at several things moving just below the surface of the water.

"Jesus, is that—"

"It sure is, hillbilly, and there are a lot of them." One of the things noticed Rick's shadow above, and reached its hands toward him, the fingers just breaking the surface of the water. The dead man was fish-belly white, and bloated. Several more white hands and fingers had broken the surface of the water when the three men heard the first thump on the hull of the barge. A shot, and then the ratcheting sound of Bourne's cold-loaded nine millimeter pistol drew Rick and Dallas' attention, and they both brought their weapons up as well. The dock behind them was filling up with the dead.

"I thought they dint go in the damn water!"

"Me too, maybe they fell in or something, and couldn't figure out how to get out until they heard you banging."

Several ghostly pale figures were had made their way to the boat ramp and stood, looking toward the dock. They turned their heads back and forth, searching. Rick took a knee and aimed his rifle at the oncoming pickled horde. "They must be blind too. Probably been in the water for so long that their eyes were taken by fish or just popped out because of the facial swelling." He got three shots off before the Hummer and the LAV showed up.

The vehicles pulled to either side of the entrance to the dock, the LAV moving slightly down the boat ramp. Pallid hands began hitting the hull of the LAV with squishy slaps.

The bass boom from Dallas's shotgun echoed across the marshy area, three of the lead creatures falling into their dead comrades, some falling back in the water.

Bourne fired again. "Hurry, Stark," he said, quite calmly.

Keleher leapt up into the turret on the Hummer and jacked the slide on the fifty cal. Anna popped out of the machine gun turret on the LAV. "Like this?" she asked into the radio.

Everyone heard Stark over the radio again, "Yeah, pull that handle back and she's ready to go. It will kick some, but the mount will take care of most of it. Use short bursts, or you'll lose control quickly."

"Okay," the young woman said, and pulled the slide on the LMG. Dallas saw her take a breath and then she squeezed the trigger. The advancing dead were taken from the right side by her copper-jacketed fire, and they fell over like tenpins, toppling into the water. The burst had lasted two seconds and she followed up with another two second burst, shifting the barrel of the weapon to the left slightly. She mowed the dead down. "This thing is awesome!" she shouted with a maniacal smile.

Bourne also noticed that the monsters were falling fast. "Murray, hold your fire! Save the fifty, and check your six!" A dead woman, looking fresher than the folks from the water but still missing her right arm, was stumbling toward the back of the Hummer. Murray shot her with his sidearm.

Seyfert, Androwski, and Wilcox showed up, the jittery kid unslinging his rifle. Androwski grabbed the kid's rifle barrel as he was starting to aim, and jerked it up yelling and pointing toward the LAV. Wilcox nodded and, switching to single fire, started picking off the dead near the LAV. Androwski and Seyfert began working on the vehicle, but neither Dallas nor Rick had any idea what they were doing or why.

There were three former humans left on the dock when the LMG clicked empty. Anna had her right pinkie finger in her right ear and was moving her jaw around trying to dissipate the ringing from the weapons fire. Rick and Bourne took care of the last three advancing dead, but there were several still near the barge or sloshing out of the water. The new target seemed to be the Hummer, and Murray, Biggs, and Keleher were shooting them with pistols as they got near. Bourne continued to give radio orders. "Murray, bring the Humvee down the dock halfway. It will put you out of danger from all directions except the rear, and it will block any oncoming hostiles from getting to us."

Private Wilcox was knee deep in the water near the LAV covering his friends when Bourne saw him. "Wilcox! Get out of the water now! Move!" Wilcox backed up the ramp, and none too soon as two infected broke the surface of the water five feet from where he had been standing. The private shot both, but more ripples behind them indicated there were others to follow. A savage scream echoed over the marsh, sending icy tendrils down the boy's back. He spun his weapon in all directions but couldn't see the screamer.

Bourne re-loaded his pistol. "Everyone stay out of the water, we have submerged hostiles, and you can't see them."

Androwski and Seyfert moved to the rear of the LAV, the SEAL lieutenant calling the colonel, "LAV's ready, sir."

Dallas had overheard. "Ready for what?"

The colonel was peering into the water next to the barge. "Amphibious incursion into the Mississippi River. Murray, how many on the dock behind you?"

Keleher turned in the turret and looked behind. "Eight sir, but there's a pack coming through the boat yard."

"Copy, destroy the ones on the dock and get up here ASAP. Dallas, Rick, help me cast off. Keep the two end lines around the cleat but loose, dump the spring line in the middle. Androwski, get your team in the LAV. Stark, get in position in front of the barge, you're towing us."

Gunfire erupted once again as Keleher fired his M4 from the turret. Stenner and Murray leaned out the Hummer's windows and also fired on the dead on the dock. The contingent of infected coming through the yard had grown. There were dozens now. Keleher took in the scene quickly. "Sir, we're about to have a shit-load of company!"

"I see them. We need to work fast."

The LAV moved into the water as Wilcox slipped in through the turret. Androwski and Seyfert were riding on the outside of the hull, and Seyfert jumped onto the barge when the vehicle was close enough. The SEAL grabbed a heavy line and started making loops with it. He threw it to Androwski, and the two of them made a triangle with the rope, the top point attached to the LAV, and the two bottom points attached to the front corners of the square barge.

Keleher spun in the turret and jacked the charging handle of the fifty caliber M2, aiming at the oncoming horde. He seemed to have an epiphany, and lowered the barrel considerably before he opened fire. The weapon was extremely loud, and when he was done his ears were ringing as the colonel came over the radio demanding to know why he fired.

"I took out the part of the dock where it meets the land. It's history, sir, they can't get up without climbing now. It will slow them down."

"Good thinking, Corporal," the colonel said as the vehicle pulled up to him. The barge swayed slightly as the Hummer drove aboard, three of the men jumping out to assist. Dallas had let his line go and already had the chains out of the box. He was covered in rusty stains as he looped the chain through the welds in the barge and on the vehicle. He attached the hooks to the links in the chain after pulling it taut. Rick also cast his line away, he, Murray and Biggs copying Dallas' chain attachments, and soon the vessel was ready for transport.

"Okay, Stark, let's get underway."

"Copy that, sir. Everybody hold on to something."

The flat barge lurched forward once, twice, three times, and then they were pulling away from the dock. A fat infected man in shorts, running extremely fast for being so large, sprinted from the crowd of dead, leaping across chasm onto the splintered dock. He landed hard, and got up slowly, mouth agape and growling. Dragging his left leg, he limped quickly down the dock, screaming as he came. The barge was ten meters from the end of the pier as the infected man jumped with his arms straight out, trying to get to the men on board. He hit the water after a two meter flight, floundered for a few seconds and sank.

Rick sighed as he and the others looked at the spot where the man had gone under. "Poor bastard. Add another undead lurker to those beneath us.

How many do you think are down there right now reaching up for us as we pass?"

Bourne looked ashen. "Damn it, I didn't think of that." He got on the radio for all to hear. "Listen up, when we get across the river, and we are about to make land, check the water for hostiles. We should be quick about it as well. Stark, pull us up on the beach, and we'll drive right off the barge. Everyone get back in the vehicle they were in before we hit the river."

Stark maneuvered the LAV out of the causeway and into the river proper. The Mississippi wasn't at its widest here, but it was still a kilometer across at least, and the going was slow as the LAV was pulling considerable weight. Several partly submerged pleasure boats were barring the passage, and Stark worked his magic by avoiding the wreckage time after time. The survivors were less than one third of the way across the river, Bourne daring to think that it was a beautiful day, when he felt a tug in his right shoulder, and lost his balance. He spun half way around and fell to the deck of the barge, disoriented. The colonel put his hand to his shoulder and it came away bloody. Then the pain set in. He had about a half a second to think *Jesus, I'm shot!* before he heard bullet plinks off of the LAV and barge over the roaring in his ears.

Rick and the men hit the deck, but Dallas was still standing, unsure of what just happened. Biggs grabbed the big man's arm and yanked him to cover.

Androwski raised his MP5SD3. "Return fire, that red boat to the left!" Two speed boats came rocketing from the other side, spewing gunfire as well. Everyone on the barge began firing. Bourne heard someone yell *The colonel is down*! before he reached across his body and drew his sidearm. Pain lanced through his entire right side, and he almost dropped his weapon. He closed his eyes as the whole world went green, and suddenly Seyfert was at his side kneeling over him with a wide, flat bandage, and a silver package that looked like pop tarts.

"Dallas, help me get his shirt off!"

Bourne was unprepared for another spear of pain when the SEAL and the Texan rolled the colonel on his side. They began extricating the officer from his shirt as bullets whizzed by overhead. The roar of the Bushmaster atop the LAV drowned out most of the rest of cacophony, but Bourne heard Seyfert say *It's a through and through.*

Dallas was unstringing the bandage as Seyfert tore into the silver package with his teeth. "What is that?" the Texan demanded.

"Kwik-clot," the SEAL replied, and Bourne's blood went cold. He had seen the trauma chemical used in triage, and had heard how much it hurt. "S…Seyfert, unh…don't…" But the SEAL had already dumped a portion of the package on his back where the hole must be. This was a new level of agony, and the colonel gritted his teeth against it, cursing.

"Dallas, put the bandage on the exit wound, hurry!" Dallas applied the compress to the wound, which had already stopped bleeding, and they lay the soldier back down, "That wasn't so ba…" began the colonel, but Seyfert dumped the remaining powder from the package into the entry wound in his right pectoral muscle. Bourne screamed.

The gunfire seemed to have slowed down, with sporadic plinking, then the turret on the LAV rotated, and the Bushmaster fired once more, five quick shots. Stark had never stopped moving forward the entire time, and Bourne noticed that the far side of the river wasn't so far away anymore, before unceremoniously passing out.

29

Dead grey hands reached for him from all sides as he used his empty rifle as a club to keep them at bay. His son, his mother and father, his uncle Joe, his next door neighbor Harry, they were all there, hungering for him. His shoulder hurt fiercely for some reason, so he looked down briefly to evaluate it, knowing that taking his eyes off of the enemy in a critical situation such as this would be his demise. His rifle was suddenly gone, and so was his arm from the shoulder down. A nub of white bone protruded from his fatigue T-shirt where his humerus used to be. He looked up just in time to see his dead wife open her mouth and lean forward, her fetid breath an olfactory horror.

Bourne opened his eyes. A ceiling fan was above him, and the most horrible black and white wallpaper imaginable assaulted his eyes as he scanned the area. He was on his back on a bed in a cheap motel room, his right arm in a sling. He was terribly parched, and he attempted to reach for the glass of water on the nightstand next to him, but his left hand was cuffed to the bedpost with a set of long manacles that you would see a dangerous prisoner wear to court.

He was beginning to worry until a giant of a man came out of the motel's bathroom wiping his hands. The colonel breathed a sigh of relief. "Dallas," he croaked, surprised at the sound of his own voice. The Texan jumped as if someone had put firecrackers in his skivvies, then smiled his big country smile when he saw their commander awake.

"Dammit, pard, ya 'bout gave me a coronary!"

"Why am I cuffed to the bed?"

"Oh. Yeah, sorry 'bout that. We didn't know if ya was gonna make it, so we trussed ya up some ta keep ya off'n us should ya...ya know...turn." The big man fumbled through his pocket and produced a key. With some effort he was able to unlock the cuffs, and the soldier was free.

He tried to sit up, but everything got woozy, and Dallas caught him before he slammed back into the pillow. "Easy there, pard, ya been down a full day."

The colonel reached for the water, but Dallas beat him to it and handed it to him. "Where are we?"

"The Cockroach Motel, an' that's no lie. Damn critters're huge, an' twice as scary as the livin' dead. Bout forty miles east'o the Mississippi." Bourne heard *Missippy* from the southerner.

"What happened?"

"Ya got shot."

"Yes, but what happened after?"

The big man stood and grabbed his radio from on top of the ancient tube-style TV. "Damn place ain't even got HBO." Dallas pulled a rickety chair over next to the bed and gingerly sat down, as if he expected that the furniture wouldn't hold his massive frame. "Well, they came on us fast, bunch a yer black-camo asshole buddies. They started firin' from one o' them half-sunk boats, and Andy thinks you done took the first round. Then a speed boat come zippin' at us from th'other side." Dallas shook his head. "Dumbasses was shootin' at a tank expectin' ta' win. Anyways, that kid Wilcox opened up with the big gun and turned their boats inta Swiss cheese, and them fellers with 'em, but not before…"

Bourne furrowed his brow. "Before what?"

"Biggs. He got shot, almost in the same spot's you did. He bled out on the barge, we couldn't save 'im.

The colonel was used to loss, but he still felt a personal responsibility for his men. "Did we lose anyone else?"

Dallas nodded in the negative. "The Kelly-kid took one in the hip, but it wasn't too bad, and I got this," the big man rolled his pant leg up and showed the colonel a bandage on his right calf. "I can see yer face, so nah, it ain't a bite. I got grazed in the fire fight, it ain't but a scratch."

"So how did we get here?"

"We drove," he shrugged. "Got this far and Androwski pulled us in here for some R&R. Said we was gonna burn out, an' that you needed to lay down proper like, or you might get infected. Ya' bullet hole I mean," he added quickly, "not with th'plague."

"We need to move," the colonel said sitting up, "we're running out of time."

"No can do there, Colonel, we're outta gas. Seyfert, Murray and the blonde kid, Stover?"

"Stenner."

"Yeah, I been callin' him blondie, he hates it. Anyways, they went lookin' fer some diesel. The Hummer's on fumes, and the LAV's got about a quarter tank."

"How long have they been gone?"

"Couple hours. Listen, I gotta call Andy and let 'im know you ain't dead. He wanted ta' talk t' ya the minute ya woke up, or know iffn' ya kicked it."

Dallas put in the call, and Androwski showed up two minutes later with Rick. They congratulated the colonel on not dying, and Androwski related their story again with little difference. One thing he did add was that they had briefly captured a Triumvirate soldier. He was in his mid-twenties, and certainly had not been military trained. He had been on the partially submerged pleasure boat that had originally opened fire. His partner had been fatally shot in the chest during the fight, but he hadn't seen it, and the man had turned and bitten him in back of the leg. Androwski and Seyfert questioned him, and the young man said that the Triumvirate wanted Bourne back, but they all thought he was a prisoner, kidnapped from the checkpoint and moved across the country under duress. The soldier was horrified to learn that the colonel had been shot during the fire fight. Seyfert drew his combat knife, and the man apologized vehemently, telling the SEALs that he and most of his compatriots had been forced to join the Triumvirate, and then forced to do its bidding regardless of how tasteless any duty may be. He divulged the fact that there were hundreds of people out looking for Bourne, and Brooks was among them. Bourne's captors were to be taken alive if possible for questioning, but dead was just as good as long as Bourne was alive and well. Seyfert thanked the man, then shot him in the head, citing that he was infected.

"Sir, we're set to move in the morning," Androwski continued, "as long as we get the fuel. Our guys were carrying two cans each, so that's about thirty-three gallons. Should be plenty to get us to a fueling area."

"Well done, Lieutenant. I'm concerned about remaining in one place though. It seems every time we stop, the dead find us."

"Agreed, sir, but there hasn't been any Lima activity since we got here. This town is totally abandoned."

"That's what scares me."

"Roger that. We're all jumpy. We're prepped to hump out of here pretty quick once the fuel arrives though, and if the fuel team doesn't get back by zero-four-hundred, we're jumping in the LAV and heading for the gas station to look for them."

"Where exactly are we?"

"Wisconsin. Approximately forty miles east of the Mississippi, and sixty miles north of Illinois." He put his finger to his ear and held up the index finger on the other hand. "Roger that, Stark. Be there in two mikes. The fuel is here."

"Again, well done, Chief."

"Thank you, sir. I'll help fuel the vehicles. Glad you're vertical... or will be soon. Sir."

"Me too."

Chris, Anna, and Rick were waiting outside the door, and Anna poked her head in as Androwski left. "How is he?"

"He's alive," Bourne answered, trying to sit up.

"Lay your ass right back down, soldier," she said sternly. "It won't do to have you opening that wound after I stitched you up. Bullet missed your lung and your shoulder blade, you were lucky. You can get up tomorrow."

The colonel raised his eyebrows, but conceded and put his head back on the pillow with a grimace. "You stitched me?"

"I did," she stabbed an index finger at him, "so imagine my displeasure if you open it up again."

The survivors left the crappy motel at zero-four-hundred the following morning, never seeing a single infected while they were holed up. They travelled for the better part of a day, with sporadic undead sightings, but no hordes. The Triumvirate didn't bother the group either, and they drove in relative quiet, only stopping to relieve themselves and walk the dog. They turned south before they would hit Lake Michigan, and at fifteen-fifty hours, Bourne called a halt to inspect something. It was getting difficult to traverse the country now without hitting populated areas, and Chicago, the third most populated city in the United States, was just under one hundred miles to the east.

Before the plague, if you had googled the population of Dixon, IL, you would have found out that approximately fifteen thousand people had lived there. A quaint arch with the town's name in bold capital letters would welcome you should you visit. Now Dixon, like most cities and towns in the United States, was a ruin. It didn't smolder anymore, the fires having died weeks ago, but something else odd had happened here. The main street through town had abandoned and wrecked vehicles as had the other towns that the survivors had visited, but the vehicles were pushed to the side, some into storefronts, some tipped over. Everything on the main street, from the destroyed vehicles, to the downed power poles, to the store front bricks was covered in a dry brown stuff to about three feet high. It may have been a liquid once, but it had dried, and now it was mostly just a stain. Not a single window remained in any standing building, and even the trees were dead, the smaller ones uprooted and knocked over, the larger ones wilted and droopy. Only a few bodies remained in the streets, also covered in the brown substance, and these were so badly broken as to be almost unrecognizable as human. Against anything solid, such as a wall, or one of the aforementioned vehicles, the brown material had accumulated in drifts of sludge, like someone had spackled the cars to the road with brown goo.

Nothing was alive in Dixon, but there didn't seem to be any dead either. At least none moving. The team stopped mid-way down Main Street, and a very cautious Murray and Stenner got out of the Hummer and took a quick look around. Everyone was on high alert, but no one had detected any movement, and the thermals in the LAV weren't displaying any out of the ordinary heat signatures.

Murray regarded the nearby sludge drifts and the stains. He inspected some vehicles and even got on one knee and examined something in the middle of the road while Stenner covered him. Murray pulled out his combat knife and pried something from the street. It was stiff and brown, and when he pulled it up, he wrinkled his nose and pulled his head back. He stood up puzzling for a moment, then looked around, and held his wrist in front of his mouth and retched. "It's people," he said into his radio and gagged again. "This brown shit used to be people." He walked to one sludge pile. "You can see bits of bone and clothes, the rest is…pulp. Jesus. I, ah… I want to leave."

Anna was skeptical. "What could do that to a human being?"

"I've never seen anything like it," admitted Bourne. "We should keep moving."

Two hours and six towns later, the group had gotten used to the sight of the brown stains. Wherever there was a tight spot, such as a road with buildings, or a traffic jam on the highway, or a bridge, the human pulp was present.

After more driving, the LAV and the Hummer crested a small hill and in the center of the road was a Blackhawk helicopter, the pilot taking a piss off the side of the road. Four men scrambled to get back in the bird, but the vehicles reached the helo before it could take off, and Seyfert popped his head out of the turret to tell them to power down. Although the weapon was already charged, he jacked the charging handle on the LMG and pointed it at them for emphasis. The men exited the helo with their hands raised.

Murray and Stenner got out of the Hummer and frisked the men as they were covered by Seyfert, confiscating sidearms and stowing them. Each man wore black camo with a gold III stitched over the left breast. Androwski came from behind the LAV. "Now what are you boys doing so far from home? Still looking for your missing colonel?"

The men gave sideways glances at each other, but no one answered. Several other questions were thrown at the Triumvirate soldiers, but they wouldn't respond. Colonel Bourne strode out from behind the LAV, and upon seeing him, all four men stiffened and saluted.

They looked confused. "We thought you were captured, or dead, sir."

"I'm neither, Captain, as you can plainly see. Why is your bird parked in the middle of the highway, and not in the air? Step forward, Captain, and report."

The tallest man moved up and addressed Bourne. "Begging the colonel's pardon, but we're not supposed to divulge—"

"Dispense with that shit, Captain. Judging by the looks on your faces and the fact that you called me colonel, you know who I am. I'm giving you a direct order, answer my question: What are you doing out here?"

"Monitoring the swarm, sir."

Bourne had no idea what the man was talking about. "Repeat that."

"The swarm, sir, our orders are to follow at a distance of about fifty miles behind and report on any direction changes. We're conserving fuel by hanging back and shutting down. It's difficult to get fuel while—"

"Captain, what the hell are you talking about? What swarm? Fifty miles behind what?"

The man looked incredulous. "The swarm of Fallen, sir, the vanguard passed by this way a week ago. Actually, it takes them about a week to move the whole horde about two hundred miles."

Bourne looked at Androwski, who shrugged, and the Triumvirate soldier to the left of the captain said, "He doesn't know, Bill."

The colonel stabbed his index finger at the man who had just spoken. "You be quiet," - another stab at the captain - "What don't I know, Bill?"

"Sir, there's a massive swarm of Fallen moving west. It started in the northeast, and has been steadily moving westward at about one mile per hour. It turned south when it hit Lake Michigan, then west again when it got past the tip of the lake. It destroys everything in its path, and picks up more Fallen as it moves."

"We haven't seen any swarm, Captain, and how would you know about it anyway? Your HQ is a few hundred miles west of here."

The man shifted nervously. "May I reach into my flight suit for a sat-scan image?"

"Slowly."

The pilot pulled out a folded piece of paper and passed it to the colonel. "Brooks was looking for you. He was adamant that we find you, but your captors kept slipping through his fingers. He took a platoon of regular Army to a big facility in rural Missouri, I flew one of the Blackhawks. We lost thirty men to the Fallen, but Brooks said that we needed to get to a satellite terminal to scan for that," he pointed at the LAV, "and that when we found it, we could get you back."

The colonel looked at Androwski again and Anna, Chris, Dallas, and Rick, who had come out of the LAV and were listening too. "When he was looking for you with the satellite, he noticed the swarm."

"How many undead are in this swarm?" demanded Rick.

"Almost eight hundred thousand, near as we can tell. I can't believe you didn't see them."

30

The Blackhawk hovered at thirty six hundred feet of altitude, just short of three miles behind the swarm. The machine was high enough that the creatures on the ground couldn't hear the engines or rotors. Bourne had commandeered the vehicle and its pilot so he could view the vast horde of dead. The pilot's cohorts were back by the LAV, under close guard by Androwski and the others, while Bourne, Seyfert, and Rick hitched a ride to inspect the walking tide of death.

Rick pointed out the starboard window and spoke into his headset. "What the hell is that black cloud?"

"Insects," Schellenger, the pilot, replied. "They follow the Fallen in droves, it's disgusting, but you can see the cloud two miles out from the ground on a clear day with flat terrain. They're a good early warning system, but it hasn't helped anyone yet."

"What does that mean, it hasn't helped?" Bourne asked as he looked at the swarm through binoculars.

"Only one of the small encampments we've seen has tried to bug out when the Fallen approach, and that one got caught in it. It's three miles wide and two deep."

"Wait, you've seen encampments?"

"Yes, sir, the more easterly you go, the more live people you find. Of course, the opposite is also true, there are more Fallen. The Triumvirate has absorbed several small camps, and we have tabs on several more. Anyway, whenever the cloud appears on the horizon, people in the camps hunker down and try to defend. Unfortunately, they have no idea the size of the swarm, and they inevitably get overrun."

"Has Brooks tried to stop it?"

"There isn't enough ordnance. We have the A10s, but we don't have any more bombs. We tried strafing runs with the Warthog's 30mm guns, but all that does is cut a line in the horde for a few seconds. There was a

Hades bomb in an armory in South Dakota, but the men who went to get it never came back."

"So what's the plan, how are you going to stop them?"

"My guess is that we won't. There have been plans to divert them, but each time we try, they end up just moving west again on the same path. It's like they're drawn west."

The colonel turned to look at the pilot. "What is the track in relation to the stadium?"

"You mean in Lincoln? Dead on. They'll reach HQ by the end of next week, and with the lack of any changes in direction, that's where the brass thinks the Fallen are headed."

"Jesus, all those people..."

"Are probably gonna die. Brooks and Recht are already prepared to leave with the capable fighters and most of the weaponry, but only the pilots and upper brass know. There simply aren't enough vehicles to evac the civvies."

"You son of a bitch," fumed Seyfert. "How could you leave those people to die?"

Schellenger smirked. "I didn't. I hand-picked my crew for this mission personally, and none of us have families back in Lincoln. Brooks and Recht would certainly kill any of our families should we desert. The point is, tomorrow at 0800, word is going to get out that there's a swarm coming and that Recht is preparing to abandon his flock to the Fallen." The pilot smiled wider. "That should go over like a shit sandwich."

"What did you mean by desertion?" Bourne asked.

"Well, first off, Brooks came to me personally prior to lift off for this mission. He told me that you were a traitor, and if I found you I was to kill you immediately, you were not to be taken prisoner." Bourne raised his eyebrows. "It's true, sir. Most of the men suspect that Brooks is off his rocker, but that confirmed it for me. He ordered the assassination of the ranking military commander in the area," Schellenger harrumphed, "as if. The men I picked for this mission are my friends and I trust them. I told them we would monitor the swarm until my guy in Lincoln spread the word about what was coming. He will also inform as many as he can about what Recht has been doing. Then we're bugging out and heading north to Canada to fish and farm. None of that matters now."

"Why not, soldier?"

"Because we're out of gas." Schellenger tapped the fuel indicator. "We've got enough for two hundred miles, and then this bird is six million bucks worth of scrap metal. Every airport and fuel depot within five hundred miles is either overrun, or has men loyal to Brooks guarding it. Not to mention that my crew and I seem to be prisoners. I guess what I'm saying is: Request permission to come aboard, sir?

"No room," Seyfert said immediately.

"While I don't share his enthusiasm, Captain, he's right, we can't fit you."

Seyfert had his pistol in his lap. "Due respect, sir, I just don't trust this Triumvirate douche."

"Careful, sailor, I was a Triumvirate douche too."

"Roger that, sir. Sorry, sir."

Rick pointed out the window. "Is that the main body of it?"

"Negative, those are just stragglers." The pilot pointed forward, about twenty degrees higher out the forward windscreen. "That's the swarm."

"Holy shit," Seyfert and Rick whispered at the same time.

31

"You at least could have tried to get some folks out," Seyfert told Schellenger as they packed a case of water and some MREs into the Blackhawk, "and fuck you for taking our food."

"I didn't take shit, your CO gave it to us. If you want to go back to Lincoln, I can get us most of the way in my bird, but then you get to deal with Brooks and his cronies. He'll know what you're about before you can ever spill the beans, and how is one man going to save ten thousand people? My helicopter will take ten at most, and that would be if I had any fuel, and if I don't get shot on a whim, and if Brooks lets me take anyone. I've done plenty to redeem myself for working with those evil bastards." Schellenger wiped his hands on his flight suit then folded his arms. "Fuck you and your insinuations that I could have helped. I did help. Go on, go back and get eaten. You'll see how ridiculous your efforts are as the Fallen are chewing on you, or when you starve to death in a cell surrounded by them."

Fifteen minutes later, Bourne was saluting the Blackhawk crew as they took off. To Seyfert's amazement, the crew saluted back. The bird flew north, with two HK 416 battle rifles and two hundred rounds of ammunition in addition to the food and water. Before they left, the four men had been searched head to toe, and Stark and Androwski had disabled the helicopter's radio.

"Too bad. Usin' that chopper woulda gotten us ta Boston quicker if we had the gas."

The colonel turned abruptly away from the departing aircraft. "Agreed Dallas, but it couldn't carry us all and it *was* almost out of fuel. Saddle up, people, we leave in five."

The group took a southerly track after they separated from the crew of the Blackhawk. Taking back roads and going overland as much as they could, there was still no way to avoid major populated areas after they turned north.

The mission team picked up a young guy named Bill in a dead town in southern Pennsylvania. He had been hiding in a food distribution warehouse, but was caught outside by a few dozen creatures when he made a break for a dentist's office to pull one of his own teeth. The team had saved him just in the nick of time, and had almost shot him as he showed up disheveled with a bloody mouth after pulling a broken and rotten tooth. The reward for saving him was extreme, with all the food and water they could carry in the LAV and the Hummer. They were now pulling a small landscape trailer laden with all kinds of sustenance. Ramen noodles, packages of snack food, and boxes of juice drinks were now crammed against the inside hull of the LAV as they rumbled northeast.

They assisted an armed encampment under siege by the dead in Hillsdale, New York. The zombies had easily been destroyed using the LAV's wheels, and Bourne had insisted that some of the food they were carrying on the trailer be left for the folks there. Bill had also decided to stay and help, as he wanted no part of travelling any further east after the folks in Hillsdale told them what they were in for. Anna asked Bill if he would take her new dog Joe with him. When everybody looked at her, she looked away. "Where we are going is no place for a puppy."

Anna looked at the rear of the LAV as they drove away without Joe.

The dead were extremely prevalent as they got closer to their destination. The towns in the Commonwealth of Massachusetts had fared no better than any other state they had come through, but these towns were full of homes jam packed together. Although many of the states the survivors had travelled through were larger in population, they were also significantly larger in area, which in turn would mean that the undead were spread out, or concentrated in the cities. Before the plague, Massachusetts was ranked twelfth in population, but forty-fifth in area, meaning that the potential for six million undead, all concentrated in a small locale was significant.

What really slowed the LAV down, though, was the traffic. There were tens of thousands of vehicles abandoned everywhere. It looked as if the entire state had tried to escape west, but were turned back by the same military type checkpoints the team had seen along the way. The citizens were turned back and died by the thousands, only to re-animate and come back to the blockades as dead people who made more dead people. Dead people who were still in the area.

It was decided that they would travel south, and hook north to avoid the majority of the populated suburbs west of Boston. South of Boston was less populated but still had the potential for huge numbers of walking dead inhabitants. They saw plenty. The roads were packed with abandoned vehicles, many with struggling forms inside. Many more had windows broken in and blood marks on the upholstery.

As the survivors got closer to the coast, the going got tougher. The LAV was able to negotiate areas that not many other vehicles could, but the Hummer was having real trouble. The vehicle was hampered by terrain and obstacles that the LAV could skirt, wade, or crush easily, and when they reached Braintree Massachusetts on Route Three, they had to abandon the Hummer. The numbers of dead were too significant to keep leaving the safety of the armored vehicles to move abandoned or wrecked cars. Anna was almost bitten when the group was shifting supplies from the trailer and the Hummer to the LAV, and half a dead woman pulled herself from under an abandoned tow truck. Now eleven rode in a vehicle designed for significantly fewer personnel.

The crew took back roads to Quincy Harbor, where they quickly appropriated a Sea Ray Sundancer 610 that had forty one hours of total usage on the engine display. The keys were in the ignition, and when Murray started it up, the fuel tanks were full. *Brilliance* was the name on the stern. Stenner limped into the living room and stared around in amazement. "This thing is better than any house I've ever been in." The back door had been open and several cases of water were on the deck but they appeared to have had been there a while. There was no sign of anyone living, but the dead showed up in droves shortly after loading the boat with the remaining supplies they were carrying. The Sundancer started on the first turn of the key, and they cast off before the dead could get even moderately close.

The original team from Alcatraz stayed on the LAV except Seyfert and Dallas, who elected to join Bourne's group of five on the boat. Stark drove the LAV down a boat ramp into Quincy Bay, chasing the Sea Ray. "I had no idea there were so many islands in Boston Harbor," commented Stark as the LAV chugged slowly through the water.

Rick was looking at the port monitor from the passenger's seat up front. "Yeah, there's quite a few, but it looks like that one wasn't spared." He pointed toward one of the islands, the bridge that had spanned from east to west missing a large piece in the middle. Stumbling forms reached for the LAV from the beach, but they wouldn't enter the water. "That must be Long Island, the bridge gives it away."

"I thought Long Island was in New York?" Dallas said over the radio.

"This is a different Long Island..." Rick seem lost in thought. "Shit, Colonel, we should head northeast for a mile."

"Negative, Rick, we're too close to our mission objective to go on a foray."

"Sir, there's a fort on George's Island, Fort Warren. It would be a perfect place for scared people from Boston to hide out, the place is huge with giant walls."

"All the more reason to bypass it. I don't want to get in a firefight with scared civvies looking to protect their assets, or have the LAV appropriated by anyone who appears friendly and then draws weapons on us."

Rick acquiesced, admitting to himself that the colonel was probably right.

As they got closer to the city, evidence of the plague grew easy to distinguish. Several of the taller buildings that could be seen from the water were covered in scorch marks, dozens of their glass windows shattered or missing. Any smoke plumes had long since faded as the fires in the city burned out. As they moved past Logan Airport on their right, the bones of several aircraft were splayed at every angle on the tarmac. One seared fuselage was half in the water, its grisly inhabitants doomed to remain belted in until the seatbelts or the occupants themselves rotted enough for release.

The inner part of Boston Harbor was devoid of any type of ships other than the roof and upper deck of a submerged ferry boat. A lone zombie walked the deck like a trapped pirate. Unwilling to get its feet wet, it was ensnared by the waist-high railing on three sides and the harbor on the fourth. It stared at the LAV as it chugged past, its eyes full of iniquitous desire. It didn't reach, but put its sodden hands on the railing

The route that the team had decided on would take them into the heart of the city by way of the Charles River. MIT was located immediately next to the river, and using the waterway to gain access seemed the safest way to progress. Rick's ex-wife and the rest of the scientists were on the sixth floor of the Computer Sciences and Artificial Intelligence Laboratories building. Rick had been in there several times to visit his wife (when they were married), and he related to the group that because of the various projects going on in this particular building, security had been extensive. Heavy steel doors with both mechanical and electronic locks secured each floor. Just getting into the building prior to the plague took an act of God, even for an off-duty cop. It was the largest building on campus, and Rick told everyone that the architecture was…weird.

Boston was eerily quiet as the vehicles made their way up the Charles. Androwski was manning the turret in the LAV, and he noticed Seyfert come out on the deck of the *Brilliance*, rubbing his eyes and stretching. "You took a nap?" Androwski asked into his throat mic.

"Damn skippy. Still tired too. I could have slept another ten hours if we weren't so close to the friggin' AO."

Androwski flashed his middle finger and Seyfert blew him a kiss in return.

32

Half of the Harvard Bridge was missing. There were cars on both sides of the missing span, apparently attempting to travel in both directions as the span was taken out. Lurching forms appeared to the sides of the bridge when they heard the motors of the two vehicles. Several overzealous creatures fell or were pushed off the jagged edge of the broken road into the river, or spilled over the rails.

The undead population was light in the immediate area considering how large a city Boston had been. That would all change soon though, as the noise from the LAV and the *Brilliance* resounded through the silent streets. Bourne gave the order to cut the engines and drop anchor at 1535. Seyfert tossed a line to Androwski, and they lashed the boat to the LAV. Bourne, Dallas, Murray, and Seyfert moved to the LAV, while Wilcox and Anna moved to the Sundancer.

A small incursion team of Androwski, Seyfert, Rick, Murray, and Dallas would seek to gain entrance to the required building and assist the scientists with any gear they had. Stark would, of course, drive. The rest of the team would attempt to appropriate three armored trucks from the Steele Securities and Transport Company further up the river. If the trucks weren't there or were not operational, Bourne would appropriate any vehicles he could to get the scientists and their gear back to the river.

The *Brilliance* would carry the scientists and the military men as they moved toward the as yet undisclosed location that was hinted at during Rick's ex-wife's previous conversations with Rick and Bourne.

The colonel took a deep breath as he picked up the radio microphone in the LAV. "This is Wanderer for Brenda Barnes or anyone in the Strata Building at MIT, do you copy, over?"

Rick harrumphed. "She hates being called Barnes, her maiden name is Poole."

"Sorry, Rick, I'll call her Poole."

Rick smiled a wicked half-smile. "Don't. It will piss her off to no end."

Bourne raised a graying left eyebrow, "Repeat this is Wanderer calling…"

A panicked man's voice cut him off. "We're here! I mean, we read you! I mean, we copy! Have you come to help us?"

"I need to speak with Brenda Barnes, repeat Barnes."

"Barnes? There's nobody here by…"

A small scuffle was heard over the radio, with several voices speaking at once. A woman's voice came on in a few moments. "This is Brenda *Poole*, to whom am I speaking?"

Bourne looked at Rick, who mouthed: *That's her.*

"Ms. Barnes…"

"Poole!"

"Ms. Poole, you called me and your ex-husband on a jury-rigged phone last month. What is your husband's name?"

"Rick Barnes. He lives in San Francisco, and he's with my daughter, Samantha."

"And my name, do you remember my name, over?"

"I believe it is Bran or something. I wasn't the one who called you, Kerry did."

"Kerry Cushing? Major Cushing's wife?"

"Yes. Where are you? When can you get here? We're down to stale pretzels, the Snickers bars were finished this morning."

Bourne was still apprehensive. "Would you please put Mrs. Cushing on?"

There was a small pause before Brenda answered, "I'm sorry. She's dead."

"How many of your original eighteen are dead?"

"There are four of us left," she answered. "How far away are you?"

"Depending on the presence of hostiles, the amount of equipment and supplies you need to carry with you, and applying the fact that there are only four of you left, we can probably have you out of there by the end of the day."

"You mean today? The end of today?"

"Affirmative, Ms. Poole."

There was excited banter and even a small cheer from the other end of the mic. "Ms. Poole, I need tactical information to better assess the situation. Can you see any undead in your area?"

"Undead…yes."

"Can you make an accurate count?"

She paused, "Uh...no, there are too many."

"Where exactly are you in the Strata Building?"

"We're on the sixth floor of the CSAIL lab. We hold the fifth and sixth floor, but the seventh…" Again, a hesitation.

Bourne picked up on it. "The seventh floor?"

"The seventh is compromised. There are infected up there."

"Okay, we're coming to get you now, is there anything else you want to tell me that could help us?"

"Help you? No. But we could all really use a sandwich."

33

Murray looked at his feet and noticed water sloshing around. He swallowed hard, "Uh, are we…?"

"Relax, Army," Seyfert cut in, "we won't sink."

The LAV motored toward the north bank. Several undead had heard the engine and had shown up to investigate. As there were only four scientists left to save, Bourne had decided to join the party even with his injury. It would be a tight squeeze to get everybody in, but they were only going to have to travel a quarter of a mile to the building, and assuming they were able to retrieve the scientists quickly, they could be back to the boats by midnight with the survivors and their data or samples.

Bourne had taken stock of their ammunition before they began the trek overland. They had two hundred rounds for the bushmaster and eleven hundred rounds for the LMG. The coaxial LMG hadn't been used yet, and that had been loaded to capacity as well, with four hundred rounds. The various small arms that the team possessed were all cleaned and loaded prior to the incursion, and everyone had a decent amount of ammo and spare magazines except Dallas. He only had fourteen shells left for his shotgun.

"I got this though," he said and patted his rebar. Stenner had given him two M9 tactical pistols, one of which was suppressed. Three magazines extra was all he had left, and he fortified the big Texan with those as well. "Now we're loaded fer bear! I jus' hope they ain't zombie bear."

They sailed the amphibious vehicle upriver until they found a breach in the embankment. Spitting mud and river rock, the LAV gained access to the MIT campus, and rolled toward Building Thirty-Two. What should have been a two minute drive proved to be significantly more difficult than previously imagined. Apparently the students at MIT had tried to build barricades to slow the advance of the tide of dead. Elaborate structures and traps some still containing squirming victims, were placed at seemingly random locations throughout the campus and its streets. These had to be skirted or run over in order to gain access to the quad next to the Ray and Maria Strata Center, also called Building Thirty-Two, which housed the Computer Sciences and Artificial Intelligence Laboratory, CSAIL, as Brenda called it. In addition, there were the same abandoned vehicles that every other city had, and some emergency vehicles, including a huge yellow fire truck with its ladder fully extended toward the sky.

The LAV turned the corner between two dormitory-style buildings once connected by a recently destroyed glass skyway, and stopped dead.

"Oh," Stark said aloud. "Oh fuck me…"

Bourne turned and looked at the forward monitor in front of Anna. What looked like a sea of tall white penguins was ambling toward the vehicle. "Stark, get us out of here! Back up, move! Androwski, get on the Bushmaster! Seyfert, the LMG!" Everyone except Dallas and Rick already had their headsets on, and the two civvies scrambled for them. Androwski was already firing the coax, tearing through the undead forerunners.

The gears ground as Stark hastily threw the LAV in reverse. The noise from the transmission and all other sounds were drowned out when Androwski opened up with the Bushmaster. The sound got more intense when Seyfert popped the top hatch and reached for the swivel LMG, as did the smell. Even with the noise dampening headsets, the roar of the gun was so loud Seyfert couldn't hear himself gag.

"Wanderer, this is Brilliance, we hear fire, SITREP, over?"

"Brilliance, this is Wanderer Lead, we've engaged hostiles and are bugging out for now. Do not leave your position! Repeat, remain on station, do you copy?"

"Five by five, Lead, copy, out."

Rick put his hand on Bourne's shoulder. "Colonel, unless we go out on the street out front, we have to go through the quad to get to Building Thirty-Two. If we back up slowly and have them follow us, we can use Plan B and move around Building Sixty-Eight," Rick pointed to a long building on their left, "and come at Thirty-Two from the northeast."

"Murray, let me sit." The Army corporal slid out of the seat in front of the cabin monitors, and Bourne slid in. The colonel punched a few keys and a globe showed on the screen. He punched another few keys and the globe spun and zoomed in. Boston, the Charles River, and the MIT campus came zooming on screen. Rick pointed, then traced his finger on the screen, "There, around here, boom." He tapped the screen in finality.

"Good intel. Stark, did you copy that?"

"Roger that, sir, moving now." Stark kept the LAV in first gear and backed up. Androwski and Seyfert continued to thin the herd in front of them, but they had slowed down their shots considerably. "Androwski, Seyfert, ammo?"

"Under two hundred!" Seyfert bellowed.

"Coax is down to half, Bushmaster has about one-fifty left."

"Conserve as much as possible, but we still need to take out as many as we can. Cease fire at fifty rounds on the Bushmaster, and one hundred on the LMGs."

The LAV backed up and the dead followed. Stark did a three-point turn and put the nose north, speeding up Ames Street with the Koch Biology building, also known as Building Sixty-Eight on their left. He stopped the vehicle halfway up the street and revved the engine. The horde rounded the corner of the structure and came at them as fast as their rotten legs would allow.

These creatures were black with rot, some having been dead for more than two months. Many were missing appendages, and all walks of life were represented. Men in business suits, teenagers in cut-off shorts, a fat woman in a bridal gown, a small boy in filthy pajamas. The plague had been thorough and hadn't left anyone out. All of them were hungry too, and they knew that the LAV held fresh vittles.

When the festering black and yellow palm of a former soldier in camouflage gear made a wet slap on the rear hatch of the LAV, Stark threw it in gear and high-tailed it up the street taking a left into the quad. There were still dozens of undead milling about, or crawling from the wounds they had received in the earlier hail of ordnance. That didn't bother Stark though, and he crushed any unfortunate creatures which got in front of the vehicle under the wheels.

They reached a fire escape on the east side of the building, and Seyfert opened fire on a small crowd that had meandered too close. The SEAL climbed out and, standing on the hull of the LAV, was able to leap to the black iron rungs of a ladder locked in the upright position. He pulled himself up and undid the catch, the ladder slamming down on the nose of the LAV, making a sound reminiscent of a gong echoing across the quad. Seyfert began climbing, as Rick, Dallas, Bourne, and Murray exited the armored vehicle via the gun turret and climbed to the first wrought iron landing. "Pass the packs up, quick!" Androwski passed three ALICE packs up and Murray handed them further up the chain. He then pulled up the ladder and locked it back in place while Androwski looked on. Androwski turned his head around, scanning for signs of the horde. The front line was just coming into view on the north side of Building Sixty-Eight when his eyes settled back on Murray. With a casual "Good luck!" he shut the hatch, and Stark gunned the engine, the LAV heading back to the river to wait.

A shirtless young dead man in shorts stumbled close and reached his left arm for the folks on the fire escape, the other arm and shoulder missing. Several broken ribs were visible below the gaping chasm where his shoulder had been. Soon more dead showed up and reached toward the men climbing upwards. The diesel drone of the LAV was faint as they got to the third landing.

34

It was at the fourth landing where Murray stopped to take a look below them. In the minute it had taken them to climb the iron-grated stairs to the fourth floor, twenty or so undead had made it to the base of the fire escape. Murray swept his gaze east and saw the tide of putrid bodies making its slow way toward the building and the living humans. There were a lot of dead people.

A thud behind him made the window shudder and his heart leap into his throat. Murray spun, weapon extended, and saw a dead woman in a lab coat looking at him with blood red eyes. She smacked the glass again, putting her mouth on it and leaving a smear of vile fluids which dribbled down the pane.

"Jesus!" The soldier extended his middle finger to the dead woman. "Fuck you, dead bitch-nerd. You're stuck in th…" He stopped talking, eyes going wide as a flood of undead materialized out of the darkness behind the initial woman, and they surged forward, all hitting the glass at once. The glass didn't break, but the silicone used to affix it to the frame gave way and the entire windowpane pushed out from the bottom. The low end of the pane slid into Murray's shins and he screamed, falling backwards against the iron railing. Fresh blood rained down into the greedy maws of the dead below. The rest of the team heard the commotion and noticed a score of undead spilling out onto the structure beneath them. Murray pushed the glass back toward the building, but several dead had made it out and were scrabbling at the man through his clear obstruction. Murray was backed against the railing, the glass pushing on him with a dozen dead a quarter of an inch away. Bourne fired three shots with his pistol destroying three dead, but there were many more still in the building. One industrious dead man in a blood-stained lab coat had fallen to his hands and knees and crawled past the barrier on the right side. The thing grabbed Murray's leg and sunk its teeth into his calf. Murray screamed again, and stopped pushing to try and shake the thing away. The railing on the fire escape buckled outward and Murray looked up into Bourne's eyes before the black iron let go, dropping Murray and eight undead over the edge to the quad forty feet below.

Three more undead simply walked off the edge, following Murray to the ground. Another noticed the survivors above and started climbing the iron stairs. The rest of the dead followed, slowly up, or quickly down. "Go," yelled Bourne, "get to the sixth!"

Dallas grabbed Seyfert. "Tell me ya brought it!"

Seyfert undid a flap on his tactical webbing and pulled out a small white square. He molded the clay on to the portion of the fire escape that was bolted to the building as Bourne, Rick and Dallas fired into the growing crowd coming up the steps. The zombies in the rear were falling over the re-killed ones in the front trying to get to their meal, so progress was impeded some. Seyfert stuck a small cylinder into the plastique. "Go, go, go," he yelled, "it's ready!"

The team climbed the steps quickly. When they reached the sixth floor window, Dallas began pounding on it, and a tall Asian man arrived in seconds, pointing a fire extinguisher at him through the glass. "Hold on," Seyfert yelled, and he double clicked the device in his hand. A small explosion made the fire escape shudder. Several windows exploded, but not the one near the sixth floor fire escape.

Dallas bellowed at the scientist through the closed window. "Let us in, dumbass!"

The man nodded, wide-eyed, and undid the catch on the top and bottom of the windows. "Just let me get the scree—"

Dallas put his boot through the screen and stepped into the room. "Don't move a muscle, young fella," he said to the tall man pointing his shotgun at him. The main raised his hands and started breathing fast. Dallas looked around at all the laboratory gizmos and benches and whirring computers. Then he looked up and noticed the florescent lights illuminating the room.

"Now how in hell do you have power?"

"We have a direct line to the Pilgrim power plant. It's a nuclear facility, and it's still operational. We…" he trailed off as the noticed the newcomers.

Rick, Bourne, and Seyfert had followed the big man into the building. "They won't be climbing up after us," Seyfert said, "but we aren't going back that way either."

Bourne was all business. "Where is Doctor Poole?"

"She went down to five when she heard your tank pull in. She took Ravi and Phil with her."

"Okay, son, sit in that chair and keep your hands where we can see them."

"And relax nerd," Seyfert added, "we're here to kick the shit out of the forces of evil."

"Aptly put, Seyfert. What's your name, son?"

"Henry Cho. I'm a post doc working on—"

Dallas cut him off. "Colonel, they have power." The Texan pointed to the overhead lights.

"How is this possible, Henry?" demanded Bourne.

"As I was saying to your friend, we have a direct line to the Pilgrim nuclear power plant. It's still operational, and before we lost contact two days ago, it was still throwing juice."

"Losin' contact ain't the best news there, pard."

"The loss was on our end. We have a computer linked via satellite and we could speak to them. We even had video. We've theorized that the satellite's orbit must have degraded because of the lack of personnel, and…"

"Okay Henry, we understand." Bourne looked to the SEAL. "Seyfert, go get Doctor Poole. Dallas, provide cover."

Dallas tensed as Henry raised his hand. "I uh… I could just call her."

Bourne nodded, raising his eyebrows. "Please do."

Henry stood slowly and reached for a gray phone. He pushed the SPKR button and a key on the right side of the instrument. "Brenda, are you there? The cavalry has arrived."

"The damn tank drove away, Henry, they couldn't get to us. Something blew up outside too, the whole building shook."

"Brenda, I'm looking down the barrel of a very large gun. They're up here with me now."

"With you?" a man's voice said, *"How did…?"*

"If you could all come back upstairs please," Colonel Bourne was polite, "we can get down to business."

"We'll be right there."

The glass entry door whooshed open a few moments later, two men and a woman walking in. The woman and an Indian man were wearing lab coats, and the third newcomer was in jeans, work boots, and a green T-shirt. The MIT folks were all smiles until they saw the weapons. The woman saw Rick and her eyes went wide in surprise. The look vanished almost immediately and she put her hands on her hips, "Rick! What are you doing here? Where's Sam?"

"Sam's safe, she's with my father."

"Your *father*!" she almost screamed. "How could you leave her in California? I can't believe you left my daughter three thousand miles away! Actually I do believe it! Are y—?"

Seyfert and Dallas looked at each other sideways, Seyfert making a face.

"Doctor Poole, calm down!" Bourne's voice was one that didn't need raising for folks to know who was in charge, so he generally kept it moderated. Still, Brenda shut right up. "Rick showed intelligence in leaving your daughter behind. In fact, the only reason he was allowed on this mission is because he knew this facility and how to get here. From what I hear, Alcatraz is guarded by a nuclear submarine and a team of SEALs. We've lost several men, one just now, and quite frankly your daughter would have been a liability en route. We've come a long way, and we're here to take you where you wanted to go. We've also brought you some food. While you eat, we need details on this facility you need to go to, where it is, and what it is, so we can best plan on how to get you there."

"I understand. I'm sorry." She had directed this at the colonel, and didn't look at Rick. "This is Ravindra Thandayuthapani, and this is Phil."

"Please call me Ravi. Thank you," the Indian looking man said, and extended his hand.

The other man extended his hand as well. "Guess I'm just Phil."

Introductions were made, and then the colonel asked where they were going.

"Colonel," Rick cut in, and all eyes focused on him, "I have a question for them. When we spoke on the phone a month ago, you said you had prior knowledge of this virus. What knowledge?"

All eyes focused back on Brenda.

35

"The facility we are in is aptly named CSAIL," Brenda said between spoonfuls of noodles, "the Computer Sciences and Artificial Intelligence Laboratories. You must understand that the people employed here are the apex minds in these fields. So last year, when the NSA came to our director and asked us to come up with a solution for an extremely nasty and aggressive viral worm based on the Stuxnet architecture, he didn't hesitate to accept the challenge. Especially with the price tag associated with the project. Funds were nearly limitless."

The two military men, the Texan, and Rick looked as if they had no idea what she was talking about.

She stopped slurping her soup long enough to realize they were confused. "Stuxnet? Iranian nuclear facilities? Operation Olympic Games? Don't you people watch the news?" Bourne folded his arms, and Brenda got the message. "Okay, Okay, sorry. Stuxnet was a computer worm...a program hidden inside other programs to wreak havoc on computer systems. This particular worm was like nothing anyone had seen before. It didn't just shut down hard drives, or gather information, it actually targeted specific functionalities in several nuclear reactors and either shut them down or took them over, completely locking out the facility technicians and not allowing the workers there to do anything. Equipment was destroyed, research lost, and people died."

"Fascinating," admonished Seyfert, "and the zombies?"

She took a sip of Gatorade, giving Seyfert a dirty look. "I'm getting to that. Stuxnet went through several iterations; Flame, Abyss, and finally Abaddon. The source code for each virus was far more advanced than the last. The Abaddon virus was the pinnacle of human code writing. Scary stuff. At first none of us here could even get inside the code, then Kerry devised an algorithm to..." Brenda had been speaking quickly, and she suddenly looked up from her bowl and noticed she had lost her audience again.

"This new virus could shut down anything. A hospital, an aircraft carrier, even your car. Things with the most basic of programming to the most advanced cyber security in the world began becoming infected. Independent systems with no link to the outside. Totally secure. Two systems at the NSA, three at the FBI, a critical system at the CIA. You remember that Russian sub that was lost with all hands in October of last year? Abaddon. That was when the NSA came knocking on our door. Russian subs are okay to lose I guess, but not American subs. The NSA was being proactive."

"Jesus Brenda!" Ravi almost shouted. "This is…this is treason."

"Relax, Ravi, the NSA is as dead as everyone else. I don't think confidentiality agreements and gag orders are going to be enforced."

Bourne was shaking his head. "I never heard of anything like this."

"You wouldn't unless you had SCI clearance. Nobody knows about this. We weren't even kept in all the loops. So, back to Abaddon. Nobody could figure out how it could infect independent systems. Either a super spy network was infiltrating every three letter intelligence installation in the country, or there was some type of signal that could penetrate hard lines. The NSA was sure it was a bunch of spies, and so we were tasked with coming up with a counter virus to clean out Abaddon."

She looked at Ravi. "We did. We worked day and night at their secure facility. We came up with a deadly, and I do mean deadly anti-virus. Rama. It not only undid the havoc that Abaddon had wreaked, but it re-wrote source code on the fly. It could prevent Abaddon from taking hold, and also save critical systems that had already been damaged by putting them in a slave mode allowing the systems to be operated by anyone who had the proper key code. Damaged systems were repaired."

She paused and looked at the colonel. "Dead systems came back to life."

"Holy shit," said Seyfert, understanding. "You did it. You created the plague."

"No," she said, "no we didn't. All of our research and development was halted as soon as we came up with the first Rama prototype. The

NSA took our product and shut us down. They escorted us from their facility and revoked our clearance."

Ravi harrumphed. "They wouldn't even let me get my iPad from my locker, they bought me a new one."

"That was months before the plague first hit Boston. Of course, you understand as soon as they shut us down, we started up again without telling them."

"Now *that* sounds like treason," Bourne said accusingly.

"You can shoot us later. Anyway, Ravi and I worked on this constantly, even after the plague broke out. There was one critical point that we never did figure; how Abaddon infected closed systems. When there were eighteen of us, and we were stuck in here, we tried to figure out how that could happen, so after we fortified the building, we brainstormed. We came up with nothing until Dr. Linda Martin, a neurologist and a pioneer in artificial intelligence and organic computing, came up with a radical idea. She postulated that the only thing that was common to every scenario was that there was human interaction.

"These NSA spooks, they undress all the way before they go in and out of the computer labs, and they made us do the same. No clothing, jewelry, or electronics of any kind. They had prescriptions for our eyeglasses before we even got there. When we were totally naked, we were escorted through a metal detector and each of us had a full body MRI. This was each time we entered or left a lab, and guards were rotated every four hours. Their computer labs were totally independent, no outside lines or wireless anything, and we were underground. Nobody could possibly have hacked a system to upload the virus, but it still infected three of the systems in lab two, and all of them in lab three.

"Dr. Martin came up with the idea that we must be carrying the virus and transmitting it with some type of hidden signal. She studied each of us and herself and there was nothing anywhere. Then she put Kerry in a magnetoencephalography machine. An MEG works by recording the magnetic fields that are produced by the human brain's naturally occurring electrical currents. Kerry's alpha wave patterns were like nothing Dr. Martin had ever seen. She put us all in the machine, and we all had irregular patterns. In addition, alpha waves are supposed to diminish when your eyes are open, but ours were super high in amplitude all the time, and the patterns didn't look right."

She lifted the bowl of soup and finished the broth. "Rama was being transmitted via alpha waves."

"Still a theory," Ravi added. "Thank you."

"Yes, but it makes sense," Brenda countered. "It makes sense that if the alpha waves are just a signal, then they could carry a *hidden* signal, but we were still back to square one. How did the signal penetrate a wireless network? That was when Phil reminded us that alpha waves were magnetic signals, and even wired computers are just signal machines."

Everyone looked at Phil, who shrugged. "I'm not without skills."

"What's your field of expertise? Bourne asked.

"Cleaning. I'm the janitor."

"Oh... I'm sorry, I just thought..."

"Well, I was gonna get my PhD, but then everybody woulda' called me Dr. Phil. You understand."

Rick, Dallas, and Seyfert smiled. Bourne did not.

"Anyway, we argued back and forth on how the signal could carry a virus, and how we thought it was just too coincidental that this plague popped up at about the same time we created an anti-virus for Rama. So we acquired some test subjects and began testing on the seventh floor. That's where the MEG was kept and..."

"Wait," Seyfert raised his index finger, "wait a second. Test subjects?"

"Yes, we needed to determine how or even if it was either Abaddon or Rama that was causing this plague. We captured seven subjects, and began testing immediately. Once we—"

Seyfert interjected, "Where are the test subjects?"

"Two are down the hall, the others are...they're up one floor."

"Ya' mean ta tell me ya' got the livin' dead on this floor with us?"

"Of course. How else could we run our tests? It's completely safe, I assure you. After what happened upstairs, we beefed up our security and contamination procedures. The precautions we've taken ensure that—"

"Where exactly is your holding facility?" demanded Bourne in his *I-will-not-be-fucked-with* voice.

"It's right down the hall in the AI lab, I'll show you."

Rick, Seyfert, and Dallas all checked their weapons and clicked safeties off.

They walked down the long hall to another lab with a few larger instruments. It didn't look like a computer lab. A large glass window looked in on the room.

"There, as you can see, they are quite restrained." Two creatures, both naked, were strapped to gurneys. The first, a male, at least six feet in height, appeared clamped to the table with leather restraints and metal straps across its neck, chest, waist, and knees. The other was only most of a torso, nothing below her ribcage was left, and her arms were gone as well. Both were, as the doctor had said, very well restrained. Some slight movement came from each, but they were mostly content.

The colonel rubbed his shoulder wound and made a grimace. "Would you please open this door?"

The lab was hermetic, and the primary door whooshed as it was opened. "We have to step inside, the inner door won't open until the outer door is closed. There are Tyvek suits on the wall that we will need to wear as well, but there are only four. If you would…"

"Seyfert, with me. Doctor Poole, please remain outside."

"What? Why? What do you intend—?"

Ravi gently grabbed her by the arm and pulled her back. "Get out of the airlock, Brenda. Thank you."

The door closed and Seyfert began looking around. He found a green cordless drill with a charger next to it and pulled the battery from the charger. Brenda began banging on the glass, but Seyfert and Bourne couldn't hear what she was yelling. Seyfert garbed up with one of the Tyvek suits and put a shield over his face. The banging intensified, and Bourne folded his arms and turned around to look at her briefly. Rick was trying to talk to her, but she was shaking him off and pointing at the glass, obviously yelling.

Both creatures were agitated now, but they couldn't move because of the restraints. Both undead wore blindfolds, and the male was growling.

Seyfert tested the drill, and the creatures grew significantly more rowdy, straining at their bonds and mewling or snarling. He moved to the full specimen, whose head was restrained with two crude, wooden two-by-four blocks on either side of its cranium. He used the drill to sanitize the thing, drilling into its forehead. It stopped its pathetic thrashing immediately, and Seyfert moved on to the next one. He repeated the process and put down the drill, and began to strip off the white suit.

Bourne nodded to him and they moved through the airlock.

Doctor Poole looked ashen. "What have you done? Do you have any idea what we had to go through to obtain those specimens?"

Seyfert was incredulous. "And you were going to do what now that we're here? Take them with us? Got a big fuckin' suitcase, ma'am? Earth to science lady: not happening!"

"Stand down, sailor." The colonel looked at Brenda. "He's right though, we couldn't very well take them with us, and if we're going to be here for a few hours, then I for one don't want them around."

"Me neither," agreed Phil. "Never did like them in here with us. They killed eleven of our people up on the seventh floor."

Brenda whipped around. "I could have told them that," she spat with venom.

Phil just shrugged.

"Enough. Tell us what you need to bring with you, and we'll help you pack. You are each allowed to bring thirty pounds of equipment and data, and we will assist by carrying thirty pounds each as well. Any more and you may slow us down, so figure out what you need. Seyfert, begin working on an exfil strategy. Dallas and Rick, check the perimeter, stay close and check all of the barricades. This mission is not over. Let's get to work. Doctor Poole, you will also need to tell me where we are going, and how best to get there."

36

"Seriously? That's the best ya got?"

"Easy, Texas, there's no other way. The fire escape we came in on is destroyed, and the one on the other side of the building is crawling with Limas, I checked."

"But I don't like climbin'. There ain't no other way? *None*?"

"No. There *ain't*," Seyfert said the word in a southern drawl. "Yeah, it sucks, but what else can we do? It will bring us right into the loading dock, which is the only part of the facility that isn't as secure as the rest."

"I'm not sure if that's a good thing or not," Bourne added, "but I don't see any other options."

Rick let out a deep breath. "C'mon, hillbilly, the colonel had a bullet in his shoulder a week and a half ago, and he's gonna climb down."

Bourne rubbed his shoulder again, and Dallas scratched his head. "I'm a mite prickly with heights is all."

"Don't look down then," Phil chimed. "If you don't look down, it will feel like you're on a step ladder three feet in the air. Just look right in front of you."

"Yeah, I heard that b'fore."

Seyfert spread his hands wide on a table, flattening out a rolled up blue-print he had gotten from a hanging print closet. MIT was constantly upgrading or altering wiring, so blue-prints of the facility were a must to the scientists who worked there. "We're here." The SEAL pointed, tracing his finger across a hallway and down an elevator shaft. "It's about sixty six feet from the entrance of this shaft on the fifth floor to the base of the shaft at the loading dock. It will be a long climb on the service ladder, but we can do it. We'll lower the data and gear down first and follow. Ravi says that the loading dock is relatively small, so the amount of Limas down there should be negligible."

"It's true, the area is small, but there's still an issue," Ravi pointed out.

Seyfert looked up, "What issue?"

"What if the loading dock door isn't closed?"

"Shit."

"Shit? Izzat the best ya got? Shit?"

"Okay, so we tie the bags off just below the second floor, and everybody waits on the ladder while Dallas, Rick, and I clear the dock area. If we can't clear the area, we climb back up and figure something else out."

"That's a lotta climbin' boy."

"Shoulda laid off the pasta and cheeseburgers, hillbilly."

"Damn, Rick. Don't be sayin' cheeseburgers in front o' me no more. Might be ya get bit by a live person instead of a dead-un."

"Enough. Seyfert's plan is good. Well done. Are there any questions before we begin?"

Ravi looked at Brenda, and they both looked at Henry, who raised his hand.

"Yes, Henry?"

"We, uh, we need the RAID on seven?"

"What is radon seven?" Bourne demanded. "Some type of chemical agent?"

"What? No. No it's a system of computer hard drives. Redundant Array of Independent Disks. *RAID*. It's on the seventh floor. In the magno lab."

Dallas looked at Henry. "But you said the seventh was fulla dead people?"

Ravi let out a breath. "It is. There are eleven of our friends, plus…plus five test subjects," he said sheepishly.

Brenda immediately started on the defensive. "The test subjects were necessary to—"

Bourne cut in. "Forget the subjects. Where are these discs and how do we get to them?"

"The array is on a lab bench in the magno lab," Henry explained. "It's a black box about this tall," he put his palm about two feet from the floor, "but it's heavy. Forty pounds anyway."

Bourne let out a sigh as he rubbed his eyes with his palms. He folded his hands then steepled them with his thumbs under his chin and looked at Henry. "And of course all of your data is on those hard drives correct?"

"Not all of it."

Seyfert threw himself into a chair. "Un-fucking-believable."

"Secure that tone, seaman, this was the mission from the get-go."

"Roger that, sir. Sorry."

The colonel looked at Brenda. "So there are sixteen undead upstairs, and you need a black box that's in the middle of them?"

"Actually the magno lab is at the *back* of the building," Henry said.

"Oh, I'm startin' ta dislike where this is goin'."

A half hour later, Seyfert, Rick, and Dallas were looking up and down a stairwell. Henry Cho was with them, looking nervous. "Seventh is only one floor up, but the whole stairwell is clear from the basement to the eighth."

"That's good news at least." Seyfert pulled his black tactical facemask up. "Henry, we move together, use the hand signals we taught you to communicate, and for Christ's sake stay with us."

The scientist looked around anxiously. "Why don't I get a gun?"

"Because I don't want to worry about Limas *and* getting shot in the back."

Dallas pulled his rebar from his belt. "Here ya go, kid." Henry grabbed it, but Dallas didn't let go and the big man looked him in the eye. "Do not lose this." Henry nodded and they began climbing the stairs.

A gray steel fire door with a yellow 7 on it greeted them when they reached the landing after two short flights. Light poured from a small window at face height into the dimly lit stairway. Seyfert held up a fist and pulled out an inspection mirror, which he put in front of the window so he could see into the room. "Looks like a glass cube," he whispered.

Henry whispered back, "It's an airlock. The whole floor is hermetic. My keycard will get us in this door and the next, but it beeps when I use it."

Seyfert took another look in the mirror. The immediate area was clear, but there were shadowy forms moving down the hall. "Dallas left, Rick right, I'm center. Henry, you stay inside us, bottom of the pyramid. Open it."

Henry moved forward, pulling a card on a lanyard from around his neck. He put the card in front of a reader, which emitted a quick beeping sound, and the red light on the reader turned green. There was an audible click, and Seyfert pulled the door open wide. The heavy door made the loudest sound of all as it opened, but no one came to greet them. Viscous fluids of many colors coated the airlock pane on the other side of them, with hand and fist prints covering the upper part of the glass as well.

Seyfert glanced in all directions through the airlock glass. He looked apprehensive. "I don't like this. Okay, I'm going to smack the glass with my rifle until we get company, then we fall back and smoke them as they fill the stairway. Henry, give me your key card, and get back and hold the sixth floor door." Seyfert turned and spoke into his shoulder mic, "Actual, do you copy?"

"Loud and clear. SITREP?"

"We are about to breach, but no hostiles in sight. Blood on the airlock door indicates unfriendlies inside as we were told. Objective is to draw them out a few at a time and take them in the stairway. We need someone down there to open the door for Henry and keep a lookout. Stair team will fall back to six if necessary."

"Copy that. Door is open. Good luck."

Henry passed the card to Seyfert and wasted no time in beating a hasty retreat back the way they had come. Seyfert rapped the butt of his weapon on the door several times. Someone stuck their head out of a room a few meters up the hall, and looked in the other direction. The SEAL gave another light whack to the glass, and the thing turned and looked its red eyes at the stairway team. Its eyes widened and its mouth opened as it came at them in a slow plod. "Back up to the door behind us, Rick hold it open, Dallas back me up with the shotgun, but don't shoot me." He went over the load of his weapon in his mind and mentally ensured see he was fully loaded. As the creature got closer to the airlock, the team could hear it moaning. Seyfert looked back and nodded to his friends. "Here goes."

He put the card in front of the reader just as the thing started scratching at the glass. The reader beeped, the light turned green, the door whooshed left, and the dead woman fell forward on her hands and knees, as she was leaning forward for a particularly hard pound on the glass. The smell that wafted out of the lab was almost unbearable. Seyfert shot the thing in the back of the head with a cold-loaded round before it could stand, and put his foot in the door to stop it from closing. The woman had a huge chunk of her neck missing, and a semicircle bite on her forearm. She looked freshly killed, a few days at most. "Come on out, pus bags," yelled the SEAL, "I got something for you!"

Three more undead came from forward of the team. One was walking oddly as it had no right foot. Seyfert, his foot in the door, sighted and took them out one by one. "Is that it?" called Seyfert. "Where are the rest of you dead fucks!" Dull thuds could be heard in the lab area down the corridor, but nothing else came out to play. "Shit. Okay, we go in. I'm on point. Watch your corners and check our six."

The three men moved forward slowly, stepping over the three corpses along the way. There were several doors off of a long corridor, then the corridor opened up into a large research area with lab benches and equipment. A glass wall, covered in gore, waited for them fifteen meters past that. Blood and gore spatter coated the walls and floor of the laboratory they were in, evidence of attacks as well. Overturned chairs and a parts bench, a computer monitor on the floor with a cracked photo of a long white beach flickering. Dallas shone his tac-light into the first door on the left, an empty office. He closed the door. Rick did exactly the same for the first office on the right. The next door on the left was smashed in and held the barely moving corpse of someone in a red cape. There was nothing left of the front of this thing. All of its muscle tissue had been eaten away, and the chest and abdominal cavity were empty. Eyes, face, both arms and one leg were totally gone, bones and all. The other leg ended at a gnawed stump at the knee. The door was destroyed and could not be closed, but the thing in the room would never move of its own volition again.

The thudding continued.

Two more offices held nothing, but the last one on the right contained a lone zombie, back to the door staring at posters on a wall. This one too had a mostly red cape, which the team silently acknowledged as a gore covered lab coat. Seyfert made to shoot it, but Dallas stopped him with a hand on his weapon. The big man stepped into the room and went for his rebar...only to realize he had given it to Henry. He gave a sharp intake of breath upon realizing his mistake, and the zombie whipped its head around and screamed, its hands clawing for the Texan. Seyfert shot it twice in the chest as Dallas backpedaled quickly. The thing fell on its back, and Seyfert put one through its forehead. Dallas swallowed hard, nodding his thanks to his friend. He closed the door and moved on.

They reached the end of the corridor and came upon the glass wall. It was another airlock, the right side of the small cube pushed in. The source of the constant thudding was now apparent: four undead pounding on the glass door creating a slowly spreading spider web of cracks. They were crowded into the airlock, trying to break the door down. Three wore lab coats, and looked as newly dead as the ones the team had encountered in the hallway. The fourth was barefoot with a pair of cutoff jeans and a ragged, fluid-spattered T shirt. It was also putrescent and impossible to tell what race or gender it had been, although it had long hair hanging in filthy strings. Its skin was a shiny black and pieces of its flesh were being left behind as it smacked the glass, the right hand worn to nothing but yellowish bone, the top portion of its fingers missing.

The living men checked their position, nothing was behind them and all the doors were closed except for the one that had been smashed in. The lab area the men occupied was as trashed as the one up front had been, equipment broken, and blood on everything. Rick and Dallas kept an eye out behind and to their respective sides as Seyfert moved forward. He stepped to the side of the first lab-coated zombie and shot it in the side of the head. It crumpled instantly. The ratcheting mechanism on the suppressed weapon was an odd sound in the partially enclosed area, and the shot was louder than Seyfert liked but the three remaining undead either didn't notice or didn't care. Seyfert shot the gooey one next, and then the other two. None had turned to look at him even when their fellows fell.

After making sure they were truly dead, Seyfert glanced in the window of the last lab. A large machine, with a short arm and small dome on the end of the arm, looked like a giant old-style hair dryer. It held a single occupant, a struggling zombie strapped in tight. Two corpses, one wearing a lab coat and one not were splayed on the floor in the room as well, and two more animated corpses were strapped down on gurneys to the far right.

Dallas and Seyfert pulled the re-killed zombies from the airlock as Rick stood watch. *"Stair team this is Lead, SITREP, over?"*

"Twelve Limas down, three restrained. Breaching the lab now."

"That leaves one Lima unaccounted for, seaman."

"Copy that, Lead, we are toes down. Another SITREP in three, out."

Seyfert looked at both his friends, nodded, and smacked his weapon barrel against the cracked pane of the airlock. The creature strapped in the machine became more agitated, but that was it, nothing else came stumbling. "Double shit," the SEAL said. He ran Henry's card past the reader and the cracked glass slid to the right. "Anybody home?" he asked.

A disheveled female zombie stood up from behind a rack of computer components in the back of the room. "Dammit," Seyfert said, and began to aim his weapon.

The creature raised its hands as well. "Don't shoot, please," croaked the timid voice.

Rick and Dallas looked at each other in awe.

Seyfert raised his eyebrows, but lowered his rifle. "Actual, we've got a live one."

37

Ravi and Brenda were all smiles as their friend wolfed down a bowl of beef flavored ramen noodles. Dr. Linda Martin had quite a story to tell. The lab folk up on the seventh floor had been experimenting on the undead they had captured. One had broken loose of its bonds somehow and clamped its teeth on the neck of one of the students leaning over it. The student had succumbed to her injuries within minutes and turned quickly. She had bitten two others while they fought her, and in the ensuing madness, Dr. Venn, the artificial intelligence specialist, dropped to the floor and died as well, probably from a heart attack. He also turned quickly, but he decided to come back with upgrades, and he sprinted around the lab tearing into every living person he could find, infecting and killing the rest of the students and post-docs.

Linda was able to get inside the magno lab, but as she did so, two of her infected colleagues also gained access while chasing her. She put them both down with a fire axe, but there were several more shuffling around, and Dr. Venn was running everywhere, spitting and destroying anything he could.

Ravi, Brenda, and Phil had been downstairs on the sixth floor when all this had happened. When they came back up, they noticed their former friends and colleagues on the other side of the airlock were dead, so they assumed the worst and gave up on the lab, quietly escaping back downstairs without being noticed. The magno lab is devoid of any type of phones or intercom system, as communication equipment can interfere with the instruments, so Linda was trapped. Dr. Martin did what any scientist would do in her situation – she continued working.

"I made some discoveries," she told them, "not the least of which is that the alpha and theta waves of an AD's brain are off the charts. More than that, not only are the ADs devoid of beta waves, they focus on them! I believe that's how a blind AD with headphones on can track a human being."

"What's an AD?" Dallas asked aloud.

Dr. Martin looked at him strangely. "An ambulatory deceased. What do you call them?"

"I call 'em pus-bags, but them military folks calls em Lima Deltas, or jus' Limas."

"Interesting. I like it. Anyway, as I was saying, *Limas* (she looked at Dallas) don't breathe, so they can't smell, so it isn't our scent that attracts them. I removed the eyes of the one I was testing, and covered its ears with headphones, and filled its nostrils with silicone caulking, but whenever I got close it turned its head toward me. It knew where I was. It always knew where I was. It was reacting to some other stimuli. Then I tested its brain waves and voila! The alpha and theta waves, which are associated with the mundane tasks we do, or outright sleep, were off the charts. It didn't make any sense!"

"Neither do dead people walking," interjected Seyfert as he tossed his suppressor on the floor, "but I'm used to it." He removed another steel tube from his load-bearing vest and screwed it in place.

"There's more," Dr. Martin continued. "I have had this theory for years about beta waves. The betas from one person have a frequency and amplitude relatively the same as the next person. Stick two people in a room together, and the frequency and amplitude of the signals don't change, but the power of the signal is amplified to approximately four point five times what it was with one person, meaning the sum of the power of the waves is greater than just two people should generate."

Everyone, including Ravi and Brenda, just stared at her. Phil was nodding his head like he understood, but he stared too.

"This means that the more people you have together, the stronger the power potential of beta waves. The Limas (she looked at Dallas again) find prey primarily through sound, but once they are in range of someone, two feet maybe, then can find them without using the five senses we use, and the more people, the farther away the signal travels! A large group of people would generate a significantly stronger signal."

"Excellent," Seyfert chortled, "wonderful. So the more people we have with us, the more danger we're in. This also means that enclaves of survivors will throw off a big damn beacon for a free lunch."

Dr. Martin looked over the rim of her bowl as she finished gulping the last of her soup, "Correct. It also means that everyone who was in even a remote contact with a Rama infected individual or computer would be instantly infected themselves, and capable of transmitting the virus unknowingly." She wiped her face with a napkin. "I've also got a theory on the faster creatures."

"Issues with the way their brains work," said Phil.

Everyone looked at Phil again. Phil simply shrugged.

"Yes. People with certain psychoses, even those who can control the psychoses, or haven't manifested any symptoms, could be immune to the shut-down effects of the Rama virus. They would still contract it, but it wouldn't work the same. It may not shut down or take over as many critical systems, or it could spiral off in other ways. Just a theory, mind you."

"A good one though," Ravi agreed. "Drugs or certain sounds or visual stimuli can alter alpha and beta waves. But if we're all already infected, why don't we just shut down right now? Why do we need fluid contact from a victim that is already dead?"

"I've hypothesized on that as well. Rama was always in a dormant mode in all the computers until it received some type of signal to activate. I believe this signal could be the introduction of fluids from an individual where Rama is running the show. Or death, that could start it off too. Somehow Rama kicks in when one of the vital systems of the human body shuts down. The virus then takes over the system that controls all the others. The nervous system. It doesn't need other systems, like digestive or endocrine, and it can slow, but not stop the degradation procedure, so the dead can walk, but they rot, albeit significantly slower."

Rick rubbed the back of his neck. "So then why do the infected want to eat us?"

Dr. Martin sighed. "I don't know. Perhaps to infect others, or to spread the virus. Maybe just to destroy, but that's not my area of expertise. Honestly, the whole Abaddon-Rama thing is just a theory."

Bourne picked up his radio. "This is good intel, but it doesn't change the mission. We have your data, your gear, and you. Let's get you to where you can work in safety. Tin Can, do you copy?"

Tin Can was the call sign Bourne had given to the LAV prior to the mission. *"Five by five. Ready and waiting. Our position is clear of hostiles."*

"Copy, no hostiles. Exfil within the hour, stay frosty. We've got all of your hostiles here. We will be coming plus four with the loss of Murray."

"Roger that, we saw it. Previous intel indicated only four breathers."

"We've got an extra. Three males, two females."

"Copy. Tin Can is ready."

38

"Uh-uh. Nope. I may be dumb, but I ain't stupid."

Dallas backed up two steps from the open and unfriendly looking maw of the service elevator shaft. The elevator was on the sixth floor, and the humans were on the fifth looking down. With two basement levels, it was more than eighty feet to the bottom, but with no lights in the shaft the darkness below was impenetrable after just a few feet. Still, the knowledge of what they were preparing to do filled the non-military survivors with dread.

Seyfert, down on one knee and holding the left elevator door open, peered over the edge and then looked back at Dallas, shaking his head. "Sissy." The SEAL jammed a large flat-head screwdriver into the carriage of the door, and stood up and kicked it. The door stayed open when he let it go. "This is it, hillbilly, you coming? Way I hear it is that there's no chow left here. Man up and prepare to climb."

He pulled three green chem lights out of his tac-webbing and snapped them. He shook them as he swung out into the shaft and deftly grabbed the ladder. He dropped two of the lights clipped a third to his webbing, and proceeded to climb down. *"Check check."*

"Read you loud and clear, Recon," Bourne answered the radio check. The colonel and Rick watched Seyfert descend until he was nothing but a green light bobbing on the left side of the shaft. The lights below him looked a hundred miles away.

"The climb isn't too bad, the rungs are dry. The glow stick throws a lot of light and I can see the ladder all around me. Passing the third floor doors now."

Dallas was shaking his head, "Dammit. I don't like heights. Don't like 'em."

"I told you," said Phil, "don't look down and you're only a foot off the ground."

"Now that's the dumbest thing I ever did hear. O'course yer off'n the ground."

The radio crackled again. *"Shit."*

"What's the problem, son?"

"Second floor elevator doors are open," he whispered. *"It's dark in the corridor and I can't see more than a foot in."* Seyfert hooked his arm around a rung and dug for another glow stick. He pulled one out, cracked and shook it, and tossed it into the open door, where it rolled against a body. *"Dammit, we've got a body just inside the corridor."*

The colonel flexed his right fingers and looked at his palm, obvious discomfort on his face. He rubbed his wounded shoulder. "Moving?"

"Negative, truly dead. Continuing down."

There was a full minute of silence before Seyfert's voice came back. *"About to breach the first floor doors now. SITREP in two minutes or I'm dead and find another way."*

The SEAL jammed another long screwdriver in between the elevator doors and began to pry. Spread eagled across the doorway, he slipped his fingers into the sliver of space between the stainless steel plates and pulled, the doors opening slightly. Peering in, he couldn't see much as the area was dark. He pushed the doors open wide and brought up his weapon, tactical light scanning. Just like so many times in the past few months, in most of the buildings he had been in, there was blood everywhere. Footprints, handprints, drag marks, and directional drop spatter decorated the floor and nearby walls. A dried pile of viscera was at his feet, but he was used to such sights as well. Two bodies were splayed out in front of him by some shelves, one with no head, the other with its face and cranium crushed. He still wasn't used to the smell though, and he swallowed hard breathing through his mouth. He heard movement to his left and tensed, thinking of missing heads, as two dead men appeared out of the shadows.

The ratcheting sound from his suppressed MP5 couldn't be helped as he destroyed the two things. He cursed to himself as the moaning started, and he backed up to the elevator shaft, keeping the emptiness and the safety of the ladder to his back. Going to one knee, he kept his firing stance ready and swept his tac-light left and right until the beasties appeared. Seyfert took a deep breath and let it out slowly as he sighted down his weapon. The holographic reticule on his optics having died with the batteries weeks ago, he used an open sight picture and fired in succession.

Pffft! *Pffft!* And so on until eight body thieves were sent back to hell permanently. Although he had only used ten rounds, he still quickly exchanged magazines in his weapon, then whistled, high and loud.

Nothing else came. He whistled again then called out lightly, "Hey boys, free dinner!" More shuffling steps came from his right; what was left of a female student in shorts stepped into his sliver of illumination. She may have been pretty once, but now her tattered skin was a slimy black, with patches of yellow and purple, what was left of her long hair a matted mess. Seyfert no longer wondered what happened to the misplaced head, the dead girl was cradling it like a crying child. She let it fall when she saw the live human. It sounded like someone dropped a cantaloupe, and it broke open somewhat when it hit the floor. She came at him quickly, but she was no runner. He dropped the thing with a single shot, then waited a solid five minutes, making soft noises before he stood.

"*Recon, SITREP.*"

"Sweeping the room now, sir, initial hostiles down. Clatter tactics ineffective or hostiles are hiding."

"*Copy that, triple check the corners and your six. Waiting on further SITREP.*"

"Roger that, Lead. Wilco." The SEAL walked softly in half-crouch, weapon at the ready. He panned the light back and forth as he moved, pausing between shelves and clearing each section before moving on. Besides the elevator shaft, the only other ways into or out of the loading dock were a fairly large roll down door at the loading area, and a set of double doors that were thoroughly barricaded. Initially, it didn't make sense to the SEAL how the whole room was dead. Then it dawned on him that one of the folks in here had been infected when they barricaded themselves in. Seyfert pictured the scenario in his mind: The folks in the loading dock barricading themselves against the undead hordes both outside and in the building. Hunkering down and being quiet, waiting for the dead to pass. One of them already infected, and either didn't tell anyone, or didn't know. They start to get sick and no one notices or they refuse to believe that it's the plague. The person dies, turns, and attacks the nearest people, all of whom are trapped in a blockaded room with no escape except into the teeth of the mass of undead outside the room. It must have been a bloodbath. The SEAL wondered how many times and in how many places this exact situation had played out across the world.

He checked the entire room three times, put on a pair of blue latex gloves, and dragged the bodies and pieces in a corner, covering them with a thick packing blanket. As he removed his gloves, he noticed he had forgotten the chewed head, and made to move it with his boot. He pushed it and the eyes and mouth moved, "Jesus! Bitch was carrying around a pet head. Yuk." Not wanting anyone to get bitten, he grabbed a push broom and unscrewed the handle. He broke the end off and jabbed the point through the left eye. He used the broom stick to push the now motionless head under the blanket with the rest of its body. He left the stick.

The roll door had four tinted oval windows, ten by twenty centimeters spaced evenly at waist level across the door. He ventured a look outside and saw minimal stumblers in the area. The main body of the horde must be to the quad side of the building, waiting for the humans to come back down for dinner.

"Wanderer Lead, this is Wanderer Recon."

"Go ahead, Recon."

"Area is clear of hostiles, but infected fluids are present so all should be careful as to what they touch. You can send down the packs."

"Roger that, Recon, area is clear. Packs are on the way."

Phil had come up with the idea that sending the ALICE packs down by rope would be easier than climbing down the shaft with them on their backs, and Bourne agreed. Unfortunately, there was no rope. Phil again showed his ingenuity by coming up with two fifty foot lengths of extension cord that he used to power the floor buffer. He knotted them together and tied one end to a pack full of hard drives, DVDs, and notebooks, and began lowering it down to Seyfert.

The SEAL grabbed the first pack and radioed back that he had it. The next two packs came down the same way, and then the humans followed.

Dallas gave one last look over the edge into the shaft and reached his hand for the ladder. "Survive a damn zombie apocalypse to die of a heart attack 'cause I'm afraid o' heights. Now thas' jus' embarrassin'."

"Remember," said Phil, "just don't look down."

The big man grumbled an unintelligible reply and began his descent. The colonel came next, followed by Brenda, Linda, Ravi, Henry, Phil, and Rick.

"Why I gotta go first anyway?" demanded the Texan.

Bourne replied without humor, "In case you fall you won't take anybody with you."

"Sounds familiar. Didn't like it then neither, but I had to go second."

Dallas was sweating as he passed the second floor elevator doors, the green glow from Seyfert's chem light illuminating a small area inside the corridor. He pressed on and suddenly he was staring the SEAL in the face. "Howdy," was all Seyfert had to say. The seaman grabbed the big man and helped him from the access ladder to the first floor.

Dallas breathed heavily. Whether it was exertion from the climb, or a sigh of relief, he wasn't sure. "That's it? I thought it would be worse."

"Help the rest of them off the ladder, I'll keep watch behind."

"Didn't ya clear th' room already?"

"Yeah, but better safe than..." Yelling from above made him stop and look up into the darkness of the shaft.

39

"You got any fours?"

"Nope. Any kings?"

"Go fish."

Anna had found a deck of cards in one of the galley cabins of the *Brilliance*. She, Stenner, and Wilcox were occupying themselves with a game at one of the galley tables while they waited for word from the rest of the team. The *Brilliance* was anchored in the center of the Charles River, and the day was getting hot.

The radio crackled to life. Keleher, the lookout, called from the top deck. "Stenner, we have company."

"Live or dead?"

"Living, unless the dead can operate a Boston Whaler. Four contacts, all armed, coming up on our stern slowly."

"Military?"

"Negative. Or they changed gear and went native."

"Shit. Call them on the radio and..."

"Already tried. No response."

Anna and Wilcox grabbed their weapons and checked the loads. Stenner limped up on deck and they followed behind. All were armed.

The boat with the newcomers stopped moving forward about ten meters from the stern of the Sundancer. The weapons on the Whaler were a mixed bag. A shotgun, a hunting rifle, an old M1 Garand, and a wicked-looking crossbow. The man with the shotgun pointedly laid it on the deck and put his hands up. "Hello. My name is Tim Straith. We would like to know why you're here."

Stenner called back, "We are elements of the United States military on a mission in Boston, that's all I can tell you."

The man visibly brightened, and looked at his friends. "The military! Have you come to help us?"

"Uh, no. As I said, we're here on a mission."

The woman with the crossbow shouted next. "We're from Fort Warren. We're in desperate need of medical supplies and information."

"I can give you what information I can, but we haven't got any meds, sorry."

"Can you tell us when we'll be rescued? We've been on that damn island for months! There are more than a hundred of us now. When is the government going to send soldiers, or have they just written us off in a quarantine?"

These people were completely ignorant of how global the pandemic had become.

"I'm sorry to tell you, sir, there is no more government. This plague isn't just in Boston, or on the east coast. The entire world is infected. Every major city on the planet is dead or dying."

All four survivors in the Boston Whaler looked at their feet. "So that's it then," the woman with the crossbow said. "It's over."

The man with the hunting rifle looked at her. "I told you. Didn't I tell you a hundred times? There's nobody left to save us. Nobody to come get us."

The man who had the shotgun, Tim, sat in one of the fishing chairs on the bow of the small craft and began to sob.

Stenner felt absolutely helpless for a second, then he got angry. "Listen up," he shouted, "I know this must be hard to take, but believe me when I tell you, if you're on that island and you're not near infected, then you're doing better than most of the rest of the folks in America. Hell, most of the world is dead, you folks are lucky! You should go back to your island. I will speak to my CO about stopping in when our mission is complete. We can have a long talk and let you know what's happening out there, what we've seen. The bottom line is you shouldn't give up! You're alive!"

Tim wiped his face with his arm and nodded. "Let's get back."

"Monitor channel six," Stenner shouted, "we'll contact you at some point."

The taller man with dark sunglasses and the M1 shouted back, "And if you don't?"

"Then we're dead."

The woman with the crossbow waved to them as they turned the Whaler around and made for Boston Harbor.

Tim turned to his three friends as he picked up his shotgun. "What do you guys think?"

The woman sighed. "We're all going to die."

"That about sums it up," said the man with the hunting rifle.

The taller man with the sunglasses was sitting down, looking back at the *Brilliance*. Tim asked a second time, "I asked what you think, I know you're kind of new to Warren, but your opinion is important buddy. You're part of the family too."

"Greg?" Tim smiled and picked up a wet rag from the deck of the small vessel. He squeezed the water out of it, crunched it into a ball and pitched it at the guy with the sunglasses. The man whipped around and caught it in mid-air.

"I'll never get tired of that," Tim said with a small smile. "What do *you* think, Brooksy?"

"We'll have to wait and see," the man said, looking back at the *Brilliance*, "we'll just have to wait."

Dallas yanked Seyfert back by his tac-webbing as a body flew past them, impacting the bottom of the elevator shaft with a sickening crunch. The yelling above continued, and the SEAL and the Texan were able to make out panicked yelps. Both men flashed their lights down and saw barely perceptible movements coming from a body a few feet lower in the shaft. Seyfert put a round in the broken thing's head and shifted his beam up so he was able to see someone fighting on the ladder above.

"Get it off me," screamed Henry. "It won't let go!"

An undead thing had snaked its arm and shoulders through the open door to the second floor, and had latched its dead hand on to Henry's dirty shirt. Dallas and Seyfert helped the colonel and Brenda into the loading area. As they were helping Linda, they heard Rick yelling, "Quit moving, I can't get a shot!" A single shot rang out, and three pings echoed in the elevator shaft. Seyfert and the Bourne dove for cover, but Dallas, Brenda, and Linda stood their ground.

"Ricochets," growled Seyfert. "Get down!" They moved further into the room as another body came crashing down. Ravi leapt into the room, Seyfert grabbing him. Another body fell, and another. Three more shots sounded, and then silence. Seyfert shone his light into the bottom of the shaft. "Dammit." He fired twice, and then Phil and Rick were coming through the doorway.

Rick wiped his hand across his face. "One of those God damned things grabbed him and they both went down."

"Where's Henry?" demanded Ravi.

"Dead," the SEAL said, shining his light into the bottom of the shaft. "Truly dead."

Linda put her hands to her mouth, "You shot him?"

Seyfert pulled the screwdriver from the base of the elevator doors. "He was already dead. He landed on one of the Limas, and another landed on him. There was blood everywhere, I could see..." The SEAL sighed. "He was dead."

"One of the students grabbed him," Phil said helplessly, "and then the whole damn campus was coming down the hall. Rick shot two through the door, and then he nailed the wedge holding the door open. It closed before the others could get to us." He looked at Rick. "Damn fine shot."

"Too damn late more like," Rick said

Bourne put his hands on Ravi's shoulder. "Did he have any critical data on him?"

"Yes, he had—"

"Is that all you can think of?" screamed Brenda. "The data? A man just died. Your man shot him!"

"Ms. Poole, we didn't come—"

"He's dead! He was alive two minutes ago and now he's dead because of you!"

"Because of us," Rick whisper-yelled. "Us? Dammit, woman, look around! He's dead because of this plague!" He pointed his finger at her in the dim light. "If anything, he's dead because of you! Now shut the fuck up and do what you're told, or so help me we will tape your damn mouth closed."

Brenda looked shocked, but she kept quiet. Seyfert was already looking through the tinted glass on the garage door, but everyone else was looking at Rick, Dallas with a small smirk.

Seyfert broke the tense silence with a whisper. "Multiple hostiles outside, sir, a hundred at least coming this way."

Bourne looked directly at Brenda. "Nobody yells again." He picked up his radio. "Tin Can, Lead. We need a smash and grab, hostiles imminent, over."

Seyfert was prying the elevator door back open when Androwski's voice came back, *"Copy that, Lead, inbound now, thirty seconds. We have a visual on the loading dock doors. Be ready, over."*

Seyfert climbed down the last few feet into the bowels of the elevator shaft and retrieved two hard drives and a notebook from Henry's corpse. Dallas gave him a hand up and they closed the doors again. The growl of the LAV's engines, and then the roar of the Bushmaster were heard. Tin Can was close.

"Seyfert, Rick, cover," Bourne said, holstering his sidearm. "Dallas, you and I will hoist the door. Civilians, get close together in the center behind the weapons." He pointed at Rick and the SEAL. "We need to do this quickly."

Two steel L-shaped slide-locks held the door closed. Dallas and the colonel reached down and put their hands on the locks, ready to pull them and push the door up when the LAV made its grand entrance.

"Lead, you have two Limas in front of the door, we can't fire or we could hit you...disregard, they are tracking us. They walked off of the loading dock. Ten seconds, over!"

The rumble of the heavy vehicle was loud even through the steel door, and the group inside the building heard a hatch open followed by five quick reports. "Open the door, quick!"

The last was shouted, but not over the radio. The colonel and the big Texan slid the locks and threw the door up. Seyfert and Rick turned left and right and both shouted, "Clear!" The ramp to the LAV was descending, an army of the living dead thirty meters and closing. Androwski popped back into the open turret and got on the light machine gun. "Move it, people!"

Rick and Seyfert ushered the civvies in followed by Bourne and Dallas, and finally themselves. Seyfert slammed his hand against the red button and the ramp began to ascend. It closed, and he jerked the yellow lever locking it in place. "Piece of cake," he said and sat down with his back against the hull.

"This is nice," said Phil as he looked around the inside of the LAV. Stark didn't need marching orders, and he gunned the accelerator, the standing occupants in the back stumbling. There was no way around the oncoming horde, so Stark plowed through them at medium speed.

Linda looked horrified at the first thump. "What was that?"

Ravi looked at her. "Undoubtedly an assembly of former Beantown residents."

Eight minutes later, the LAV entered the Charles River.

"*Brilliance*, this is Tin Can, we are in the Chuck, with the city of Boston in pursuit. Personnel transfer will commence at the mouth of the river, there are too many hostiles too close, and the natives are restless, over."

"*Copy that, Tin Can, we see you. Copy on the rendezvous.*"

Ravi, Linda, and Brenda were looking at the water sloshing around their feet. Brenda and Linda lifted their feet out of the water and put them under their legs on the seats. Ravi reached down and stuck his finger in the water. He pulled it back up and smeared his fingers together. He opened his mouth to ask a question, but Seyfert cut him off with a sardonic half-smile. "Relax, professor. We won't sink."

40

The orange and pink glow of the sunset was heartening, even if it was over a ruined town. The last vestiges of a dying day glinted off of thousands of small wave crests in Massachusetts Bay. A dingy olive drab military vehicle, looking much like a floating tank, stuck out in stark contrast next to a large pleasure boat in the harbor of the tiny town of Marshfield. The town had not been spared from the plague, and evidence of hasty retreats and watery graves were present at the small dock the survivors had chosen for anchorage. Several boats had been attached to a fuel dock when the dock had exploded. Burned pilings, and the ruin of several piers held melted fiberglass hulks that used to be boats. Bullet holes and brown stains covered a small shack near one end of the semi-sunken dock. A corpse was in a fetal position on the charred boards. Not much more than a skeleton, the body had been picked clean by sea birds and anything else brave enough to dine.

"I'd rather not leave her moored like this, sir; I think solid ground would be better."

Bourne looked up from his torn and folded atlas, the GPS in the LAV having ceased to function through an internal fault a half hour before. "I understand, Stark, we should only be a few more minutes here and we can get underway."

The grind of a bilge pump echoed through the LAV as a black-eyed Stark ducked back in the top-side turret. The survivors had been anchored at the last unburned dock for approximately an hour, working out how they would get to a small industrial park in the low hills outside town. The park was actually an NSA front for computer research and training. Ravi told Bourne and his crew that there were four buildings on three acres surrounded by a nine-foot-tall stone wall. An electric fence twenty feet inside of the stone wall was another barrier would-be spies or terrorists would have to surmount should they attempt to break in to the facility. In addition, the entire computer research installation was underground, and it was six miles away.

Not everyone would fit in the LAV, so another ride would have to be appropriated. The *Brilliance* would move a half mile off shore with everyone but the three SEALs, and Stark, Androwski, and Seyfert would commit grand larceny, stealing a local vehicle.

Two hours after they left, Stark and Androwski returned, rowing a small boat out to the *Brilliance*, who had seen them and moved to intercept.

"Where's Jersey?" demanded Dallas, nervously looking about.

Androwski held up a finger telling Dallas to wait a second, his hands on his knees and breathing heavy on the deck. "With...with your new vehicle."

"Ya winded, Navy?" Dallas folded his beefy arms. "Thought SEALs was tough."

Androwski switched fingers. "You try rowing for half a mile, Chief. That is if the boat would haul your giant, sasquatch-ass anyway."

Seyfert and the new vehicle, a blue dualie Ford F350, were in a good spot, and he would rendezvous with the team as soon as they radioed him. It was decided that after an hour's rest, they would get underway. Stenner, Wilcox, Anna, Rick, and Dallas would use whatever new vehicle they had, and the rest would ride in the LAV. Phil adamantly refused to leave his scientist friends.

"I'm surprised you didn't want to go with your wife," Anna said to Rick when they were once again, anchored almost a mile from the beautiful beach.

"Ex-wife." Rick sat on the plush couch and put his dirty, booted feet on the glass table, closing his eyes. Dallas sat down beside him.

Anna whispered to Wilcox, "Not surprised anymore."

Stenner called from the above decks, "They're out of sight. And none too soon, the beach has some tourists."

Anna climbed out from below decks and made her way to Stenner. He passed her a bottle of water and pointed toward the coast. Two figures were walking the beach, very close together.

She stuck her hand out while she was drinking from the bottle and Stenner passed her the binoculars. She raised them to her eyes with one hand. "Oh shit, that's awful."

"What?"

"Those two dead people are hand-cuffed together."

"Aw shit, that *is* awful… Lemme see."

40

The town of Marshfield Massachusetts is small area-wise in comparison to some towns in the United States. Approximately thirty square miles of land, with several miles of beautiful coastal seashore, complete with gorgeous beaches and dunes. Approximately twenty-five thousand people live in the small town year round, but in the summer time the population swells to over seventy thousand, even higher during holidays like Memorial Day, or the Fourth of July. Some simple math on a winter month indicates there are almost eight hundred thirty-five people per square mile. Triple that for a summer month, and you are at about twenty-five hundred people per square mile. Frustrating for townies when they have to deal with "Cape traffic," but down-right deadly when it's not just your neighbor, your mom, and the local constable that are trying to eat you, but thousands of tourists as well.

The plague hit the town just after Memorial Day, and the Department of Public Works had put up dozens of street signs announcing the three-hundred-eightieth birthday celebration for the town at various spots and beaches throughout the area. When the dead started rising, poor Marshfield had been cursed with a full house.

The streets, both wide and small, were teeming with shambling victims close to the beaches. They had invaded the shops and restaurants, homes and businesses with no thought to nautically themed porches or carefully manicured lawns. With a single-minded objective, they converted all in their path to their cause with no hesitation, no mercy, and no remorse. Other than the sound of the breeze through the marshes, or the occasional shrill cry of a seabird, the only noises were those the dead intermittently made. It was deathly quiet.

The rumbling roar of a Detroit Diesel 6V53T engine coupled to an Allison MT653, 6-speed transmission, sounded like thunder in a breadbox as the LAV made its way past abandoned vehicles, the debris from burned-out houses, and the ever-present forms of the dead. A blue Ford truck followed close behind. Every creature, living or otherwise could not help but hear the vehicles make their way westward. The living ones were no longer ignorant of the inclinations of the stumbling former humans, so they stayed put in their hidey holes. Dogs, cats, rats, and even one horse kept out of sight. The dead did no such thing. They came from behind smashed doors, from dumpsters and under cars, from fire stations, and summer cottages, even from the candy shop. The unearthly quiet that had settled upon this picturesque little town disappeared when the LAV thundered down the garbage strewn streets, but soon the moans of the hungry dead became just as loud.

In minutes, a veritable river of dead people flowed behind the LAV and the truck, emanating frustrated, mournful noises.

With the abandoned vehicles, and unrepaired road damage, it was slow going initially. After about two miles, the salt air was behind them, and the dead thinned considerably. They still stumbled onto the road, however, Stark avoiding them where possible. The teams arrived at the long winding driveway to the Marshfield Hills Industrial Park just before 1500 local time. There were no living or dead in sight.

A large white sign with red letters reading, *Please report to the gate house to check in prior to entering the industrial park. Speed Limit 10 MPH,* was posted on the left side of the driveway.

When they reached the empty gatehouse, Ravi pointed at the forward monitor. "We want the building to the center left over there."

Stark turned and looked back at Bourne. "Sir, that's a serious gate."

The gate was a yellow monstrosity of tube steel stretching across both lanes with the guardhouse in the middle behind it. A second identical gate was twenty or so meters further up the road with a second guardhouse. In between the gates were six cylindrical pistons extending upward from the driveway, three in each lane. A pretty stone wall spread in both directions from the gate and hooked back toward the compound at about a hundred meters to the east and west.

"Sir, I can blow the gates," Seyfert tapped on the view screen, "but I can't do those pistons."

Bourne looked at the group. "Suggestions." It wasn't a question.

Stark was shaking his head. "I can't run over those pistons, but I might be able to crash the wall."

"Negative, I like the wall as a defensive barrier. We can shore up the gate area after we get in."

"What about destroying the pistons with the tank weapon?"

Bourne looked thoughtful. "This is an LAV, Ravi," he corrected. "We could damage the pistons enough that we might not be able to get in, and I want to conserve ammo, but I'll keep it in mind."

Phil, sitting on the bench and cleaning his fingernails with a pocket knife, pointed to the screen. "Light's on in the guardhouse."

Everyone looked at him.

He shrugged, but didn't look away from his nails. "Power's on. Why don't you just open the gate and lower the pistons?"

"*Wanderer One, this is Two, what's the hold up?*"

"Big damn gate," Stark answered. "Stand by."

"*Copy that, out.*"

"Sir, I'll check the guardhouse then?" Seyfert asked.

"Stay frosty, I don't see any Limas in our area, but that doesn't mean they aren't there. Check for living hostiles as well, this is a government facility. Chief, go with him."

"Roger that, Colonel," Androwski confirmed.

The SEALs exited the LAV via the top hatch and climbed down to the road. The pistons were lowering in fifteen seconds, and the both gates swung wide as well. A second chain-link gate rolled back on wheels, allowing access to the facility.

Seyfert scanned the area as he and his partner walked the vehicles through the perimeter fencing. "This whole place screams to be left alone, I've got to admit it has me uneasy."

"Me too, I don't like it at all. Where the hell is everybody? I would think an installation like this would have tons of people hiding out behind the walls."

"Maybe they're inside."

"Yeah, maybe."

Seyfert hit the buttons in the guardhouse to shut the gates and ran toward the rolling fence. He had to jump through sideways as it was almost closed when he reached it. The gate locked into itself as it closed.

As an afterthought, Androwski moved to the inner gate house and in seconds a little red light appeared on top of the gates, and at every post along the chain link.

"Electric fence," he said when he returned to the group.

The vehicles and the pedestrians made their way to the building that Ravi had previously indicated. The front entrance lights were on, and the glass doors had been prevented from closing by two wooden wedges. The building was wide open.

The back of the LAV opened and the scientists and the colonel came out stretching. Four doors on the pickup opened and the rest of the team stretched as well.

Androwski pulled his balaclava down to cover his face and checked his weapons. "Everybody stay frosty, something's wrong."

"How do you know?" demanded Linda.

"Because this place has ridiculous security, a huge wall, a secondary fence, a gate system that could stop an Abrams," he pointed to several locations, "and cameras everywhere."

"So how does that make something wrong?"

"Because there's nobody here to greet us or stop us and the damn front doors are open."

"Androwski, Seyfert, Wilcox, and Keleher, exterior recon of the buildings, then report to me. Dallas, you're in the back of the pickup, Keleher, you drive if we have to bug. Rick, get up on that tower with one of the rifles," the colonel pointed to a small radio tower with several antennae approximately thirty feet high, "and provide cover. Everyone else gather around. Except you Stark. Sorry, I want you in the LAV."

The obligatory *Yes, sirs* and *Wilcos* sounded off, and people started checking their weapons and radios before they got on the move.

Forty minutes later, the recon team returned with intel that the other buildings were secure. No signs of anything ambulatory in any of the main structures or outbuildings. A silver Lexus was in the parking lot behind one of the buildings with the door open and the keys in it, but the dome light was off so the team assumed the battery had died. Androwski didn't want to attempt turning the vehicle over for fear of giving their position away. Wilcox told Stenner that the gargantuan, eight-wheeled LAV had given them away already and they chuckled under their breath.

No evidence of struggle, no blood, no people, and most importantly, no Limas had been detected. Bourne had heated up some food, and distributed some MREs as well. Androwski and Seyfert pulled their masks up and flipped on their safeties. "What's next, sir?"

"Recon team," he looked at the four he had previously sent out, "get some chow and hit this building. Standard two-by-two cover formation, check rooms and lock doors as you go. Do not split up, Androwski is Team Lead. Ravi, Brenda, can you give us any intel on the building?"

Ravi handed Bourne a piece of paper. "I took the liberty of drawing you a map while we were eating. Perhaps Brenda could check it for errors. Thank you."

"Thank *you*."

Ravi nodded as the colonel unfolded the paper, the incursion team surrounding him in a semi-circle.

"Pretty much as I remember it," Brenda told them, "but what's this block in corridor B by the elevators?"

"That is a soda machine."

"I could use a Dew." Seyfert looked around; everyone was staring at him. "A Mountain Dew? Nectar of the Gods."

"After we secure the first floor," Bourne scolded. "Three minutes to study the map gentlemen, then go."

The colonel handed Androwski the map, and three minutes later the recon team was passing through chocked open glass doors, Seyfert still chewing a brownie from his MRE. "Eating while on recon, squid?" Seyfert just looked at the colonel and swallowed. Other than the few leaves that were stacked against the front desk, and the small bird's nest in a darkened lighting fixture, the place was in good shape. No signs of anything anywhere. Androwski grabbed a red Sharpie marker from the attendant's empty desk and handed it to Wilcox, who put it in his tac-webbing.

The lieutenant made hand signals as he moved forward, shining his light in each room even though most of the lights were on. Private Wilcox closed each door as each room was checked, and marked the front with a large red X. Nine offices were cleared this way, and then the team came upon another desk next to a heavy blue door at the end of a corridor. The other office doors all had small oblong windows, but this one was solid.

They had passed the soda machine ten feet before; Keleher walked back and put his hand on it. He nodded in the affirmative, and pointed to one of the press bars on the machine. "Mountain fucking Dew," he stage whispered.

Androwski tried the handle on the door. It was locked.

"Wanderer, this is Recon, we're at a blue door at the end of one of the corridors by the soda machine. There's a desk here, but the door is locked, over."

"Roger that, Recon, stand by. Recon, intel indicates there is a button under the desk that will open the door."

"Roger that, attempting now."

"Recon? Intel also says thank you."

Androwski used hand signals to tell Seyfert and Keleher to cover the door and Wilcox to cover the rear. He moved behind the desk and looked under. He found two buttons, one red, one green, and a holster for a weapon attached to the underside of the desk. The weapon would have been within easy reach of whoever sat at the desk. The holster was empty.

"Wanderer, there are two buttons, repeat two buttons, one red, one green, over."

Fifteen seconds of silence followed Androwski's last transmission, and he was about to call again, when the colonel came back on, *"Recon?"*

"Five by five."

"Pick one, out."

Androwski looked at Seyfert, who shook his head. "He didn't tell *me* to pick one."

The chief frowned, "Fuck me," and he hit the green button. There was a click, and all weapons went up. Androwski moved from behind the desk and put his hand on the door handle. He faced his team, and silently counted down: "Three, two, one," and he pulled the door wide. Another room, this one with a metal detection system that would rival an airport check-in, waited for them. There was a walk-through detector that would alert the folks in the room to any threats, and a conveyer x-ray machine to look into containers.

An elevator door was at the far end of the short room, and Androwski relayed this information to the colonel.

"Good work, Recon. The rest of Wanderer is en-route to your position. Sodas are on me."

41

The entire group (with the exception of Stark and Keleher, who had remained in the LAV) showed up six minutes later. The elevator door needed a key card that nobody had, but the SEALs pried the steel panels open and they looked down the shaft. There was a square of light coming from the bottom. Seyfert took a pull from his Mountain Dew and put the plastic bottle on the x-ray table. He checked his gear, then swung in on a ladder in the shaft.

Dallas looked down the shaft. "Another damn climb? How come nobody never puts stuff on one floor no more?"

Seyfert did his climb and his recon, and soon the group was filing through an open elevator three stories down. The light had been coming through the top hatch of the elevator. A long cinder block hallway, painted in utility gray with steel doors along the sides, greeted them. "This is where we worked," Brenda told everyone. Another set of stainless steel elevator doors shined past all the other entries.

They moved as a group through the corridor and wound up at the second room on the left, which was a computer lab. Stenner and Wilcox were sent back up to tell Stark what was happening as communications were impossible via radio through the structure.

The SEALs and Bourne had found a security room and were looking through camera feeds. The scientists were looking over equipment and attaching the hard drives to a computer system. Rick, Dallas, and Anna were talking amongst themselves about the journey. Phil had found a magazine and was thumbing through it, when the colonel came out of the security room and addressed Brenda.

"Ms. Poole, what's on the level below us?"

"I don't know for sure, we were never allowed down the elevator, but I heard talk that there are huge servers down there with vast amounts of storage capacity."

"Would you come with me please?"

They filed into the security room, curiosity dragging the others with them.

Bourne pointed at one of the security monitors. "Who is that?"

A bearded man in jeans and a green T-shirt was sitting in a wheeled chair throwing a tennis ball against the floor and wall, and catching it on the return flight. The monitor had a digital code on it, and SVR_ RM_1_SUB_LVL_2 in bold white letters across the bottom of the screen.

"I don't know, I've never seen that man before."

"How about this man?"

A second man, duct taped into a second wheeled chair, was moving feebly. There was so much tape on his arms, legs, and chest his clothing looked gray. The chair was tied to a desk with a short length of cord and the man had layer upon layer of tape over his mouth.

Phil, his magazine folded under his arm, pointed to the screen. "That guy's dead."

"So it would seem. Brenda, Ravi, do you know him?"

"I do not."

Brenda shook her head no.

The man with the tennis ball leaned over and spoke to his roommate, then bounced the ball off his dead head and pointed to a monitor. The live man wheeled his chair over to a bank of computer screens and began punching keys.

The colonel folded his arms. "Let's go meet him then."

Dallas and Phil helped the two SEALS grab yet another ladder in yet another elevator shaft, and the men climbed down. They watched them quietly climb through the emergency hatch and into the open steel box. These doors had been wedged open as well. A few minutes went by as the duo stared down the shaft. "Least I dint haf' ta climb down this 'un."

Phil glanced at Dallas sideways and then looked back down the shaft. "Oh man, I am so sorry about this," he said, and used a spinning back kick to push the Texan into space. Dallas didn't even have time to pinwheel his arms, and there was no scream, as he tumbled two stories and crashed into the steel roof of the elevator. Phil shook his head and made a sorry face. "Dude, that just wasn't fair." Dallas was not moving. Phil pulled a small pistol from a back holster and a suppressor from an ankle brace, then closed the doors and moved toward the security room as he screwed the suppressor onto the weapon.

42

Seyfert nodded as Androwski brought his dead holographic sight to his eye and leveled his MP5SD3 at the server room door. The open sight picture granted a full view, as the battery-powered optics had failed along with Seyfert's some weeks before. Seyfert held up three fingers, and it was Andy's turn to nod.

The SEAL from New Jersey put his hand on the door handle and counted silently to three. He shoved the door open and they stepped through, weapons at the ready. It was relatively loud in the room, as the blade servers in multiple racks and chilling towers that cooled them were humming away. The man in the chair had his back to the door with his feet up on a parts-and-wire ridden desk, and hadn't heard the SEALs come in. His compatriot was facing the newcomers, however, and became extremely agitated at their entrance.

"Whasamatter Tim," the bearded fellow half-yelled. "I told you, we can watch the last part of *The Holy Grail* when the level four data is done compiling. Don't get your panties in a bunch, buddy!"

Seyfert moved to the left side and looked down the rows of server racks. Androwski covered him. "Clear," he mouthed.

Androwski nodded and pointed his weapon at the man, but kept his finger on his trigger guard. "Sir!"

The man whipped around and stood up, eyes wide and breathing fast. He blinked hard a few times, turned his head to the dead man and said something.

"I didn't catch that, sir," Androwski said. "Would you please repeat that as you put your hands on your head?"

The man swallowed hard putting his hands on his head. "I asked Tim if he sees you too. He says yes."

Seyfert stepped up next to the man and frisked him. "He's clean."

"Who are you guys?"

"We're US Navy. We've brought some scientists here to help work on a possible cure for the plague."

"Why the hell would you bring them here?"

"You have the computers and some data they need to work, and this facility is secure. Where is everyone else?"

"The important folks got airlifted out when the Army pulled out of Boston. The big boys realized that this place wasn't as impregnable as some others, and they wanted to take the smart people to someplace they could control them. At least that's what I think. Most of the nerds were eager to get on the helicopters, but I knew better. Probably staggering around out there someplace right now or under the jackboots of *The Man*."

"You said most, where are the others?"

"One level down. You can see them on the monitor there if you'll let me…" he let the question hang but pointed toward a monitor.

"Go ahead, but do it slowly."

He looked at the zombie, who was still struggling. "I know, right? As if I would do anything to get shot." The man pressed a soft-button on his monitor screen, and the camera feed switched from another server room to a waiting area, then a lab, then to a wide open space. "That's them."

They were all dead. Savaged and covered in dried blood, the inhabitants of the large room milled about, stumbling by the camera with vacant stares and red eyes.

"They needed someone to maintain the servers up here while they stayed safe down there. You see there's no way down there other than the elevator, and it's stuck. Won't move now that it's down there, so you would have to climb, and who's crazy enough to do that? I mean other than us, right Tim?"

"What happened to them?"

"They died. Well, one of 'em died, and then ate the others. Actually, I guess she only kind of died, because she was up again in a couple minutes. She was fast though, not slow like them. She attacked some others, then they turned and did the same. It was absolute bedlam, people in total panic, running every which way. Bullets from the security guys flying into both the living and the dead. The last guy to go was hiding in that bathroom for a couple days before they wandered in there and got him." He looked at the zombie again. "At least we think that they got him, right buddy? Nobody came out again, the door opens in. Anyway, it took almost ten days for the fast chick, I dunno her name, to starve to death, and now she's not so fast anymore. I'm Bob by the way." He stuck his hand out.

Androwski shouldered his weapon and shook Bob's hand. "Call me Androwski, that's Seyfert." Seyfert nodded.

"What is that place?" Androwski asked, pointing to the monitor.

"Bunker. Supposed to hold one hundred people for twenty years or something. Nuke bunker I think." He turned to the dead man and chuckled, "Bet they never thought of the living dead getting them from the inside, huh Tim?"

"Neither did NORAD. How did Tim die?"

"He's right here, dude… Me and Tim were checking the power couplings on the chilling towers and he got a tad too close. He got zapped and kicked it. Electricity must have done something to him, because he didn't turn for hours, and I was able to…restrain him before he attempted to snack on me."

"We need to sanitize him, I'm sorry."

"Yeah, um, he's in the room Mr. Androwski, you can talk to him. What does sanitize mean?"

Seyfert had had enough. "It means shoot him in the fucking head so he doesn't infect us." The SEAL raised his weapon and pointed it at Tim's head.

"Don't."

"Don't what? Kill it? Why? It's already dead, your friend is gone."

"Yeah, I know, I'm not a complete crazy person. But if you shoot that weapon in here the Halon system might trigger and we're all dead in four minutes. And you can't kill him if he's already dead anyway. Duh." Bob lowered his eyes. "I thought about whacking him with a hammer, but then I wouldn't have had anyone to talk to. I've got food and shelter and there's a shitload of guns down in the bunker, but I can't get them."

Seyfert perked up. "Guns?"

"Yeah, like a vault full or something. The security guy's…" Bob swiveled in his chair and studied the monitor, he touched the screen

indicating a dead man in a blue uniform, "right there! He has the keys."
Bob touched the screen to indicate which man had the keys.

43

Colonel Bourne had a gray phone receiver in his hand and was looking at a printed sheet of numbers at the base of the camera monitors when Phil sauntered in. The colonel casually glanced at the man as he moved toward the small group. "Where's Dallas?"

Phil stopped with his hands behind his back. "Shit-kicker heaven." He drew the suppressed Walther PPK and shot the soldier three times center-mass. Bourne collapsed against the monitor table and fell to the floor, clutching his chest. Rick and Anna went for their weapons, but Phil beat them to the draw. "Don't. Drop them and kick them away, hands on your heads." They did as they were told.

Phil turned to Bourne who was gurgling and trying to pull his own weapon. "Traitor," he said, and shot the dying man once more in the forehead. He raised the gun and pointed it at the shocked scientists. "Same gun James Bond uses."

Brenda had the back of her hand to her mouth, Linda was sobbing. "Phil, what have you done?" demanded Ravi.

"My duty. Now it's time for you to do yours." Phil stepped over Bourne's lifeless body and grabbed the dangling receiver with his left hand. He briefly depressed the phone hook with the tip of his suppressor, and then began dialing, "Sir, it's Lynch. Yes, sir, the colonel has been sanctioned. Three of use, maybe one more that was already here. Yes, sir, two SEALs on the level below me, and four targets above with the LAV, plus two civvie hitters. Roger that, sir, I'll be waiting."

"Where's Dallas, you son of a bitch?"

"Dead. I'm sorry about that, I liked him. He was one of those dangerous-type personalities though, and big. Damn that man was big. Hopefully when your SEAL buddies stick their heads up through the elevator hatch, he'll bite them off."

Anna was quietly seething. "You bastard! We saved you. Dallas saved you, and…"

"Save it, girl-scout, you didn't do shit. I could have left MIT at any time. My mission was to keep an eye on her," he nodded toward Brenda, "and get her here when the time came. Don't for one second think that I needed you. I know what your little group is all about, and I know what your commander was going to do with the…" Phil paused as he caught a glimpse of something in the monitors, "Oh shit." The monitor switched to a different picture automatically, and he pressed the CAMERA button three times until he got back to the view of the parking lot in front of the main structure. The LAV was backing up to the building as a massive swarm of undead beat at the chain-link gates. The ones in the front were sizzling and popping against the electricity as it flowed through the fence and into them, the ones in the back pushing against their dead comrades. The fence was buckling fast. Wilcox and Stenner were running into the facility at top speed.

Phil raised his pistol. "Don't move." He picked up the phone and dialed again, "This is Lynch. Sir, the compound is about to have a shitload of company. Yes, sir. I can't tell, but there are more than a few hundred. Yes, sir. Roger that, Viper inbound. ETA? Copy. Thank you, sir." He hung the phone up and wiped his sleeve across his brow. "Change of plans. You five come with me, I'm going to get you to a more secure location down a couple of levels. Help is on the way. Hands on your heads and move back to the computer lab, we're going to get some equipment and go down a level until the cavalry arrives. Oh, and I'm one of the good guys."

"What about the men up top?" demanded Rick.

"Bad day for them, now move." Phil gestured with his pistol to get them going, and the five put their hands on their heads and moved out the door. Phil picked up Rick's M4, following. As he walked out the door, a giant fist impacted the side of his head and he went flying two meters down the corridor, his weapons clattering to the floor.

"I hate elevator shafts, you sumbitch! Uh, sorry ladies, m' language suffers some when I get angry."

Anna threw herself around Dallas and hugged him, crying, as Rick picked up the M4 and held it on Phil. Anna backed up a step, then launched a jab at Dallas's shoulder, "Don't die again!"

"Ow! I jus' fell down a damn elevator shaft, woman!" Dallas spit blood. "See?"

Rick put his fingers on Phil's neck then backed up quickly. "Holy shit, hillbilly, you killed him."

"He pissed me off."

Phil's right foot began to twitch. Anna picked up the PPK and shot Phil above the right eye. "James Bond my ass." She looked at Rick and Dallas. "Pissed me off too."

The scientists were aghast, Dallas was all smiles.

"What are you smiling about, you crazy Texan?"

"Just figgered out I ain't a scared o' heights no more."

44

The undead that were pressed against the fence hissed and popped, their brothers pushing behind them. The electricity was a deterrent to living foes, but dead ones just held on until their brains cooked away, unable to understand why they were catching fire.

The entire rest of the team was incommunicado. Stark and Keleher couldn't raise anyone inside the structure, but they may be down a few stories if what the nerds said was true. The fence was buckling and wouldn't hold for long, and there were a lot of Limas wanting in. A lot. Stark sent Wilcox and Stenner running back inside to quickly provide intel to the team in the facility.

As the fence came down, all Stark could think was that the aroma of cooking dead people smelled absolutely fantastic, and he had never wanted a steak as much as he did right now. The red lights on the chain-link posts failed and Stark looked at Keleher. "We are in a world of shit, Army."

Keleher sighed. "Well they can't get us in here Navy, but we won't be going anywhere anytime soon."

Stark smiled. "It's okay, I got a deck of cards. Wanna run over some pus bags?"

"Indeed I do."

Stark put the LAV in low and the armored behemoth rumbled forward. The rotted carcasses of the dead came apart at the seams as they impacted the front of the vehicle and were crushed and torn asunder when the eight-wheeled monster rolled over them. The men could hear the thuds of dozens of fists on the exterior of the hull.

Stark threw it in reverse and backed up, crushing all in his path, but more continued to pour through the breach in the fence. The electricity must have ceased as well because the creatures against the chain link were no longer sizzling.

The wheels began to slip in under two minutes, and Stark was happy that this hadn't happened sooner. He put the LAV in park, and unbuckled his seat belt, putting his feet to the side and stretching. "Well, the cards are in..." Keleher watched the right side of Stark's body disintegrate as the LAV shuddered and tore apart, armor-piercing incendiary rounds ripping through the top of the hull. He had a split second to wonder what the hell happened before shrapnel and rounds the size of railroad spikes shredded him to a bloody pulp. A Hellfire missile finished the job, leaving the LAV and a hundred or so undead in smoking ruins.

45

Wilcox looked up at Stenner when they were halfway down the first elevator shaft, as the unmistakable sound of an explosion reached them. "What the fuck was that?"

"I don't know, but we have to get inside and let the colonel know about the damn zombie horde at our door."

They continued their climb and eventually found Anna administering first aid to Dallas in the corridor outside the first computer lab. Rick, his M4 slung on his shoulder, stood next to them, as Ravi, Linda, and Brenda were fiddling with some of the gizmos in the computer lab. A slumped form outside the doorway of the security room got the kid's attention. He silently tapped Stenner and pointed. "Is that Phil? What the hell happened?" He flipped the safety off of his M4 and backed up a step.

Anna continued to work on Dallas as she answered the question. "Phil wasn't a friendly. He tried to kill Dallas, and he…he shot the colonel."

"Bourne? Where is he?"

Rick moved toward the security room. "C'mon"

Stenner sighed and nodded when he saw the body. "There are hundreds of undead about to get into the parking lot. We closed the front doors, but they're made of glass. I closed the door into the first room with the metal detector, and the elevator doors closed behind us, but I dunno if that will stop them from getting down here."

"Don't forget the boom," Wilcox added, staring at the colonel.

"Yeah, there was an explosion of some kind up there too."

Rick's brow furrowed, and he repeated what Phil had done with the cameras earlier. When he reached the feed for the front of the building, he could see the destroyed LAV burning in the background, and at least a thousand undead milling about the facility grounds. He slumped into a chair. "Dammit Stark."

The phone on the desk next to him rang, causing everyone to jump.

"Rick? Where's the colonel?"

Seyfert saw the look of horror come over Androwski's face, and demanded to know what was happening. Androwski ran to the monitors and punched the soft keys until he was looking at the same view of the parking lot that Rick was seeing.

Androwski backed up a step. "We need to get back upstairs."

"But the colonel… "

"Bourne's dead."

Seyfert was visually taken aback. "What? How?"

"Let's get up a floor and find the fuck out." He looked at Bob. "Don't leave this room, okay?"

Bob nodded, and Seyfert drew his knife. He flipped it around so he was holding the blade and passed the butt end to Bob. "Through the eye, or up under the chin are your best bets. Try not to get any infected shit on you."

The SEALs made their way toward the elevator to climb up the ladder.

The Viper AH-1Z gunship made a secondary pass over the destroyed LAV, but she kept her guns quiet. She climbed and hovered at sixteen hundred feet, the man in the forward gunner's position relaying what was on the ground to the three Blackhawk helicopters inbound to the facility.

"Roger that, sir, the LAV is no longer operational. Negative, the compound is not clear, repeat, not clear of hostiles. Estimate numbers in the high hundreds, possibly one thousand. Affirmative. Talon One can soften them up, but we don't have the ammo to clear the compound, and rockets may damage the structures if fired close. Talon One has AP rounds not HE, so effect will not be maximized."

The pilot interrupted, "We're bingo in twelve."

"Sir, what is your ETA? We have eleven minutes of fuel before we need to RTB. Copy that, six minutes out. Recommend incursion teams drop on to the roof of the primary structure in the center of the compound. LZ is very hot, no room for birds on the ground. Roger that, sir, Talon One engaging, out."

The Viper nosed down to five hundred feet and the M197 electric Gatling cannon went to work, its three barrels spitting twenty millimeter destruction. Between the LAV and the undead, five hundred of the seven hundred fifty rounds of armor piercing ammunition had been expended when the barrels stopped spinning. The gunner wanted to keep two hundred rounds in reserve to cover the transport choppers which had just appeared on the Viper's Longbow radar system.

The dead were still pushing and shoving to get inside the complex, and the gunner thought the parking lot looked like that of a rock concert or a football game. "Steady to two twenty-five, vertical spread, firing hydras in three, two…" When he got to one, fourteen Hydra rockets erupted from the LAU-68C/A launcher, and the pilot dropped the nose of the aircraft slightly and steadily as the gunner fired to maximize the effect of the rockets over a wider vertical scale. The line of dead streaming into the parking lot were blown limb from limb, some bodies and parts flying ten meters in the air. The entire exterior guard house and road into the facility simply ceased to exist. Amazingly, not all of the creatures had been destroyed, and some of them began to rise, or drag themselves toward the compound using whatever appendages would carry them forward.

The distant thrum of several helicopter rotors was heard by the undead as the Viper moved to eight hundred feet and hovered. The creatures searched, but were unable to determine the source of the sounds until the helos burst into sight over the trees. The first Blackhawk hovered ten meters above the roof of the main building, and four black lines descended from it. Eight soldiers in two teams slid down the lines head first and righted themselves immediately prior to impacting the gravel on the roof. Several bags followed them down. A quick sweep left the soldiers with nothing to shoot at, and they took up covering positions for the next teams. The lines were retracted into the Blackhawk and she moved off. The procedure was repeated twice more, the very last man down in a black T-shirt striding forward with a radio. Twenty-four men had been deposited in less than two minutes.

The Viper swooped down and fired her remaining rounds into the crowd which was still swarming into the facility, then she moved off as well.

An assortment of weapons was pointed at the roof access door as a man with a ram signaled he was ready to force the door. One whack and the door slammed open, revealing a stairway leading into darkness.

Tactical lights switched on and the black-clad warriors moved forward, weapons at the ready.

Two men with sniper rifles remained on the roof for a moment to assess the undead activity that couldn't be seen from the helicopters. They looked over the side of the building at the same time then reacted identically: "Oh shit."

"Yeah, I ain't stayin' here." One man quickly yanked up his balaclava and pressed his throat microphone. "Delta One, this is Far Eye, rooftop cover not effective with this many Fallen, request permission to regroup with Delta One?" The man looked shocked when he pulled his mask back down.

"What?"

His partner looked back over the side. "That's a negative on the regroup. We're to remain on station until called for."

"Are you fucking kidding me?" The second man pointed at the stairway. "We don't even have a door!"

"Would you rather face the Fallen or Brooks?"

Both men slung their rifles and reached into one of the black bags, removing two P90 submachine guns and a single Benelli M3 shotgun. "Let's see if we can fix the fuckin' door, yeah?"

46

The SEALs and Rick stood over Bourne's body, Rick had covered the top half with a lab coat. "So he just shot him?" demanded Seyfert.

Rick looked solemn as he nodded. "He called him a traitor."

"Motherfucker," Seyfert said through gritted teeth. "You should have left the prick for me."

"Talk to the hillbilly about that. Killed Phil with one punch."

Both looked incredulous. "Bullshit!"

Rick half-smiled. "No bullshit. Phil also made a phone call."

Anna called from the computer lab. "Rick! Rick, come here!" Rick hurried off.

Seyfert glanced at the video feed and sighed. "Fuck me."

Androwski looked at the screen and saw several extremely well-armed figures moving with military precision down a stairwell until the camera switched. The SEALs looked at each other. "We can better defend a level down, more cover."

"Agreed," Seyfert said, still looking at the screen. He looked at his friend and grinned, "but I can leave some surprises up here."

"Do it," Androwski said. "I'll exfil the nerds downstairs." Seyfert began to move off, but Androwski grabbed him by the shoulder. "Take Stenner, but don't throw your lives away. A burst, maybe two, and get your asses downstairs."

"Roger that, buddy."

Seyfert held up what looked like a half moon of white play dough with a bunch of metal keys, paperclips, pens and precision screwdrivers sticking out of one side and he looked at Stenner. "At least a ten-foot kill radius, maybe more in a confined area like the corridor." Stenner nodded, eyes wide. "I want you in the shaft, on the ladder. That end of the hall will be dark, but they'll have Starlights. As soon as I see them, flip the glasses down, I'll turn on the lights at this end and fuck with their eyes. You fire your whole mag with a light spread down the hall the second the lights come on, then get your ass down the shaft, I'll be right behind you. If I'm not there in thirty seconds, you blow numbers two and three, got it?"

"Roger that. You just get your ass down there too."

"I am way too fucking pretty to die," the SEAL replied and ran toward the far elevator. Stenner could see him placing the homemade IEDs in strategic locations in the corridor in the security room. The Army man got into his elevator shaft, with his feet on a rung, and half twisted, aiming his M4 at the now closed stainless elevator doors down the hall. He swallowed hard as he heard gunshots from what seemed like a million miles away. They were coming from the floor above.

Seyfert returned and set himself up to the right of Stenner in the last lab, just inside the door. A three-way light switch for the corridor within easy reach. He flicked the switch and they were bathed in darkness, waiting.

47

"Contact behind!" screamed a black-clad soldier and he fired his belt-fed Squad Assault Weapon into the growing crowd of dead. Tracer rounds ripped into the approaching mass as the soldier's squad mates frantically tried to open the steel door. Others joined the battle and fired their assorted weapons, some on selective fire, some on full auto. The man in charge calmly reached behind a desk and smacked something the door opening. A soda machine in the hall was peppered with high-velocity projectiles, sparks and carbonated liquid spraying the creatures who were stepping over their fallen comrades, slavering at the meal to come.

The man with the SAW actually stepped toward the horde. "Get through the fucking door!" he bellowed over his shoulder. The rest of the team filed quickly through the portal to relative safety, taking up defensive positions to guard the door behind them. The man who was dressed differently than the others, obviously the commander, slipped through the door last with a catlike grace.

The man defending his mates with the big gun was ankle deep in bullet brass, and there were considerable enemy casualties in front of him, but the mass moved forward, paying little heed to his hail of lead. When the things were an arm's reach away, some began to lunge, and the soldier deftly backed away, skirting their advances to their utter frustration. He began a quick retreat and backwards-jogged to the door firing his weapon the entire time. To his horror, the door was closed. He kicked the door with his boot, screaming for his friends to let him in, but his calls went unanswered.

The man in the black T looked casually at the men around him. "They're too close to the door, if we open it we all die." He strode through the metal detector, which sounded a familiar tone, and he produced a clear plastic card from a lanyard around his neck. He ran the card through a reader next to the stainless steel doors and a ding sounded. The men in the room with him looked at each other and at the door behind them.

Several more frantic kicks thumped and then the machine gun went silent. Black T shirt whistled *The Girl from Ipanema* while reports from a sidearm could be heard from the other side of the door. Two quiet seconds passed and the elevator doors opened. A last shot made the men's blood run cold, and then the sounds of scuffling came through the steel. The first thump of a fist thundered through the quiet room, interrupting the whistling.

Black T walked nonchalantly into the elevator and leaned against the back wall, crossing his feet at the ankles. "It will be tight, but we can fit maybe fifteen of us in here." Men quietly filed into the box with him. "I'll come back up for the rest of you as soon as we get down."

The men left behind looked apprehensive, especially when multiple fists began striking the steel behind them.

The elevator doors closed, and a man near the metal detector spoke, "Harris and Billings on the roof and now Beck three feet from us? What the hell is with this guy?"

"He don't give a shit about us, he wants whatever is in here and we're expendable," answered another.

"I'm not dying for that son of a bitch's agenda!"

"Then keep up, and don't be last. Last guy gets eaten."

48

Stenner saw the doors open at the end of the hall, and men come out in cover formation. There were many of them, and they didn't expect the darkness. Eight men moved forward slowly and quietly. Seven stayed behind in the elevator weapon barrels scanning. Stenner heard: "Switch to IR," and the men reached up to snap down their goggles. They each took another two steps, and then the corridor flooded with light, the men holding their hands up to shield their eyes. Stenner leaned to the right and fired a twenty round burst down the long hallway with a light left to right spread and return, the fore-grip of his weapon bucking in his hand with the auto fire. Two rapid explosions followed, and men screamed.

Seyfert was disgusted that he had to fire on former US Army, but he knew he had no choice. None of the eight boys in the corridor would likely survive Stenner's hail of lead, much less the IEDs he had planted himself. He switched the lights back off just as return fire left pockmarks all over the corridor. He looked to see if the Army kid had followed orders, and indeed he was gone. The return fire ceased because of the yelling of a man to stop shooting. Cries and wails of pain mixed with the ringing in the SEAL's ears. The smell of freshly fired weapons made his adrenaline rush even more, and he slid through the lab door and dashed two meters to the shaft.

He hadn't been as stealthy as he needed though, because gunfire erupted as he moved. He almost made the ladder before he felt two tugs in his right leg, one in the back of his upper thigh, and one is his calf. A hammer blow to his lower back propelled him forward, and he fell into the shaft reaching for the ladder. He caught it with both hands, but felt something pop in his right elbow, and searing pain leapt up his forearm. His MP5SD3 went clattering to the roof of the elevator cab twelve feet below.

Another few rounds came pinging over his head, and Seyfert thought that the shots he'd taken didn't hurt near as much as his elbow as he began an agonizing climb down.

49

Shrill laughter echoed through the server room, mostly drowned out by the noise of the many servers themselves.

Bob tried to catch his breath. "Seriously? You seriously thought it was *alpha waves*? Awesome! Now I've heard some shit before, but this! Classic!"

Between guffaws, Bob noticed no one else was laughing, and his mirth fled. "Oh. You really are serious." He wiped his eyes and looked at Tim who no longer struggled at his bonds. "Tim, they...oh yeah." He looked at Brenda. "Look, Doc, that's just crazy, and I know crazy. How in hell do you hijack alpha waves? It's totally insane."

Anna harrumphed, "Yeah, because dead people walking is a paragon of sanity."

"Touché. But the thing is, Rama never escaped this facility. It's still in the servers here, locked away under a mile of code." Bob shook his head. "Nope. Didn't get out, I'm telling you. Didn't."

The scientists and Bob began to discuss and debate the virus. Androwski, Wilcox, Rick, and Dallas looked at the monitors, and Anna was checking into the general health of Bob as he spoke.

Several small explosions shook the ceiling ever so slightly. "What was that?" demanded Bob. Brenda and Linda also looked scared, Androwski smiled. "That was Seyfert buying us time." He turned to Ravi. "What do you guys need?"

"We have zombies below. We have paramilitary forces and more zombies above. We need to work, but I do not understand how this is possible under the circumstances. It may take weeks to finish, perhaps months if we can ever get a prototype antivirus at all."

"It's possible," Dallas answered, jacking a round into the chamber of his shotgun with one hand, "cuz we're gonna kill em all. Ain't that right, Navy?"

Androwski turned from the monitors, looked over his shoulder, and smiled a half smile, "Damn skippy, hillbilly." The monitor showed the laboratory corridor above, with men dead or dying from Seyfert's handy work. Blood covered one wall, as did black scorch marks that looked like pepper. Several of the men were holding their ears, and a medic was checking others. One soldier with a suppressed MP-5 was firing into the skulls of some of his downed squad mates. All of the black-clad men had a gold III embroidered on their left breast.

The soldier who had sanitized his comrades pulled his balaclava down and glared into the camera with hate. He gave a long middle finger to the lens and mouthed the word *Traitors* before raising his SMG toward the camera. A white flash and the feed was gone.

Androwski hit a button and the feed switched to the same scene as viewed from the far end of the corridor. The elevator doors opened and more men came out in defensive postures.

"Shit."

Seyfert more fell than climbed through the hatch on the top of the elevator car. Stenner helped him as best he could, having retrieved the SEAL's rifle first. "You okay?"

"Do I look okay to you?"

Stenner looked more closely. The SEAL was bleeding profusely from the leg, and limped, cradling his right arm to his chest.

"No. You're a mess." Stenner put the SEAL's left arm over his shoulder to help him down the hallway. "Medic!"

"Both leg wounds are through and through," Anna Hargis said and moved to Seyfert's back. "If the Kevlar was an inch shorter, the bullet would be in your liver, I would be helpless and you'd be dead in fifteen. Lucky bastard."

"Don't feel lucky."

"Let me see your arm." She felt around the elbow and touched a few places. "Yup, dislocated. Put your arm out, palm up. Now make a fist." She put her hand in the crook of his elbow and pushed his fist back toward his body slowly. An audible pop sounded and Seyfert hissed a quick intake of breath. "That's all I can do, try to move it."

He did as instructed and moved his arm around. To his amazement, the agony was replaced with a dull painful throb. He opened and closed his hand and flexed his bicep. "Holy shit, when did you turn into a doctor?"

"Along the way. *That* little trick I learned when I was a kid and dislocated my elbow." She began bandaging up his leg with supplies from the LAV. "No arteries, or you'd be bleeding a lot more. You really are lucky."

"I got shot three times and fell down a hole. How is that lucky?"

She looked at him with incredulity. "Because you got shot three times, fell down a hole, and we're having this conversation. Don't you think if..."

She was interrupted by the ringing of the phone on the desk.

Androwski picked it up immediately, but didn't say anything. He put the phone on speaker, and a jovial voice flooded the already loud room, "Hello? May I speak to whoever is in charge please?

Androwski sighed. "That'd be me."

"Who's me?"

"Cut the bullshit, pal, who are you?"

"No need to be hostile, sir, my name is Brooks. Special Agent Brooks of the recently defunct Central Intelligence Agency, and...other, organizations. Now I speak for the Triumvirate, the new ruling body of—"

"Don't you need three for a triumvirate?" Androwski looked at the jacket covering Bourne. "Because I'm looking at a dead colonel, but I'm guessing you know that already."

"Ah yes. Colonel Bourne was a loose cannon who wanted to steal a cure to this plague and sell it to—"

"Back to bullshit, are we? The colonel was a damn fine soldier. I followed him halfway across the country, and he wasn't out to steal shit. I'm guessing it's you who's the fucking thief." A few seconds went by and the phone remained silent. "What? No snappy comeback or truckload of bullshit?"

"I didn't get your name."

"Lieutenant Trent Androwski, US Navy."

"Well, Chief, here it is in a nutshell, I outrank you, and I have been given leave by the President of the United States to accomplish my mission by any means necessary. I'm ordering you to give up the scientists and any data that they have—"

The SEAL harrumphed, "President? You just told me you no longer work for the United States, dick-nose."

Bob laughed out loud. "Dick nose. Classic."

The man on the phone continued unperturbed, "The President is dead, but I'm still following orders, as I'm sure are you. Give up the scientists and my men and I will leave you alone. You have my word."

"The word of a CIA spook. Fuck you spook, come get them."

The phone gave an audible sigh. "Pity. I was hoping it didn't have to come to this. We'll be right down."

50

"Perhaps this man will listen to reason," Linda said. "If we went with him, we could still do the research, and you would all be alive."

Seyfert shook his head. "The moment he has you, he'll kill all of us. Probably one of you as well, as incentive."

"We need to get down a level," Androwski said, looking at the staggering forms in the monitor. "Bob says there's weapons and food."

Bob pointed at the screen, "Yeah, and a shit load of *them*. I realize you guys are tough and whatnot, but even if you go all Clint Eastwood on them, there are too many. And he," he pointed at Seyfert, "isn't one hundred percent anymore."

Seyfert raised his middle finger and winced at the pain.

"I rest my case."

It was Androwski's turn to shake his head, "Upstairs are superior numbers, fire power, and training. I have three fighters and a bunch of civvies." Anna narrowed her eyes and was about to say something when the SEAL raised his hand, palm out. "You three, have more than proven yourselves, I should have said six fighters."

Seyfert stood up. "The chief is right, we need to get down there and see what we can see. If this is the type of facility I think it is, there will be gobs of goodies down there. Maybe even enough to hold this CIA guy at bay, or even kill him. Plus, I'm betting dollars to doughnuts that there's an emergency escape out of that hidey hole. The powers that be would have realized it was a deathtrap without another egress point."

"That's true," Rick agreed. "We're fifteen miles from a nuke plant, which would certainly have been a target of a ballistic missile. The upper floors of this building would have been irradiated if not completely destroyed if a missile hit the plant." He looked at the monitor. "They must have had another way out."

The big man cut in with his southern drawl, "Yeah, but don't that mean there's another way in?"

51

The man called Brooks got up from his seated position at a desk. He rubbed his forehead with the palm of his hand in annoyance. "Well, that didn't work."

A black-clad soldier passed him a bottle of water. "They killed my friends. I don't give a shit what they want, I'm gonna kill them."

"Yes, and they know that too. From what I hear, SEALs are pretty tough. You think you really could kill them?"

"Fucking cowards are dug in and hiding. They left IEDs for us like a God damn insurgent. I will eat those Navy traitor-dicks alive."

"Traitors yes, cowards no. They came from San Francisco, Captain. San Fran-fucking-cisco. That's three thousand miles through hostile, infected terrain, with absolutely everything trying either to shoot or eat them. They lost most of their crew getting here, and they got the nerds before I did, and I'm good at what I do. I wish I had ten like them. All I got out of what you just said is that you eat dick. Now shut up and get ready. I'm going back upstairs to get our last two guys. We're going to need them."

Brooks strode to the elevator and used his card to access it. The doors opened and he stepped through. He began humming *The Girl from Ipanema* again as the steel box ascended. In just a few seconds, he was back at the first floor. He was fiddling with his radio, thinking that he should have called the rear guard first when the doors opened with a *ding*. More than sixty blood red eyes stared at him through the open door. He frantically pressed the Door Close button, but the stainless panels didn't even make it halfway before rotting hands stopped them, and the elevator flooded with the dead.

"I don't like this," a Triumvirate soldier said to his comrade. "He's been gone too long and he won't answer the radio."

"Relax, Jack," answered his friend, "here he comes now." He pointed at the elevator floor indicator above the doors.

The doors once again made a *ding*, and Hell poured out and swarmed the two men. One gave a half scream as he was savaged, but the other was engulfed without so much as a sound. Three other men came into the hall to investigate, and were immediately taken down as well. Another stuck his head out of a doorway and noticed a small horde of dead munching on his buddies. He ducked his head back in the room and slammed the door, but not before he had seen Brooks at the back of the elevator waving to him.

The elevator made eight more trips, until the entire corridor and several of the labs were wall to wall with staggering, blood-covered forms. Several of them were clad in black camouflage with gold III's embossed over the left breast.

"Now these are soldiers," Brooks murmured aloud from the back of the hallway. Instantly a dozen or so heads turned in his direction, and some creatures began stumbling toward him. *"Although I should keep quiet apparently,"* he thought. *"Troops that will never need food, or feel fear or compassion for the enemy. The perfect army, and they are legion. What commander has ever had such a force at his disposal? Pity they stink...*

He looked once again at his new squads as they milled around searching for prey, and made a snap decision. He raised his eyes and smiled to himself, shaking his head. Initially he wanted a vaccine so he could give it to his troops of live soldiers, and some civilians to keep the plague in check. Now he realized he didn't need a vaccine. Not only that, but anyone who could even remotely envision a vaccine was potentially devastating to him. Yup. Dr. Brenda Poole needed to take a dirt nap as soon as possible.

52

"I mean, really?" The Texan looked down the last elevator shaft, then back at Androwski. "There's somethin' wrong with ya, boy."

"Radically," answered the SEAL.

Anna shouldered her friend. "Thought you weren't afraid of heights anymore, big guy?"

"That was easier t'say when I wasn't lookin' down another damn elevator shaft."

"Seyfert, you and Stenner rear." Seyfert was taken aback, but Androwski placated him by raising his hand, "I'm more worried about the bad guys with guns than the Limas. Cover us. The rest of us are going to climb down the shaft, Wilcox and I will drop into the elevator, Rick and Dallas follow quickly after, be as quiet as possible. Anna, you cover Ravi, Linda, Brenda, and Bob, but stay on top of the elevator until we call..." Bob raised his hand, Androwski looked at him questioningly.

"Can I stay up here? I really, really, really don't want to go down there."

"Bob, you might get killed down there, it's true, but I'm telling you for an absolute God damned fact that this guy that's coming will not let you live."

"Okay. I'll come."

"Seyfert and Stenner will buy us some time, same as before, but only if necessary. I hope to have the bunker cleared before they have the courage to come down a level, but make no mistake, they will come, and this time they'll be prepared when they open the elevator doors."

"I'm shit out of SEMTEX anyway," Seyfert said. "No C4 either. I don't even have a firecracker."

"As soon as I go in there," he pointed at the empty hole, "no more talking. At all."

Everybody nodded.

Radio and ammo checks were performed, and Androwski swung into the shaft, grabbed a rung and started down, the others following. When the group was on top of the steel box, the SEAL pulled a compact mirror on an extendable rod from his tactical webbing and extended it into the elevator. Moving it back and forth for a moment, he pulled it back up and packed it away. Putting his finger to his lips, he nodded, screwed his suppressor on to his MP5, and dropped quietly into the elevator, Wilcox following immediately. Rick and Dallas dropped in soon after.

They surveyed the area in front of them, a large granite lobby with exquisite stonework. Androwski stepped through the doors and scanned both directions before motioning for the others to follow. A small waiting area, with a lone undead woman, was to the left. She had her back to the small group, and the SEAL drew his knife. He dispatched her efficiently, noting that the door to a large common room was open, and several undead could be seen lurching about or standing still. Some looked to be seated, waiting. The place was a mess, with furniture overturned or smashed, and a quiet jukebox against the far wall with spinning silver CDs inside.

Rick and Wilcox appeared in cover formation with Dallas behind. The four men looked into the room. They backed up and out of sight.

The SEAL spoke in a low voice, "Rick, Wilcox and I will fire suppressed rounds until they catch on. Dallas, you provide close cover with the shotty. If they get too close, call it and move to point. Don't move in front until you call it! I'll fire a single shot into the jukebox to distract them, then fire at will down your firing lanes. If it looks like we're going to get overrun, Wilcox, you're in charge of closing this door, then we fall back to the elevator and get on top. Wilcox and I on one knee, Rick standing, Dallas cover. Wilcox, do not stand up until you call for clear and get a reply! Cans ready on three?"

The three men nodded, indicating they were ready, and the foursome moved as a unit back to the door. True to his plan, Androwski fired a single suppressed round into the juke box, which began to hiss slightly. The effect was immediate, and the things in the room began to shuffle toward the machine. The ones that had been sitting began to get up.

The living men began firing single shots at the dead ones, who began dropping where they stood. More dead began to appear from doorways, making their way to the popping juke box. A young dead woman stumbled and fell, and as she righted herself, her blood-red eyes looked directly into Private Wilcox's soul. She gave a low throaty growl, and Wilcox ended her misery, but not before the jig was up. Several dead people turned and saw the men, and began to come for them. In only a few seconds, the entire mobile population of the bunker was on its way.

"Loading," cried Wilcox.

Rick shot a man in jeans and no shirt, the thing's spine visible through its empty chest cavity. Androwski dropped a bearded man whose scalp had been torn off, his bared skull making him appear bald. The SEAL switched targets and took out a young man with no hands, nubs of bone reaching toward the men. Androwski clicked empty. "Loading!"

Wilcox began firing again, and eliminated threats to the left as they approached. Rick scored eight head shots before he missed and his round hit a fire extinguisher, the contents discharging quickly in a powerful gust of powder. More than twenty creatures were down, when Rick called that he was reloading.

"Dallas, move up! Wilcox, be ready with that door!"

Rick and Dallas switched places and all sound was drowned out by the bass roar of the shotgun. The Texan fired into the crowd obliterating skulls with buckshot.

"I'm loaded," yelled Rick over the din of Dallas's weapon. Most of the creatures were down, but there were still some in the room and more were coming from the antechambers and doorways.

A shell jammed in the ejection chamber of the shotgun, and Dallas looked at Androwski. "They's all spread out!" He passed his weapon to a confused Wilcox, and drew his rebar with his right hand and his suppressed sidearm with his left. "Cover me if they get too close, we needs t' save ammo."

Dallas strolled into the room and stove in the head of a dead man in blue BDUs. He raised his pistol and fired at another, the thing's head snapping back as it caught the round under the nose, and then the big man swung the metal pole in a sideways arc nearly decapitating a third undead with the rebar. He heard a hissing growl to his rear left, and he spun to face it, but Wilcox put it down with a single shot. The Texan dealt with three more stragglers, and there were only breathing men in the room.

"Let's get these doors closed," the SEAL pointed at the various exits from the room, "and we can check the other rooms one at a time. Wilcox, get the civvies down here too, and figure out if we can seal that elevator door somehow. Dallas, you're with Wilcox. "

"Roger that, sir."

"You got it, Andy."

Dallas and the kid moved off, following orders. "This place is a mess," Rick said. "There's contaminated…goo everywhere."

"Yeah, we'll have to clean it up. Don't get any on you if you can help it. Let's get this door first, you cover."

Rick and the SEAL moved to the door and they closed it in short order. They moved to the second of six doors and a dead woman stumbled out and into Androwski before either of the men could do anything. She latched on to him and tried to bite him as they went down. She missed her first attempt, and raised her head back for another go, when Rick thumped her in the head with the butt of his M4. She fell to the side, and Androwski scrambled backward. Rick raised his rifle to shoot her, but another undead woman lurched out of the same door and grabbed the barrel of his rifle. The thing pulled the barrel toward her and Rick fired two rounds into its upper chest, one below the right collar bone, the other center mass. Neither round had the desired effect, and the creature pulled the rifle to the side and lunged at the fresh meat. Rick let go of his weapon and fought the woman off as Androwski stood and aimed his MP5SD3, "I don't have a shot!"

Rick didn't answer, as he continued to fight the zombie who had him. She had managed to grasp his right wrist and his tac-webbing, her grip was like iron. The thing that had initially grabbed the SEAL grabbed at his ankle and latched on to the pant leg of his BDUs. He shot her in her snarling face, and took a quick two steps forward using the butt of his rifle to imitate what Rick had done moments before. The thing's head snapped to the right, but she didn't let go, and had begun to growl. The SEAL put his suppressed weapon to her head and squeezed off a single round. She let go of Rick immediately, and dropped to the floor, but not before two more undead stumbled from the door, and another from another door.

"Shit, back up! This is getting out of hand."

Both men hurriedly moved back to better assess the situation, as more undead staggered out into the common room. The men took them down with single shots, and soon it was quiet again. Androwski looked at Rick. "You know we have to try closing those doors again."

"Yeah, but I'm going to shine my light in them from ten feet away first. Then I'm going to let you close it while I cover you. From ten feet away."

"Pussy."

Rick smiled. "*Tactical* pussy." The men closed four of the six doors when Wilcox and Dallas returned with the rest of the party. Seyfert and Stenner were with them. Stenner's face was ashen.

There was a thump on the back of the fifth door shortly after the duo closed it, and when Rick shone his light down a long hall through the sixth door, several forms lurched toward them. Androwski was about to shut the door when Rick stopped him. "Hold on, let's get those ones from here."

"Good call," the SEAL replied, and the two men fired several rounds down the dark corridor before they closed the door. The thumping continued behind door number five.

"Okay, we can talk at normal levels now," began Androwski. "Anything that was down here already knows we're here. Be extremely careful about getting any of these fluids on you. I don't think we'll be able to use this room much until we bleach the shit out of it."

"That won't work anyway," said Brenda. "The virus isn't a normal virus."

Bob shook his head, "I'm still not buying your alpha wave theory, Doc."

Brenda became heated immediately. "It doesn't matter what you believe, we—"

"Okay, stow it. We can worry about that later." Androwski looked at Seyfert. "What's the word from upstairs?"

Stenner and Seyfert looked at each other, then back at the chief. "We, we ah, should probably talk about that in the cone of silence."

"Honestly, I'm too damn tired." He pointed at the scientists. "They're going to find out anyway, so spit it out."

"We checked the monitors before we came down this shaft…"

"Yeah, and?"

"And we've got a hundred Limas at least two levels above, where the labs are."

"So they got the spook, but they can't get down here, that's good news."

Seyfert and Stenner looked at each other again.

"What?" Androwski demanded.

Stenner looked scared. "We were looking at the Limas wondering how they all got in the labs so fast, when we saw one of them pushing through the crowd. He was wearing a black T-shirt and sunglasses, and he…"

"He looked at the camera, smiled, and fucking flipped us off," Seyfert finished.

"This is not possible," Ravi said.

Rick sighed. "It is."

Everyone looked at Rick.

"He's right," agreed Dallas. "I seen it too. Guy named Billy could walk right pas' them pus bags an' they wouldn't s'much as look at 'im. Course Billy was a lil'…off."

"We'll need to talk about this later. Right now, we need to seal this elevator so this guy can't bring his dead pals down here on top of us."

"Well, that's easy." Everyone looked at Bob. "This is a nuke bunker." Blank stares. Bob rolled his eyes, walked over to an open panel and pushed a button. A second panel, next to the elevator door slid open. A small wheel with a red handle was recessed into the wall, as was a keypad.

"This place," he spread his arms wide, "was made for *important* people. The powers that be didn't want anybody freaking out and trying to leave if the surface was irradiated, and they certainly didn't want anybody coming in. If we turn this wheel, a big steel door will close from the ceiling down. I don't know how thick it is, but it will keep out the zombies. We need to find Dr. Crisp, and Major Mello's bodies. They have the keys to activate this door." Bob pointed to the keypad where two round key holes were evident. "I gotta tell you though, once the steel drops, it locks in place, and can't be raised again for, like, ten years or something. There's enough food and water down here to last us."

"Gotta be another way out of here," Wilcox said, looking around.

"If there is, I was never told about it, and I was one of those guys who kinda knew about that stuff."

"You are forgetting a vital piece of information," Linda said. "All of our equipment is upstairs. We still need to work."

"Not all of it," Ravi said, and put down the heavy backpack full of hard drives.

Androwski stepped in the elevator and looked up. The hatch was still open, and he could see light from the floor above. He stepped back into the ante room. "Can't work if you're dead. Find those keys, there's no way to close this door and keep it closed from the outside." Thumping continued from some of the closed doors in the common room, everyone looked in that direction. "And we have more work to do."

53

"Tall and tan and young and lovely, the girl from Ipanema goes walking." Brooks looked at his dead captain. "I just can't get that song out of my head, you know? It must be the elevator. Triggered that song or something, I don't know." The dead man took a step toward Brooks, but Brooks fell silent and the thing stopped, looking at him quizzically. It was just Brooks and the dead soldier in the elevator. The agent made a face. "Ew, you're a mess." It came at him again, and stopped when he stopped talking. It reached for him, but didn't grab, then it put its hand down.

A swift kick with a combat boot to the solar plexus that probably would have killed a living man, sent the creature sprawling. It got back up slowly, but immediately, and turned around, surveying the confines of the elevator. Brooks drew the captain's knife from his side scabbard and stabbed the dead man between the shoulder blades. There was no reaction, and the thing continued to look about the steel walls. "Got to tell you, Cap, I like you better this way."

The elevator opened, and dozens more dead came traipsing toward it. Brooks stepped out and pushed some in and then stepped back in himself. His tally was one hundred and fifty-one, a sizeable force to attack the traitors and scientists with, and IEDs were unlikely to destroy his soldiers unless they suffered severe head trauma. The CIA man couldn't wait to get back to Nebraska to talk with Recht. The swarm that would certainly have not reached the stadium yet consisted of more than eight hundred thousand. Almost a million soldiers if he could figure out how to control their movements. *This is better than a bare-handed strangulation! Recht might have his own personal army of thugs, but lookey what I have.* He smiled. *When I'm done with that sick preacher, I'll move on to Alcatraz and have some more fun. It's like Christmas!*

54

The dead major and the dead security guy were easy to find, and their keys were appropriated. Dr. Crisp was another matter. He was nowhere to be found. Androwski began to get nervous. "He's got to be in one of the other rooms."

Bob raised his eyebrows. "Dude, those doors don't lead to *rooms*. This is an entire *facility*, just as big down here as up there." He pointed up. "There are buildings down here, and a swimming pool, and a supermarket, and a geothermal power station. There's even a series of fish ponds full of, like, ten species of fish. It will take you a week to check everything.

"Don't have a week. They'll get in here unless we close that door. Where would be the most logical place for this Crisp guy to hole up, or go if, well if exactly this happened?" Andowski spread his arms indicating the re-killed dead.

"The labs. Guy couldn't stay away from the computer labs. Most administrators administrate, but Crisp is extremely hands on."

Brenda raised an inquisitive eyebrow. "Wait, there are computer labs down here too?"

"Yeah, it's a *fa-cil-ity*. You didn't think a nuclear holocaust or zombie apocalypse would actually stop the work these guys did, do you?

Dallas stepped up. "Where's the labs, kid?"

"Through there," Bob indicated the door that the pounding was coming from.

Dallas rolled his eyes. "'Course. Prolly another damn elevator shaft too. How come we's always findin' secret unnergroun' places anyways?"

"Wilcox, Stenner, cover. Seyfert, you, Dallas, and Anna cover the civvies. Fall back if we get overwhelmed, but take as many out as you can. Rick, you get any roamers. Breach on one. Three, two…" Androwski pulled the door open and a lone dead woman fell forward. The SEAL stomped on the back of her neck twice, and she flopped in place. He kicked hard, her head snapping back, and the un-life left her. She was the only creature at the door.

Androwski didn't turn around as he shone his tac-light into the yawning darkness of the doorway. "Cover. Wilcox, do not shoot me."

The SEAL panned the light back and forth, then stepped through the door. In a few seconds, the corridor was bathed in florescent light as he had discovered a light switch. A short corridor ended at a glass door, and beyond was a large area with many desks and computers. Oddly, although the corridor had held a dead woman, there wasn't much blood, and the far door was closed.

Androwski came back through the door. "Okay, head count. We line up these bodies and figure out how many are missing, then we find them. Bob, how many were down here."

"Forty-three with me and Tim, so forty-one."

Seyfert moved to help with moving the bodies, but Anna stood in front of him. "And just where are you going, Sergeant Dumbass?"

"I… I was going to help with…"

"Nope. You're gonna sit down." Everyone was looking at her as she righted a wooden chair. "Right here. There's no goo on this chair so plant it." She pointed at the chair and the SEAL groaned as he put his bottom on it. She looked down at him, arms folded. "Screw with my bandages again, and I'll shoot you myself."

"I'm not a sergeant…"

Dallas started to chuckle as he looked down at Seyfert. "He he. Tough as nails except in the face o' wimmin. I bet—"

"You too, Redneck," she said and righted a second chair. "A concussion, bullet to the leg, and getting thrown down an elevator shaft? Sit! You can both provide cover with your asses in those chairs."

The big man did as he was told, the SEAL grinning at him. "Shut it, pard, not a word." Seyfert raised his hands defensively.

When the bodies were lined up, Androwski counted them three times. "There are only twenty three. That's eighteen potential Limas unaccounted for."

"This place is huge, you can't possibly think that everybody got killed right here. The bathroom," Bob pointed, "did you check the bathroom?" Androwski and Rick looked at the unassuming wooden door. "I saw some wander in there on the monitor. I was pulling for the guy that was hiding, but he can't have made it. Door opens in."

They worked the bathroom as they did every door they came across. The SEAL would push the door open, and Rick and Wilcox would blast whatever was on the other side, while Stenner would be a backup. "On one…" Androwski counted down from three and kicked the door on one. It moved forward a half inch and stopped. There was dead weight behind it. "Excellent." He moved forward and knocked on the door. The team waited a full minute without hearing any signs of undead before Androwski pushed the door open. The light was on, and there were two destroyed zombies on the floor apparently taken down by blunt force trauma. The SEAL moved into the room and was covered by Rick and Wilcox, Stenner holding the door. The four stalls were kicked open one at a time, but revealed nothing but toilets.

Bob showed up a moment later. "Huh."

Wilcox looked at him. "What? What huh? Huh what?"

"Well, the guy that was hiding in here was a black dude, don't know his name. Neither of these folks is black. That's a huh-able conundrum, don't you think?"

Androwski started looking around again and was confounded. "So where the hell did he go?"

Rick pointed at the wall, and everyone turned to look. "In there?" A large vent grate was above the last stall. Androwski stood on the back of the last toilet and shone his light through the grate. He then slung his rifle, reached up and pulled the grate off with ease. "Rick, take this." He handed the grate to Rick and unslung his rifle again. Shining the light down the vent, he could tell that it went for about six meters, and ended in a T-junction. "He must have gone in here. There's no place else to go."

Bob ran his fingers through his thinning hair. "So this means we have a potential zombie in the air conditioning?"

"Unless you want to go find him." Androwski cupped his hands in front of his mouth. "Hey! Anybody alive in there?"

"Aw man, the zombies came in this bathroom almost two weeks ago. There's no way that guy is alive in there now, or at least he's damn skinny with no food."

"We can't worry about that now, we need to find that key." The group left the bathroom, and Androwski started giving orders. "Dallas, Seyfert, you watch the civvies. Wilcox, you cover the elevator, and let us know if anything comes down. Everybody else," Bob pointed at himself and raised his eyes questioningly, "yes, Bob, you too. Everybody else come with me." As an afterthought, the SEAL asked Ravi to come too.

The corridor to the lab was bright, and mostly clean, and the lab doors were hermetic. "Looks familiar," Rick said as he peered through the glass. "How the hell do you get funding for something like this?"

"You're kidding, right?" asked Bob. "This is the US government. Their funds are, like, limitless."

Androwski turned his head. "Focus."

They moved into the labs in cover formation, checking corners and behind desks. No blood, no undead, no living people in the first lab. Bob accessed the second lab with his security ID badge, and it was much the same. The last door, made of steel with a small window, where the others were glass, remained locked as it would not accept his card, "Thought this might happen. I needed clearance before I could access these last labs. Somebody always had to go in there with me."

"So how do we get in there?"

Bob knocked on the door. After ten seconds, he knocked again. "Well, at least we tried. I don't know if there's—"

A scared voice came over the door intercom, "Yes?"

"Doctor Crisp?"

"Yes, who is it?"

Bob pressed the intercom button. "It's Bob! I'm here with some military types, and some scientists from MIT. They need your key to shut the elevator down so the army of zombies that is on the floors above us can't get down here and eat us."

A moment passed before the person on the other side responded, "Bob who?"

"Bob, the IT guy! You and me used to play cards. You sucked and I took all your money."

"Where are all the infected people that were out there before?"

"Dead. Well, dead-*er*. Re-killed? I told you, there are Navy SEALs out here."

The doctor peeked through the window and Bob waved. Dr. Crisp seemed to waver a moment, then opened the door and stuck the barrel of an M16 in Bob's face. Bob put his hands up.

No one raised their weapons. "Dr. Crisp?" The man's gaze flicked to Androwski. "We're here to work on the virus with you. We've brought people you may know."

Ravi stepped forward. "Hello, Allan."

"Ravindra?" Crisp lowered his weapon. "I don't understand."

"Dr. Crisp, we need that key now."

"Of course." He pulled a chain from around his neck and produced a key, just as the lieutenant received a panicked call from Seyfert.

Private Wilcox leaned against the door frame to the elevator room, his back against one side. He was thinking that this place could be made to be extremely safe if they could close the door. If there really was food and water down here, that's all they really needed. Again, if they could close the door. He was thinking about hot fudge sundaes when the elevator doors closed. He flipped the safety off of his M4 and strode forward. The elevator was rising.

Wilcox ran out into the common room and shouted for Seyfert, who stood with a groan. "Dallas, cover the civvies." Dallas stood with a groan, and checked the action on his shotgun.

"What is it, Wilcox?"

"Elevator is going back up!"

"What did you touch?"

"Nothing! It just started on its own!"

"Uh...that's bad." Seyfert accompanied the young man back to the elevator lobby. The car was already on the way back down. The doors opened with a soft *ding* when it reached their floor, and the survivors had a side view as they opened. A dead man clad only in a filthy tank top moved out of the elevator and surveyed his surroundings. He looked left and noticed the living men. The reaction was immediate, and the thing started toward them moaning. Several more undead followed their comrade, and they traipsed toward the men, who immediately fired a volley of bullets at them. The men backed up and shut the lobby door, but not before Seyfert saw the doors to the steel box close, the elevator returning to higher floors. Seyfert and Wilcox ran back to the scientists and Dallas as the pounding and scrabbling started on the other side of the door.

"Androwski, come in! Come in, over!"

"*What is it, Seyfert?*"

"Elevator is carting Limas down by the dozen!"

"*Have Dallas get the scientists down the lab corridor, you and Wilcox cover! We're on the way!*"

"Dallas, you heard, get them there and get back here ASAP! Wilcox, start pushing some of this shit up against the door." Seyfert indicated the overturned tables and chairs and the bloody couch. There wasn't much.

Dallas, having sat back down, groaned again as he stood, and hurried off with the two women as the SEAL and the Army kid began to push the ruined couch against the door to the elevator lobby. The door was heavy wood, but the frame was already beginning to shake as the things shoved from the other side. They could hear the needful cries through the oak.

"Come on, pile up more shit!"

They were pushing the juke box against the couch when Androwski, Stenner, Anna, and Rick came running in the common room. All four newcomers immediately began assisting in the barricade. When every object in the room, including a three-hole punch and a stapler were packed against the door, Androwski started giving orders. "We hold as long as possible here, then we fall back to the labs. There's a heavy door at the last lab that we can use against them, they won't be able to get more than two or three to push on it at once. Rick, you and Anna use the sniper rifles to cull as many as possible, get them coming through the door, and try to clog it with bodies. Dallas, we're trading weapons, you take this." He handed the big man his MP5SD3 with three extra magazines, and the Texan reluctantly passed his SPAS12 to the SEAL. "Aim true, there won't be any drop in such close quarters. Selective fire is here." Androwski pointed to a small lever on the side of the weapon. "Switch to full auto only if you need. Dallas, Rick, and Anna, stay to the rear and get any strays. Don't shoot us! Only fire if you have a five-foot clearance on either side of one of us, you guys fire right down the middle. The rest of us will move forward to ten feet from the targets in two teams right and left, and fire at them as they come through. Do not run in front of friendly fire! Wilcox, you're with me, let's go!"

When the four living men were five meters apart on either side of the lobby door, Androwski shouted for an ammo check. Magazines were ejected, inspected and replaced. Dallas put two extra mags on the floor next to him and the last in his pocket. Rick swiped his arm across a table in the lab corridor clearing it of various paper supplies and dragged it out into the common room. He and Anna set their bipods on the table for support Rick put the earbud for his XM408E in his ear. Anna was using Martinez's SR25. She looked over at Rick. "Cheater." He smiled and winked at her. "Don't miss."

The door held out significantly longer than the group thought it would. A good fifteen minutes elapsed before the couch moved slightly, then the lock on the door gave way, and the door itself moved in a little. The barricade began to slide toward them, slowly at first, then with more speed. The first undead through had been a construction worker, and he still had his tool belt, sans tools, as he stumbled forward, pushing at the couch with his knees. The ear piece beeped and Rick started to squeeze his trigger, when Anna fired a suppressed round, dropping the former construction worker with a perfect head shot. "Damn, this rifle is long with the suppressor!"

Androwski and Wilcox could see through the partly open door, and there were more than just a few undead. Wilcox sighted his rifle on a thing in blue scrubs and ventilated its cranium. He did the same with a teenage girl, who looked freshly killed, and a bald man, his entire neck and lower jaw missing, the head lolling to the left, held on by spine alone.

Tainted former humans of all ages, genders, and races pawed at the door, the barricade, and their brethren as they tried to get to the living souls. Wilcox clicked empty after twenty rounds. "Loading!"

Androwski stepped toward the door and fired the shotgun. He fired again, and again, preferring the semi-auto mode to the pump action. The door moved forward again, and more creatures began to push to get in the room. The team was constantly firing, but the doorway kept filling with dead people, all with a desperate need to get in the room.

Androwski was doing the math, and he figured that there were at least fifty dead either pawing at the failing barricade or crumpled on the floor with head trauma. Fifty wouldn't fit in the elevator, so they were either coming in from another location, or the bastard upstairs was sending down multiple car loads of Limas. When he clicked empty, he yelled to his friends, "Alright, we lost it! Cease fire and retreat to the lab doors!" Everyone rushed back through the common room and into the lab corridor. The lieutenant was the last through and he shut the door behind him. The heavy oak wouldn't stand up to the onslaught of the dead forever, but there were stronger doors in front of them that they could put between the Limas and themselves.

When they had reached the first glass lab door, the scientists were waiting. Ravi looked concerned. "What is our status?"

Bob looked at the heavy-breathing faces of the team. "Screwed."

"Not yet," Seyfert heaved. "We still have the steel security doors."

Androwski stood. "Is there anything in these labs you guys need? We're going to pull back and fortify at the last door. Make a list and we can carry what you want. You've got two minutes."

The new guy, Dr. Crisp, looked worried. "We have everything we need in the Data Lab, but there's an issue."

Dallas sighed. "Prolly another floor down? More elevator shafts, huh?"

"Uh…no. This is the bottom level…well, mostly. The issue is that there are other ways in here. Each of the four sections has a causeway to another. All the sections lead to the common room."

"Are you fuckin' shittin' me?" exploded Wilcox pointing at Bob. "That's critical, NEED TO KNOW information!"

"Stow that shit, Private! Dr. Crisp, can we block off or seal the causeway to this section?"

"Maybe, but if we do, we can't get to the PX or the kitchen. Those are in the next section over."

Androwski pinched his nose, then pointed at the ceiling. "Just one thing! Just one thing to go right," he opened his hands, palms up, "please?" The SEAL turned to look at everyone. "Get back to the steel door. We fortify, and fall back. Wilcox, Stenner, take Dr. Crisp and check out this causeway, check all areas on the way and don't get bitten, there are Limas unaccounted for. Constant contact."

Stenner gave a curt nod. "Affirmative, sir. C'mon Wilcox, let's get 'er done. Dr. Crisp, you're with us."

"Wait," said Androwski. "Dr. Crisp, is there a weapons locker down here?"

"Yes, it's near the PX. Major Mello had the keys."

Androwski fished the keys out of his pocket and tossed them to Wilcox. "Check it out."

The three moved off at a brisk pace.

"There's a security room just like the ones upstairs in each module down here," Bob said nervously. "We could monitor where the zombies are with the cameras."

"Seyfert, you're with Bob." He pulled his friend aside while Bob moved down the hall. "Stay frosty, we just met him, and I don't want another Phil."

"Roger that, buddy." Seyfert limped off after Bob.

"You three," the chief pointed at Ravi, Linda, and Brenda. "We're here, what do you need to work?"

"Now? You want us to get started while there's an Army of those things a hundred feet away?"

"Yes, Doctor Poole. Our mission was to get you here. You're here. I'm adding a mission objective, and that's to protect you, but you need to get started. Figure out what's what, and Rick and I will fortify our position to the best of our ability. Dallas, you and Anna keep an eye on them and provide assistance. Anna, monitor the redneck's injuries."

Dallas raised his eyes in question, the SEAL tipped him a wink.

"Doctors, don't go anywhere, especially not to the bathroom, alone. Tell us what you need, and we'll get what we can for you."

Ravi was already working on attaching the heavy RAID array to one of the networked computers. "We will need network access, and to perhaps disable password necessity. We will not be able to log on to the system without an initial password as ours were disabled at the end of every work day. Thank you."

"Will Crisp have this ability?"

"Yes. He should be able to give us access when he returns."

"I won't have the equipment I need to further my research on the wave theory, but I can help with the computer analysis," Linda said.

"Whatever you need, ask. Rick and I are going to start barricading the entry doors. Do not come looking for us alone, you all come together, is that clear? In fact, I don't want any of you out of the other's sight at any time." The two men moved off to provide what security they could to the already-solid door.

55

"Look all I'm sayin' is that I never heard of one is all."

Seyfert grunted as he sat down in a wheeled chair staring at the back of Bob's head. Getting back up was going to be a bitch. "So you think that all these important people were going to come down here, a nuke drops and the elevator caves in, and then what?"

Bob, was pushing buttons on a console. "I feel you, dog, but I dunno where it is!" He was clearly frustrated. "If there is some kinda emergency egress from this place, Crisp might know where it is. I don't."

The phone on the desk rang, and the two men looked at each other.

"Probably Androwski. You can get it and pass it to me, huh Bob?" The SEAL rubbed his calf.

Bob shook his head. "SEALs." He picked up the phone. "Hello? Bob here, is—?" Bob's face got deathly serious. "Yes. Yes," he handed the phone to Seyfert, who had to move forward as the cord wasn't long enough. "It's for you."

"Androwski?" asked Seyfert as he extended his good arm for the phone.

Bob shook his head in the negative and Seyfert showed a confused look. "Hello?"

"*This is not the same voice I spoke to earlier.*" A strange voice said to him. "*Where's the lieutenant?*"

"Busy. You must be the dicknose."

Bob smiled, Seyfert scowled.

"*Turn your camera to feed six there, Navy, and look behind you at the camera so I can see your face.*"

Bob turned to six, and Seyfert saw the back of the black T-shirt guy leaning back in a wheeled chair with his feet up on the security console. The guy dipped his left shoulder and absently waved to the camera. He was wearing dark glasses, and looked like any other guy you might see on the street, or would have if they weren't all dead now. Unassuming, but with an air of confidence.

"So, is there any way you might open up some doors so I could come down there and talk?"

Seyfert spun towards the camera. "You shot me." He pointed to his leg.

"Through and through?" The guy looked genuinely concerned. *"Damn, I'm sorry about that, I really am, but you did kill a bunch of United States soldiers with your terrorist act. What were we supposed to do, cuss at you? Besides, I didn't fire a shot, it was Wilkes. Wilkes is staggering around with the rest of the team."* The man made a face like he'd just heard nails on a chalkboard. *"He's looked better."*

"US or *Triumvirate* soldiers?"

"Now you sound like your chief! Anyway, I just wanted you to know that I've stopped sending dead people down on the elevator. I've got a better plan." The spook put his feet on the floor and spun in the chair. Seyfert was still looking at the camera, but Bob told him to turn around and look at the monitor.

Brooks was attaching small red parcels that looked like oversized candy bars, to something with a strap belt. The thing had treads and a long arm sticking up out of the front it. *"This is my 510,"* he said while he worked, *"and these,"* he held up one of the candy bars and shook it for emphasis, *"well, if you set up the IEDs, then you know what these are."* There were sixteen bricks attached when he was done, and he counted them off.

Bob pointed at the screen. "What is that?" Seyfert remained silent as he stared at the monitor.

When he was finished counting, Brooks produced a tablet, and powered it up. *"See this?"* he pointed to the tablet. *"Detailed schematics of your really nice facility down there. Did you know it was actually fabricated for key members of the government who just might be around if we were going to get nuked? I'm not talking about governors, or senators, but* important *people. It was called the Basement, and it was officially decommissioned in nineteen eighty-eight, but they kept it stocked. Anyway, the only way in or out is the elevator, and I'm going to take care of that for you. Ever been buried alive?"*

Brooks picked up a remote control that looked like a video game controller, and moved his thumbs around on two sticks, the robot moved forward and to the left. *"Hey, it works great! Now the average 510 pack bot remote couldn't communicate through thirty feet of concrete, but this is a special one."* He sounded like a middle school teacher giving a lecture.

Seyfert fumed into the phone. "I'm going to kill you. I swear to God I'm going to kill you."

Brooks broke into laughter. *"No, you're not. You're going to starve to death, maybe fighting off your friends for the last Saltine. Or maybe your dead friends who have already starved to death, or the rest of the horde down there if the boom-boom opens a door or two. I guess what I'm trying to say is: toodles!"* Brooks hung up the receiver and opened the door to the security room. Two dead men immediately came in the room, but he ignored them. He piloted the explosive ordinance robot out the open door and the dead followed, leaving the room empty. Many shadows could be seen moving past the open doorway.

The SEAL stood with a wince and a sigh. "We need to get back to Androwski."

"What was that thing?"

"Trouble."

56

"Jesus this place is huge," Wilcox said as he looked around at Crisp.

"Well, it was made for..."

"Tsst!" Stenner cut him off with a raised fist. "A little noise discipline goes a long way," he whispered. "We don't want to advertise our position."

Dr. Crisp nodded and kept his mouth closed. They walked down a long corridor; all the doors were closed, and there was no evidence of anything wrong save an overturned chair. That changed when they got to the end of the hallway at a T-junction. Bloody hand prints adorned the plain, gray concrete wall, and a huge dried blood smear complete with drag marks and directional spatter covered the floor, disappearing around the corner.

Stenner held up his fist again and they all stopped. He pointed to himself then to his eyes. The other men nodded. Stenner removed a stick from his tac-webbing, and telescoped it out. A small inspection mirror was on the end and he used it to look around the corner in both directions. He retracted it and turned to his group, holding up three fingers, then he pointed back the way they had come and they all moved about fifty paces.

"Three Limas right," he stage-whispered. The soldier drew his M9, and began screwing a suppressor on it. "Wilcox, you stay back and cover the doc. Doc, listen, this is a *can*." He chin-pointed toward the suppressor he was still screwing on to his weapon. "It doesn't sound like it does in the movies. It will be loud in the corridor, so be ready for the noise." Crisp nodded. "If they get me, or if anything unexpected happens, you two high-tail it back to the others. Wilcox, he's more important than you and me right now, got it?"

"Yeah, I get that a lot."

Stenner smiled. "Watch your six." He moved down the passage and used the mirror again to check the position of the enemy. Stepping out into the corner, he took up a firing stance and carefully fired three rounds.

The reports were louder than Crisp had thought they would be, but they sounded like they came from everywhere at once, and not just in front of the doctor. Seyfert fired once more, then motioned for the men to join him.

"Three tangos, I mean Limas down," he said when they reached him. "Wilcox, write that down, and get their IDs if they have any. Stay out of the fluids." Wilcox turned over the first thing and did as instructed.

"Dr. Crisp, we need to secure this module from the others, and see about food and weapons."

Crisp pointed at the door the undead had been congregated at. It was a steel fire door, probably with a bar handle on the other side that the dead had been unable to negotiate because it opened toward them, "That leads to the common room, through another short corridor and then another door." Stenner moved toward the door but Crisp put his hand on his shoulder. "There could be some on the other side."

He nodded. "Where does this go?" He used his weapon to point behind them down the other side of the T.

"The kitchen, cafeteria, and the PX. Both have everything we need."

"I don't like this, that door could open at any time and spill the whole common room on us," the younger soldier said.

"Agreed. We can't recon the PX until we secure this door. Options?"

The kid thought for a second. "It opens this way so we can't block it." He raised his eyebrows. "What about welding it closed?"

"Got a welder on you?"

"I do," the doctor said, "not on me but back at the lab. There's an S.M.A.W we used for making the steel tables longer.

The army men looked at each other, then at Crisp. "You have a SMAW? What the hell are you talking about?"

"Shielded-metal arc welder? It's a welder, isn't that what you asked for? It will seal that door for certain."

The military men chuckled lightly. "Shoulder-launched, multi-purpose assault weapon. SMAW," Stenner whispered

Crisp looked confused.

"Big damn rocket launcher? Forget it. We hump back to the others, report, get the welder and seal the door. We can seal the door to the common room in the lab module first."

"We haven't fully reconned this area, Stenner."

"Agreed, but we can't seal that door and I don't want fifty of those damn things on us while we're in the kitchen."

"Me neither," Wilcox said nodding. "Let's book."

57

"Twenty kilos at least."

"On a 510?"

"Yeah, he was already done wiring when we came to report."

The SEALs, Rick, Dallas, Anna, and Bob stood in a small circle while the scientists worked. Rick let out a grunt. "So what now then?"

"Twenty kilos of Semtex will certainly open that oak door," Androwski chimed while he rubbed his chin in thought, "but the roof of the common room was, what, five meters high, and the walls maybe twenty meters apart?" Nods all around. "So the explosion will dissipate through the air, the only problem is it has no place to go while we're underground."

Seyfert saw the looks on the faces of the civilians. "He means the explosion might bring down the roof."

"I'm more concerned with it throwing the door frames out of whack such that we can't close them."

Stenner's group returned huffing right then, and relayed the information about the doors to the PX module and the fact that they didn't complete their reconnoiter.

"So we weld the door to the PX module closed, then fortify it. Then we do the same to the living quarter's module." Androwski looked at Crisp. "Will that seal us in?"

"Yes. The power station is under the lab module. All the techs are either dead, or down in it though. Oh, and there were several people that made it into the living quarters, although I was the only one to make it to the labs."

"Then we seal ourselves in and go door to door."

"Um, hello," interjected Bob. "What about the explosives? Boom remember?"

"We need to worry about things we can change first. There are what, sixty Limas between us and the elevator? That prick will want to drive the 510 right up to the door before he blows it. The Limas will get in the way, so we have maybe a half hour."

"So somebody has to go out there and stop that robot then right?"

"You wouldn't get out the door. The only thing you would achieve is letting the Limas in. We would never be able to close the door once you opened it."

Bob shook his head. "We have both sets of keys now. We can close the blast doors at the elevator, and the robot can't get down here. I've seen those doors tested, and I don't care how much explosives that dude has, he won't scratch those doors."

"Boy, we ain't gettin' back into that there common room without our asses gettin' chewed off."

"I can," Bob said sheepishly.

58

"Are you sure about this," demanded Androwski.

"Hell no. Absolutely not. No way... Let's do it."

Bob had launched into a story about how undead Tim never got agitated or even seemed to care that Bob was in the room. Bob had tied him up when he died, but Tim never made so much as a sound, and never once struggled against his duct tape bonds until the SEALs had entered the server room. "I still didn't have the stones to go come down here with all the zombies though," he admitted, "and there was nothing up above I needed for at least another couple months. I never took the tape off of poor Tim's mouth, but during the initial outbreak I saw dozens of videos of zombies that were chained or tied to something, and they did everything they could to break out and eat whoever was near. Tim never did that once. Then, when you guys said that you knew a guy that the zombies wouldn't touch, I thought long and hard about Tim and how he never tried to chomp on me. I must be immune too."

"You *think*."

"Yeah, I think. I would say let's test the theory, but the clock is ticking."

Androwski and Rick stood at the hermetic security door with an extremely nervous Bob, who seemed to be looking everywhere at once. Rick pressed the intercom button and said hello. There was no response from the other side other than the distant thuds of undead fists on wood. "They don't seem to be in yet," Rick said. Everyone who had a weapon had it aimed at the door when Rick opened it wide. No undead were in the corridor yet, but the door at the end of the hall was already beginning to show signs of failing.

Androwski handed Bob a suppressed MK23 handgun with three extra magazines. He had already shown the computer guy how to fire and re-load it. "They should flood this corridor the second you open the door and get confused when there are no food sources," the SEAL said. "Get past them and to the elevator and lock us down. Get back to this corridor and thin them out with your weapon, then close the far door again and get back in here. Move as quickly as possible without drawing attention, and if you panic, they will probably tear you apart. I know we've already discussed this, but once I close this door, I won't open it again until there are none of them left moving between the doors. Good luck."

Bob swallowed hard and nodded.

The steel security door closed with a *whoosh*. "Just like Star Trek," the terrified man said and moved to the end of the corridor.

Bob put his hand on the doorknob but hesitated. *"I'm dead either way, I'm dead either way,"* he chanted in his head. He turned the knob and the push-lock popped. He stepped back and out of the way as several dead people stumbled into the room and walked right past him searching. He didn't go unnoticed for long though, and within seconds one of the things snarled and lunged for him. Bob didn't move. He didn't raise his pistol or scream or try to run. All of those things did nothing as the freshly killed man clad in black camouflage grabbed him by the wrist and leaned in to bite. Bob closed his eyes and waited to be torn asunder, but the bites never came. He opened his eyes and looked. Twelve dead eyes stared at him, but he focused on the face of the thing that had him by the wrist. If it were possible for a severely lacerated face to show need and confusion at the same time, this creature had pulled it off. Bob thought the thing looked pissed off with its feral expression until it and all of its friends just moved away. Unfortunately, the dead man didn't let go of Bob's arm, and it began to pull him along with it as if trying to bring him to something of great importance. The thing's grip was like iron, but Bob rolled his wrist inward and forced the zombie to let go of him. It didn't look back as it lurched about looking for prey, a gas mask dangling from its tactical webbing.

The creatures still filed into the corridor, but none had decided that the steel door at the far end held any goodies, and they milled about seemingly aimless. Bob knew better. He knew their aim. The living man was unable to get through the constant stream of ambulatory dead through the portal, so he tentatively shoved. Two of the things fell down and started to get up, but Bob was committed now, and shoved some more. He was able to gain access to the common room, but immediately wished to be behind the protection of the steel door. At least fifty creatures reeled and staggered about. Bob did the same. He moved at a slow walk toward the elevator lobby. Some of the things noted the way he moved, and came to investigate, but they all moved away after coming within a meter or so.

Bob reached the access door and slipped though.

59

"Jesus, he made it," Seyfert said and tapped the monitor. "I would have bet against that crazy kid."

Androwski was still frowning. "Well, if he's legit, and doesn't try to kill us like Phil did, then he's earned a spot."

"Who's Phil?" Crisp asked.

"Tell you later." Seyfert pressed a button on the monitor until they could see Bob in the elevator lobby. The only creature in the lobby with him was the one they had dealt with when they got down there, and she wasn't moving. Bob pushed one of the round keys into the appropriate slot, then moved to do the same with the other key. After he had the second key inserted, he tried to turn it, but it wouldn't move. He returned to the first key but it wouldn't move either. Bob ran to the elevator lobby desk and began searching for something. He leaned over and began doing something frantically with his right hand. Bob ran to the camera and held up a hand-written note for the people in the security room to see:

"Need to turn both keys at the same time! Can't reach!"

"Jesus, he can't do it," Seyfert breathed. Bob sat down in the desk chair and put his head in his hands. Just as quickly as he sat down, he sprang back up and ran to the elevator. He began removing his shoes.

"What the hell is he doing now?" Rick demanded as he stared at the screen. Bob was removing his shoelaces. The group tucked safely in the security room watched in amazement as Bob tied his shoelaces together and then tied one end to one of the keys. Moving quickly to the second key, he strung out the now single lace behind him. Head bobbing three times as if counting, he attempted to turn the key and pull the shoe lace at the same time. It wouldn't go. He pulled harder and harder until the lace snapped.

The phone rang on the desk next to Seyfert, who immediately answered it, "*Hey, I'm having some technical difficulties with this 510 bot, do you know how to make it go down stairs? I just tried and...*" Seyfert hung up.

"Well?" demanded Androwski

"Spook being a dick."

They all watched as Bob, shoeless, sprinted back into the common room. Seyfert switched feeds until they found him. He was surrounded by undead, all reaching for him. He remained motionless, and the creatures all stopped once again and ambled off. Visibly shaken, he positioned himself behind one of the dead soldiers in black and drew his suppressed Sig. He aimed the weapon at the back of the creature's skull and then froze. He looked at the weapon as if it were broken, shook his head and released the safety catch. Bob fired one suppressed round into the thing's cranium and it collapsed to the floor. The effect on the other creatures was immediate. Every one of them instantly became hyper-agitated, although they didn't know in which direction to move as the suppressor had created confusion. Bob stood stock-still as the things searched, and only after a full minute of pants-shitting stillness did he move. He began removing the dead man's tactical webbing and searching through it. He stood up and carried the webbing back to the elevator lobby, and Seyfert switched back to the lobby feed on the monitor. Bob was attaching the webbing to the left side key. He stretched it out across the elevator door reaching for the other key with his extended right hand. The group viewing Bob on the monitor watched in horror as a dead girl in filthy pajamas lurched into the room and came directly at the man's back. Either unaware or focused, Bob didn't turn around. He pulled on the webbing and turned his key at the same time the dead girl put her hand on his right shoulder.

Two things happened right then, Bob whipped around and pushed the girl away, and an alarm klaxon began to sound throughout the entire facility. An emergency light dropped from the ceiling and illuminated the small lobby in a red glow. Shortly after, a steel wall began descending in front of the closed elevator doors. The rumble of the door machinery was loud and steady as compared to the *Bah... Bah... Bah* of the klaxon. Holding his left hand in his right, Bob ran back to the door only to be confronted by a steady stream of the undead as they flooded into the room searching for the source of the rumbling sound. The living man stood to the side of the door and let the dead come in. They began beating on the descending wall, and Seyfert was happy to see that three of the creatures were crushed as three tons of tungsten steel alloy moved relentlessly downward.

The lobby filled quickly, and Bob moved out the door, closing it behind him. Seyfert switched the feed again, and noticed that eleven dead people still milled about in the common room. They approached Bob as he moved the couch back against the door with the broken lock. He stood to the side and let them come, his eyes wide. Once again, the things stopped short and began to mill about in different directions. All but one. It had been an elderly man, perhaps in his seventies, but it was big, and towered over the little computer technician. It stared down at him, and he back at it. It reached for him and Bob side-stepped, but the thing would not be deterred. Bob moved toward the corridor, and the safety of the steel door, and the thing followed at as brisk a pace as its dead legs would allow. The man turned and used both palms to shove the elderly zombie away as he had done the young girl minutes before. This time the creature went absolutely ape-shit, and started a horrible caterwauling that set the others in the room off doing the same thing. They all moved at Bob at a quicker pace than he thought possible, and he broke and ran for the corridor door.

"Chief, get the fucking door open! The jig is up! They're almost on him and the corridor is clear!" Seyfert's voice screamed over the radio. Androwski, Rick, and Dallas were waiting at the steel door when the call came through, and the SEAL immediately began to open it. The door opened out, and when the three men rushed into the corridor, they saw Bob at the end of the hall pushing against the heavy oaken door to the common room. The old man zombie had the upper right side of his torso in the door, and Bob was fighting to keep the dead man and his friends on the other side. It was a losing battle, and the door was moving forward. The back of the door on Bob's side was slick with blood and Bob was moving slowly but steadily backwards.

Rick was the first down the hall, and he threw himself against the door to help Bob. They heard ribs crack as the undead in the door was pinched, but the thing paid no heed, and continued to reach around, grabbing Rick by the shirt.

"Not today, pard!" Dallas yelled, and smashed his rebar into the side of the zombie's head, clearly fracturing its jaw, but the thing stood its position howling that mournful sound.

Androwski took up a firing position six meters away as Dallas whacked again, this time killing or knocking the big dead man out. He didn't fall, but was held up by the door and the frame. Several hands reached around their fallen brother to get at the meat on the other side of the portal. Dallas lent his considerable weight to pushing on the door, but Androwski noticed that there was no way it would ever close with the dead man stuck in it and several others pushing on it. "On three, I want you guys to run back towards me and get behind me. We're gonna let them in and fall back to the lab! One, two, THREE!"

The men let go and sprinted back down the corridor as four ex-Massachusetts folks spilled through the doorway, falling to the floor. In single-fire mode, Androwski fired before the things could rise, re-killing three, but there were more behind, and they began to file into the corridor, moaning and lurching. The radio blared to life: "*Andy, get the hell out of there, they're coming from the elevator lobby now! Get back inside!*"

Androwski clicked empty and reached for another magazine only to find he had none. Letting his MP5 dangle on its single point sling, he pulled his side arm and chose targets. The boom of Dallas' shotgun next to him made him miss his third shot, and Rick began firing as well. "Get the fuck back inside the lab dammit, I'm right behind you!"

"Door's locked, boss," Dallas' bass drawl roared. "You gots the keycard!" The shotgun went off again, and Rick kept firing his M4.

"Keep them off of us for five seconds!" Androwski stood and sprinted the fifteen feet back to the steel door, cursing himself for a fool. He fumbled with the card for the door as his friends fired into the growing crowd. "Fall back ten feet!" he heard Rick scream. The door wouldn't open.

"What the Hell! It won't open!" Androwski started pulling on the door. "Seyfert, the damn door won't open with the card," he screamed into the radio.

Rick stopped to jam in a fresh magazine. "Androwski, it's getting real up here!"

"I know!" Androwski fumbled with the door for another second and then turned around drawing his sidearm again. The creatures were less than four meters away from his friends, and he ran up and joined them on the line picking targets. Three shots in, he heard through the ringing in his ears, Private Wilcox behind him screaming to get in the door.

"Fall back! Fall back!"

Rick and Bob turned and fled. Dallas tried, but a dead man lunged forward, and a rotted hand grabbed the back of Dallas' XXL BDUs. The huge Texan pulled the scrawny dead thing, towing it down the hallway.

Wilcox aimed his M16 at Dallas and fired once, the creature falling off of Dallas. The Texan was the last through the door, and both Wilcox and Androwski slammed it shut.

Three seconds later, the wave of dead plowed into the door with a thud. The beating and pounding commenced instantly.

Dallas was huffing and rubbing his calf. "Wil...Wilcox," he said between breaths, "I swears, I felt that bullet go by!"

"Jumpin' Jesus! Motherfucker was gonna bite our hillbilly!"

Dallas looked at him, then at Rick, and then everyone but Bob burst out laughing. Bob began chuckling not too soon after.

60

Things had gone well after Bob had dropped the blast door, although the phone call from forty feet above them hadn't been very pleasant.

"Honestly, and I just said this to somebody else, I wish I had ten like you guys. You think on the fly, and take zero shit. And you got civvies in the playroom too! You remind me of me. But as far as I see it, you've taken yourselves out of the equation. There's no way out of that bunker for thirty-five years, (I looked it up) and you've got dead friends down there for company. I left the explosives near that door you lowered. I must admit, that thing is thicker than the main vault door at Langley. Well, anyhoo, there's a pressure sensor set to the boom-boom. When that door opens, or if there's a speck of dust that hits the sensor, anything near it goes away. Far away. I was scared shitless setting it, but I digress. While I admire you guys, you have severely pissed me off. This will not stand, so I'm going to take it out on Alcatraz. I just might be able to get my hands on the launch codes for an ICBM, and if I do, I will turn that ridiculous rock into radioactive glass. If not, I will hit that island with whatever I can, including a freighter full of my new soldiers. Have a nice life down there."

Androwski scowled as he made a reply, "Screw you, you son of a bitch! We're going to… Bastard hung up on me."

They watched through the exterior monitors as the man in the black T-shirt strode past the dead, patiently weaving his way through the ambulatory corpses until he reached a certain point outside. He looked up and spoke into a hand-held radio. A drop line from what could only be a helicopter smacked the ground near him. He made a quick knot, attached a carabineer to the line, and was hoisted up by what must have been a bewildered crew. As the man began to disappear from the camera's view, he gave a mock salute to those he had left behind.

Rick swallowed hard. "I have to get back to Alcatraz."

EPILOGUE

The torn and faded map had a huge brown blood stain completely obscuring Candlestick Park. Cyrus thought that the dim light of the loft and the circle of people studying the map, made the place look like a scene from a Jimmy Cagney movie. Cyrus had heard quite enough, but he didn't think interrupting his son while his son was formulating a plan was supportive, and would not slight him in front of his minions. When Doc Murda was finished speaking, he dismissed five of the nine gang bangers and turned to his father with a broad smile. The giant Pee Wee, and the gunman Masta G remained as well, as they were Captains in Doc Murda's army.

"So, what do you think?"

Cyrus seemed to consider for a second before he approached his son. "I think," he slapped Murda hard across the face, "that you are an absolute buffoon."

Masta G raised his eyebrows and looked at Pee Wee, but the big man remained impassive. Murda cringed slightly and covered his stinging cheek with his palm as his father continued. "Am I to understand that you knew there were survivors on Alcatraz with food and supplies? Furthermore, you *warned them* that you were coming to attack them? *You warned them?*" The volume of Cyrus' voice hadn't changed but it seemed much quieter in the room.

"Still looking for praise, Malik. Still looking to be the big fish. Still going off half-cocked when you're angry. Your previous plan's only flaw was that you were the one to come up with it. An intelligent person would have sailed over there under cover of darkness and crept into their fortress unawares, slaughtering and pillaging at will." Cyrus shook his head. "Fool."

His face reddening, Malik Phillips looked at his father. "Doc Murda."

"Excuse me?"

"Malik Phillips is gone, I am now Doc Murda."

Cyrus smiled. "Then there may be hope for you yet."

"I wanted them to know that they were going to die for crossing me," continued Murda, "I needed them to feel a new fear."

Cyrus put his hand gently on his son's shoulder. "Undoubtedly they did. I'm sorry I lost my temper, but you know that we both have issues in that area. Revealing your plan to the enemy was foolhardy, but also water under the bridge. Something else I must bring up, however, is the wonton murder of your troops when they appear inadequate. This must stop."

"If they fail me, they die. Fear will keep them focused."

"Agreed. However, too much fear is also a bad thing. Fear can lead to dereliction, defection, or even outright revolution. Should you keep killing the soldiers for small mistakes, you will lose half of your army in punishment alone, the other half will try to kill you, or just leave."

"We find more every day. They join or they die. If they run, they die. You're right though, I will administer a less permanent measure of chastisement in the future."

Cyrus beamed. "My son, you will be great, I can see it. Now, back to the problem at hand. We can't get to the Alcatraz because it just happens to be guarded by a United States nuclear submarine?"

Murda sighed. "Correct. There are military on the island as well now, and they have begun to fortify their position. They sunk one of our tug boats, but the other was allowed to leave. In addition, our TOW missile attack was successful in that there was structural damage and fire on the island afterward. The inhabitants of Alcatraz know for certain that there are other parties interested in their little sanctuary."

"Soldiers, fortified positions, and a ballistic submarine. Have you considered just letting the island alone?"

Murda looked at his father aghast. "No! They slighted me! They—"

Cyrus raised his index finger. "Calm yourself, Doc Murda, I only wish to understand the situation."

Murda visibly pacified himself, and took two deep breaths before he continued, "They have better weapons than we do, and disciplined, trained men to use them. Eventually, their supplies will run low, and they will need to come to the city to forage. That will diminish our supplies. War is the only answer."

"Now that is the most intelligent thought I've heard yet. Let me ask you this though; wouldn't it be easier to maintain constant vigilance over the island, and attack the foraging parties to weaken them? When they have lost enough men, they will not be able to stand up to attack."

"But the sub…"

"A technological marvel like that submarine needs dozens of people to run it. Kill enough, and that sub is nothing more than floating metal." Cyrus appeared thoughtful. "Unless we could sink it…"

"We tried. We fired one of the missiles at it."

"Ah, but did you have training on those missiles? Perhaps a small team on a small craft sent out with explosives could disable the sub enough such that they could not affect repairs."

Murda looked pleased. "A fine idea, sir. As it happens, I have some explosives lying around."

THE END

And just for kicks...

"Have you ever felt left out? I mean, totally neglected when you know for an absolute certainty that you should have been allowed in?" *The young man covers his eyes with his hands simulating a headache.* "Well, I know how you feel. I was left out. Left out of this stupid book! What kind of dummy leaves out everybody's favorite? I know I'm your favorite because I'm *my* favorite. Well, fear not Bugs Bunny fans, because I will not take this crap any longer!" *The blond man, a scar on his jaw, points at you, Dear Reader.* "I will not fail you! I will up the tally, providing you with comic relief in the form of busted zombie heads before you can say Jack Robinson!" *The kid cups his chin in his hand.* "Come to think of it, I don't know who Jack Robinson is... But who cares? The bottom line is that I've missed you as much as you've missed me. So much in fact, that I have pushed my way to the forefront of this guy's," *he chucks a thumb toward a guy sitting at a computer, typing furiously while glancing at the old fashioned clock on the wall,* "mind. I guess what I'm trying to say is: See you soon!"

Acknowledgments

Honestly, this is harder than writing the damn book. There are so many people without whom I couldn't have put all this together. Thanks to all the folks on HPoTD for persuading me that my writing didn't suck. Thanks to my family who constantly tells me I don't suck. Appreciations to my friends, who occasionally tell me I suck, but hopefully they don't mean it. A special thanks to all the reviewers of the first book who really liked it and said it didn't suck. Those who think it *did* suck, I'm sorry you didn't like it and screw you for being mean.

Thanks to J.R. Jackson and the Ward Room https://wdrmmta.wordpress.com/ for making this book suck less.

Thanks to Joy and Eve for telling me I don't suck.

Thanks to Zombiefiend.com for helping me along the way.

Thanks to Chris Rawding for his inspirational drawings which *never* suck.

Thanks to Dusty, my now deceased cat, for pissing on the couch. I hated that couch.

Thanks to Tufo, Recht, Bourne, Brooks, Romero, Campbell (Bruce), Monchinski, Schannep, Frater, and Keene. You guys drive me, half of you don't know me, and none of you suck.

Thanks to you, yeah you, who took the time to read both the book and the acknowledgements. You don't suck.

If I missed thanking anybody, sorry, but I suck.

CHECK OUT OTHER GREAT ZOMBIE NOVELS

Z BURBIA
by Jake Bible

Whispering Pines is a classic, quiet, private American subdivision on the edge of Asheville, NC, set in the pristine Blue Ridge Mountains. Which is good since the zombie apocalypse has come to Western North Carolina and really put suburban living to the test!

Surrounded by a sea of the undead, the residents of Whispering Pines have adapted their bucolic life of block parties to scavenging parties, common area groundskeeping to immediate area warfare, neighborhood beautification to neighborhood fortification.

But, even in the best of times, suburban living has its ups and downs what with nosy neighbors, a strict Home Owners' Association, and a property management company that believes the words "strict interpretation" are holy words when applied to the HOA covenants. Now with the zombie apocalypse upon them even those innocuous, daily irritations quickly become dramatic struggles for personal identity, family security, and straight up survival.

ZOMBIE RULES
by David Achord

Zach Gunderson's life sucked and then the zombie apocalypse began.

Rick, an aging Vietnam veteran, alcoholic, and prepper, convinces Zach that the apocalypse is on the horizon. The two of them take refuge at a remote farm. As the zombie plague rages, they face a terrifying fight for survival.

They soon learn however that the walking dead are not the only monsters.

 SEVERED**PRESS**

CHECK OUT OTHER GREAT ZOMBIE NOVELS

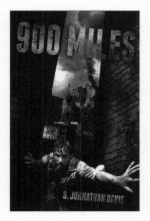

900 MILES
by S. Johnathan Davis

John is a killer, but that wasn't his day job before the Apocalypse.

In a harrowing 900 mile race against time to get to his wife just as the dead begin to rise, John, a business man trapped in New York, soon learns that the zombies are the least of his worries, as he sees first-hand the horror of what man is capable of with no rules, no consequences and death at every turn.

Teaming up with an ex-army pilot named Kyle, they escape New York only to stumble across a man who says that he has the key to a rumored underground stronghold called Avalon..... Will they find safety? Will they make it to Johns wife before it's too late?

Get ready to follow John and Kyle in this fast paced thriller that mixes zombie horror with gladiator style arena action!

WHITE FLAG OF THE DEAD
by Joseph Talluto

Millions died when the Enillo Virus swept the earth. Millions more were lost when the victims of the plague refused to stay dead, instead rising to slaughter and feed on those left alive. For survivors like John Talon and his son Jake, they are faced with a choice: Do they submit to the dead, raising the white flag of surrender? Or do they find the will to fight, to try and hang on to the last shreds or humanity?

CHECK OUT OTHER GREAT ZOMBIE NOVELS

VACCINATION
by Phillip Tomasso

What if the H7N9 vaccination wasn't just a preventative measure against swine flu?
It seemed like the flu came out of nowhere and yet, in no time at all the government manufactured a vaccination. Were lab workers diligent, or could the virus itself have been man-made? Chase McKinney works as a dispatcher at 9-1-1. Taking emergency calls, it becomes immediately obvious that the entire city is infected with the walking dead. His first goal is to reach and save his two children.
Could the walls built by the U.S.A. to keep out illegal aliens, and the fact the Mexican government could not afford to vaccinate their citizens against the flu, make the southern border the only plausible destination for safety?

ZOMBIE, INC
by Chris Dougherty

"WELCOME! To Zombie, Inc. The United Five State Republic's leading manufacturer of zombie defense systems! In business since 2027, Zombie, Inc. puts YOU first. YOUR safety is our MAIN GOAL! Our many home defense options - from Ze Fence® to Ze Popper® to Ze Shed® - fit every need and every budget. Use Scan Code "TELL ME MORE!" for your FREE, in-home*, no obligation consultation! *Schedule your appointment with the confidence that you will NEVER HAVE TO LEAVE YOUR HOME! It isn't safe out there and we know it better than most! Our sales staff is FULLY TRAINED to handle any and all adversarial encounters with the living and the undead". Twenty-five years after the deadly plague, the United Five State Republic's most successful company, Zombie, Inc., is in trouble. Will a simple case of dwindling supply and lessening demand be the end of them or will Zombie, Inc. find a way, however unpalatable, to survive?